A Virtuous Killer

J H McCullough

ISBN: 978-1-914933-44-8

"Something is broken. Beyond race. Outside
colour or history. Something has cracked."

Chronicles from the Land of the Happiest People on Earth.
Wole Soyinka.

John H. Mc Cullough

Part One

Copyright 2022

i2i
PUBLISHING

i2i Publishing. Manchester.
www.i2ipublishing.co.uk

Chapter 1

Fatma guides her little troop across the busy flyover that descends into Kano's main market. Maimouna, her daughter, is wrapped across her back, soft feet poking out either side of her mother's narrow hips. Asibi, her stepdaughter, walks beside her, tugging at her arm.

Maimouna keeps wriggling! Why is her baby so restless? She's normally such a good sleeper. Fatma turns her head to one side and tuts. She's been so intent on getting them in and out of the market, she's forgotten her daughter is not lying across her back, but on the fake explosives packed tightly between them. How can she prove herself worthy if she can allow her focus to drop so easily? She wishes she could explain to Maimouna that it won't be long; the men will remove this package as soon as they get this drill over with. Then she'll be reunited with the warmth of her mother's back and can sleep as long as she wants, while her mother basks in the praise of Abdullahi, their leader. Her husband, Muhammed, will be proud of her too, but it's not his praise she craves.

This is the first time the three of them have been out together on their own. Fatma feels no sense of liberation, unlike Asibi, who points at one thing after another: a ragged boy with firewood piled high on his back; a woman gliding past in a purple robe, a basket of mangoes balanced on her head; and now a Chinese man who cuts in front of them. His scowl implies they've no right to be there, getting in his way. He quickens his pace and the smoke from his cigarette drifts back in their faces like a parting slap. He wouldn't be so disrespectful if he knew who she really was. Why did Abdullahi insist on her bringing Asibi? Okay, he said it would make them look more innocent but this child's just holding her back.

Through a gap in the flyover wall, Asibi marvels at a cluster of coloured parasols below, insisting they're giant mushrooms. Naturally, she wants to stop and look. Pulling her along is like dragging a reluctant goat to market. The straps of the empty shopping bag are too broad for Fatma's narrow shoulders and keep sliding off. Her impatience gets the better of her. She kneels down in front of Asibi, taking hold of her arms:

'Look, I know your father lets you get away with everything but I'm in charge of you today and you'll do what I say. If you keep stopping to point at every little thing — listen to me!' She grabs Asibi's chin and pulls her face round so she has her full attention. 'If you keep stopping and pointing like this, you'll be snatched by the market witch. The one with the sharp, pointy teeth who lies waiting for naughty little girls like you. And, you know what she'll do?'

Asibi swallows hard.

'Put you in her stew and eat you for supper.'

The tears roll down Asibi's cheeks, her mouth screws up and she starts to bawl.

'But if you listen to me and do as you're told, I can protect you, okay?'

Asibi nods.

'You promise to be quiet and keep moving?'

Asibi sniffs and nods again. Her bottom lip is up; she stands still and lets Fatma wipe the tears and snot from her face. Fatma knows she's been harsh, but there's important work to be done and no time for catering to the whims of little girls. Abdullahi's words are lodged in her head:

"Don't rush, don't look at anybody and don't stop."

He had spoken like a father, not the way he speaks to his men, barking commands and issuing threats. "Feel invisible, and you will be!" She'd thought he was joking when he said that, but he stared at her, letting the words sink in, and she realised he wasn't. She should've known better; he never lies to her. She nodded as if she'd understood, afraid he might take back this opportunity for her to show how useful she could be to him.

Abdullahi had told her to marry Muhammed when she'd reached puberty. Muhammed's a fierce fighter; tall and strong, but shy with her and ... boring! He hardly opens his mouth when they're alone, and he does whatever she asks. Imagine, a warrior like him in thrall to someone half his age and half his size! He could snap her in two if he wanted! She was thirteen when they married, still a girl. And still thirteen when she had Maimouna. Now she's a woman, a wife, a mother, and, at last, a fighter! Who will they choose to blow up the market? Probably one of those schoolgirls who think they're so high and mighty. It doesn't matter. Once she's done this trial run, they can choose whoever they want. She'll have done her job, showed that she's ready to take the next step towards being a real fighter.

They exit the flyover and have to wait while a stream of auto-rickshaws and motorbikes muscle past, stopping anywhere to put people down or pick them up. The blare of horns is so constant, she no longer hears them. She uses the break in their journey to look around. Muhammed told her the market used to be surrounded by huge mud walls with the entrance through a big arch supported by two sturdy towers. Over the years it has spilled into nearby streets, swallowing up any available space. The crowd flows predominantly in one direction which can only mean the centre of the market. She will follow it and keep walking until it thins out and she reaches the other side.

Abdullahi is a great leader. He's promised her a phone when she completes her mission! There was no need, but it makes her happy. She hadn't always looked up to him. After her abduction, she couldn't speak for six days. But he'd taken a special interest in her; said she'd reminded him of his daughter whom he hardly saw anymore. He'd explained that in time she would realise how stupid her parents and all those other villagers had been and he was right. They were like sheep. She knows that now. They deserved to die. He had rescued her from all that and given her a purpose. Alhamdulillah!

The fevered conversation of Kalangu drums neutralises the rattling drone from the generators but not the smell of diesel, or the voices of traders, indignant but resigned to being pushed to the last price. Tethered goats, cattle, and camels express their own displeasure. The stink of dung and vegetables on the turn is masked by the acrid smells of smoked fish and freshly tanned leather. The brightly-coloured cloth in traditional West African designs looks like it might catch fire. The old men in the election posters seem to stare down at her with disapproval but she keeps her little band moving forward, navigating the clamour with a mix of fortitude and grace. Plain grey hijabs encircle the faces of the two girls. Their black tunics brush lightly against their skinny legs as they walk between covered stalls, mostly under the shelter of the market roof but at other times in open spaces where the sun's heat is unrelenting. Nevertheless, Fatma is surprised by a bead of sweat that drips off her nose and onto her lip. It's hot and dusty as usual, but she has walked much further than this without tasting salt on her tongue. She hopes the fever is not returning, then remembers she is carrying the weight of two babies on her back.

Activity in the market is picking up. Sometimes they must step aside and wait for a space to clear, other times, they are brushed out of the way. People seem to be looking at them more and more, and the attention makes her uneasy. Maybe she's imagining it. Asibi pulls on her arm and makes her stop. She looks up at her and says:

'You're hurting me!'

Fatma swallows hard. She's been holding Asibi's hand too tightly. She relaxes her grip.

'I'm sorry.'

She's aware of another drop running down her face. It's not sweat this time, it's ... a tear. What is happening to her? They draw level with the market mosque. Two beggars are propped against the wall looking for eye contact with anyone passing by. A worn-out towel lies in front of them, displaying a few Naira, anxious for company. One of the beggars stares at her before nudging his companion and pointing a grubby finger at them.

Humph! Who do they think they are pointing at her? Asibi points back in response, asking loudly why the men's legs are like balloons. It didn't take the child long to forget about the witch, but that's okay, someone had to put these infidels in their place. As she ushers Asibi away, determined to pick up the pace. Asibi doesn't like it, but Fatma bends down and whispers in her ear,

'We can't walk side by side anymore. It's too crowded. Walk in front of me.'

They press ahead, her hand resting on Asibi's neck and shoulder. Despite the bumping and shouting, they make progress though Fatma still feels they are standing out from the crowd too much. Fortunately in the bustle of the market, eyes don't have time to settle. They reach a narrow intersection. People are impatient to pass and while not hesitating to push forward, make it clear they don't appreciate being pushed from behind. The drumming is louder, but Fatma sees no drummers. It's not drumming she's been hearing but a throbbing in her temples that's been getting louder the closer they get to the centre of the market. She is distracted by a wiry man in a torn white vest pushing a rusty trailer stacked precariously with cases of bottled water. He ploughs through the crowd towards them, issuing warning shouts, looking like he has no intention of stopping. People step aside without thinking. Such is the way of the market; they know he knows if he stops he will lose momentum and won't get his load mobile again. Fatma moves back too, pulling Asibi in close. Her arms drop over Asibi's tiny shoulders and her hands press against the little girl's chest. The movement causes the bag to slip off Fatma's shoulder and hang from her elbow. The strap is snagged by the wheel of the passing trailer, pulling Fatma's arm roughly and dragging her off to one side. She cries in pain and manages to untangle her arm from the bag. She loses her balance and stumbles backwards alongside the trailer, trying to grab its rail to avoid falling on top of her baby.

This is not supposed to happen. She hears people shouting as she struggles to stay upright. She catches the fear in the man's eyes. The wrath of the crowd will fall upon him if he injures anyone, and it will be merciless. But Fatma doesn't fall on top of her baby. The explosion is thunderous and she is thrust violently upwards then thrown back on the market floor like a lump of meat. She can barely see. Perhaps it is the whooshing noise in her ears that makes her think she's in the middle of a waterfall. Or maybe, it's the warm, pink mist of blood and water falling back to earth and caressing her face. She hears snakes hissing around her and is afraid. She cannot move. The snakes come closer, dancing around her like flames. They brush against her and her face burns. She is plunging down a deep well which she fears will lead to hell. As the final seconds of her life drain away, she thinks of Maimouna and Asibi. She thinks of her parents. She thinks of Abdullahi and Muhammed and as death engulfs her forcing the last breath from her shattered body, she knows her betrayal is pure and complete.

Chapter 2

Abdullahi surveys the chaos from his vantage point behind the unfinished breeze-block wall on a nearby rooftop. There's little to match the intensity crammed into those few seconds between pressing the detonation command, hearing the blast of defiance, and feeling the shift of warm air on his face. The surge of energy that command releases feels like it has come directly from Allah using his body as a conduit. He watches a cloud of grey smoke billow up majestically into the empty blue sky, fascinated by the way it turns over and over into itself. Allah is expressing His approval. Below the cloud, a section of the market has been reconfigured into a jumble of collapsed stalls, bent corrugated steel roofs, burning wooden frames, and broken bodies, entangled and shrouded in dust and blood. The screaming begins. A couple of survivors make tentative steps towards the injured but most scatter. It's time to go. There will be time to celebrate later when they watch the video. He hands the detonation phone to Muhammed. Another fighter guides the drone that has been monitoring Fatma's every move, back to the rooftop, and packs it into a holdall. The three men are quickly down the dusty concrete stairs. They pause at the doorway for the all-clear. The engine of the builder's truck is running, and they clamber inside. The vehicle slips quietly out of the narrow street and merges with the road. It displays no black and white identifying flag, just a paint-splattered rag, fluttering from a ladder protruding at the back. Election posters of the Governor have been pasted on the sides of the vehicle, obscuring the name of the firm to which the truck belongs.

Ten minutes later, they've put sufficient distance between themselves and the mayhem they've left behind. While retaining a watchful eye on the road ahead, they can sit back in their seats and relax a little. They approach another market, its stalls running along the roadside. The throng of pedestrians, rickshaws and traders causes the road to narrow, and their truck slows to a stop. People cross in front and behind them as if the traffic doesn't exist. Their truck inches forward inducing slaps on the bonnet and demands they give way. Abdullahi makes a mental note to revisit this place and make these infidels pay for their insolence. Thoughts of revenge are soon set aside as the familiar black shape of an armoured car looms up ahead. Their fingers curl round the triggers of their AK-47s, muzzles brushing the floor.

The armoured car is now six car-lengths away. Its lights flash and its claxon bellows like an angry camel and is turned off. It doesn't seem in much of a hurry. It could bully its way through or go off-road, but it seems content to align with the traffic. Abdullahi knows these infidels fear another bomb could await them at their destination and they have every right to be fearful. He would have been glad to provide them with a special welcome, except that it would have required more time and resources and delayed their escape. No need to be greedy; too much ambition can be an enemy. This scum will remain free to poke through the devastation he has caused, looking for information they have no capacity to find and wouldn't know what to do with if they found it. Both vehicles draw level as if for a pre-arranged meeting. He sees the sweat glistening between the rims of black berets and sunglasses. One of them glances down at their builder's truck. While Abdullahi knows he might be better served to look away, he chooses defiance and looks back. Two metres of sticky tarmac separate deadly enemies but only one of them knows that is the case. Abdullahi and his men might be outnumbered, but they are better armed, and will be sure to strike first. More importantly their resolve is stronger. When have these infidels ever had to fight in close and battle for their lives? The policeman locks eyes with Abdullahi expecting him to be cowed, but Abdullahi returns his stare with interest. The bustle of the market and blare of car horns seem to recede even though the gaps in the side windows remain as before. Abdullahi and his men focus on their prey like hyenas. The air above both vehicles shimmers. Is it the impact of the Kano sun or the sign of another energy source mobilising?

The curiosity in the policeman's eyes turns to suspicion but not yet to realization. A second policeman follows his comrade's gaze. They exchange words, prompting a third to lean round from the back and peer down. Such swagger. They think they're checking out a few workmen on their way to a building site. Men they'd love to drag out of their truck, slap around, demand papers from and relieve of any Naira they can find. But maybe they're beginning to doubt. Abdullahi always seeks out an edge. If he is going to act it will have to be now as the element of surprise is dissolving. His men are primed, he senses their willingness for him to make the call. Half a minute is all they need, and, unlike these infidels, they will not hesitate to drive through anyone or anything blocking their path. A space opens in front of the police vehicle; its engine roars and it moves away. The sounds of the market return, and the builder's truck moves off in turn. It is Allah's will.

The truck leaves the road and pulls into an unremarkable side street comprised of modest houses most of which await completion. They approach the safe house.

They will rest up for twenty-four hours, except for the meeting he and Muhammed will have later with Ado, the Senator's errand boy. There is no need for the driver to honk his horn, a tall metal gate swings open, they pass through and park under a corrugated steel roof. Everyone gets out, Abdullahi issues a few commands and equipment is stored, weapons brought inside, and security checked. As soon as the door closes behind them, he bids his comrades gather round. He takes out his phone, holds it up for them to see, and plays the video footage captured by the drone. They cheer and embrace. He steps back to address them:

'My brothers, today we have hit back hard. Alhamdulillah! The President and his security forces have told the world that *Jama'atu Ahlus Sunnah lid Da'awati wal Jihadwe,* is on the run. The Governor has told the people that Kano State is secure in his hands. He will have to tell them something else and they won't believe that either. The end of times is coming. Allahu Akbar!'

'Allahu Akbar!' they respond, fists punching the air.

He raises his hand; they fall silent and drop to their knees. He leads them in prayer:

'In the Name of Allah, Most Gracious, Most Merciful. All praise and thanks are due to Allah, and peace and blessings be upon His Messenger. As-salamu `alaykum wa Rahmatu Allah.'

They regain their feet.

'Where's the bitch?' says Abdullahi.

'In your room. She's sleeping, sir.' The boy is about fifteen, not yet ready to fight.

'"She's sleeping sir!" What is this, a fucking hotel? I'll soon wake her up! Go up on the roof and keep your eyes open.' He lets the boy run past then stands on the first stair to address his men again.

'Muhammed, we leave at seven thirty. Make sure everything is ready. And all of you, remember this day, be thankful, be proud. Now, rest up. Tomorrow we have a long journey back ... with no screaming babies or whining bitches to put up with.'

Everyone laughs apart from his second-in-command.

'Why the face, Muhammed? Oh I see, you lost a wife and two daughters today, and it bothers you. Don't be so fucking weak! Fatma was like a daughter to me, do I look like I'm grieving? No, because I know she's in paradise! I've told you before, all of you, you must be prepared to sacrifice anything for your faith. "We belong to Allah and to Him we shall return." When it's your time, Muhammed, Fatma will have seventy-two virgins waiting to welcome you.'

He smiles, 'But don't expect to join them just yet. Allah has more work for you to do here, on earth'.

'Inch Allah,' says Muhammed.

'More work for all of us!' says Abdullahi.

'Allahu Akbar!' his men respond.

Chapter 3

Senior Nursing Officer Jamilah and her colleagues had heard the explosion and feared the worst. She mobilises efficiently and calmly: visitors are politely but firmly asked to leave; doctors and administrators are consulted; her team is briefed on a pathway; additional space is created; supplies are gathered; orderlies are told to supplement their stretchers with chairs and boards; cleaners and catering staff are instructed to stay and act as assistants; shift workers are contacted and requested to come in. And still, when the aftermath of the explosion reaches their door, the worst surpasses anything they could have imagined.

People haul the injured from the backs of trucks, auto-rickshaws, motorbikes, and taxis. Some bodies are pierced with shrapnel, while others are badly burned, their skin divided into black, brown, and white patches like antelope hide. People are missing limbs and in a few cases, body parts have been retrieved and placed in hope beside their owners. Other casualties have stopped breathing, many seem about to. The walking wounded stagger in like dust-covered zombies. A surge of arrivals becomes an invasion. The hospital struggles to stay on its feet. Nurses and orderlies stop going out to meet the incomers and Jamilah's focus shifts from treatment to triage, assessing new arrivals and prioritizing only those her team can help. This is what she's good at; holding up under pressure, keeping a grip on her emotions and, however much they resent her, galvanizing the team. At times she loses patience and shouts at them. Yes, it's heartbreaking to stop treating someone who is dying, but if two lives can be saved by letting one go, let it go. She imagines this is what it's like on a battlefield. Colleagues she expects to show courage, find it hard to focus, while the quieter, more timid ones concentrate and get on with the job.

The doctors work flat out; for them too, procedures that are quick and save lives are the order of the day. There's no time for micro-surgery or trying to reconnect limbs. Survival takes priority over future life improvement. All available space becomes an extension of the Emergency Room. Jamilah supervises her team as they dress burns, extract fragments, stem bleeding, clean, suture, and bandage. Before long there is no blood left to transfuse and the supply of bandages is running low. She instructs the cleaners to take sheets from the cupboards and cut them into strips. Dr Salim has mobilized all the junior doctors and interns, and Jamilah experiences the synergy of team integration like an electric current surging through the room. She's content to leave it to the better qualified to ration the oxygen cylinders, but now they are running out of suture needles and it's up to her to do something about that. She sends an orderly to mobilise the cleaners to collect the needles from her nurses, disinfect them and bring them back for re-use. They are being overwhelmed but Jamilah holds the team together, sometimes with shouts, occasionally with gentle urging, and always by example. A General Hospital like hers, with eighty-five beds, was never designed to function in a war zone, but that's what Kano state has become, and it's not alone. Her anger at what has happened is compounded by her frustration at seeing standards compromised − not the only frustration in her life − but she keeps the team going and the line holds.

Jamilah's uniform is damp with sweat and stains of red. Tears of blood fall from her scrubs onto her ankles and quickly transfer into her plastic shoes, filling the spaces between her toes. Concern for her patients competes with a fear of contracting HIV. She'll make sure she and her team start post-exposure prophylaxis treatment as soon as they come off duty – and get tested in a fortnight. Supplies of plastic gloves is the next thing to fall dangerously low. She tells the cleaners to provide basins of hot water with disinfectant for her colleagues to immerse the gloves in before moving to the next patient and keep doing it. It's yet another thing to offend her standards but the option of using bare hands or spreading blood from one patient to another is inconceivable. The air-conditioning fails but Jamilah and her team keep functioning. The old generator clears its throat and coughs up some light, though dimmer than before. The rusty overhead fans creak into life trying to do their best but offering only limited relief to those directly below them. People keep coming and, of course, it's the children, the most innocent, who are hardest to deal with. Some scream in pain, some are unconscious while others stare in silence, unable to understand where they are and why their mothers are crying. Poor souls lie waiting outside, unattended. Thankfully, off-duty nurses and volunteers begin to arrive, including private sector nurses who bring welcome supplies. All are drawn to Jamilah who directs them to where they can best make an impact.

Eventually, the cries of despair and anger become less frequent, only erupting again at death. People stop arriving. A blanket of misery covers the building bringing no comfort. As early evening sets in, heads are still shaking in disbelief and sobs steal outside to merge with the stridulation of cricket wings. Finally, the staff can do no more. They've been treating the injured for over five hours and exhaustion bites. Of those who made it to the hospital, thirty-three are dead and more are bound to join them in the coming hours and days. Jamilah wonders how many dead were left behind at the scene or died en route? More than that, she wonders how the guilty can be rewarded in paradise for such evil while the innocent are left to suffer?

She heads to the locker room. Thankfully, the showers are working, and she can wash the blood and sweat from her skin. She has less success in washing away the images and sounds she's experienced on the ward, but she's not going to bring them home with her, though she knows, Aminah, her sister, will be full of questions. It is one of her goals in life to maintain as much normality as she can in the lives of her brother and sister — her little family. They'll have seen the news and will expect her to be late. She texts that she's on her way. She opens her locker. She would love to change into her running gear for a stress-busting jog around the grounds. It's the only place in the city where she can run, and even then she still gets looks, but it's already late and it would be inappropriate tonight, especially as there are reporters still hanging around. As she pulls on her jeans, one of her colleagues comes in.

'What are things coming to Sister, when a person can't even go to the market without being blown to pieces? These people ...'

'They're not people,' replies Jamilah. 'I don't know what they think they achieve by killing and maiming innocent souls, especially children.'

'Have you heard? People are saying it was a child who carried out the attack. A teenage girl with a baby and young child. Another suicide bombing. How can ... She must have been brainwashed or drugged. Why doesn't the government do something?'

It's a rhetorical question for which the answer is too long and painful, so they both shake their heads and fall silent having exhausted the usual clichés. With no patients on which to focus her attention, Jamilah's tiredness allows her guard to drop and unwelcome memories of her younger self rush in to intrude on her thoughts. She's a teenager again, like that young suicide bomber, like her sister Aminah. She spends her time helping her father bring up Aminah and their brother Ahmed, after their mother had died trying to give birth to a third child. It's not the market that is burning, but her village. Scrawny men drive away on whining motorbikes, waving guns and machetes. Some scowl, others laugh but they're all exhilarated. Minutes later, an open lorry filled with vigilantes screeches to a halt. A king-size police sergeant, with jowls and stomach to match, emerges from the front, looks around and catches Jamilah's eye. She had developed quickly for her age and knows the meaning of that look. He barks a command, and vigilantes jump down, so very brave with their sticks and machetes. They scatter like ants amongst the smouldering huts and broken bodies. They pounce on her father and uncle rushing back from the fields and bring them in front of the policeman. They assure Sergeant Giwa that her father and uncle are collaborators. If not, how come they have been spared by the terrorists? And why are they sweating so much? They are collaborators, it is clear. In fact, they are known to them.

Jamilah fights back the tiredness, determined, as always to prevent the sense of injustice from overwhelming her. She pushes the images back into their cell and locks the door. She stands up and adjusts her blouse. These people: police, vigilantes, terrorists, politicians — they're as bad as each other. It's always the innocent who suffer. But such words are not spoken aloud in a government hospital by an SNO, especially one who's still resented by her peers for her fast-track promotion and whose opinions would be seized on to undermine her. She fastens her trainers and resorts to another cliché, which she addresses to the floor. 'Yes, something must be done. We can't have more days like this.' She lifts her bag. 'I'm off. Don't forget to pick up your post-exposure prophylaxis at the pharmacy.'

'I won't.'

'See you tomorrow.'

'Inch 'Allah.'

'Inch 'Allah.' Jamilah makes the customary response, less through belief in the faith into which she was born, more through the need to keep her job. When Sergeant Giwa and his brave vigilantes left her village those ten years ago, her faith left with them. It creeps back sometimes like a missing cat but never stays for long. She checks in the mirror for the one thing that always comes back. She knows it's there because she can feel it; the patch of acne on one half of her left cheek that since that traumatic day flares up at times of stress.

Chapter 4

Abdullahi and Muhammed have taken cover behind a dilapidated wall that looks across to the car park of the old mosque. The wall feels like it's being held up by the shrubs and weeds that have reclaimed it and the rest of the old tyre factory — one of many construction projects built back in the seventies when people believed the country had a future. Abdullahi's father was one of them, but building a factory was one thing, running it was another and the only thing that did function effectively was the pervasive greed and corruption which slowly strangled the life out of it. His father never found another full-time job and like most other families moved away, but he still brought his son back to the mosque. Only the Sheikh remains as a living link to the past and like the mosque, he too has fallen into disrepair but remains an inspiration to Abdullahi, both spiritually and in his obstinacy to stay put. There's no more evening prayer, no more congregation; the only thing that remains is the smell of rubber.

A car approaches, its headlights dimmed. Muhammed stops chewing his miswak and inches forward to take a look. 'Here he comes,' he says over his shoulder. 'Thinks no one will recognise him if he wears old clothes and drives a beat-up car.'

'He should stop pushing himself up the senator's ass every time a TV camera comes into view', says Abdullahi.

The handbrake is yanked up painfully and the lights switched off. Ado, the driver, looks from side to side. They will keep him waiting out of disrespect. Abdullahi makes out a dull flickering light from within the mosque. Ado probably sees it too. The Sheikh is taking tea by candlelight. Abdullahi gets on the back of the bike and they ride into the car park, pulling up alongside Ado's unassuming Corolla. Unlike the shiny black 4x4s the Senator's entourage usually run around in, this rust heap bears the scars of growing up fast in the back streets of Kano. Muhammed keeps his scarf across his face, Abdullahi doesn't bother. He dismounts, opens the passenger door and gets in. Muhammed manoeuvres the bike round so it's facing the exit, then switches off the headlight. The car park is in total darkness.

'As-Salaam-Alaikum,' says Ado shifting in his seat.

'Wa-Alaikum-Salaam,' replies Abdullahi.

'Don't you ever wash?' Ado winds down his window.

'Those of us who do what we say, are obliged to live with the consequences. I might smell of the earth, you smell of something worse. We both know what that is.'

'The earth? Don't you mean, a sewer? And your breath.' Ado turns his head away in disgust, 'it smells like a dead dog in the sun'.

Abdullahi puts one arm across the steering wheel and slides the other over the top of Ado's seat behind his head. He stares directly into Ado's face, pauses, then asks, 'Would you like to be a dead dog in the sun?'

Ado's bravado unravels like the loose stitching of his cheap kaftan. He pulls his head away from his aggressor, his side pressing hard into the door. But there's nowhere to go. He clears his throat and talks to the windscreen.

'Senator Yakubu is pleased with your work. Coming after the Governor's big speech on getting tough on security, the timing of that explosion couldn't have been better.'

'The Governor's an old man.' Abdullahi relaxes his grip on the steering wheel and rolls back into his seat. 'The only thing tough about him is his ass.' He scratches his groin then turns to look at Ado, 'You think your Senator will be any better?'

Ado avoids looking back. 'Senator Yakubu will bring stability back to our State. Make the people of Kano more prosperous.'

'Save your campaign speeches, I can guess which "people of Kano" you're talking about. As for bringing stability ... For now, our interests align. If your boss ever becomes Governor, that may change.'

'When the Senator becomes Governor', Ado winds down the window a few more revolutions, 'I'm sure we can work out a new modus operandi for mutual advantage'.

'A new what? I'm tired of your bullshit. Just do your master's bidding, errand boy.'

'It's in the boot. It's all there.'

Abdullahi gets out of the car, 'Stay there'.

'Wait', says Ado leaning forward, 'Kidnapping girls ... The Senator wants you to do more. It gets the attention of the western media and brings even more grief to the Governor's campaign'.

Abdullahi leans inside the open door. For the first time, he observes what looks like a self-inflicted dent in Ado's Fula cap,

'We're not kidnapping girls. Who's ever received a ransom note? You? Yakubu? The Governor? We're waging jihad. You're too much of an infidel to know what that means. We take these young women captive because it's our right. We teach them how to behave. We sell some, we keep some, we even marry some. Either way, they serve us, as we serve Allah.'

He snatches Ado's hat from his head and throws it into the back of the car.

'Tell Yakubu, if he ever becomes Governor, to remember who helped put him there. We'll expect his support in exchanging some of these young women for the women the security forces have taken from us, as well as any of our fighters they haven't slaughtered yet.'

Abdullahi goes to the back of the car. Muhammed rolls across on the bike to join him. Abdullahi is sure Ado is watching in the rear-view mirror, so enjoys pulling up the boot lid to obscure his view. He shines a torch inside and slides a knife through the black plastic covering. He sees what he needs to. The two bags are packed tight with Naira. He hands one to Muhammed and keeps hold of the other. He gets on the bike, puts his bag on the seat in front of him and takes the other from Muhammed and places it on top. Muhammed pushes back against the bags wedging them tightly between passenger and driver. They leave the boot open and drive off, passing a figure walking slowly towards them along the side of the mosque. It's the old Sheikh probably come to investigate the noise. Abdullahi hears the boot being closed and Ado's car starting up. He shouts into Muhammed's ear,

'He's shitting himself in case the Sheikh recognises him. The Sheikh couldn't recognise his own reflection!'

Muhammed joins in the laughter as they speed away. He steers imperceptibly between the potholes, like a wildcat that knows where to put its paws on a well-trodden trail.

Chapter 5

Jamilah unlocks her apartment door and announces herself with a cheery hello. Aminah is at her side in a flash with a wide smile and warm embrace. Jamilah hugs her back.

'Thanks for waiting!'

'Sista, how could we start without you?' Her face switches to concern. 'What a dreadful day.'

'We did what we could, but these people ... If they could see the consequences of what they do.'

'It wouldn't bother them,' says Aminah.

'No,' says Jamilah recognising herself in her sister. She strokes Aminah's face and heads to the kitchen to start dinner, pausing to ruffle her brother's hair. As usual, Ahmed is tapping at his phone. He raises his hand in a lazy welcome and grunts.

'Wow,' says Jamilah, turning towards her sister, 'you've done everything! Thank you'.

Aminah joins her at the kitchen entrance. 'Least I could do seeing you've been feeding me all week.'

She gives Jamilah another hug, and Jamilah looks at her sister with pride. Aminah wears Islamic clothes. It's the school's influence but it suits her. Mind you, anything would. The rich blue headscarf that encircles her face adds serenity to her beauty. Aminah is so sure in her faith. She would say that's where her serenity comes from, not her looks.

Jamilah turns her attention to Ahmed. 'Come on mister, the least you can do is set the table.'

'I'm not a can-do guy. Thought you knew that.'

'Aren't you curious to find out how much your sister's cooking's improved?'

Ahmed drags himself from the sofa and yawns. 'Don't you mean "if" as opposed to "how much"? Anyway, she didn't cook last time she was here.'

Aminah is determined to be a doctor and Jamilah is equally determined to make it happen. Over dinner, she fields Aminah's questions on the day's events in a professional manner, so her sister learns how clinicians talk. From time to time, Jamilah glances over at Ahmed, concerned in case his silence is due to something more than having to share a table with two chattering females. She doesn't want him to think she favours Aminah over him, but it's not every week they have their sister home.

'Well Bro, what do you think of the new menu? Or are you only interested in that girl you're texting all the time?'

'Funneee!', says Ahmed, back on the settee and back on his phone. 'Pepper soup has taken on a whole new meaning.'

Aminah swings round to stare at her brother.

'Don't listen to him,' says Jamilah, 'it's the best Egusi he'll taste in his entire life, and he knows it'.

'Listen, sis, I have to go out.' He stands up.

'Noo,' says Jamilah, 'It's Aminah's last night, I thought we'd spend it together. And don't forget, you have to get up early to take her back'.

'I know. Sorry.' He kisses Jamilah on the side of the cheek. 'Great dinner, Minah, I'm sure you'll make someone a good wife one day — if you ever manage to find a husband.'

Aminah reaches out to thump him, but he moves sideways and avoids her.

'Where are you going anyway,' says Jamilah, 'it's nearly ten o'clock!'

'To see a friend — not a girlfriend. A guy who's selling a part for my bike. It's on the uni auction site. He's accepted my bid; I have to go now, or he'll sell it to someone else.'

'Humph, what a story,' says Aminah. 'Mind you it's more convincing than him going to meet a girl. Who'd have him?' She sticks out her tongue. He laughs.

'Do you have enough money?' asks Jamilah.

He nods.

'Be careful, there'll be more roadblocks than usual. Don't be late. Don't forget your key.'

The door closes.

'Don't look so concerned, he'll be back in no time', says Aminah, pulling her chair closer to her sister.

'He's always going out late. I wish he did have a girlfriend. If you weren't here, he'd be staying over with one of his friends. Do you talk to him much when you're away?'

'About once a week. We text too.'

'That's good', says Jamilah.

'He always changes the subject when it comes to girls though', Aminah laughs.

'He's secretive about everything! I mean, going off to meet someone in the middle of the night. Why can't he buy things in normal hours like everybody else? Leave that, you did the cooking, I'll clear up. Go pack for tomorrow. I'll make us some tea before we turn in.'

'Look sis,' says Aminah, 'he's almost twenty-one, he's at university. He likes to hang out with his friends. It's normal. He's fine'.

'I suppose so', says Jamilah, proud at how mature her sister's becoming.

'And I'm okay, seeing as you ask. We're all grown up now, so *you* can start living your life too and stop worrying about us.'

'What do you mean? I do live my life. I have a demanding job, a career, I've got you two, and we've got this place!'

'Yes, and that's all great. But sooner or later he'll find a girl and get married, Inch 'Allah. I'll go to university and maybe not in this state. You're a young woman, sis. And despite what you say, a beautiful one. Stop blushing!' she laughs. 'Maybe the next time one of those doctors asks you out, you'll say yes and stop using us as an excuse!' She laughs again.

'Huh, you don't know what men are like, especially doctors. Only interested in the one thing. They think when they float into the wards all the nurses should fall at their feet. Some do, not me. No thanks. I'm happy to say no, very happy.'

'All right, sis. But … maybe they're not all the same.' She kisses Jamilah on the cheek and heads off to the bedroom.

Jamilah remains at the table feeling a little put out at getting advice on how to live her life from her younger sister. At the same time she can't but admire what an intelligent young woman Aminah is becoming; able to think beyond her immediate future and care about her family. But what's she getting at? Even if the pair of them go away, they'll always be her family; the only one she needs. Besides, no man will be interested in her once they learn about her past. She touches the rough edge on her face and looks around the room. Her eyes rest on Ahmed's empty plate. She stares too long allowing the cell door to spring open again. Unwelcome memories elbow their way out determined to trample over her thoughts. Her little brother Ahmed is crying. Stop! She bangs the door shut. That was ten years ago. Why can't it stay there and leave her alone? It's like that stupid boy in the market who keeps following her around, pushing his cheap rubbish, despite being told to go away.

Her elbows rest on the table; her hands cover her eyes and capture warm tears. She knows she can't change the past, but she can make sure Aminah and Ahmed have a better future. It would be nice if Ahmed found a sensible girl, got married and had some kids. Aminah is right, she must stop acting like his mother; go back to being his sister. Their real mother would be so proud of them ... living in the city, she an SNO with a degree in nursing, Ahmed at university and Aminah set to go in a couple of years. She wipes her eyes and gathers up the plates. They're doing really well. She's doing fine; she doesn't need anyone to come in and spoil everything.

Chapter 6

Senator Yakubu sits at the head of his Louis XIV-style dining table wearing a floor-length *babban riga* of blue and gold with matching Hausa cap. The ivory handle of his cane leans against the side of his chair. A line of froth from the first gulp of his morning smoothie forms a thin white moustache above his lip. Half a dozen plates heaped with yam, eggs, meat, fish, sausage, potatoes, plantain, rice, and beans are reflected in the boss's sunglasses. They await their fate in dignified silence. An ornate silver teapot stands sentinel over assorted bread rolls. Rectangles of butter, still in their gold wrapping, float in a bowl of melting ice.

Ado is used to being invited to a breakfast meeting by the Senator, and never being offered breakfast. Just as well he doesn't share the boss's appetite. Even if he felt hungry it would be difficult to eat while being stared at by a hundred of his own images reflected back from the ornate mirrors opposite and behind him. If that weren't enough, an impression of his face keeps glancing up at him from the surface of the mahogany table. He is reporting back on his most recent meeting with Abdullahi.

'I was having none of it. The insolence! I soon put him in his place. "You don't make demands," I told him.'

'What demands?' The Senator stops chewing and wipes his mouth.

'Well ... when you become Governor, he expects you to order the release of his women and fighters.'

'When I become Governor, that stinking little rat will be exterminated and shoved back down the sewer he crawled out of.'

'Insha'Allah.'

'At your next meeting, I'll have guns trained on him from every direction.'

'Alhamdulillah.'

'When I'm Governor, the people of Kano and the President of this country will see what real security looks like.'

"Alhamdulillah. Our state is blessed, Excellency. Our country too, but … are we sure the security forces can be trusted to carry out their duty?'

'Woman, where in the name of Allah are you? Get in here!' The Senator's third wife hurries in. 'Bring me water and charge that phone. What's the matter with you?'

'Sorry, sir.'

'And pour Mr Ado, some tea. He's been sitting here for ten minutes, and you've offered him nothing. Do my guests have to die of thirst?'

'No sir. I'm sorry sir.'

It's a challenge to handle the boss, even for a man of the world, like himself. How does this young woman manage it on a daily basis? As she pours the tea without spilling a drop, he admires her long, elegant fingers and fine features. No such displays of admiration from the boss; he ignores her like the hippo ignores the oxpecker walking on its back. Ado dreads to think what it must be like for her to share the old man's bed. At least the hippo leaves the bird in peace. Ado expresses his gratitude with a thin smile and a nod, both of which she reciprocates. She places the teapot back on the table and lifts the Senator's phone. Ado resists the temptation to look at her any further.

'Don't be concerned,' says the Senator, 'I won't leave you alone with that vermin. I'm taking out insurance on your behalf'. He pauses to spit out a bone. 'I've been in touch with an organization,' he pauses to extract another bone, 'experienced in fighting terrorists across Africa. You'll meet their leader this morning. He's coming in to make a presentation and talk terms. His unit will take charge of this little operation and many more like them'.

'Mercenaries?'

'No aid workers, what do you think?' He shovels more food into his mouth but still manages to speak.

'Been here a week. Staying at the Abuja Hilton. Sanctioned by the President.' He pauses to chew.

'If any State wants them, they have to pay for them from their own budget. I want them in Kano on the day I take control of this State. You have an incentive to ensure I get what I want. Your life could depend on it. Negotiate hard and find the money.'

'Another masterstroke, Excellency. I will ensure it's done.'

While he'll be glad to see the back of Abdullahi, Ado could do without the extra work at this time. The Senator's step up to Governor is assured given the incumbent's unpopularity, the money the Senator has spread around, and the promises made. Nevertheless, there are still a lot of tasks and negotiating to be done before he can think about identifying funds for post-election contracts. His boss is gulping as if he's having difficulty in swallowing. He downs some juice. Ado is unsure if his audience is over. Maybe the boss is going to offer some suggestions as to where such funds might come from. That would be a first. The Senator looks as if he's going to add a few more words; instead, he releases a low-pitched belch that sounds like it has escaped from a breach in the earth's core. With a wave of his hand, he bids Ado go, then buries his fork in some plantain.

Chapter 7

Dusk is Abdullahi's preferred time for this kind of attack. As daylight fades, people trudge home from the fields, tired, hungry, and less alert than when they started the day. In the towns, they squeeze onto beat-up buses filled with diesel fumes, clamber into auto-rickshaws or risk all on the backs of okadas driven by youths high on Tramadol and amphetamines. People are tired, distracted and want to be somewhere else. Before dusk gives way to night, he will order his men forward with enough light to guide their attack and enough darkness to obscure their exit.

The millet field provides excellent cover. It has been cut back a good twenty metres from the narrow road that runs past the boarding school opposite. Abdullahi and his men kneel down out of sight, the millet spears project motionless above their heads. Abdullahi watches closely as the new security detail pulls up in front of the school gates. He counts them off the back of the truck: ten infantry, one officer. The men being relieved waste no time jumping on board the truck to fill the spaces left by the new arrivals. The latter fall in, and the officer says a few last-minute words, before climbing back on board the truck and settling into the passenger seat. The truck roars away as if needed urgently elsewhere.

The men left behind look morose. Guarding the school at night brings a heightened level of danger. They pass through the gate and form a huddle behind a ramshackle brick shelter hastily built for their protection. No one seems to be in charge. Abdullahi shakes his head. It seems they've just been told to stay there and keep their eyes open. If that's supposed to be a deterrent, it's insulting. Six of the men break off into pairs and slink off to take up positions around the perimeter wall — just as they've done every night for the past week since that pathetic excuse of a Governor used his visit to the school to proclaim to the TV cameras that Boko Haram was finished, and the electorate could trust him to make the state secure. Huh, not while his troops stand shitting themselves, with rusty old rifles in their hands. What sense of allegiance can these men have when their officer can't be bothered to stick around and support them? Poorly equipped and ill-fed; poorly paid and paid late, anyone can see they'd rather be somewhere else, but here is the only place he and his men want to be. Allah continues to clear a path for them. Sometimes he wishes He would make things harder.

Two of the detail go into the small guard house where a light bulb flickers into life. The other two remain behind the shelter. They think they'll be safer there than out in the open. They'll be trying to convince themselves that as no one has attacked them since they started this detail, then why should they bother tonight? The three pairs of men reach their positions. A few show their familiarity with the terrain and sit on the ground, backs against the perimeter wall; a couple perch half-on, half-off. Another man stands and stretches. When they look out across the road, it's towards Abdullahi and his men but unlike them, they see nobody looking back.

Darkness edges down, taking control of the horizon. The millet field transforms into what must seem like an impenetrable black wall. There's nothing for the infidels to see, so they stop looking. They will have to depend on their ears. Abdullahi smiles at the thought and stands up. He steps over a farm worker who stares up at him with dead eyes that had seen too much. He whispers in Muhammed's ear:

'Time to do Allah's work.'

Muhammed takes off silently, AK47 in one hand, mobile in the other. Less than a minute later he texts that everyone is in place and ready. They will attack in four groups reflecting how the infidels have stationed themselves. Muhammed returns and creeps forward to join another fighter in an advanced position, less than two metres from where the millet ends, and the open space before the road begins. The man is lying on his stomach on a stiff inflammable sheet. He looks like an extension of the Serbian-made Zastava M02 Coyote heavy-machine gun that extends out in front of him. His elbows press into the ground as if they are part of the weapon's sturdy tripod. His chin rests on the butt; his left hand forms a fist around a metal hand grip, beyond which the body of the gun forms a compact bridge to the barrel that stretches out like a mini runway. The index finger of his right hand points at the gate, impatient to slip onto the trigger to start the assault. Muhammed lays his AK47 to one side, drops to his knees, pats his comrade on the shoulder and lies down alongside him.

Abdullahi releases a cry of 'Allahu Akbar!' which is taken up and repeated by his men. The Coyote roars into life. Muhammed is there to ensure the belt feeds smoothly from the ammunition box, but this machine works so well it's unlikely that he'll be needed. How they love this weapon. Accurate up to 1500 metres, its shells have no problem finding their target just a stone's throw across the road. They rip into the makeshift shelter at a speed of 700 rounds per minute. It takes seconds for the wall to disintegrate and after a slight pause, the guard house follows suit. It's inspirational. The Coyote is allowed to pause for breath and Abdullahi's fighters stream past eager to mop up. Muhammed leaves his AK47 on the ground and using the sheet to protect against the heat from the barrel, helps the gunner carry the Coyote forward a short distance onto the open ground. As Muhammed goes back to retrieve his rifle, another fighter picks up the ammo box and takes Muhammed's place. Together they set the weapon up again, this time trained not on the school but in the direction from where the soldiers' truck arrived. Abdullahi, joins them, machete in hand, Muhammed at his side. They kick discarded millet stalks in front of the barrel of the Coyote to give it some cover; satisfied, they dart across the road. Any soldier who has not fled will be dead or dying but as they pass through the gate, Abdullahi hopes that one or two might be hiding somewhere. He sees a couple of women and a man running towards the dormitories. They should have run away.

Chapter 8

Jamilah's mantra to Aminah and their brother has always been, "live in the present, don't be a prisoner of the past". Her sister has led by example. While the memory of that awful day when she was a little girl has never gone away, Aminah has comforted herself by believing that lightning couldn't strike twice. But it has. Even with an armed platoon outside to protect them 24/7 and despite the Governor giving them his personal assurance he'd keep them safe. It had been all over the media: the smiling benign politician on the campaign trail talking paternally to respectful, demure schoolgirls. Words don't provide protection, but they can provoke a reaction. Tonight it has arrived. There is gunfire in the school grounds, her classmates are screaming, and they are far from safe.

'Come away from the window, Aminah', her teacher urges. 'They'll see you.'

'What does it matter? They know we're here. They've come for us.'

The crack of gunfire echoes against the building. Is there a more foreboding sound? Their attackers are coming closer. Men are running. The hunters outnumber the hunted. A caretaker comes into view, sprinting towards their building. His face is distorted by terror and hopelessness. Another crack and he is propelled forward, coming to a halt face down in the little rose garden they had planted before the break. His hand reaches out and grips a thorny stem and he tries to crawl forward. A tall man in black, a scarf across his face, approaches. She sees the flash of a machete and turns away. The windowpane shatters and plaster falls from the wall opposite on to a screaming classmate crouched below. The bullet lodged in the wall, could have been lodged in Aminah had she stayed at the window. She surprises herself by not panicking. Her senses are sharp. She is on edge yet composed. The teacher turns out the light.

'Girls get down on the floor. Try to stay calm. We've rung the police. They'll be here soon. Pray for Allah's protection.'

Aminah feels calm though she knows she should be terrified. In the darkness, she rings her sister. No response. She tries again and this time uses the voicemail, speaking in a half whisper:

'Jamilah, it's me. Boko Haram have come for us. We need help.' She sounds business-like, as if she's filing a report for the local newspaper. 'Call someone. Please, hurry. I love you, and Ahmed ... always.'

Maybe she's in shock? Like those patients Jamilah told her about the previous day who were intent on comforting staff when they were the ones in need of comfort and didn't seem to realise it. The downstairs door is being smashed in; her pulse quickens. Evil is at their door and impatient to meet them. Screaming in the dorm intensifies. She feels sorry for her teacher. What words of reassurance can she offer her pupils now? Aminah crawls across to her bed and, reaching underneath, exchanges her flip-flops for her trainers. She opens her bedside cupboard and, using the light of her phone, takes out sanitary towels, toothbrush, and pen. She hears footsteps charging up the stairs and rejoins her classmates huddled together at the end of the room. Like the wings of a swan, their teacher's arms reach out across her pupils' shoulders, drawing them in. The door bursts open, and the light is switched on. Some of the girls can't look and brace themselves for the clamber forward and the inevitable molestation. It doesn't come. A tall man fills the entrance. He has the shape of the man she observed earlier from the window. He carries a rifle and a machete smeared with blood. Two men enter behind him and position themselves either side of the door. They wear black kaftans and trousers, and soldiers' laced-up boots. Black scarves cover their heads and faces; the whites of their eyes are visible through horizontal slits. A bearded man of medium build makes an entrance. He too carries a machete but is dressed differently from the others. He doesn't bother to cover his face and wears military fatigues and a vest of dark green pouches. The tall man picks up a chair and sets it down facing the girls. The shorter man sits down. More men push in now and spread themselves across the room, staring at their captives with lustful eyes. The girls edge back against the wall. A gulf is created between the intruders and their captives. On one side: aspiration, kindness, femininity; on the other: evil, brutality and masculinity. The teacher stands up and raises her palms in a conciliatory gesture. The man raises his eyes to the ceiling as if he cannot bear to look at the stupidity in front of him. Lowering his head, he raises a finger to his lips. His fingernail is filthy, but his gesture has the desired effect on the teacher and the entire room.

Aminah recalls that day when Boko Haram arrived on motorcycles to attack her village. A wild-eyed bunch of brigands in shabby clothes, carrying an assortment of weapons. These men, on the other hand, have the air of a military unit, with leadership and discipline. But the salacity in their eyes is undeniable and she shudders. In the silence, she smells the oppressive body odour these intruders have brought to the dorm. When the leader smiles at their compliance, it is through rotten teeth the colour of his beads.

'My name is Abdullahi and in the name of Allah, I have come to liberate you.' His voice sounds like it is coming from hell itself and cuts the air like a razor. 'The education you receive here is forbidden. These infidels', he scowls at the teacher, 'are brainwashing you. They put blasphemous ideas in your heads, allow you to think you are independent when all they are doing is subverting you from the purity of the Qu'ran. The words of the Prophet, peace be upon him, are all you need to learn in this life. That, and how to serve Him and your husband better. We will prepare you for both. You are too ignorant to appreciate this now, but one day you will look back at this night and see it as your moment of liberation and be forever grateful'.

He stands up and pulls the teacher away from the group throwing her roughly onto a nearby bed. The sudden violence agitates the girls, and their sobs intensify. He turns to look at them, pointing a controlling finger at the teacher. 'Shut up! I will say this just once: I do not tolerate disobedience.' The room falls quiet again. He turns back to the teacher, 'I was told there would be a lot of girls here tonight. At least a hundred, yet I count only twelve. The downstairs dormitory is empty, as are most of the beds in here'.

'Please do not harm these girls, sir'. The teacher sits up and presses her palms together. 'They are children, good Muslim girls. We teach them the way of Allah.'

The man rips off the teacher's hijab, grips her by the hair, and forces her on to her knees.

'How can you teach them something you know nothing about? Now, I asked you a question.' He holds the blade of his machete at her throat.

'It was a school break last week, sir. All our pupils should have returned this afternoon ready to start tomorrow, but most have stopped boarding and stay with relatives each night. They will be back tomorrow morning.'

'So that's the kind of discipline you instil in this place. These girls come and go as they please. How could you ever teach them the true path when they don't respect you or your rules.' He throws her onto the floor.

'We will undo the harm you have done!' He glances at the girls. 'Put them back on the straight path. Are there non-believers, amongst you?' His eyes slide across them. Aminah feels them burn into her, then pass.

'Good. You are coming with us. Hand over your phones as you leave, don't be stupid enough to try to conceal them.'

He snaps his fingers. His men move forward and bundle the girls towards the door. Aminah tries to go to the aid of her teacher but is pushed back into line. She pushes the hand of the fighter away.

'Go, Aminah,' says her teacher.

Aminah moves off, looking anxiously over her shoulder. Her teacher remains on the floor trying to put her hijab back on. Aminah is the last girl to leave. She hands over her phone and is manhandled towards the door. She steals a final look back. Her teacher remains on the floor, supporting herself with her elbows. She stares up at the man towering over her, his feet placed either side of her legs. His weapons lie on the bed. He is loosening his clothing. Aminah beseeches Allah to protect her teacher.

'Be quick,' says Abdullahi. 'I never want to see this bitch again.'

Aminah is pushed down the stairs behind her classmates and finally her tears flow. She weeps for her teacher and for the despair she feels for herself and her friends. Ten minutes ago, they had been schoolgirls, brimming with hope and ambition, excited at seeing each other again after a short break. Now they're a commodity and soon they'll be slaves.

Chapter 9

'You're not drinking, Colonel? I'm told it's the best. What's it called again, Ado, Stolenback?'

'Stellenbosch,' says de Witt, before Ado can respond. 'Excellent choice, Senator, but I haven't drunk alcohol in fifteen years.'

Ado glances at the boss. He knows that look. A rare goodwill gesture spurned. Alcohol isn't normally on offer at the Senator's table. Ado's not best pleased either, considering the effort he put in to procure it. Aren't these people supposed to drink like fish?

'The catfish is delicious,' says de Witt, possibly sensing the Senator's irritation. No reaction. 'I've caught quite a few in my time. Kuils River, Western Cape — just down the road from Stellenbosch. Those slippery bastards can fight, man. I'm telling you.'

In his well-cut business suit, crisp white shirt and cropped grey hair, de Witt looks as sharp as the power-point he delivered earlier. He is clean-shaven, but any impression of being a desk man is tempered by a tanned, pock-marked face and steel blue eyes that hint at ruthlessness.

'We try our best.' The Senator helps himself to more yam. 'I've been to South Africa. Our countries have much in common.'

'Our countries are the giants of Africa. We're blessed with great resources but, frankly, we should be doing much better.'

'I agree,' says the boss. 'Too much corruption and poor management.'

'You will change that, Sir,' says Ado.

'Yes,' says the boss, 'and the Colonel here will help rid me of some ... obstacles to progress. Ado, run us through what we agreed today'.

Ado reaches for his iPad. 'Okay, gentlemen, the headline stuff. We will engage Soteria Security Services for six months at a monthly fee of $225,000, to be transferred, in advance, to Cayman National Bank. Accommodation and per diem costs to be split fifty-fifty. Start date — when newly-elected Governor Yakubu takes office.' Ado's deferential nod goes unacknowledged. 'In return, SSS will provide us with ten experienced military advisers under the command of Colonel de Witt with the aim of enhancing the capacity of our State Security Forces to eliminate local insurgents. This includes direct engagement with same, and use of extreme force, as necessary. Our new Governor,' Ado nods again in the Senator's direction, 'will ensure federal support for military equipment and supplies are delivered to State Security Forces in a timely manner, including a list of surveillance equipment and military hardware (to follow) for use by SSS. The Governor will facilitate communications between SSS and State Security Forces. Blah, blah, blah ... Contract can be cancelled by mutual agreement at no less than one month's notice ... deployment by SSS to other states to be agreed by the Governor in advance. Colonel de Witt to report directly to the Governor.' Ado looks up. 'Have I left anything out, Colonel?'

'A few details,' de Witt rolls his head, 'but we can work them out later. 'Otherwise, ja, good to go.'

The boss nods.

'I look forward to doing business with you gentlemen,' says de Witt, raising his water glass. 'And here's to a successful election.'

The Senator and Ado respond in kind. Ado remains concerned at the cost of de Witt's services. As he drinks, his eyes are drawn to the deep lines on de Witt's neck and his weather-beaten face. The act of raising his glass draws attention to the bulge of his biceps pulling at his suit. Physically he is imposing but … he's older than Ado had expected. The boss seems to read his mind.

'You've been doing this work for some time, Colonel.'

'Twenty-five years, man. Throughout Africa and the Middle East.' De Witt leans back and spreads his thick, gnarled fingers along the edge of the table. 'We're contracted by half a dozen African countries, but mostly it's the US, UK and the UN who seek us out. We've saved the ass of more than one UN peacekeeper, I'm telling you, man.' He laughs and leans forward. 'We guard embassies and contractors. Help governments deal with insurgents. The boys I've brought with me are highly experienced in this arena. Special Forces-trained. We'll get the best from your people. We'll soon rid you of your problem.'

'You have no concern about your people's capacity to function in our terrain?'

'We may not be in the spring of our youth, Senator, but we're fit and strong. Our lives depend on it. We'll use plenty of younger legs and fists from within your ranks when we need them. Tracking and bush craft are our meat and drink, and my boys are the best out there. I've a world -class chopper pilot, unrivalled in hunting down insurgents in the bush.'

The boss stops chewing, a clear sign of interest.

'We could access more men,' says de Witt. 'Russian, French, whatever, but we don't need them. We're not up against a large force and they operate in cells, only coming together for bigger ops, less than a hundred or so at a time.

Use a lot of paid help too. Your security forces have a numerical advantage but it's how you deploy them that counts. I've only been here a few weeks, but we've done our research and, if I can speak freely ...?'

The Senator waves a chicken leg.

'There's too much competition between the different elements of your forces. A lack of synergy, strategy, and a winning mentality. We can change that, but we will need good intelligence.'

'You'll have whatever it takes to rid us of these vermin', says the Senator. 'What they're doing to my state and elsewhere is intolerable. People no longer feel safe in the market, at school, or even in the mosque. It's monstrous.'

'They're fearless in fighting villagers and capturing girls,' says de Witt. 'Wait 'til they come up against a trained military machine. We'll see how brave these bastards are then, I'm telling you.'

'I was a military man myself', says the Senator. 'I wish I were young enough to be out there with you.'

'If you were in charge of our country's military, Sir,' says Ado, 'we wouldn't have this problem'.

'Who's in charge of state security, on the ground?' asks de Witt.

'The CP — State Commissioner of Police', says the boss. 'Another spineless incompetent. When I take over, he'll be replaced by Giwa, the Deputy CP. The Governor thinks Giwa's loyal to him, but he's my protégé from way back. Rough at the edges, but he gets things done. One final thing', the boss raises the chicken leg in emphasis, 'discretion. Keep a low profile. Be mindful of the media. If you're asked what you're doing in this country, stress your role as technical assistants, here at the invitation of the

President, to train our troops in guerrilla warfare and modern weaponry. And *not* to do any fighting yourselves.'

'We appreciate the external sensitivities', says de Witt. 'The media like to present companies like ours as undisciplined mercenaries — trigger-happy, getting drunk every night, out for a quick buck. In reality, we're trained, disciplined professionals, providing security services to governments and businesses across the globe.'

'You're also white and South African,' says the Senator.

De Witt puts down his knife and fork. 'Look, we've worked in West, Central and Southern Africa. For political reasons, our own government treats us like bloody criminals. They live in the past, we don't, and the rest of Africa recognises our value. Presidents talk to one another, that's why we're here. I respect good soldiers irrespective of their colour. I'll leave it to your communications people to deal with the media. We'll not give them anything to write about. And I can assure you, Sir, once the bombing stops, the attacks on villages reduce, and more and more insurgents are killed or captured, no one will be interested in who we are or where we come from. We'll be under the radar, and not seeking any credit.'

'Good. Let's have some tea.' The Senator rises slowly to his feet. 'Woman, where the hell are you?'

The Senator's wife comes in immediately. Two maids hover behind her.

'Clear these things away. We'll have tea in the lounge.'

'It's ready, sir.'

'Why didn't you say so? What's the matter with you? Go, go!' As usual, the boss doesn't bother to introduce his wife to his guest. De Witt will assume she's one of the maids.

'Excuse me, Senator, the rest-room?' says de Witt.

'Through there,' says the Senator. 'She'll show you. We'll wait for you next door, in the lounge.'

As de Witt follows the Senator's wife out of the dining room, the Senator holds out his ebony cane in front of Ado, motioning him to stop.

'What do think?' he asks.

'Of de Witt?'

'No, my wife's ass.'

'Seems to know what he's about. Impressive track record. He inspires confidence, but he's not cheap.'

'You get what you pay for, isn't that what you always tell me? We'll get them up and running as soon as possible. Make them work for their money. If they're as good as he says they are, this could be one of our more profitable investments.'

'It doesn't leave much time to pull the money together, Sir.'

'That old fool of a Governor is still telling himself he can win another four years so he won't clean everything out of the coffers — not that we won't say he hasn't. You'll find a way.'

'Yes, Sir but —'

'No more buts. Do you want to be Deputy Governor of Kano State?'

'Yes, of course, Sir, it will be an honour to —'

'Do you want insurance at your next meeting with that Boko Haram piece of shit?'

'Yes, Sir. I —'

'So find the money and stop whinging. Come.'

The Senator takes a step forward then stops again, 'The thing I can't stand about these Afrikaners is their fucking arrogance. Did you see the way he sat there, picking at the food, not drinking the wine, and telling *us* what's wrong with *our* country? Been here five minutes and he knows everything. Only whites, it seems, can be trusted with security in Africa. No wonder our brothers in South Africa disown them.'

'That accent,' says Ado, 'the sound of white oppression. These are the bastard sons of the men who imprisoned Mandela. Steeped in Apartheid, steeped in African blood.'

'Yes, but we'll pay them to shed more African blood, only this time it will be of our choosing. If he does his job, I will be known as the Governor who rid his state of terrorists. Nigeria will take note. It will be an important step towards the ultimate prize.'

'President Yakubu', Ado bows.

The Senator rests his hand on Ado's shoulder, a rare hint of a smile on his lips, 'Let's not count our chickens. We'll let these Boers do the work and we'll take the credit. After that, we'll get shut of them. He's coming back. We'll discuss it later.'

Chapter 10

Abdullahi unclenches his fist. The sand slides through his fingers, flowing back into the hollow from which it had come. This, he reflects, is how he and his men are absorbed back into the forest after an operation. Night is falling. Behind him the men are quiet and alert, waiting for his signal. From the covered lorry nestling under a cluster of bushwillows, comes a low whimper from the new consignment. Most of them sit on the wooden benches running along the sides, others huddle together on the floor. Abdullahi sniffs the air. He's been in the bush so long he can't imagine living anywhere else. Faded by the sun and infused with dust, his clothes, vehicles, weapons, and tents blend in with the Sahelian grassland. This is where Allah wants him to be and where Allah provides for his needs.

He scratches his groin, then hearing the distant hum of a helicopter, stops and looks up. At last, they are coming. He presses his rifle into the sand to help him stand up and signals to his men to lie low. He rejoins them pressing a finger to his lips. He orders one of them to point his rifle inside the truck to maintain silence. It's all unnecessary. Men in a helicopter would never hear them; it's more about discipline and training these princesses in obedience.

The helicopter is higher than it should be. Maybe they have heard about the Coyote. A beam of light tries to find the road, but it has too far to travel and dissipates. The pilot seems equally half-hearted, more intent on keeping his craft on a straight line than following the turns in the road. It tells Abdullahi that the crew is more concerned with getting back to base than finding them. The chugging of the rotary blades overhead reminds him of the Sakara drums of his childhood. His fingers tap in rhythm along the shaft of his rifle, now strapped back across his chest. Displaced air passes across his face and soon the swish of the blades slicing through the night grows faint. He laughs and turns to his men.

'You see how stupid these infidels are? They pass above us and see nothing. They'll radio that there's no sign of us on this road, and yet, here we are. They'll be ordered to direct their search elsewhere, but ... not until tomorrow, because for now, they have to be home before their supper gets cold!'

Some of the men laugh, others shout 'Allahu Akbar!' drowning out the sound of girls weeping. It's always the same. One starts, the rest join in like sheep. He walks to the rear of the covered truck and his men fall silent and gather behind him. He pulls the cover aside. He can make out their shape, hear their blubbering, and smell the soap on their skin. He's energised by their presence. A group of females over whom he wields complete power. Not for the first time, they edge back in fear except for one who stands up and has the audacity to speak to him:

'This is wrong. You should take us back to our teacher. It is against the Qur'an. We are the daughters of Allah, the Most Merciful. You cannot treat us like this. You must take us back.'

Abdullahi ignores her, takes out a torch and casts the light around the interior, assessing his haul for a second time. He is still angry that it is so small — someone will pay for that — but he is pleased with the quality. They are older than the usual consignment, practically women. The men will like that. They look healthy and are surely all virgins. Only the one who remains standing returns his gaze. He makes a closer inspection: trainers; long legs; athletic type;

well developed; indignant look on her stupid face — he'll soon get rid of that.

'We're pulling out,' he says. 'If you want to relieve yourselves, now is the time.'

The girls look anxiously at each other. The defiant one starts up again,

'Why are you doing this? It is wrong.' She turns her attention to the men, speaking over his shoulder, as if she expects a different reaction from them. 'You must take us back. Now!'

He grabs her by the throat and presses his face into hers, pausing to breathe in her scent. His desire is strong and urgent: this is how he is in the bush. Her face screws up in disgust and she turns her head away. He strikes her hard across the side of her face with the back of his hand, opening a cut. She reels back. Almost absentmindedly, her hand reaches for her cheek, and she slides down against the legs of other girls who are too shocked to react.

She's not looking so defiant now! He's seen it all before. They cry and scream as if that will change things and now and again, there's one who thinks she knows better than the rest. Not brave, just arrogant and ... stupid. She will have further to fall than the rest and she can't see it. He steps back and motions to one of his men to undo the back of the lorry. The girls descend tentatively and silently and are directed to the side of the truck. This is another lesson for them. They can look as embarrassed as they like. If the men want to look at them relieving themselves so be it. They will soon learn to do as they are told when they are told.

They clamber back inside. The canopy and the back of the lorry are secured. Abdullahi raises his hand. An armoured Hilux pulls out and stops beside him. A door opens, and he gets in the back. It moves off, the lorry follows, then another. Two more Hilux emerge to complete the convoy. They bump along guided by the light of a crescent moon. There is no need to switch on the headlights. Their eyes adopted to the darkness long ago.

It's an hour since the attack, in another hour they will be back at the camp. Abdullahi knows which of these young women will honour him tonight. He tastes her blood on his ring. It's the old way, the way of the Caliphate. The defeated army must yield up its women. The security forces hold his own wife and daughter prisoner in their barracks, but he is not defeated, he knows this is how the infidel fights.

Chapter 11

Jamilah shows the last patient out of the consultation room, saying goodnight and leaving her with the smile she has developed especially for Dr Salim's clientele. Her real smile is reserved for her family and Salim especially when he tells her a joke. She has a work smile too for the patients on the wards, especially the children; but at the clinic, Salim told her early on that the clients expect her to smile when they arrive and again when they leave, whether she's pleased to see them or not, so she does her best.

Salim works at the hospital too, but it's during these four evenings per week at his private clinic, that he makes his money and she hers. The framed certificates (copies of those in his office at the hospital) confirm he's a member of the Royal College of Obstetricians and Gynaecologists and a graduate of the universities of Zaria and Liverpool. These would count as wallpaper if it weren't for his network of the great, good, and not so good, that ensures a regular flow of daughters, wives, girlfriends, and mistresses — women who expect the best care, paid for by wealthy men who appreciate a discreet, professional service. As this is what Salim delivers, the clinic receives a steady flow of visitors. Jamilah has little to do compared to her day job, but Salim tells her she adds value, not only by being trained in midwifery but in offering a reassuring female presence — in the tailor-made nurse's uniform he provides for her, complete with the clinic's logo. Of course, while he would never say it, she also brings experience of the thing that all women live in fear of. Anyway, no time to think of that now, it's time to head home.

There is no receptionist. Discretion is total. Salim accepts appointments on his clinic mobile number and

Jamilah greets them at the door. She's grateful for the money. How else could she support Ahmed at university, pay Aminah's school fees and keep a roof over their heads? But it's also a way of repaying Salim's kindness over the years. It was Salim who had examined her at the hospital after her ordeal. He'd looked angry when she told him who had been responsible, but he'd advised her not to take it further. Sergeant Giwa was a powerful man; it would put her and her siblings in more danger. Maybe he had felt guilty about that, but for whatever reason, he has been a significant presence in her life and especially after his wife died. He's a good man. He sent his maid to look after Ahmed and Aminah, so she could focus on her nursing studies, and even lent her money to pay the rent. She hasn't given up trying to pay him back, but he just laughs, telling her it was an investment. She knows there are plenty on the team who think she got her promotion because she slept with him. Too bad. He has filled their father's boots for a long time, and she's not bothered about being popular. Besides, she couldn't do her job properly if she got close to them.

Salim holds the door open for her and they exchange goodbyes. She leaves him to lock up and hails her usual auto-rickshaw driver. Settling into the back, she takes out her phone and notes two missed calls and a voice mail notification from Aminah. This is worrying. Aminah knows she has to keep her phone on silent during consultations. Clients expect her undivided attention. She plays the message. She can't hear it completely, but she hears enough for her chest to tighten and her throat to dry. She tells the driver to pull over, gets out and replays the message, listening hard. Aminah speaks calmly against a background of girls crying and the crack of gunfire. She rings Aminah's number. It rings out. She calls the school. Voicemail. She calls Ahmed. He picks up.

'Hi Jam —.'

'Ahmed, listen. Something terrible has happened. I got a message from Aminah three hours ago. I've only just played it. The school was being attacked and she wanted me to call for help. She's not picking up, I can't get through to the school. Has there been anything on the news?'

'I haven't heard anything. I'll check online.'

'Okay, I'll be home in fifteen minutes. I'll try the school again. See what you can find out.' She gets back in the auto-rikshaw and tells the driver to hurry. She tries the school again and leaves a message with her number. She checks an online news site on her phone. The News Flash sucks the breath out of her. It's hard to take the words in. She doesn't want to read on but of course she must:

"Reports coming in ... dozen girls taken ... eight policemen slaughtered ... two missing. Three teachers dead ... three missing. The Governor assures relatives and the public the perpetrators will be brought to justice ... brave men will not die in vain ... thoughts with relatives ... full update in the morning. Security forces employing all their resources ..."

Yes, but what about the girls? She reads on praying she's not going to come to a list of missing girls with Aminah's name on it.

"Commissioner of Police confident of early arrests and return of the girls. Next twelve hours crucial."

And that's it. There's no list, just a number for relatives to ring for information. She calls it — engaged. Only twelve taken, there's hope. There should be six times that number at the school. Aminah is a smart girl and, like her, she can run. She'll be hiding somewhere, waiting for daylight. That's the smart thing to do. She'll go out there and find her little sister. But why hasn't she rung again? Maybe she lost her phone, or her battery died or ... someone took it from her.

Jamilah closes her eyes. It's hard to deny the unescapable truth, her little sister was there in the middle of it, surrounded by terrorists and calling for help. How could she get away? There have been no more calls. They've taken her phone. They've taken her. Jamilah looks despairingly up at the crescent moon. Can Aminah see it too? Where is she now? Jamilah calls the number again. Engaged. She will find her. Her phone rings. It's Ahmed. He speaks immediately, his words an uncanny echo of her thoughts:

'They've taken her.' His voice lacks its usual easy confidence.

'We'll get her back, Ahmed.'

'I called the number. It was **State Police Force Command**. They wouldn't confirm, but it seems only a dozen girls were there tonight. From what Minah said on your voicemail ... they must have her. The police took my contact details. Said they'd be in touch as soon as there's any news.'

'And that's it?'

'They gave me the name of a counselling service.'

'Didn't they say what they're doing to track them down?'

'Nothing. They'll let us know. And they request we don't talk to the media as the Governor will be making a statement in the morning.'

'So Boko Haram can walk into a school, kill the guards and staff, walk out with the pupils and we have to keep quiet and not make a fuss? Meanwhile, the Governor goes back to bed and gets someone to sit and write him a speech. Why isn't he giving updates about progress in chasing these people down? They must have ways to track them. Are they even out looking for them at all?'

'Sounds like they won't be doing anything more until daylight.'

'So what was "the next twelve hours are crucial" all about?'

'Wanting to sound as if he is doing something. If his daughter had been taken, no one would be sleeping in the barracks tonight. They'd be turning the country upside down.'

'Well, I'm not ready to curl into a ball and wait for something to happen. Not again, and not when it involves our beautiful sister.'

'Nor me,' says Ahmed, but almost in the same breath, his voice cracks, 'What are we going to do, sis?'

'I'm outside now. Get your bike, we're going to the State Police Force Command. Let's find out what's going on.'

Chapter 12

The heavily fortified State Police Force Command building looms up ahead. Ahmed pulls over.

'We'll have to walk from here', he says, 'if I drive any further, they'll start shooting'.

They walk at a slow, deliberate pace, through an avenue of bright lights surrounded by swarms of flying insects colliding in a demented dance. Election pennants flap in the breeze. The Governor's face looks down at them from a billboard, trying to look statesmanlike but in Jamilah's eyes, he's a symbol of incompetence. How could he let this happen? Ahmed holds his arms away from his body to show he has nothing in his hands. She follows suit. They pass imposing blocks of concrete set out at intervals to deter car bombers and head towards a security bunker positioned between a row of trees. Its strong corrugated iron roof slopes over thick banks of sandbags at the front and sides. In the gap between the roof and top of the sandbags Jamilah sees helmets and faces of two guards. She is concerned that one of them is pointing his rifle at Ahmed. She recalls that a few hours ago these men lost comrades, maybe friends too. The flickering red lights of cameras provide a modicum of reassurance that these men will surely keep their emotions in check. A strong voice from within the bunker tells them to stop and asks what they want.

'As-Salam-u-Alaikum', says Jamilah. 'We seek news of our sister. We believe she was taken from her school tonight by terrorists.'

'Turn around slowly and keep your arms away from your sides ... Okay, who are you?'

'I'm a Senior Nursing Officer, my brother here is a student at the university.'

'We are closed, go home, there's nothing to find out tonight. Come back tomorrow.'

'Please Sir, I only want to know what is happening.'

'We are on their trail. Go home, there will be an update tomorrow morning.'

'Please, Sir,' Jamilah moves a step closer with her arms spread out, 'if you or any of your comrades were ever brought to our hospital, like all those people I treated yesterday from the market bombing, I will never turn you away. Neither you nor your family. We are on the same side. Let me talk to someone.'

The guard turns to speak to his colleague, then addresses Jamilah again,

'You can ask at the desk. But they won't tell you anything different. Come forward slowly and put your ID here, where I can see it ... Okay, stand back.'

He examines their ID and hands it to his colleague who looks like he is writing down the details.

'Go through there.'

Jamilah follows Ahmed through a turnstile gate set in the middle of a tall metal fence. The guard comes out of the back of the bunker and tells them to stand legs apart, arms outstretched, then runs a handheld scanner over them. He makes no apology that it is him scanning her and not a woman. He hands them back their ID.

'Follow the path up to that lighted window.'

'Thank you, Sir,' says Jamilah and they do as he says.

The window slides across and once again they are asked what they want. They hand over their IDs and phones in exchange for a reclamation tag. The policeman joins them outside and tells them to follow him. He walks ten metres, opens a door and indicates with a nod that they should go inside. They find an unmanned front desk facing half a dozen wooden benches.

'Wait here. The Sergeant will come.'

'Thank you, Sir,' says Jamilah turning around but the man's already gone. They sit.

'I didn't think we'd get this far,' says Ahmed, running his hand across his head. 'And we haven't had to dash anyone.'

Jamilah takes his hand, and they sit in silence suppressing their unspoken fears. Old posters hang crookedly on the wall advising the public about the dangers of drug abuse and appealing to them not to participate in corruption. On the wall, behind the front desk, are large, framed photographs of the President and the Governor, separated by a motto and crest; below these are smaller photos of men in uniforms, whose faces she can't make out. The strip light above them is blinking. It's probably been doing that for a while.

Fifteen minutes later, a door behind the desk swings open. A Sergeant walks in briskly, his stripes boldly proclaiming his authority. He beckons them forward and looks at them sternly. He's thin, wiry and wears a blue shirt with black epaulettes. A beret with a silver badge sits on his shaved head,

'Ten of our men were slaughtered tonight protecting a school. But I am asked to break off our investigations to come and tell you people what you've been told twice already. Ten grieving widows are sitting at home tonight comforting children who've lost their fathers. Have any of them insisted on coming here tonight demanding a personal consultation? No, they're too busy arranging funerals for the morning.'

'May Allah give your comrades an easy and pleasant journey and shower blessings on their grave,' says Ahmed.

'May Allah give you patience,' says Jamilah.

The Sergeant doesn't acknowledge their condolences, but they seem to calm him.

'We lost someone tonight too, Sergeant,' says Jamilah. 'Our dear sister was taken by the terrorists who murdered your men. We're afraid she might be murdered too. We want to know for sure if she was taken and what the security services are doing to catch these murderers and rescue our sister.'

'And avenge your comrades', adds Ahmed.

'We'll catch them. If your sister was at that school this evening, she's been taken, otherwise she'd have turned up by now. The only females we found there were teachers who had been shot and in the case of one, raped and butchered. We'll confirm tomorrow when we have concluded a full search, but they came to take girls, not kill them. The Governor will give an update in the morning alongside the Commissioner. If you're thinking of going out to the school tonight, don't. It's been cordoned off while we investigate the murder scene. You'll be wasting your time and getting in our way.'

Jamilah hears the words but has difficulty assembling them into meaning for her eyes are focused above the Sergeant's head on a framed photo of a man in uniform she hasn't seen in ten years. He seems to be sneering at her and her brother. She realises the Sergeant has stopped talking.

'Who's that?' Jamilah points at the photograph.

The Sergeant swivels round and his face lights up. 'Deputy State Commissioner of Police, Giwa. If anyone can bring your sister back, it's him. Now, I have work to do. Good evening.'

He walks out leaving them standing. Jamilah goes back to sit on the bench leaving Ahmed to stare at the photograph.

Her mind is racing. Ahmed is eleven years old but like her, tall for his age. He is spared because she offers herself to Police Sergeant Giwa. She loses her virginity roughly in the back of a police lorry, staring past his uniformed shoulder at the dusty sky as his belt buckle grinds into her stomach. Splinters from the wooden floor pierce her buttocks and lower back. Her father and uncle lie on the ground waiting to be slaughtered. Waiting, because she can hear the vigilantes' executioner talking on the phone to his girlfriend. He laughs, assuring his "darling" he'll see her that night and no, this time he won't be late, it's a promise.

What went through her father and uncle's minds as they lay there on their stomachs, wrists tied behind their backs, the worn-out flip-flops of vigilantes pressing their faces against the hard earth? What went through little Ahmed's mind as he sat below her, his back against the wheel of the lorry, watching that butcher, phone in one hand, cigarette and machete in the other, cruelly delaying the execution? She found out later that the brave boy had kept his hand over the eyes of his little sister the whole time. Now, ten years later his hand is on her elbow urging her up from the bench. The gesture draws her back to the present. They collect their phones and ID and are soon outside walking back to the bike.

'Are you okay Jam? I never thought I'd see that man's face again. I'd stopped thinking about him.' Jamilah doesn't reply. He slips his arm around her shoulder, and she leans her head against him. 'They've made him Deputy CP! Can you imagine? Rewarded for his outstanding police work.' His voice is hoarse with anger.

No matter how many barriers she puts in the path of these images, they find their way back to her. Everything was pushed to one side and left to fester. There wasn't even an inquiry into the deaths of her father and uncle. How could a village girl seek justice? Salim had counselled that if it ever got to court, Giwa would say her father was a terrorist collaborator killed by vigilantes and he had stepped in on time to stop them executing the boy. He would manufacture witnesses to prove it while she would find it impossible to find a witness to risk his or her life to say otherwise. As for violating a minor, Giwa would either deny it or say it was consensual and he hadn't realised she was so young. That was another complication. She couldn't accuse him of rape. She'd proposed it. There was no screaming, no fighting him off. She hadn't sold her body; she'd traded it for her brother's life, to a man whose job it was to protect her and her family. She was a girl, a young girl! Why did she have to make such a bargain? No witnesses came forward, there was no inquiry, no resolution but people in the village knew what had happened and she was tainted by it. She shudders. She can still smell his breath, hear his grunts, feel his weight crushing her. And now after all this time, she's heard his name spoken, seen his photograph adorn the wall and he's been promoted. In the eyes of his men, he's some sort of hero. Aminah has been taken and this is the person they must depend on to get her back. They reach the bike. There are tears in her eyes, but her voice is firm, 'We can't let this overwhelm us, Ahmed. We have to stay strong for Aminah.'

'Inch 'Allah. But we can't rely on these people.'

He's right. He's always been her little brother, now he's got to be a man; ready to step up and fight alongside her. More than ever they need Allah to protect their sister and to get help to get her back.

Part Two

ONE MONTH LATER

Chapter 13

Aminah lies still and alert. There are ten of them in the tent; she's the only one trying not to sleep. They are kept apart from the Christian girls for whom this life of captivity is even worse; it almost makes her ashamed to be Muslim. She and her classmates get to eat at least once a day — always millet, occasionally goat — and, apart from that first night, have been left alone. Those poor girls, having refused to convert to Islam, are the slaves of the fighters and their wives. They fetch water, search for firewood, wash clothes, scrub and cook and for their hard work they are beaten, raped, and have to live off scraps. Mostly, they seem to survive on the leaves and drumstick pods of the moringa tree as well as crickets they trap and roast. They don't even have a tent, just a ragged sheet spread over branches they have managed to wedge into the hard ground. Aminah admires their conviction and courage. At least one of them has been murdered; she had stayed true to her faith, even when they beat her. Aminah saw her being dragged off by two fighters, heard two shots and never saw her again.

She thinks back to the night of her capture. The lorry had stopped for a second time and Lami and Fa'izah had managed to loosen the cover and squeeze out the back. Aminah was on the verge of following them when her friend Abbiah had gripped her arm and begged her not to go, saying the escapees were bound to be caught and would suffer for it, and she didn't want Aminah to suffer too.

Touched by her friend's concern, Aminah had suppressed her instincts and stayed put. She had thought Abbiah was looking out for her, but she was only thinking of herself. She was too scared to move and didn't want Aminah to leave her. Abdullahi was furious, his men fearful. He picked two of them and beat them fiercely. Loud threats and insults filled the air, a few shots were fired but they didn't spend much time looking for the escapees. Soon, the convoy was on its way again, and this time the fighters were twice as vigilant.

Within minutes of reaching the camp, Aminah did suffer. She was raped by that … animal. He had slapped her again and again as if he wanted to see more emotion from her, but she had taken his blows, his thrusts, and his bites without a saying a word, keeping her eyes shut and praying for it to be over. The stench of his breath and the stink of his body was nauseating. She had thought of her teacher left behind with Muhammed, and how he had finished with her in minutes. Abdullahi was the same. They are like any other animal in the bush; they spread their seed quickly and move on. He'd left her lying on the grass outside his tent where she'd curled up into the foetal position and closed her eyes trying to come to terms with the shock. She was still alive but what if she'd contracted HIV or was pregnant, would that still be a life worth living? She'd felt something pull at her feet. At first, she'd thought it was an animal but when she looked up she could see the silhouette of a woman undoing the laces of her trainers. For a moment Aminah felt more outrage at being robbed of her precious shoes than her honour. But she was too sore and defeated to put up a fight and when the woman dropped her old sandals on to Aminah's chest, she'd been obliged to accept the exchange. The humiliation didn't stop there.

Unashamedly, the woman had rummaged through her clothes, taking her sanitary towels, pen, and torch. When she was satisfied there was nothing left, she had pulled Aminah to her feet and handed her a threadbare towel, pointing to the blood they both knew was not due to a period. The woman pushed her towards a tent where her classmates were sitting in a huddle, afraid to look at her, as if by doing so they would have to accept their new reality. For her part, Jamilah had a sense that she had taken part in a ritual that occurred each time Abdullahi returned with new captives. Abbiah averted her eyes while Jamilah looked at her with contempt. To this day she has no time for her.

The courage of the Christian girls strengthened Aminah's resolve not to go to pieces or even kill herself, which is what she would have imagined doing before all this happened. Their example also strengthened her resolve not to lose faith in her own faith. If these Christian girls could stay true to their God when they were suffering more than her and her classmates, then she could at least do the same. Their captors are not true followers of Islam but dedicated to a perverse version of it that makes them inhuman. She decided that the best way for her to be true to her own faith was to disobey her captors and escape. If she had followed her instincts, when she'd had the chance, she could have been home with her family now. Oh, how she misses them! They've never been apart this long. They have not communicated at all since she sent her sister that last text. She remembers how Ahmed teased her on their last night together: "I'm sure you'll make someone a good wife one day, if you ever manage to find a husband." She'll never have a husband. She's come to terms with that. Look at Jamilah. As soon as word spread that she'd been violated, her sister was no longer wife material. The circumstances counted for nothing. Now it's her turn. It doesn't even matter whether she was raped or not, it will be assumed she was and that will be enough for mothers to keep their sons away from her. Well, there are worse things that could happen. Allah has other things in store for her.

The unit moves camp every couple of weeks. Abdullahi and Muhammed come and go more frequently and will be back tomorrow when they will leave the Mandara mountains for a bigger camp, deep in the Sambisa Forest. There, she will have the "honour" of marrying a fighter. This is why she has been left alone since that first night. Two senior fighters want her and she has declined them both. For the time being, they compete for her attention. Abdullahi finds the contest amusing. She knows these men are on edge and increasingly impatient. It won't be long before she receives an ultimatum. Abdullahi says that under Islam, a single woman must be married, and at her age she should have been married already. Her above-average height and physical development appear to have made her more attractive to these brutes, but she has no intention of giving her life away. She wants to be a doctor, not the bush wife of an illiterate killer, and never, ever, the mother of his child.

The tent is filled with the movements of poor sleep and the sound of tired breathing. On a normal night, she too would be praying for sleep to come quickly and not let go. Tonight, she is awake, resolute, and anxious for the time to pass. She raises herself on her elbows and looks around. Her eyes have learned to adjust to the dark like they did when she was a girl in the village. On the far side, three girls huddle together, arms reaching across each other, fear masquerading as tenderness. Her supposed friend, Abbiah lies across from her beside the youngest girl who sleeps with her thumb in her mouth. Spread around the tent are plastic bags containing odd bits of clothing, worn plastic bottles and the exercise books they have been given to record verses of the Qur'an.

It's time. The two tent pegs she's been loosening for the last couple of hours, slide out easily. She squeezes her head underneath the flap and looks around. No guards nearby, no moon, no stars, just dark clouds offering their protection. Allah is protecting her. Is it Him making the crickets sing so loudly so as to drown out the sound of a false step? Or maybe it's because her ears, like the rest of her body, are on high alert. They do not bother to assign a fighter to sit outside their tent to guard them. They think their promise to cut the throat of any girl foolish enough to try to escape will suffice to keep them trembling in their tents. There are always a couple of sentries high above on the rock and she knows they will not surrender to the lure of sleep for fear of incurring the wrath of Abdullahi. But the sentries are focused on what might be in front of them, not below.

She pulls the rest of her body out of the tent, crouches down and waits. The crickets become louder as if they are telling each other she is on the move. It is forbidden to leave the tent at night, but if she is spotted now, she can say she has a fever and must relieve herself outside. She slips on her sandals. Based on the rising of the sun and informed by overheard snippets of conversation from the wives, she has chosen to go east, towards the border with Cameroon. She heads down the slope, keeping low to the ground and resisting the urge to run. It's hard to see ahead but also hard for her to be seen, and with each careful step forward the night shifts its cloak of darkness further around her shoulders. She goes sideways at first, then diagonally as she moves steadily downhill. She picks her way between the rocks and reaches the tree she had chosen earlier as a marker. No shouts, no warning shot! There are less rocks; the terrain is flattening out. Silently and steadily she slides through the cool, black air.

Fifteen minutes later, her breathing is hard and fast, and she's afraid someone will hear it. She reduces her pace. The ground feels different ... a trail! Alhamdulillah! Allah is looking out for her! She looks back in the direction of the overhang but cannot make it out, though she knows it hasn't moved. She bends down and touches the worn surface to make sure it's real. Her fingers trace the unmistakeable pock marks forged by cattle hooves. She shifts from one side of the trail to the other, verifying its width. It's not a road or even a path, just a trail that surely can take her forward in a more orderly way. She prays it will lead her to a village where she can seek help, not to an empty field waiting to welcome cattle in the morning. She takes off with renewed energy. So far, so good, but she won't get ahead of herself. It will be another four hours before the sentries wake up the slaves, and maybe another half hour before they discover she's gone. She thinks of Jamilah and Ahmed and her step quickens again.

Chapter 14

Sitting in the heart of his palatial new office, adorned in his gubernatorial finery, it's hard to imagine the boss in any other setting, at least until the top job comes around. He's spread out on a large sofa, hand resting magisterially on his cane. A large glass coffee table separates him from his audience of three. He addresses de Witt:

'Welcome, Colonel, I thought you should meet our new Commissioner of Police, Giwa, as soon as possible.' De Witt and Giwa shake hand. 'And of course, you know Ado our new Deputy Governor.'

'Congratulations gentlemen. I look forward to working with you.' De Witt's wearing the same grey suit. No doubt, like Giwa, he'd feel more at home in uniform but a South African mercenary in military fatigues, calling on the newly-elected Governor of Kano on his first week in office is hardly a good look.

'"Giwa" stands for elephant in our Hausa language,' says the boss, 'now he has the opportunity, I'm sure he'll waste no time trampling these terrorists underfoot!' The boss bares his teeth in a smile. He's still on a post-election high. Giwa looks pleased with himself too. His promotion has just been announced but he hasn't wasted any time in having the "CP" tag stitched on his shirt.

'Colonel de Witt is here to help us get rid of our vermin problem, Commissioner. His team will provide us with technical support drawing on their experience of pest control elsewhere.'

The boss is on form today, thinks Ado.

'I'm sure we can benefit from the Colonel's experience,' says Giwa, 'and under your leadership,

Excellency, we will restore discipline to our State and respect for the law.'

It seems the elephant is beginning to learn the ways of court, thinks Ado. He won't be ringing the Inspector of Police in Abuja for instructions every five minutes, like his predecessor.

'We'll start straight away,' says the Governor. 'Our priority target is one of their leaders, a man called Abdullahi. CP, fill the Colonel in.'

'Abdullahi is a high-ranking Boko Haram Shura member and military commander with a unit that's particularly active in our State — though he spreads his operations right across the North West and into Chad and Cameroon. His ability to stay mobile and move between different camps across large distances is one reason why he's managed to elude us. There's no doubt that he's ruthless, some say he's clever, but in my view he's been lucky. He goes for easy targets. They've slaughtered hundreds. He enjoys killing — his words, not mine. Likes to kidnap girls — and hold on to them too.' He laughs inappropriately.

'Can't be all be down to luck,' says de Witt. 'Surely he's getting help from somewhere?'

Giwa looks at the Governor. The Governor looks displeased. Ado wonders who de Witt has been talking to.

'He hasn't needed any help', says the Governor. 'My predecessor was a coward who lacked leadership. The previous CP was an incompetent who lacked willpower.'

Ado nods his head emphatically, then weighs in, 'The former Governor looked to Abuja for guidance and to the military to take on the terrorists. Abuja would send troops — mainly Southerners who knew nothing about our land or religion. Federal funds allocated for equipment and training never reached barrack level. Would you agree, Commissioner?'

'Yes', says Giwa, 'but our firepower is already improving. Just this morning, thanks to your intervention, Excellency, we took delivery of a consignment of Heckler Koch G3 machine guns, promised more than six months ago.'

The Governor nods in recognition, then raises his finger. 'If some of these western governments, who criticise our government's response to this insurrection, would focus their attention on stopping funds from the Middle East reaching terrorists in this country, and give us money to buy arms instead,' he placed the palm of his hand on his chest, 'we would end this conflict a lot sooner'.

'What weaponry does Abdullahi's group have?' asks de Witt.

'In the beginning, it was old rifles and craft guns', says Giwa, 'but they've replaced them with modern imports — AK-47s, Kalashnikovs, rocket launchers, shoulder-launched weapons, IEDs and ... under my predecessor's command, weapons they stole from us, including Hecklers, and a Zastava M02 Coyote heavy-machine gun. But their most lethal weapon is the suicide bomber.'

If de Witt is shocked by this revelation, he doesn't show it, 'What about drones?' he asks.

'They don't have any,' says Giwa. 'And they wouldn't know what to do with them. Despite all that modern firepower, they're still peasants in love with their machetes. These are unsophisticated men Colonel, bush rats led by a bloodthirsty fanatic.'

'Tell the Colonel about your little operation,' says the boss with an approving nod.

'A month ago, I found out where Abdullahi's relatives were hiding. We raided the place, killed a few of them and took the rest in for questioning, including his wife, daughter, two sisters and their husbands. They told us they didn't know his whereabouts, which we knew would be the case, although,' he pauses to grin, 'we had to make sure. We're holding them for obstructing the course of justice. We did get a contact number for him though'.

'He wants to trade', says the Governor, 'You see, this piece of shit is happy to take other men's wives and daughters but doesn't like it when the boot's on the other foot. And here's the best bit, he wants a ransom payment on top!' He shakes his head in disbelief. 'The Deputy Governor will share with you what we have in mind, Colonel.'

'I spoke to Abdullahi. He agreed to a face-to-face negotiation meeting with me at a disused tyre factory, on the outskirts of the city.'

'Sorry, Mr Ado, why you?' asks de Witt, 'and if it's just a negotiation, why can't it be done on the phone?'

'I would have thought that obvious, Mr de Witt,' says Ado. 'He needs to know the person he's dealing with has the power to negotiate. And we have to be sure he is who he says he is, especially as there might be a financial transaction. We could be speaking to anyone on the phone. We've never met the man before, and there are no recent photos.'

'So how will you know it's him?' says de Witt.

'Because', says Ado, 'I insisted he bring a schoolgirl with him, whose name and photograph I will have with me. To further prove her identity, I will ask her a question that only she will know the answer to. I will have his daughter with me to exchange. I have agreed to go alone, but of course, I won't. We've checked the place out. There's plenty of cover for you, your team, and the CP and his men in the background. You'll be lying in wait, ready to take him out. For my sake, Mr de Witt, I trust your team is as good as you say they are.'

'Aren't you concerned he'll kill you? asks de Witt. 'Wouldn't a deputy governor be a big feather in his cap. Why would he agree to meet you on his own? He's supposed to be clever, why would he risk walking into an ambush?'

This man's tone is beginning to rankle. Ado's a Deputy Governor, this Boer's a hired hand, yet it feels as if he's being interrogated like he was one of de Witt's soldiers. 'I've spoken to him,' says Ado. 'I've assured him the Governor wants to see schoolgirls freed even more than bringing a terrorist leader like him to justice. I told him, in a conspiratorial way, that coming so soon after the elections the release of these girls will be a major coup for the Governor, and make the international media sit up and pay attention. Abdullahi needs funds and wants his daughter back.'

'Doesn't seem so concerned about getting his wife back!' interjects Giwa with a smirk.

'I told him this is just a preliminary face-to-face meeting, a confidence builder,' continues Ado. 'We do one exchange and agree terms on a much larger one.'

'I can understand why you want this man eliminated', says de Witt, but surely there *is* a lot of political capital to be gained by trading first, liberating a lot of innocent girls then finding a way to kill him later?'

'Perhaps, Colonel,' says the Governor, 'but my priority is to have him eliminated as soon as possible. It will be easier to find these girls once Abdullahi is out of the way.'

'What if we take him alive?' says de Witt. 'We get one girl back, keep the money, then beat the truth out of him. Once we locate the girls you do what you want with him.'

'No! I want this vermin eliminated, immediately', says the Governor, bristling with anger and looking as if he is trying to stand up. 'Once you get your hands on these people you have to exterminate them. We've learnt that the hard way. I'm not paying you for your opinion, but to do what I want, do you understand?'

'There's another thing you overlook, Mr de Witt,' says Ado, 'if Abdullahi is captured, he could threaten to have all the girls killed unless he was released, then we'd be in a worse position.'

'Exactly!' The Governor slaps the sofa arm.

'With respect, Sir,' says de Witt, 'and I apologise for any offence, of course, this man should die. I was only seeking to offer you the added value of my experience. Isn't there a risk he would give instructions to his men to kill the girls if he is killed at the meeting?'

'These schoolgirls only have value to Boko Haram if they're alive', says Ado. Abdullahi's death won't change that. Yes, he might make that threat, but once he's gone, his men will appoint another leader and, here you have to yield to our greater understanding of these people, Colonel, I doubt the first thing his successor would do is kill off their most valuable assets. Besides, who would they have to carry out their suicide bombings?'

'Enough,' says the Governor. 'This isn't a debate. I've made my decision. The meeting with Abdullahi is scheduled for Friday night. Colonel, you will come up with the necessary plan and logistics. Consult with the CP and my Deputy. Report back to me in forty-eight hours.' He waves his hand to signal the meeting is over.

Chapter 15

'I'm sorry it's taken so long', says Lami's mother, 'but even after she was returned to us, Alhamdulillah, they told us not to let our daughters speak to anyone. But now that the Governor's lost the election ...'

'We were told not to talk to anyone either,' says Jamilah, 'but how can you just sit at home and do nothing when your child's been taken?'

'I know, it was over a week before we could get near the poor girl, two weeks before we could get her home. Can you imagine, our own daughter!'

'It must have been so frustrating', says Jamilah.

'We got to talk once a day on the phone. There was always someone in the room with her. They kept promising she'd be back with us very soon, but my first sight of her was on TV'. Lami's mother claps her hands. 'They were parading her up and down, meeting this one and that. Strangers, not even her own family. It was like she'd escaped one group of captors only to be taken prisoner by another!' She presses a handkerchief against her upper lip then dabs her eyes, perhaps out of habit, for there are no tears to be seen.

'They were holding on to her and kept telling everyone they had rescued her.'

'Hadn't they?'

'No. They escaped all on their own. They were very brave girls.'

'Yes, they were, but —'

'The old Governor was hoping their return would boost his re-election campaign. I see that now. Look, I've told her to tell you everything because you're leading the support group and you've a right to know. We never disagreed with what they said. The Governor was very generous to Lami. In a way, I'm sorry he didn't get back in. But we were so glad to get her back and now she's safe with us at home.'

Jamilah aches at the sound of those words. If only she could have her dear sister home safe. But what she had suspected from the outset was true. Despite all his talk, the Governor had not even tried to get the rest of the girls back or avenge the murders of the guards and teachers. His priority for the security forces had been to protect him during his campaign rallies and maintain order on election day. But the public had had enough of him.

'Let's hope the new Governor, Yakubu, will be better', says Jamilah. 'He's promised enough times to get our girls back and come down hard on Boko Haram.'

'I hope so. That's why the people voted for him. Anyway, by Allah's grace, we have Lami back. Alhamdulillah. We can put this terrible thing behind us and get on with our lives. Oh, I'm sorry my dear, that was heartless of me. Poor Aminah. I'm sure she'll be back with you soon. Lami talks about her all the time, and the other girls too. She's still so upset. Allah will answer our prayers. You'll see.' She embraces Jamilah.

'Insha'Allah', says Jamilah.

'Insha'Allah. Come, she's waiting for you.'

She shows Jamilah into a room where Lami is sitting alone on a sofa, absorbed in her phone. A popular soap plays in the background with the sound switched off.

'I'll bring some tea', says Lami's mother.

Lami looks up and smiles at Jamilah. She seems different, older.

'No, don't worry, if you can give us fifteen minutes?'
says Jamilah, setting down the bag she has borrowed from
Dr Salim.

'Of course', says Lami's mother, drawing the curtains
and switching on a light. 'I'll be outside if you need
anything else.'

Jamilah smiles, and as Lami's mother shuts the door
behind her, Jamilah has the impression she is not the first
person to be granted an audience with Lami in recent days.

'Hi, Lami.' Jamilah sits down beside her, and they
embrace. 'It's been a while. How are you?'

'I'm okay', says Lami, 'Just tired.'

Jamilah takes Lami's hand. Her fingernails are long
and painted orange. 'I'm sorry for what you've been
through, it must have been terrible.' She smooths Lami's
hand between her palms. 'You know me, Lami. I'm not
from the police, or the government, or the media. I'm here
on behalf of Aminah, your friend and my sister.'

Lami is wearing so much make-up she could pass for
a twenty-year-old.

'I'm sorry. I didn't mean to be insensitive', she sighs,
'it's just when you get asked the same questions over and
over again...'

Jamilah wonders why Lami is the one who thinks she
should be receiving sympathy.

'I think of my classmates every day, especially
Aminah. She was so brave.'

'Have you been on television?'

'Yes! How did you know? I've recorded two
programmes this week, but I didn't think they had gone out
yet. Have you seen them?'

'No ... it was just that you look ... different', says
Jamilah.

'Do I, how?' Lami smiles broadly, clearly fishing for a compliment. Jamilah won't oblige.

'Well … your clothes, your hair …'

'You'll never believe it', says Lami, eyes lighting up, 'I've been promised a nursing scholarship in the States. Dukes University. Travel, fees, flights, visa, accommodation — USAID will pay for everything, The Ambassador himself came to see me. I just have to stay here for another year, get my grades, then I'm off! Oh, I wish I could tell Aminah, she'd be so excited for me. She would have loved to study in the US. She wanted to be a doctor.'

'I'm sure she still does', says Jamilah. 'So tell me about the men who took your classmates, anything you can remember.'

'Sure.' She sighs, resigned at returning to a familiar routine. 'it's just … I hate thinking about it, it's so horrible.'

'I know, please, try.'

'It happened so quickly. There was a dozen of us in the dorm. The only boarders to come back on time. We were chatting, sharing what we'd been doing during the break and so on, then we heard this … cracking noise outside. When we looked out, we realised it was shooting and the school was under attack. Our house teacher came in and told us to be calm. There were guards to protect us, she said, and they had phoned the State Police Force Command. Then we heard men shouting "Allah Akbar" and got really frightened. In no time, they broke down the door and stormed inside.'

'And Aminah was with you?'

'Yes. And you won't believe it, just before they burst in, the teacher told Aminah to move away from the window. A second after she moved, a bullet shattered the glass and lodged in the wall right above where I was sitting!

Can you imagine? If I'd been standing up at the time, I would have been killed! I wouldn't be here now.'

Jamilah instantly reflects that if Aminah hadn't moved she would have been the one to have been killed. 'Why was Aminah at the window?'

'That's what I mean about her being so brave. She was trying to see what was going on. The teacher turned off the lights and led us to the back of the room. Then we heard them breaking down the front door and charging up the stairs ...' She turns her head away and closes her eyes as if she is telling the story for the first time or has been watching too many soaps. Jamilah lifts a glass of water sitting close by and offers it to her, but Lami holds up her palm, waits a second then signals she can continue.

'When the lights came back on, they surged in, waving huge machetes, dripping with blood. We screamed. I was sure they were going to slaughter us there and then.' She fans her face with a crossword magazine. 'Then this man walked in, and everything went quiet. The others were dressed in black from head to toe, but this man didn't bother to cover his face. He didn't seem to care. He was clearly in control.'

'What did he look like?'

'Horrible. Evil. Smaller than the rest of them, especially his lieutenant, a tall man he called Muhammed, but they all seemed afraid of him. He had a beard and rotten teeth. His eyes were black. When he looked at you, it was as if they were burning right through you, like coming face to face with Satan. You could tell he never took a bath. His fingernails were black, he smelt disgusting. I was sure I was going to die, especially when he grabbed our teacher by the hair and started screaming at her.' She sobs, 'I felt my heart was about to burst.'

'What did he say?'

'He was angry there were so few of us around. He told her she was not fit to teach us. The school was putting bad ideas into our heads, they had come to liberate us. They would teach us the Qur'an. According to him, that was the only education we needed. They would teach us how to be proper Muslim wives.'

'And your teacher?'

'She was so brave ... trying to protect us.' She dabs her eyes with a tissue. Jamilah can't tell if she's crying or not. 'They killed her. I didn't see it but I know it now.'

'That's shocking.' Jamilah squeezes Lami's hand.

'They herded us outside, grabbing our phones as we left. They shoved us into a lorry with benches inside.' Lami glances at her large new phone that has been buzzing since the start of their meeting. She looks at the caller's identity and reads a message. She half smiles at Jamilah, her long nails tap the screen. 'Sorree,' she says looking up, ready to continue.

'How did you get away?' asks Jamilah.

'The lorry was bouncing around and it was very noisy. It was totally dark inside and we were still in shock. The longer we drove, the more it felt we were never coming back.' She reaches for another tissue. 'Out of the blue, they pulled off the road and we waited. A helicopter passed overhead, and when it was gone, they all cheered. And that's when that awful man slapped Aminah.'

'What?'

'She told him what they were doing was wrong. Against Islam, but he just ignored her. She spoke up again and this time he grabbed her and pushed his face right into hers then he slapped her hard, full on the face. He was wearing a ring and it marked her cheek.'

'A ring?'

'One of those Prophet's Seal rings with the inscription in large Arabic writing.' She adopts a conspiratorial tone, 'The Governor, sorry ex-Governor, told me it's forbidden to wear these rings because the Prophet didn't want them reproduced. It shows how ignorant these people are, doesn't it? They told us our teacher isn't qualified to teach Islam and they don't know a simple thing like that.'

'Was Aminah okay?'

'Yes, but we were all stunned. I had thought of speaking up myself, but it was clear these men couldn't be persuaded of anything. Look at what happened to our teacher. They have no respect for women and that's against Islam too.'

'So how did you get away?'

'The convoy took off and after about twenty minutes made another stop. Fa'izah and me were sitting opposite each other at the back of the lorry. The cover wasn't tied down properly so we'd already managed to look out a couple of times and knew there were a couple of Hilux trucks behind us. We didn't hear the doors of the lorry bang shut, so it seemed no one had gotten out. We peeked out the back and saw the doors of a Hilux were open. The men inside had jumped out and were doing something at the back of the truck, maybe a flat tyre or something. Fa'izah and I had the same idea. We loosened the rope attached to the canvas cover, squeezed over the panel, and slid down onto the ground. We froze for a moment expecting someone to see us and for our friends to follow us. We took off into the bush and ran as fast as we could.

'I was sure others, especially Aminah, would do the same, but they decided to stay put or maybe it was too late. I've never run so fast. We heard shouting and knew they were coming after us. They fired a few shots but we ran even faster. When we couldn't run any more, we jumped into a ditch and lay still, gulping for air. We hadn't run in a straight line so knew they would have to spread out to find us. They probably realized it too and decided it would take too long and they couldn't remain stuck there on the road. They shouted bad things at us and fired a few more shots. I pressed myself as hard as I could into the ground. A few minutes later, we heard doors being slammed and engines starting up. It was such a relief when they drove off, but we were worried about our friends.'

'What happened then?'

'Fa'izah thought they might have left a truck hidden out of sight, trying to fool us into thinking they had gone away. So we didn't move for about fifteen minutes then we walked back the way we had come and found our way back to the road. We managed to hail a car down. We were lucky that someone was on the road at all. The driver phoned the police, and they came and picked us up.'

'But on the news, they said you'd been rescued. '

'I know, but when they interviewed us at the barracks —'.

'Who interviewed you?'

'The Commissioner of Police and his Deputy, mainly his Deputy.'

'Giwa?'

'You know him? He looks like a big bear but he's really sweet, isn't he? Got us blankets and tea and sat with us in the truck. He was like an uncle. He explained we'd have to stay at a hotel for a while for our protection and that it would help get our classmates back if we stopped saying we'd escaped, for what had really happened was they'd rescued us after a chase. We weren't convinced and we asked how it would help get our classmates back if we said that. He told us we didn't know the full picture. The Security Forces had been in pursuit the whole time, getting closer and closer. When the terrorists stopped, they had caught up with them. The bursts of fire we'd heard were not the terrorists shooting at us, but the Security Forces exchanging fire with them. They hadn't known the two of us had run off, so they continued the pursuit but lost them. It was his men who had come back and picked us up at the roadside, as they had already been out there. How could it not have been a rescue? They'd saved our lives.'

Lami's phone buzzes again. She glances at the screen and time ignores it.

'He told us the leader of the men who took us was called Abdullahi and few people had seen his face and lived.'

Jamilah wonders if this girl ever thinks before she speaks.

'He told us that the Governor believed it was important to recognise the courage of our security forces and not detract from their achievements and didn't we agree that the Governor was a wise and experienced man, and we should listen to him? The Governor had personally instructed him to ensure we were taken straight to a secure hotel and be well looked after in light of the ordeal we had just gone through. We were still confused but before we knew it we found ourselves walking through the lobby and straight into the lift. Before we went to sleep he wanted us to work on an identikit picture of Abdullahi while his face was fresh in our minds. While we were doing that Giwa kept repeating that the Governor knew what was best for us, and our schoolmates. He would ensure we came to no harm but it was essential we were on the same page in terms of what had happened that night, and in any case, his version of events was the truth, and that was the only version the media should hear. Before we could say anything more, he jumped up and left the room.

'When he returned, he was holding something behind his back and told us to shut our eyes. He presented us with brand new Samson Galaxies! We couldn't believe it when he said they were ours. He said when the Governor heard ours had been taken he insisted we be given new ones. We were so moved and of course, we agreed to help. If it was going to help get our classmates back, then we had no choice, had we? How would it help our friends if we confused the media? But you must keep this to yourself Jamilah. I know the Governor is gone now, but Giwa is still around. He's the new CP and he won't be pleased if he hears I'm talking out of turn. My mother said you should know the truth, as you've always been kind to us, but you mustn't tell anyone, not even the parents of my classmates. It doesn't change anything, and to be fair, we did stay safe, and we were well looked after.'

But they haven't got your classmates back, have they? Jamilah thinks but doesn't say. And you were afraid they'd take your new phone away.

'In any case', says Lami, 'there's a new Governor now, I'm sure he'll get Aminah back.'

'Inch 'Allah. You know your mother wants me to examine you?'

Lami rolls her eyes in exasperation, a teenager again. 'I've told them a hundred times that no one touched us, why can't she take my word for it?'

'I know,' says Jamilah taking the gloves out of Salim's bag, 'but … your mother knows best.' It's all she can think of to say.

Chapter 16

'I'm getting nowhere', says Jamilah sitting down in the patient's chair opposite Salim. It's a quiet night and they have ten minutes before the last appointment of the evening. 'It's been a month. It's like they've disappeared off the face of the earth.'

Salim's head nods in time with the squeak of the overhead fan. If things were different she'd laugh. How absurd is that? She looks down at her hands, 'Nobody cares, especially those whose job it is to care.' She hadn't planned to start opening up again, but ... who else can she talk to and he's the only one who understands her. 'Then "Princess" Lami tells me she and her friend were never rescued at all!'

Salim's head stops nodding.

'They escaped all by themselves!' says Jamilah. 'Saying it was a rescue, was part of a vain attempt to get the Governor re-elected.'

'I'm sorry to hear that, but not surprised. We let them get away with so much. I'm starting to think we get the leaders we deserve.' He removes his glasses and rubs his eyes. 'How's the Support Group?'

'Holding together, just. We started with ten families. Then we got a directive from the Governor's office telling us our campaigning was not helping his campaigning and it would be better if we kept quiet until he was re-elected — and had more time to do something. Half the families persuaded themselves he was working in their interests and withdrew. At least Lami's mother talks to me, but Fa'izah's parents never engaged with us. Her father actually thinks it was Allah's will that his daughter escaped, and it would be better if the other girls weren't found. No decent family would want them back, he says. No decent family would want their sons to marry them. Can you imagine?' There's a lump in her throat, it's hard to remain professional. 'My beautiful sister who dared to aspire to a better life; this is what they are saying about her.' A tear escapes down her cheek and Salim gets up to comfort her, but she holds up her hand and shakes her head. She's still at work, she must compose herself. Salim sits down again. 'We still get support from NGOs but it's not much.' She sniffs. 'Sometimes I think it's more for their benefit. We're linked to the "Bring Back our Girls Movement", been to the Unity Fountain a couple of times but what's the point? Aminah's been gone a month. She's far from Abuja, who knows where? I've written to the new Governor and heard nothing. What else can I do? I want my sister back, but nobody cares.'

This time she can't stop Salim from getting up. He hands her a tissue and stands behind her, resting his hands on her shoulders.

'Yakubu's only just come into office', he says, 'everyone will be seeking his attention. But he campaigned on law and order. He's staked his reputation on shifting the balance. Look, I know Ado, his Deputy; I'll ask him to meet you.'

'I'm fed up meeting people! They nod their heads, say something must be done, and I can see in their eyes they're just grateful it's not their daughter or sister who's been taken. How can we live like this? People steal our daughters, and it seems it's just another thing we're supposed to put up with. "Life's like this, bad things happen, stop making such a fuss. Accept it." The world is mad. Why should we put up with this? Why, Salim?'. She weeps. He gently squeezes her shoulders and rests his hand gently on her head.

'There's truth in what you say. I suppose I'm one of those people too.'

'No.' Jamilah shakes her head, 'Never.' She grasps his hand. She looks up at him and sees the concern in his face. They've been here before but this time she feels intimacy.

'I know you're trying to help me keep busy, keep my mind off things. You're always there to listen. I know you care for Aminah. I know you care ...' She squeezes his hand harder. He reciprocates then lets her hand go, raises his own to his mouth and clears his throat.

'And Ahmed, how's he holding up?' he says, returning to his seat.

She inhales slowly. 'I hardly see him. I think he feels he let his sister down. It's harder for him as a man. People feel pity for me; I'm sure they feel the same for him, but he's convinced that behind his back they express contempt because he couldn't protect his sister. And, of course, he's frustrated he can't do anything about it.'

'Would it help if I talked to him?' says Salim.

'Yes, that would be a big help', says Jamilah, smiling through her tears. 'We were offered counselling; he declined. Said it made him look even more of a failure.'

'We're becoming world experts in failure. I suspect the fact that you saved him when he was a boy, and he wasn't able to save his sister might be weighing on him.'

She nods. 'He thinks driving her to school that day somehow makes him an accomplice. We could've kept her for another day, like most of the other families. But I've told him it was me who insisted she go back when she was supposed to. Typical of me, isn't it? Always following the rules.'

'I know you know this but let me say it, so you can hear it. Neither you nor Ahmed did anything wrong. These people strike anywhere, anytime. They are to blame for everything. Look, I know someone, a really good counsellor —'

'He won't see them. He's getting his counselling from the bottle. One of my team's brothers saw him with a couple of friends drinking and watching a football match in one of those downtown drinking dens ... But I think if you speak to him, it'll help. There's a better chance he'll listen to you.'

'I will, but I was also thinking of you. Maybe —'

'It's hard, really hard, Salim but ... '. The doorbell sounds and she stands up. 'That's the end of my session,' she smiles, 'I'm sorry, didn't mean to offload.'

'Don't apologise. I wish I could do more.'

'You do a lot already. You know that.' She smiles again then heads for the door.

'Wait,' says Salim. 'This patient. It's not a woman.'

'What?'

'It's a favour for Ado, the man I mentioned earlier.'

'I don't —'

'It's a Yellow Fever booster,' says Salim. 'I know, not our usual service, but Ado wants it done discreetly.' The bell rings again. 'You'd better let him in. I'll get the jab,' he says heading off to the kitchen.

She dries her eyes, blows her nose, and heads out to the hall. Why would someone book an evening appointment at a private Ob-Gyn clinic to have a vaccination? A booster can be done anywhere. She takes a deep breath and slides open the locks. Drawing back the door she is shocked to find a white man standing smiling at her.

Chapter 17

'That was our new Deputy Governor.' Abdullahi puts his phone away and sends a postscript of spit hurtling into the grass.

'Did you give him our congratulations?' says Muhammed continuing to urinate.

'I know what I'd like to give that piece of shit.'

Abdullahi stares up at the sky and scratches his beard. They are en route from the Shura meeting and having skirted around the last main town, have stopped outside a village from where they hear the sound of drums and celebratory shouting. For Abdullahi, this is not a joyful sound but one of provocation.

'I think we should pay these people a visit', says Muhammed getting back on the bike, clearly of the same opinion.

'Something's not right', says Abdullahi, staying put and running his prayer beads between his fingers. 'This meeting ... he wants to set up a meeting to negotiate a prisoner exchange. I told him we'd want ten thousand for every girl we release, plus all of my family released, along with any of our fighters they haven't executed, and no re-arrests. And he can start by releasing my daughter.'

'What did he say?'

'Said he thought that could work. They'd want one of their bitches back, the main thing was to start negotiations and get movement on releasing their girls. I don't trust that conniving bastard Yakubu or his errand boy.'

Mohammed nods. Abdullahi's beads weave between his fingers.

'He says if Yakubu starts getting girls back so soon after taking power, he'll be seen to deliver on his promises. "Get a popularity boost" Ha, can you imagine?' He pulls at his beard. 'Why's he showing me his hand?' His fingers stop moving. 'Yakubu supported us because we helped get him elected. Everything we did before helped him, everything we do now undermines him. And he knows if it ever came to light that he supported our Jihad, he'd be finished.'

There's a rustle in the bushes. Muhammed spins round drawing his machete. They peer into the darkness looking for a shape, their nostrils filtering the air, their ears alert to the sound of a leaf falling. Abdullahi glances at the bike, calculating how fast they could get on board if they had to. Their voices will have carried a bit, but this is an unscheduled stop, a nowhere location by the side of a backroad. Then it appears: a pathetic mange-ridden dog, no doubt cast out of the village and looking for somewhere to die. It must have heard them speaking; maybe it had one last hope that these humans would show him more kindness. Abdullahi knows all about last hopes and he doesn't hand out reprieves. He expects Muhammed to raise his blade. Instead, he kicks the animal. It yelps and limps back amongst the branches and thorns.

'When it's our time', says Abdullahi, 'we won't go like that, tails between our legs. We'll go out in glory, giving our last drop of blood for Jihad.'

'Alhamdulillah!'

'Last time we met Ado, I told him I'd expect his boss to free my family when he got into power. These people wait for you to come to them so they can squeeze you harder. I don't feel squeezed at all.'

'So what he really wants is us', says Muhammed.

'You see the light.'

'That's why Allah chose you as our leader. Alhamdulillah.'

Abdullahi takes a few steps forward and looks towards the village.

'With Yakubu at the helm, people can sleep safe in their beds. That's the bullshit he feeds them. The Big Man will protect them, right? Well, these people need a wake-up call. You wanted to pay them a visit? Let's go.'

They get back on the bike. Allah has provided guidance once again and exposed the infidel's intentions. That errand boy will get more than he bargains for at his meeting. It's time to celebrate in Allah's name. The Shura has formalized their alignment with ISIS. They are getting stronger. The End of Times is accelerating. He tells Muhammed to get off the bike. Standing, they kiss their hands, and say,

'Praise be to Allah for this blessing. I praise Him and thank Him for His bounty.'

Abdullahi takes out two Beretta M9s and gets back on the bike. 'No fly-by,' he says, 'it's stop and kill'. He wants to get in close, see the terror on their faces, hear their pleas, smell their fear and most of all, watch the blood flowing from their wounds. The Berettas will stay hidden until the last moment. Let them drop their guard. When he empties both magazines, he will ensure his thirty-four rounds will not be wasted.

'Allahu Akbar!'

'Allahu Akbar!'

The drumming and coloured lights are ahead of them, the shouts and laughter more discernible. A sparking fire hisses under a roasting cow. A wedding celebration. Look how these infidels behave! Stopping at this place was no accident. It was Allah's will. Another bike is behind them and in a hurry. They let it go past. The driver has two women on board and gives Muhammed a friendly wave. Muhammed waves back and follows them in. They arrive together. Allah has smoothed their entrance into what will soon be a gathering of death. Another lesson for the infidels.

Chapter 18

Aminah thinks she's been walking for about an hour. In daylight she could have gone the same distance in half the time but having banged her toes more than once, her step is more cautious. The grass is hard and sharp. She left her village a long while ago and her skin has lost its capacity to cope, leaving her ankles scratched and bloody. Now and again she stops to shake out loose stones. If only she had her trainers instead of these battered old sandals.

A dog barks! Alhamdulillah! She must be near a village! The trail is turning into a path of sorts and it's winding up an incline. That's a good sign! She presses on, energised by hope. She stubs her big toe again and the pain is fierce. She hopes it isn't broken. The barking becomes frantic as if the animal is exasperated that no one is coming to investigate. The path straightens. She sees the unmistakeable shape of a building about thirty metres away. She makes out a cluster of huts with straw roofs and a pen from which she can hear the shuffle of hooves. And there's the dog, tied to a post, pulling on the rope to get at her. She tries to calm it with a few whispered words and hand gestures, but it will not be denied this chance to show its worth. The cattle sense her presence and shuffle uneasily.

A door opens. A man steps out carrying a rifle. He stops when he sees her. He looks unsure what to do. He doesn't speak. He was probably expecting cattle thieves but instead his nocturnal visitor is a girl standing alone in the dark, hands raised above her head. He shouts at the dog. It falls quiet and sits down in disappointment. He points the gun at her and takes a few steps forward. A month ago, before her capture she would have been terrified, now she finds herself adopting the same calm approach she took with the dog. There is a light behind the man and an old woman half his size shuffles forwards holding a lamp. She presses down on his arm and he lowers the rifle. She indicates to Aminah to come forward. She holds the lamp towards Aminah who lowers her head to show she is not a threat. The woman touches Aminah's chin in a gesture that implies she wants to see her face. Aminah looks up and the woman strokes her cheek. Her hands are rough but gentle. Her thumb rubs the scar on Aminah's cheek and something melts inside her. Brutal men have held her captive for a month, and now a stranger greets her with tenderness. She bursts into tears and the woman embraces her, drawing her head down onto her narrow shoulder. She smells of cattle. Aminah whispers in her ear:

'Help me, mother. Please help me.'

The woman puts her arm around Aminah's waist and leads her to a rough bench outside the door. She holds the lamp at Aminah's feet and then tells the man to bring some water. Like her, he is thin, wiry and below average height. Aminah assumes he's her son. He pours some water into an old basin and some into a cup without a handle. She nods her thanks and gulps the water down. He has some straw sticking out of his hair. The whole place reeks of dung. The woman cleans blood off Aminah's legs and feet. Another man appears. The old woman shouts at him, and he leaves. She sits down beside Aminah.

'What's your name?'

'Aminah.'

'What brings you to us in the middle of the night?'

'Mother, do you have a phone?'

'No. The Chief has one, but the army destroyed the mast. He cannot use it in the village.'

Aminah tells her story. The woman nods from time to time, remains silent and strokes Aminah's arm. The man looks on, showing no emotion and Aminah is unsure if he understands her. She finishes her account; the woman nods a while longer and neither she nor her son speak. It's as if they need more time to absorb her words, but Aminah is impatient and speaks again:

'How far is it to the Cameroon border? Can you help get me there? Or to a town where I can be safe and contact my family?'

The woman clears her throat and spits to the side. 'The border is closer than any town — maybe a day's walk if your feet are okay. We know these men who took you. They take our cattle when they feel like it. They killed my brother's son when he tried to stop them. They are evil men. You are not safe here. You will stay with us tonight. Get some rest. Tomorrow, my son will speak to the Chief. He will know what to do.'

'Thank you mother.'

'You will sleep in my hut. In the morning we will work out what to do.'

Chapter 19

'Francois de Witt. You were expecting me?'

'Yes. Come in. You are welcome.' Jamilah steps back and lets the man pass. She observes a large black 4x4 parked a few doors down the street, a driver waiting — an indication of power. She slides the bolts back in place and the man moves imperceptibly to help her.

'Maybe you weren't expecting a white African,' he says moving back a respectable distance, though not before she catches his scent in her nostrils. It's like fresh pine, masculine, unsettling. His accent, she knows it from the TV — South African.

'No, no, it's okay', Jamilah smiles her natural smile. 'My mind was elsewhere. I don't meet many people from outside Nigeria. Dr Salim has been everywhere.'

'I haven't met him yet, but you are ...?'

'His Assistant, Jamilah.'

'Pleased to meet you.' He has a firm handshake but it's his eyes. She's never seen anything like them. Grey, blue ... metallic.

'More like I'm *her* assistant.' Salim joins them in the corridor holding a chrome kidney dish covered with a white cloth. He extends his free hand. 'Welcome to our clinic, Colonel. Jamilah is being modest. She's a Senior Nursing Officer, in my view the most competent nurse in the country.' Jamilah feels her cheeks heat up.

'I'm in very good hands then,' he says turning to Jamilah.

'The best', says Salim. 'The youngest to hold the post at our hospital.'

Typical of Salim to sing her praises but it's so embarrassing and this white man keeps smiling at her and all she can do is blush! How ridiculous! Salim opens the door of the Examination Room and bids de Witt enter. He declines, insisting Jamilah goes first.

Salim sets the dish on a desk. 'Jamilah will perform the operation, Colonel. I'll speak to you afterwards. And I'll fix that meeting with Ado for you', he adds over his shoulder to Jamilah.

She takes the dish over to the sink and removes the white cloth exposing the syringe and vaccine. So he's a Colonel. 'Okay, you're here tonight for a Yellow Fever booster, Mr de Witt.'

'Ja.'

'And you've no problems having injections?'

'None. I've brought my inoculations booklet; I'd be grateful for a stamp and your autograph.'

'I'm sure we can arrange that,' she smiles again. She's flirting! What's the matter with her? 'Could you remove your jacket please and roll up the sleeve of your right arm?'

'Yes, Ma'am'.

'You can sit on the bed.' She pulls on a pair of disposable gloves.

'I thought I'd better get a booster. I read there was an outbreak and … why are you smiling?'

'Sorry. It's funny you should come here to an Ob-Gyn clinic for a vaccination. We specialise in … other treatments.'

'Ja. I know.' He smiles again. 'It's a security thing. My employers want me to keep a low profile and they tell me that Dr Salim respects confidentiality. He hasn't told you about me, then?'

'No', she says gravely, 'and relax, no one will know about your clandestine visit to a women's clinic or the intervention you required'. She can't hold on to her serious demeanour and they both break out laughing. She composes herself, swabs his muscular upper arm and administers the booster. He's not a young man but he's in good shape. Rugged, handsome and he smells good. He has an aura.

'Can you press on this for me?' She places a ball of cotton wool against the injection point. 'Just for a second.' She reaches for a small plaster and applies it to his arm. 'There, all done.' She turns away to dispose of the syringe, cotton wool and gloves.

'Thanks.' He rolls down his sleeve. 'Listen nurse, you can be straight with me. How long have I got?'

'There's a good chance you'll survive the night, after that ... we'll have to take each day as it comes.' They laugh again. 'Can I ask you a question, Mr de Witt?'

'Only if you stop calling me, Mr de Witt. My name is Francois. He puts on his jacket, still keeping his eyes on her.

'Okay, Francois, I know the Deputy Governor's arranged for you to come here tonight — that's all I know. What is he like?'

'Much like the rest of these politicians though not as loud and intimidating as his boss. The sort of man who works behind the scenes and gets things done.'

'I need him to get something done for me.' Jamilah's thoughts swing back to her sister, guilty at having been distracted by this man's visit. Laughing and flirting, imagine, while her sister is held captive by a bunch of murderers. A tear escapes which she wipes away instantly, embarrassed by her lack of professionalism.

'Are you okay?'

'Yes. Thank you. I'll show you into Dr Salim's office.'

'No, wait. I heard Salim mention Ado to you. Is there anything I can do? I work with him. If you want to see him, I can arrange that for you.'

'You could speak to him on my behalf?'

'Ja. Of course.'

He sounds so confident. 'But you haven't even asked me why. Won't you need to tell Mr Ado why he should meet me?'

'Yes. So why don't you sit on that chair and tell me.'

Before she can say anything, he places his arm around her back and steers her to the chair. He sits on the edge of the bed, looking down at her expectantly.

'A month ago, my dear sister, Aminah, was taken by Boko Haram along with eleven other girls at her school. Nobody has done anything to get them back. I formed a family support group, but the last Governor refused to see us and even told us to stop campaigning. Dr Salim says he will speak to the new Deputy Governor and ask him to see me.' She gets up. 'What I want is this new Governor to do something about it. He has the power after all.' She rubs her hands together. 'I don't want to think about what Aminah's going through. We − her brother and me − just want her back and knowing that nobody is looking for her is very hard to bear.'

'Ja. I see. Look man, I'm involved here as a military consultant. I'll make sure you have that meeting with Ado, and I'll see what I can do about getting your sister back. Write down her full name, date of birth, the name of the school she was taken from and when, and your phone number. I'll be in touch.'

'Thank you, Francois. And I'm sorry for bringing this all up when you only came for −'

'A gynaecological consultation, I know.'

As she scribbles the details on a notepad, she feels his steely eyes observing her. It makes her self-conscious, but her primary emotion is gratitude. She tears off the page and hands it to him. He looks at it, slips it into his pocket and takes out his inoculation card.

'Best you give that to Salim, the stamp's in his office.'

'Okay. It's been a pleasure to meet you, Jamilah. I'll be in touch.' They shake hands.

'It's been a pleasure to meet you too. Thanks for listening to me, I didn't mean to —'

'I'm glad you did. I'm very sorry to hear about your sister. Try not to lose hope.'

She nods. 'I'd be grateful if you didn't mention our conversation to Dr Salim. I'll tell him later.'

He winks. 'Patient-nurse confidentiality! Anyway, it won't do any harm if Salim calls as well.'

Chapter 20

Aminah opens her eyes. She hadn't expected to sleep but it's already light and she hears the sound of people up and about, of wood being chopped, and cattle lowing. For the first time in a month, she's woken up alone. Back at the camp, the girls will be up, and the men will have discovered her absence. They'll be afraid to tell Abdullahi, they'll try to find her before he gets back. They'll have already started looking. She can't stay here. The old woman appears.

'Come, I have water. Time to wash, then you eat.'

'Thank you, mother. Did your son speak to the Chief?'

'Go wash, talk after.' She shoos her out of the hut. Outside Aminah can make out the overhang on the horizon. It's closer than she was expecting, and her fear intensifies. As if anticipating she is going to speak again, the old woman presses her finger to Aminah's lips, then points her to another hut nearby.

'For women. Take bucket. Go. Be quick. Chief coming soon.'

A few minutes later, Aminah finds the old woman outside cooking. She signals for Aminah to go inside and follows her in with a plate and some milk. She tells Aminah to sit but Aminah is agitated.

'Mother, I must leave. These men will come for me at any minute. If they find me, they will kill me. That's what they do to anyone who tries to escape.'

'The Chief is coming. He will know what to do. Sit. Eat.'

Reluctantly Aminah sits down.

'Eek!' She draws back from the plate. 'Is that a mouse?'

'You have not eaten before? Try it. Sauce good. You will like it.'

'I'm sorry mother, I cannot eat a mouse ... I don't mean to be rude. But ... I can't.' Her appetite has taken flight, but she takes the milk and expresses her gratitude.

There is increased activity outside, the sound of male voices. The old woman motions for Aminah to get up and they go outside. The Chief has brought two advisers with him. All three are dressed plainly but the Chief wears some chains and walks with the aid of solid wooden cane. Aminah bows respectfully. The Chief asks her name and then tells her to explain why she has come to their village. She looks for the old woman's son but cannot see him. Surely, he would have explained, but the old woman gives her a prod, so she tells her story again, finishing with a plea to the Chief to help her get to the border. He walks off a few paces to confer with his advisers. They speak quietly, in another language, unfamiliar to her. After a couple of minutes, he addresses the old woman briefly in what sounds like the same tongue. He nods to Aminah and walks off without speaking. The old woman ushers her back into the hut.

'The Chief says it is not safe for you here. And dangerous for the village. You must leave as soon as possible. For now, stay inside. Not good that others see you.'

'Mother, they'll be looking for me. I need to get as far away as I can. If they don't find me today, I'm sure they'll stop looking. This is my chance.'

'The Chief has good plan. Go change clothes. Take off Hijab. We are not Muslim. I go find something for you. You are tall. Bigger than women here, but not men. For journey, you will look like man, not woman.'

Chapter 21

'Hello, it's Colonel de Witt.'
  'You survived then?'
    'Ja. I'm with the Deputy Governor now. He'll see you this morning. Can you be here in an hour?' He sounds different, business-like.
      'An hour? Yes, yes. How did you manage —'
      'One more thing, can you bring a recent photo of your sister?'
      'Of course.' Jamilah is about to ask why, but he doesn't give her a chance.
      'Good. See you shortly.'
      'Thanks, Francois.' He's gone. She looks at her phone. For the first time in a month, something is happening and all because of a white man from South Africa who she only met last night. She must ring Ahmed.

'You think this will really happen, Sir?' Jamilah sits facing the Deputy Governor. 'I'll really get my sister back?'
      'Inch 'Allah.' He looks at Aminah's photo, then back at her as if he is convincing himself they are sisters. Why would she bring a photo of someone else? These men just enjoy making people uncomfortable.
      'We have faith in the Colonel and his plan,' he says glancing at de Witt who doesn't respond.
      'Thank you, Sir. Thank you, Colonel.' Seeds of hope are taking root. She smiles nervously at de Witt. She'd thought they'd established, if not a bond, a friendly relationship. He returns her smile. What was that? Did her heart just skip a beat? This is ridiculous. She's getting her feelings confused. She had not expected him to be at the

meeting, but the reason for his presence had become clear
once he explained why Aminah's photo had been needed.
And, in explaining that, he had, with Ado's approval,
explained the reason for his presence in Nigeria. She now
knows what he is. In his well-cut suit and polished shoes,
he is the image of efficiency. He remains the only one in
authority who has helped her. She will never forget it. She
looks back at Ado who is studying his computer screen.

'Sir, I know His Excellency, Governor Yakubu and
you are extremely busy and that you have only just come
into office, for which the people of this State are grateful,
Alhamdulillah. Sir, I am here not only to represent my
family but also the families of other girls who were taken
from their school last month.'

Ado drags his eyes away from his screen. 'We place
great importance on getting all these girls home where they
belong. Your sister's release is the first step in a process.
You should be grateful she has been chosen.'

'Yes, I understand that Sir, and I am extremely
grateful. It's only that I don't want our Support Group to
feel I've used my position solely to plea for my own sister's
rescue.'

'Very noble of you, Madam, now —'

'Are you sure it won't be dangerous for her?' asks
Jamilah, before can signal the end of the meeting.

'There will be an element of danger,' says de Witt, 'we
are dealing with terrorists after all. But my men and I will
be there to ensure Aminah is delivered back to you in one
piece.'

'Madam, unlike the other girls she was taken with,
and the hundreds more held captive, your sister is being
given the opportunity of imminent release. I think you
should focus on that.'

'Yes, you are right, Sir. Thank you, Sir.'

'This photo, Madam,' Ado shows her Aminah's photo, 'is it a good likeness?'

'Yes, Sir. I had it taken for her hospital ID card last year when she worked as a volunteer. She wants to be a doctor, so —'

'By way of additional verification,' says Ado, 'can you suggest a question for me to ask her? Not her favourite colour, or anything like that, something it would be difficult for anyone else to know or guess.'

'Okay ... "On what day was our father ... What was the date of our father's passing?"'

Ado raises his eyebrows, 'A little morbid, but fine. Write the date down for me.' He passes her a notepad and pen.

The door bursts open and suddenly her violator is in the same room with her.

'You started without me, Mr Ado.'

She turns her head away at the sound of his voice.

'When the Deputy Governor's door is closed it means he doesn't want to be disturbed Commissioner,' says Ado.

'But I heard you had an important security meeting, so I presumed you'd be looking for me. We both know His Excellency would expect his CP to be at any — how now!' Giwa stops talking and lifts up Aminah's photo. 'Hmmm. Very nice,' he nods his head approvingly. 'You have a good eye, Deputy Governor. Like them young, do you?'

Ado snatches back the photo. 'This is one of the girls kidnapped by Abdullahi. And this is her sister, a senior nurse and coordinator of a family support group campaigning to get their girls back.'

'Ah, my apologies, Ma'am.' Giwa makes a small bow. 'We're doing all we can to get these poor girls back. You'll have your sister home soon.'

Despite the air conditioning showing a temperature of seventeen degrees, sweat glistens on Giwa's forehead and stains his shirt under the armpits. She has been bracing herself for this encounter, but still, she shudders. He had that same leer ten years ago; he's just directed it at her sister's image and now he's directing it at her. If he recognises her, he doesn't show it. How disgusting he looks, even heavier than she remembers.

'CP Giwa, at your service.' He leans towards her, hand outstretched. His bloodshot eyes staring right into hers, the same grotesque smile with the large gap between his top teeth that has haunted her dreams for years. She looks down at his sweaty hand and the large chubby fingers. She will not allow him to touch her again. She is nauseous at the thought. She stands up and moves to one side.

'Excuse me, Sir,' she says looking at Ado. 'I feel unwell. Can I use your —'

'Behind that curtain over there,' says Ado, looking concerned, more, she suspects, for the shiny surfaces of his new office, than her health.

De Witt moves past Giwa to help steady her. He supports her across the room and pushes the bathroom door open for her. She goes to sit on the edge of the bath, and he closes the door behind her. The nausea eases but she is shaking, not just from the shock of Giwa's presence but with renewed anger that such a man can operate with impunity and be rewarded for it. She runs the tap and sprinkles some water on her face. She dabs a towel to her cheeks, takes a few deep breaths, then returns to the room and retakes her seat. She is aware of Giwa slumped in a chair to the side of Ado's desk but refrains from looking at him.

'Are you okay, Madam?' asks Ado.

'Yes. My apologies, Sir. Thank you for the use of your bathroom.'

'I'm sure we can understand the stress you are under at this time,' says Ado, glancing in Giwa's direction, 'and it is to your credit that you continue to work at our hospital. Talking of which I will not detain you further but would just remind you that what we discussed today must stay within this room. Do not talk about it to your family, your support group, anyone. Your sister's life depends on it. I will ensure his Excellency is informed of your visit.'

'Oh behalf of all the families in our group, I thank you, Sir, and please extend our congratulations and thanks to His Excellency.' She stands up and bows to Ado. She doesn't look at Giwa and is grateful when de Witt appears at her side.

'I'll see you out.' He supports her elbow as she leaves and once again, he steps ahead to open the door for her. Sandwiched between the indifference of the politician, and the lust of the policeman, is the courtesy of the mercenary. How ironic that the only one of this trinity who seems to genuinely care about the fate of her sister, is a foreigner. De Witt follows her out of the room, closing the door behind them.

'You've met Giwa before.'

She remains silent.

'I don't imagine it was a good experience.'

'It wasn't. He disgusts me. If you knew what that man has done …'

'I can imagine.'

'I'm sure you can, you kill people for a living.'

'I work for an international organization that provides military services in training and operational support to governments that request them.'

'Is that a fancy way of saying you kill people for money?'

'Our services cost money. We put our lives on the line, like we'll do for your sister. And yes, sometimes it's kill or be killed, but we are talking military situations. We do not kill innocent people.'

Why is she arguing with this man? Not only has he been kind to her, he's also engineered for Aminah to be rescued before any of her classmates. He is looking at her, but she looks to one side and touches the itch on her face. She doesn't know what to say.

'I must go back in. You seem okay now.' He squeezes her arm. 'I'll call you later'. She hears the door close behind him.

What did he squeeze her arm for? Why did he say he'll call her later? What's that supposed to mean? Does he think she's available? That she's some country nurse he can have a bit of fun with between his killing sprees in the bush?

Chapter 22

Aminah bends down to embrace the old woman, 'Thank you mother, I will never forget you. I will come back one day, I promise.'

'Child, go. He is leaving.' The old woman pulls away and points toward the man steering his cattle towards the trail. Aminah bends down to kiss her, then hurries off to catch up with the herd. She turns to wave a final goodbye, but the old woman has already turned away.

She will come back one day. She will bring presents and money too. It's such a relief to be on the move again and it's not long before Aminah feels the same elation she'd experienced the night before, as each step took her further away from her captors. What's more, the herder and his cattle know where they are going and they move much faster than she did last night. Allah is with her, guiding her on the final stage of her journey. Alhamdulillah! The Chief's plan is simple but unreal. She is dressed like a man! The old woman helped neutralise the parts of her anatomy that would signal her gender. She is bulkier, she carries a stick, her hair is cut back so that the box-like hat worn by men in the village fits snugly on her head. A scarf covers the lower half of her face; it's unusual, but the old woman said it was better to look unusual than show a woman's face under a man's hat. The herder strides ahead, keeping his dozen heads of cattle moving along. She takes the smell of the village with her, not only because she's surrounded by the herd, but also because the old woman smeared her clothes with dung. She tries to mimic the herder's walk and keep herself tight within the herd so that her gait will not attract attention.

It's hard to maintain the pace and avoid being barged by the cattle, but she is determined, and it becomes easier as she becomes accustomed to their rhythm. The herder neither speaks nor looks at her. When he opens his mouth it is to shout at the cattle, sometimes geeing them up with an accompanying whack. She wonders what the Chief told him about her. He'll know she's a woman. Does he know that when they reach the end of the trail and the cattle have their pasture, she will carry on without him? It doesn't matter. Best they don't communicate. It's a good plan; simple, direct. Let it work.

Not for the first time, they pass imposing boulders, that resemble clumps of broken mountain. It's a desolate, empty place. The mountains are more like hills, the terrain is rough but surprisingly verdant. The trees that have managed to get a foothold are flourishing. The sky is cobalt blue and the air fresh though the sun is beginning to make its presence felt. She has an urge to remove the scarf around her face, but the remembrance of where she's escaped from quickly banishes that thought. Each time she glances back towards the village, she half expects to see fighters in pursuit, but instead she sees an empty trail with newly trampled weeds and wildflowers and fresh dung trodden into the ruts of the hard ground. When her captors come to the village, they will find no trace of her. But what if they start shooting people? The Chief will have to tell them about her. She tells herself to stop thinking these thoughts; this time tomorrow she will be in Cameroon, and out of captivity.

About fifteen minutes later, they pass a field dense with sorghum. Its ripening brown tips look like a host of faces at the end of thin poles, all staring at her. There is no breeze, yet they seem to nudge each other and whisper. They are not taken in by her disguise.

The herd rounds a corner and scurries up a steep incline. Below are rows of man-built terraces in which carrots, cowpeas, and other vegetables are being cultivated. Thirty metres away, a few women are bent over, working the earth, digging out weeds with metal hoes and harvesting carrots. They pause to look up, no doubt glad of a distraction. Aminah ensures the cattle are between her and their curious eyes. The herder waves and the women wave back. She makes a half wave; they don't respond. Aminah turns her head away and shoos along a cow that doesn't need shooing. She keeps her eyes fixed on the trail ahead, and soon they are alone again with it; only the clomping hooves break the silence.

She can no longer see the overhang and her backward glances become less frequent. Now it's about looking forward, scanning the horizon for what she hopes will be some sign of Cameroon, though she has no idea what that would look like. It can't be long before she will be on her own walking towards freedom, and she will walk for as long as it takes. When darkness falls, she will sleep rough and in the morning she will set off early and reach the border. She's never done anything as adventurous as this in her life but when she thinks of Jamilah and Ahmed and the joy of being reunited, she has all the courage and motivation she needs. They will fear they have lost her forever, but she will find her way back to them. Allah is with her, Alhamdulillah!

She thinks of how her siblings will laugh when she tells them about the mouse for breakfast. Ahmed will tell her not to get any ideas. But she shouldn't laugh at the old woman's expense. She was kind and protected her. She has given her nuts to eat along the way and told her about leaves that are safe for her to eat, and where to look for them. The trail descends sharply to merge with a bigger track. Two small cows are reluctant to descend but do so after a couple of thwacks of the herder's stick. Another cow having made the descent, heads up the track in the direction they have just come from. The herder shouts and the cow, confused, slows down. The man gets in front of it and waves his stick. The cow turns and skitters back to the herd.

Aminah takes the opportunity to look into the distance again. She can make out some hills and hopes they are in Cameroon. They look a long way off and if they're not in Cameroon she's going to have to walk a longer way still. She wonders if she shouldn't ask the herder. There can't be far to go now, and she'll soon be parting company with him. She doesn't know his name.

'Hey!' He doesn't seem to hear her. She calls again and still he doesn't turn round. Instead she hears the sound of familiar voices and the noise of an engine coming towards her. Even as she turns around, the doors of the Hilux have already been thrown open and her two suitors are racing towards her. Remaining seated in the truck is the old woman's son. He has brought them here. They must have been waiting for her. She scrambles back up the rocks toward the trail. She has no chance; this is their terrain. With two leaps, one of them is behind her while the other clambers ahead and cuts her off. They seize hold of her. She tries to wrestle free. One pulls off her scarf, the other her hat. Satisfied it is her, one grabs her by the hair yanking her head back, the other slaps her face twice. She falls backwards in shock, ears ringing from the blow. Laughing, they pick her up, drag her down the slope to the truck and bundle her into the back seat vacated by the son. He's talking to the herder and doesn't look at her. She is pushed down, her face squashed against the seat, and she feels the truck do a three-point turn. Why did they betray her? Did the old woman know? Tears flow, burning her face with frustration and despair. Gambo is driving, Rashidi is in the back with her, his hand still pressing the side of her face against the seat. Blood runs from her nose and gathers between her cheek and the seat's plastic surface.

'Don't care much for her perfume, do you, Gambo?'

'She stinks,' Gambo replies.

"What's she done to her hair? Why's she dressed like a peasant?'

'Huh,' says Gambo, 'spends one day with these infidels and stops wearing the hijab.'

'And starts dressing like a man!'

'I preferred her the way she was before.'

'Yeah, but she didn't want us before, did she? We weren't good enough for her, isn't that right, bitch?' Rashidi pulls her head up and she gasps for air through the blood and mucus. He shouts into her face, 'Not good enough, were we?'

She feels his spit against her cheeks and cough mixture fumes invade her nostrils. With their leader away, they are high.

'No, you weren't,' she cries. 'I would never marry a killer.'

'And you never will,' says Gambo, looking back, 'you'll never marry anyone once we've finished with you!'

Rashidi has her by the hair again and yanks her head back so that her eyes look directly up at the car's roof. He growls in her ear, 'Did you really think you could slip out of our camp in the middle of the night and walk to

Cameroon? For someone who thinks she's so clever, you're really very stupid, aren't you? The infidels in this village? We let them live. They grow food for us, let us know when the army or any strangers come sniffing around. If they don't, we take their women,' Rashidi laughs, 'and in the worst cases, their cattle.'

'We shoot their men,' Gambo joins in, 'and then burn down the village!'

'Please, let me go,' says Aminah. 'If you have read the Qur'an, you must know you should not harm me! You know this is not the way of Allah.'

'Here she goes again,' says Gambo. 'What do you know about the Qur'an? Haven't you learned anything in your time with us?'

'Whoa, these clothes are stinking out the truck!' Rashidi plucks at her clothing with disdain. 'We'll have to do something about that.'

He pulls her head back even more roughly. She feels his tongue and lips race around her neck. His slobbering makes her heave. He tears at her clothes. She tries to free her hands to push him away, but he is pressing hard against her, keeping her arm trapped by his body, her other arm squashed against the car door. This is not right. Why is this happening to her?

'Yeah, get her out of those clothes,' says Gambo. He drives the truck off the track and pulls up under the shelter of a large rock. They drag her out. She resists and screams for help. Gambo tells her to shut up and slaps her face. When she continues, he punches her in the stomach. She retches. The breakfast milk surges up through her throat and nostrils and splashes onto the ground. It is warm on her feet. She hopes it will deter them. It doesn't. Gambo holds her arms behind her back and Rashidi grapples with her clothes. She screams again and tries to wrestle free of Gambo's grip. Rashidi hits her twice in the face, the second time catching her jaw. She loses consciousness.

When she comes round, she is on her back and Rashidi is on top of her. Sharp stones dig into her buttocks and back. He grunts with each hard thrust. She has learnt to shut out the pain, but tears flow into her mouth and sideways into her ears. Her teeth are clamped together, her mouth stretched and twisted. There is a line of saliva hanging from his chin. His eyes are blotched red. She looks away only to see the leering face of Gambo. He is masturbating while waiting for his turn. She shouldn't be seeing this; she shouldn't be here living this nightmare. Why is Allah punishing her? What has she done for Him to desert her? She thinks of her family and feels shame. She wants to die. She lifts her head off the ground and pulls Rashidi's head down towards her face. He resists and pauses to stare at her. If the thought enters his mind that she is somehow responding to his sexual prowess with a desire to kiss him, it is short-lived. Their faces touch but there is no kiss. She bites into his nose as hard as she can. He screams and places one hand on her chest, the other on her face trying to extract his nose from her mouth. She puts every ounce of strength into gripping his hair, keeping his face against hers and biting as hard as she can. He tries to punch her, but she holds on to his head, restricting his leverage. Her eyes are squeezed tight, her jaw is shaking with the effort. There is a scrunching sound, and her front and bottom teeth meet. Blood gushes into her mouth. She grinds her teeth and jerks her head to the side tearing his flesh away. Screaming, but now free from her, he punches her in the eye and rolls away, blood pouring from his wound. Through her good eye she sees his hands rush to his face, he is on his knees. He neglects to cover himself and the blood drips onto him. It's also between her teeth, on her tongue, in her throat. She spits it out along with bits of his flesh. She retches but there is nothing left in her stomach. Her body is battered, inside and out and now she feels the pain. It is hard to move. Her hands reach out for clothes but cannot find any. Rashidi howls. This is a living hell. Gambo draws his machete. Good, she is ready. His foot stamps down on her face, forcing it to the side. Her cheek and temple are pressed hard against the ground. She knows what comes next. This is how her father died. Her fingernails dig into the earth. This is what happens to girls who try to escape. She offers no resistance and prays that it is quick.

Chapter 23

A bright screen displays a map of the old mosque and its surrounds. As de Witt delivers his PowerPoint presentation, Ado wonders how the boss and Giwa would have briefed their men on a covert operation in their military days. While he doesn't like de Witt, Ado finds his professionalism reassuring; it is after all what one hopes for in a man who will be at his side when his life is on the line. The lights are dimmed but sitting at his desk, the boss's profile is unmistakable: hat; sunglasses; sagging jowls; and a waterfall of robes. He looks like he's chewing, despite the absence of food in front of him. Maybe the message hasn't got through from his brain that lunch is over?

As befits acolytes, he and Giwa are positioned on either side of the Governor's desk, separated by an oak-framed glass coffee table, furnished with the obligatory bottles of water and a bowl of mints.

'Since we last talked', says de Witt, 'there's been further communication between Abdullahi and Mr Ado'. He looks in Ado's direction. Ado presumes it's a cue and speaks up,

'Abdullahi insisted his daughter be freed as a quid pro quo for giving up one of the girls. His Excellency has given his consent.'

'Freeing his daughter ought to increase his incentive to turn up', says de Witt.

'Killing him is all that matters', says the boss,

'Ja', says de Witt, 'and ensuring we extract the schoolgirl safely'.

There is no response from the Governor's silhouette.

'While we're on the subject, Sir,' says Giwa, 'Abdullahi's daughter, is her safety a priority too?'

'The opposite,' snorts the Governor. 'Can you imagine her reaction to seeing her father being shot to pieces? She'll be screaming to the media, playing the little heroine, making herself out to be some kind of champion of justice. She's the offspring of a killer, why should she live to breed a bunch of little bastards like him? She knows who her father is and has never denounced him. She goes too. Caught in the crossfire, that will suffice. Who's going to be upset? It can be blamed on Abdullahi. What's the matter, Colonel? … Squeamish?'

'With all respect, Sir, I have no issue in despatching terrorists. However, I draw the line at civilians, particularly adolescent girls.'

'Oh for fuck sake. What are we paying you for?'

'I'll spare the Colonel's feelings,' says Giwa. 'Quickly, quietly, and out of sight.'

'Good,' says the boss. 'It seems we still have to rely on ourselves for some things. Continue.'

'As Abdullahi is bringing a girl', says de Witt, showing no reaction, 'he insists on bringing along a driver-cum- bodyguard'.

'Insists a lot, doesn't he?' says the Governor. 'What an arrogant piece of shit. When you're done with him, I want to see his body so I can piss on it.'

'You won't have long to wait, Sir,' says Giwa, as if he is controlling the operation.

'I had assumed he would not be coming on his own,' says de Witt, 'but this demand offers two advantages. One, his driver will probably be a senior member of his unit, so on top of Abdullahi, we have the chance to eliminate a possible successor. And as Abdullahi insisted on a driver, he had to agree to Mr Ado being accompanied by one, in this case me — camouflaged of course.'

'We'll make a Nigerian of you yet,' laughs the Governor. Ado and Giwa are quick to join in. De Witt smiles patiently, then turns back to the screen.

'We've visited the site. Studied the layout. So, two cars, each containing a negotiator, a driver-cum-bodyguard, and a hostage. They meet here at 22:00 hours.' He circles the car park with his laser pointer. 'We've left it late to allow the CP's men to get into their position around the mosque well in advance, and to let the darkness absorb them. Our car with Abdullahi's daughter will leave the barracks at 21:15 hours. Abdullahi is sure to have someone watching our departure to ensure all looks above board. The CP will have men posted at various points en route, to monitor our progress. The CP's men', de Witt points the laser at the junction of the main road and the road leading to the mosque, 'will be hidden here. They will alert us when Abdullahi's car turns off the main road. At that time of night, there's no reason for anyone to be driving to a disused tyre factory or abandoned mosque, so they will be easy to spot.'

'We'll give them time to reach the mosque before blocking off the road behind them,' says Giwa. 'We'll block the road at the other end too, though it doesn't go anywhere.'

De Witt clicks a device in his hand and a map showing the mosque and its car park in detail appears on the screen.

'We will arrive with at least ten minutes to spare', he says. 'This will ensure we have time to park in the position we want, namely here,' he indicates with his laser, 'in a diagonal across this corner, the driver's side facing into the car park. Some of my men will be hidden on the other side of the wall, here, so the car will shield them further from view while providing us with immediate backup, as needed.'

Music to Ado's ears.

'On the other hand', continues de Witt, 'when Abdullahi's car pulls up alongside us, it will be in an exposed position, open to the rest of the car park and the mosque, in plain sight of our men. More of the CP's men will be positioned here, by these factory outbuildings', says de Witt, using his pointer again, 'here, on the roof of the mosque, and here, on the ground out front. Cover will be provided by the remains of this wall, and here by this out-building, an old latrine.'

'Kind of you to think of the CP, Colonel', says the boss, clearly happy with what he's hearing.

The CP tries to muster a laugh. Ado does better, enjoying the CP's discomfort.

'Just a joke', says the Governor. 'Surely you know your old comrade by now.'

Giwa offers his gap-toothed grin in response. The Governor turns to de Witt.

'Your men, Colonel, where will they be?'

'Lieutenant Coetzee, my second-in-command, will be with the CP in the mosque. The others will be at strategic points — here on the roof of the mosque, there behind that tree, but mainly in close, around the car park perimeter and that corner.' He circles the wall in front of the car with his pointer.

'What about the Sheikh?' asks the Governor, turning to Ado.

'Senile', says Ado. 'Alone, most of the time. The only person living in the entire vicinity. Hasn't had a congregation in years. A nephew comes round at noon with food and switches on a call to prayer. The two of them pray alone, then eat. He leaves his uncle some food to tide him over 'til the next day, then goes on his way.'

'Only he won't be going on his way on the night of our operation,' says de Witt. 'The CP will lock the two of them in the Sheikh's room and from what Mr Ado says, the Sheikh won't remember much when he wakes up the next morning.'

'Good,' says the boss. 'Ado, we need to talk about this site once all this is over. I have some ideas for redevelopment. Okay, Colonel carry on.'

'Mr Ado has given Abdullahi the details of a schoolgirl to be handed over to us. Her name is Aminah, we met her sister this morning. She's a senior nurse who heads up a family support group, so a good choice. Mr Ado has a photo of the girl and will verify she is the Aminah in question.'

'I can recall what she looks like', says Giwa, 'and I've only seen her photo once.'

'We've never met Abdullahi,' says Ado. 'Confirming the girl's identity, confirms we are dealing with him and not someone out to steal five thousand dollars from us.' Even though it's a lie for de Witt's benefit, Ado feels, as Deputy Governor, that he shouldn't have to justify himself to a thug like Giwa, CP or not. 'Besides, I'm sure when the CP presents the girl to the media, he wouldn't want to find out she's not the Aminah in question, but a frightened girl forced to take part in a scam, while her family is held hostage in a village somewhere.'

'You've made your point,' says the Governor. 'Colonel, can you get to the part where Abdullahi is eliminated.'

De Witt presents a computer-generated layout of the site on screen. 'I'm expecting Abdullahi's driver to draw up parallel with us, pointing in the opposite direction, so they can drive straight out once the meeting's over. I'd expect him to leave a gap of around fifteen metres between his vehicle and ours. Mr Ado will be in the back seat, directly behind me, the money at his feet. We'll be facing inwards, towards them. Abdullahi's daughter will be handcuffed and sitting in the back. But whatever position they park, our priority is to get Abdullahi out of the car into the open, likewise his driver. To encourage this, I'll get out of the car, as soon as they arrive, and stand beside Mr Ado's door, ready to open it. If they don't do the same, Mr Ado will wind down the window and signal Abdullahi or his driver to get out and meet him halfway. If I'm Abdullahi, I'll want to see my daughter and the money first before I get out of the car.'

'And I'm not handing anything over', says Ado, 'until I see the girl and establish she's the Aminah in the photo'.

'If there's reluctance for Abdullahi to get out,' says de Witt, 'Ado will say he's agreed in good faith to come to the meeting to discuss hostage exchanges but —'

'I'm not prepared to do so by shouting through a car window! But, if I have to', he glances at de Witt, 'I will get out first'.

'And I'll keep your door open,' says de Witt, 'so Abdullahi can see his daughter inside'.

'Once I've established the girl is Aminah', says Ado, 'I'll propose the daughter walks to her father, carrying the money, while Aminah walks to us. I'll tell Abdullahi, once that is done, we can turn to the main purpose of the meeting — negotiating the release of the rest of the girls.'

'Hopefully, things will not progress that far', says de Witt. 'We just need to get Abdullahi out of the car and away from the girl. As soon as that happens my sniper will take out the driver, and I'll take out Abdullahi.'

'We're counting on you, Colonel', says the Governor.

'That's the best case scenario, Sir, but we have to be ready for others.'

'Such as?' says the boss.

'Abdullahi may drag the girl out of the car with him. Hold a gun to her head or point it at Mr Ado. We must be patient, alert and flexible, which is why I want to stress again that, for this operation, the only people who should fire their weapons, must be me and my men. I will eliminate Abdullahi when I know the girl and Mr Ado are not in danger. It's a question of timing. The last thing we want is someone trying to make a name for themselves, taking a pot-shot at the wrong time and starting a fire-fight with Mr Ado, the girl and myself in the front line.'

'You've already made that clear', says Giwa. 'I can vouch for the discipline of my men; I hope you can do the same for yours.'

'This is crucial to the success of this operation, Governor,' says de Witt as if he hasn't heard Giwa's remark.

'I'm sure we all understand the importance of discipline on the battlefield, Colonel', says the Governor.

'Sir, it's not just about restraint in discharging a weapon; there will be a lot of men surrounding this car park. It's vital they maintain their silence.'

'I'm not in the habit of repeating myself, Colonel', says the boss, 'but I realise you are a stranger in our country and are here to do an important job, so I will make an exception. I trust our security services to do their job, especially under their current leadership', he nods in Giwa's direction. 'I further trust there won't be a need for our security forces to fire a shot, for that would mean something would have gone wrong. In which case don't be surprised if I come looking for an explanation, not to say a refund!'

Giwa looks on smugly. De Witt remains impassive. Ado is unsettled by this talk of being in the firing line, while the show of rancour between the heads of the two units he will have to depend on for his survival, is not doing much to ease his state of mind.

'My remarks were not meant to denigrate State Security Services, sir. In the event of something unforeseen happening, I have confidence in the ability of the CP and his team to perform appropriately and prevent any escape by these terrorists.'

It seems de Witt is conversant in the art of diplomacy as well as the art of war. The temperature drops and Ado breathes easier.

'I'm at your disposal to answer any questions, sir?'

'I have none', says the Governor. 'As you have said before, Colonel, you work in a results business. I expect to be informed immediately these results are achieved and you can expect me at the scene shortly afterwards. Ado, I presume our media people are on standby?'

'Yes, Excellency.'

'And you and your men know how to melt away, Colonel.'

'Ja.'

'Then, we're done. I wish you a successful mission.'

'Inch 'Allah,' says Ado, and the CP in unison. They get up to go. De Witt turns the lights back on and starts to pack away his laptop.

'Commissioner, stay back for a moment', says the boss. 'I'll order us some tea'.

'Do you need me, Excellency?'

'No, no, Ado. Thank you. I'll see you tomorrow, Inch 'Allah.'

'Inch 'Allah.'

Chapter 24

'What are you smiling at, man?' de Witt leans back on his chair, turning his coke bottle round in circles.

Jamilah shakes her head, closes her eyes and smiles even more. 'I was thinking how strange it is to have a man in my house, other than my brother.'

'Never mind an Afrikaner you didn't know forty-eight hours ago.'

'Yes,' she laughs, 'very strange'.

She sits across the dinner table from him. If Aminah could see her now! Lipstick — she never wears lipstick! And decked out in her headdress and robe which are only worn on special occasions, and never to impress a man. But this man is always well-turned out and tonight is no different. He's wearing a stone-coloured linen suit and white shirt with button-down collar and no tie. It would have been disrespectful to greet him in jeans and trainers, especially after all he is doing for her family.

'Well, you were offered dinner at what I'm told is Kano's finest hotel', he says opening his palms.

'Yes, that was kind of you, and totally unnecessary, just like these flowers.' She strokes the vase. No man has ever bought her flowers or asked her out to dinner and it felt good to be asked. 'I'm sorry I couldn't accept. It's inappropriate in our culture. The Hisbah — the Sharia police — hang around hotels waiting for such opportunities. They'd see you as a white businessman looking to spread his seed, and me, a Nigerian woman moonlighting as a sex worker — and willing seed recipient.' She laughs, then feels embarrassed. 'As for the gossipmongers, they'd have a field day.'

'But I've seen whites with Nigerian women in the hotel restaurant', he shrugs, 'dining in full view. I didn't think it would be a problem'.

'They were probably part of a group, or if you're talking about a mixed couple, probably outsiders on a working visit, staying at the hotel.'

'Ja, I get it. Apartheid is alive and well in Kano!'

'It's not the same, and you know it!' She gets up to check the stove. 'Anyway, it's only right that we should offer you hospitality in recognition of all you're doing for us. You have earned your chance to sample my pepper soup!'

'Yes, Ma'am! Smells great. I'm looking forward to home cooking. Been through the hotel menu more times ... than I've had hot dinners', he laughs.

'Well hot dinners are a house speciality here!' She smiles and sits down.

There's an unexpected silence. She wants to ask him about the exchange but feels he should be the one to raise it. Maybe he's waiting until Ahmed's here and he won't have to repeat himself. She can't make up her mind if his eyes are more grey than blue. Regardless, they display little emotion. Do they change when he kills? The things he must have seen ... and done. Can he tell what she's thinking? Maybe he's wondering why she's so made up, sitting at home in her little flat. He's a man of the world. She must look like a clown.

'How's Dr Salim?'

'Fine', she nods. 'He gave me the night off.'

'I'm grateful to him.'

She's blushing again and looks away.

'Ahmed will be here soon. I'll set the table.' She gets up, grateful for a chance to clear her head.

'Let me help.' He springs to his feet.

There he goes again. She has to ask Ahmed to set the table. This man, this Colonel …

'So these Hisbah, they give you a hard time?' He's uncomfortably close.

'No, I don't let them.' She lifts the plates. 'Can you take these?'

He does as asked while she grabs the cutlery.

'I know how they work. When they're not sneaking up on women who aren't dressed to their liking, they're searching for brothels, or in the market trying to catch the mammas mismeasuring cloth or over-weighing lentils. Can you grab that jug of water and glasses?'

She starts laying the table.

'Of course, they never try to catch the big fish stealing the real money.'

'I can guess who you mean,' says de Witt. 'Talking of which, everything is set for tomorrow night.' She sits down. 'I can't tell you where, but I'll call you as soon as we have her. Hopefully before midnight.'

'Thanks, Francois. I'm so grateful, Ahmed too. It's been over a month and not a word from the kidnappers or the police. To think Aminah could be free tomorrow night. I know they won't let me see her straightaway, but I'll be able to talk to her, right? On the phone?'

'I'll ensure you get to speak to her on my phone. She can tell you herself how it feels to be free.'

'Inch 'Allah. You're sure she won't come to any harm?'

'I can't go into details Jamilah, but I can assure you that measures are in place to ensure her safety.'

'And you'll be careful too, won't you? You'll send me a text when it's done?'

'Yes', he nods. 'Don't worry about me, man.'

Jamilah smiles warmly at him. She resists an urge to throw her arms around him and hug him, but she'll not hesitate to do so if he fulfils his promise. And she does care that he doesn't come to any harm. He's her knight in shining armour. He's looking at her and neither of them are talking. She's too shy to look back. She glances at her watch.

'Typical of my brother. He never used to be like this. I'm going to serve up, he can help himself when he comes — after he apologises for his bad manners.'

'No need for that, but I'm as hungry as a lion, man. That smell's driving me crazy!'

'Ha! Help yourself to another Coke.' She points to the fridge. 'You're going to need it!'

Chapter 25

'Bring me that Fulani bitch!'

Muhammed goes to do his leader's bidding.

'Wait, let me see those two first.'

Muhammed steps out of the tent and pushes Gambo and Rashidi inside. Rashidi has a blood-stained dressing across the middle of his face but it doesn't dissuade Abdullahi from bringing down the back of his hand against it. Rashidi loses his balance and as his hands reach out for the ground, he receives a kick in the stomach and slumps in a heap.

Gambo receives a closed fist to the face, causing blood to gush from his nose. Still upright, he takes the full force of a stomach punch which bends him double. He drops to his knees, fighting for breath.

'I go away for one night and you let a bitch walk right out of here. If it wasn't for those stupid herders, she might have walked all the way to the border. Were you fucking sleeping again?'

Their silence elicits two further kicks and a mumbled response.

'And in what state do you return the goods, uh? I'll fucking tell you. Her eye's the size of a pineapple and she's covered in fucking cuts, her face, neck, arms. I'm surprised you didn't fucking slice her into pieces and bring her back in a bag.'

He turns to Muhammed. 'Look at them lying there, snivelling like a pair of bitches. And I can smell that fucking codeine syrup on them.' He drives the sole of his boot into Gambo's chest, knocking him back. He bends down and shouts into his face, 'I warned you about that before, didn't I?' He kicks Rashid. 'Didn't I?'

'Now they can't speak,' he says to Muhammed.

'Which one of you wants to marry her now, then? You?' He kicks Rashidi who shakes his head and stares into the ground.

'You?' He kicks Gambo and gets a mumbled negative.

'Are you sure, Rashidi? No need to wait till we get back to the forest, we could have a little ceremony in the morning before we leave. Muhammed could take some photos on his phone — you and your bride covered in fucking bandages. What a fucking sight that would be.'

He stares at them with contempt. 'If it was up to me, the vultures would be feasting on your scattered remains right now — on that rock up there. Give praise to Allah that He has other plans for you.'

He turns to Muhammed. 'Get them out of my sight. I'll see the bitch now.'

Muhammed pulls the men up and pushes them outside. He returns with Aminah, who flops to the ground like a sack of cloth and curls into a foetal position. The leader nods towards the exit and Muhammed leaves. He lifts a candle, kneels down in front of her and pulls away her hijab. The eye looks bad; they've put some herbal paste on it, she'll be okay. The cuts are a mix of the deep and superficial. She'll survive, but she'll be scarred. In a way he can't explain, he likes that. She was too perfect before. She pushes herself up but doesn't try to stand. He gets to his feet. She stares back at him with her good eye. While badly beaten, she retains an air of defiance. He likes that too. He stands looking down at her. He owns her, controls her, she excites him. He draws his hand back and swings it down against the side of her face. She slumps back to the ground. He kneels down, grabs her hair and stares into her face. An old wound has re-opened up on her cheek. He recalls with satisfaction that it was he who had administered it the night he had taken her.

'I respect courage, you would make a good fighter, but you lack intelligence. Did you think you were going to walk out of here and keep walking all the way to Cameroon? You didn't think we would come after you, we who know the terrain better than anyone, we who have bikes and trucks? We who have a camp in Cameroon? No, you don't think. You know the most stupid thing of all? If you'd stayed in your tent another night you wouldn't have had to do anything. Because you will be returning home tomorrow in the back of a car.'

She looks up.

'I thought that might get your attention. There's going to be an exchange. You for my daughter. Yes, you're going home, but only if you obey me. Is that clear?'

Aminah mumbles and receives a slap on the other side of her face.

'Yes,' she says

'Yes, what?'

'Yes, master.'

'Good. I'm going to miss beating you and I know you are going to miss us too, aren't you?'

'Yes, master.'

'Well just to make our night of nostalgia complete, I'm going to fuck you again. Does that please you?' He slaps her again. 'Does that please you?'

With an effort she raises her face, and still struggling to hold her head steady, she spits at him.

'Here's more good news, on top of whatever those morons did to you earlier, I'm going to send you back to your miserable family with so much jihadi seed inside you, you'll breed a fucking army.'

Chapter 26

Jamilah makes a final check on her phone, then starts to clear the table.

'You don't think he's in any trouble?' asks de Witt.

'I wouldn't know what to think these days. I should be angry, but it feels like he's lost hope and doesn't want to think about his sister. No, stay there, I'll manage.' She puts Ahmed's unused plates and cutlery away and returns to pick up the rest. 'He carries so much guilt around even though Aminah's abduction had nothing to do with him. 'Family', she shrugs, rinsing dishes under the tap. 'Tell me about yours.'

'Ahh, that's a long tale of woe.'

'I've got time.' She comes back and sits down.

'Farmers, soldiers all. Fought the Brits first, then after we kicked the Krauts out of German South-West Africa, my grandfather moved the family there. Took the get-rich-quick approach, digging for diamonds north of the Orange River. But, he got in too late, had to work for someone else. Died in an explosion. Then came the Border Wars. My father joined the South African Defence Force. Got himself killed fighting SWAPO. My mother died giving birth to my sister, who didn't survive either. I told you it was a tale of woe.'

'No, it's okay, go on.'

'I was seventeen, my brother a year older. Somehow we kept things going even though it was hard to get people to work for us. They either saw us as the enemy or didn't want to take orders from schoolboys who couldn't pay them much.'

'My mother died in childbirth, and my father and uncle got themselves killed too. I was sixteen, the same age as Aminah is now ...'

'What happened to them?'

She spreads her fingers out on the table in front of her. He touches her hand. She sits up, pulling her hand away. 'Long time ago. It's okay, please go on,' she manages a half smile.

'My brother and I joined the SADF too. We fought Africans, Russians, Cubans. We fought hard for our land, man.'

'Your land?'

'Look, Europeans settled in the States four hundred years ago. Took land from Native Americans then imported thousands of African slaves to work it. Why are Afrikaners treated differently.'

'African land belongs to Africans, real Africans.'

'I'm an African. I know Apartheid wasn't right but ... apologies for upsetting you. I should be going.' He stands up. 'Thanks for —'

'Please sit down, Colonel. I don't know why I started talking politics, I know nothing about the subject.'

He hesitates.

'At least have some tea before you go.'

He sits down and she gets up to boil the kettle. 'Isn't there a Mrs de Witt somewhere in this story?' she says, in an effort to lighten the mood, though, at the same time, curious.

'My wife was raped and murdered by thugs. I wouldn't call them soldiers. Our farmhands ran away. Same old de Witt story. I wasn't around to prevent it and she was pregnant too. But you see, I know about terrorism from a long way back.'

Jamilah leaves the tea-making and sits down beside him. 'I'm sorry Francois'. This time it is she who touches his hand.

'It was a long time ago. By 1990, our farm was in the newly independent republic of Namibia. After Mandela went, corruption really took hold. We were eased out. My brother emigrated to Australia, I became a consultant and ... here I am.'

'And you never remarried?'

'With my job and given our family history?' He smiles. 'Who'd be mad enough to take me on? What about you? How come you're not married?'

'Never been asked.' She lets go of his hand and leans back. 'And that's fine by me. My career comes first. Always will.'

'Never been asked? Look man, I've been around. I recognise a beautiful woman when I see one. Are the men in this country blind?'

More blushing. Maybe because she finds her embarrassment so embarrassing, or because he was so open with his past, whatever the reason, she starts talking. Her voice is soft, and she looks away from his piercing eyes.

'My father and uncle were slaughtered by vigilantes who invaded our village after a Boko Haram raid. They were under the control of the man who's now the CP.'

'Giwa?'

'Yes. It was ten years ago. He was a sergeant then. They were going to kill Ahmed too. He was twelve. In order to save him, I had to give myself to Giwa. Ahmed knows this. People in the village know this. This sort of thing stays quiet until it's necessary to speak of it. That's why no man would ever marry me. I'm damaged goods.'

'Did Giwa recognize you at the meeting yesterday?'

'No. Why would he remember a dumb village girl like me from ten years ago? You can be sure there were many more before and after me.'

'Couldn't you have moved away? Started a new life.'

'What? With no money, no parents, and two siblings to look after? I wasn't a rich farm boy like you. Looking back, I can see how damaged we were.' She feels her lip tremble and knows tears aren't far off. 'We only survived because of Salim.'

De Witt, gets up, lifts her to her feet, puts his arms around her and holds her close. She freezes, arms at her sides. Does he do this when he goes to comfort the widows of his comrades? Her arms stay limp, and she cries into his chest. The strength of his arms rekindles a sense of security she had lost when her father was killed. Her arms rise involuntarily over the smooth surface of his suit. His back is wet with sweat. The electricity went off an hour ago and battery power only supports one fan. Still, this man is not her father; he never smelt of lavender or a pine forest. His lips brush the top of her forehead. She holds him now; her head nestles under his chin.

'Those were cruel things to have happened to you,' he says.

'And you,' she replies.

'People shouldn't disparage you. They should be looking up to you. A man should be honoured to have you for a wife.'

'Thank you,' she sniffs.

'And I meant what I said, Jamilah, you are a very beautiful woman.'

'It's "very" now,' she looks up, smiling through her tears. He frees his hand and caresses her neck and cheek. Her cheek burns and their lips touch, once, twice, then press together fiercely. He strokes the side of her face with his thumb and his fingers slide inside her headdress, a simple act that makes her shudder. His other arm holds her in a stronger grip than before. She finds the combination of tenderness and strength intoxicating. Her hand curls around the back of his neck and his tongue probes her mouth. She recoils but he is insistent, and her resistance weakens. All night their tongues have been talking, now they wrestle and communicate directly. What are they trying to say? I empathise with you? I like you? I desire you? I love you? His mouth moves to her neck. She is losing control and not fighting to keep it. Her fingers spread across the back of his head. She has a moment to breathe before he finds her mouth again and their tongues renew their intimacy with more intensity. He presses hard against her. She holds her ground and presses back. His hands slide down her back and grip her buttocks. He draws her into him. She gasps. His arousal is unmistakeable. She is aroused too. She's unable to suppress her desire. But with the sound of a key turning in a lock, she is obliged to. The front door opens and closes with a bang. They pull away from each other and adjust their clothes. She straightens her headdress and motions to de Witt to sit down. Ahmed is already in the room. He looks at them, closes and re-opens his eyes slowly. His mouth widens into a lazy smile, and he sniggers, inducing some unsteadiness.

'I was going to apologise for being late, but I suppose I should apologise for the intrusion!' His body shakes in silent laughter, and he looks up at the ceiling. This invokes more unsteadiness which he counteracts by moving back a pace and letting his back fall gently against the wall.

'There's no intrusion, and you can take that stupid grin of your face. You *are* late and you should apologize to our guest. Colonel, this is my brother, Ahmed.'

'Francois de Witt,' says de Witt, extending his hand.

Ahmed ignores de Witt's hand, choosing instead to stand to attention and salute.

'Reporting for duty Colonel. I apologize for the lateness of my arrival, but I was on a top secret mission to drink eight bottles of Gulder. As you will appreciate, orders are orders.'

'I do, though I suppose it might depend on who's giving them and why.'

'I can see who's giving the orders around here. My sis looks like she's on full parade and,' he sniffs, 'there's an unusual scent in the air. Very pleasant. I'm sure that's not the pepper soup.' He seems pleased with his little joke.

'Stop talking like that. You were supposed to be here two hours ago. Colonel de Witt is a guest in our house. He's helping us get our dear sister back. Remember that and show some respect.'

'Yes mother, you're right.' He runs his finger across his mouth as if buttoning his lip. He bows to de Witt. 'I apologise for my late arrival, Colonel. I hope my sister has been looking after you.' He staggers back across the room towards the opposite wall and slumps into the sofa.

'No need for apologies,' says de Witt, 'and yes, your sister has been the perfect host.'

'I can see that,' says Ahmed through half-closed eyes. 'Tell me, is that a soup stain on the side of your face?'

Why do drunks have this ability to notice things that pass sober people by? A red mark, the same shade as her lipstick stands out like a fresh cut on de Witt's cheek. She takes out a tissue and wipes it. Ahmed's head falls down on his shoulder, eyes closed, mouth half open.

'I'm sorry, Francois. He's not like this, really.'

Ahmed isn't done. 'Not like what?' he shouts, springing to his feet. 'I'm supposed to welcome a racist mercenary into my home and be happy for him to molest my sister? You don't get it sis, this man isn't here to help *us*, he's just a hired hand in the pay of the man who's responsible for Minah's kidnapping — Yakubu. If we didn't have corrupt leaders like him syphoning off the country's wealth, you wouldn't have groups like Boko Haram running around, with nothing to lose. They didn't kill our father and uncle; it was thugs masquerading as state security, led by Giwa, Yakubu's enforcer. The man who your boyfriend's hand in glove with. Yes him, who you've brought into our house, to … entertain'. There are tears in his eyes, but Jamilah is unmoved.

'This is what you and your drinking pals spend hours talking about, is it? Well this man might be in the pay of the Governor, he may be white and from South African, but he's not sitting on his backside getting drunk and talking about what's wrong with the world. He's the only one to have done anything about freeing Aminah. He's risking his life for our family and for that he deserves our gratitude and respect!'

'I'd better go,' says de Witt.

But it's Ahmed who heads for the door. Jamilah raises her eyes in exasperation as he walks past. The door slams shut.

'I'm sorry,' says Jamilah turning to clear away the plate and cutlery left out for Ahmed.

'No need. Is he going to be okay?

She sighs. 'I expect he'll go to one of his friends to sleep it off.'

They hear the sound of a motorbike starting up and heading off.

'I'm the one who should apologize. I haven't kissed a woman in … a long time.'

Why does she blush and avoid his eyes every time he says something nice about her?

'I should get going.'

'Well,' she presses her lips together, 'it wasn't the evening I'd planned, but I'm glad you could come. Thank you again for everything you're doing for us.' She goes to show him out.

'I'm glad you invited me,' he says, walking behind her.

She turns to face him. 'Please be careful tomorrow. You know what kind of man Giwa is. He's not to be trusted.'

'I don't trust any of them. Your brother's analysis wasn't all wrong. I work for men like Yakubu all the time, they kill hope as well as people and that's when you get extreme responses. But don't worry, I'll have my men with me. We watch each other's backs. We'll free your sister, I promise.'

They exchange a light kiss on the cheek. She turns and opens the door, and he slides past into the landing.

'Thanks for the flowers.'

He raises his hand, smiles, and disappears down the stairs.

'Be careful,' she whispers.

Chapter 27

With Friday afternoon prayers over, and the mosques silent, an air of calm descends over State Government House. For Ado, this is normally the time when he can settle back and pull the loose ends of the week together. The only sounds are the occasional pings from his phone and the barely audible drone of his split aircon. He doesn't mind that his colleagues are making their way home through the dust and heat, ready to settle into another weekend of the same thing they do in the office, namely, little of value. Since becoming Deputy Governor, Ado's workload has of course increased, both in quantity and quality — heavier documents, more complex negotiations, diverse budgets — while demand for his signature has never been greater. But he hadn't expected to be so engaged in the murkier side of political life, well not in such a hands-on way. Yet tonight, he will risk his life to ensure his new-found position of power will not be derailed by a terrorist who believes himself an agent of Allah. And this afternoon, there's little chance of him getting much work done because there's only one thing occupying his brain: the role he will play tonight. He will risk his life while the boss lies in bed in front of his big screen, his alluring wife on hand to satisfy whatever sordid demand he makes on her.

He looks at de Witt talking on the phone. There's a man who knows when to talk and when to stay quiet. There's a rap at the door. Instinctively, he prods the cash-laden holdall a few inches further below his desk. An official enters carrying clothes. Ado tells him to put them on the table and wait outside. In an hour, he and de Witt will set off for the barracks where they will get something to eat, pick up Abdullahi's daughter, then proceed to the "meeting." He yawns — the consequence of being up half the night going through his lines. De Witt, on the other hand, looks bored. Probably a good thing. Bored means calm, doesn't it? He's coming to speak to him.

'That was Coetzee, my second-in-command.'

'I know who he is, what did he say?'

'The old mosque is secured. The Sheikh's in poor shape. His nephew brought him medicine but it's a job to get him to take it.'

'Probably thinks someone's trying to poison him.'

'The nephew offered to take him back to his house, but he refused. Prefers to die in the mosque, it seems.'

'It's a popular venue for death', says Ado, regretting it immediately.

'Giwa's locked them in for the night. Everyone's in position apart from those who'll be outside around the car park. They'll integrate themselves when night falls. No point in sitting out in the sun, exposed to view. Coetzee will oversee things from the roof, with Giwa in tow.'

'You sound confident, Colonel.'

'That's my job. Providing everyone sticks to the plan, we'll be fine, though you've always got to be ready for the unexpected.'

'Indeed,' says Ado nodding his head as if he were a veteran of such situations. 'And you're happy with the CP … you trust him?'

'That's a strange question, coming from the Deputy Governor', says de Witt.

'I mean, do you have confidence in the ability of the CP and his men to play their roles.'

'As you know from the plan, the success of this mission rests in the hands of me and my men. I have full confidence in my boys. I know who they are and what they can do. If you had the same confidence in your own security forces, you wouldn't need me. All the CP and his men need to do is stay out of the way and be quiet. Stop worrying man, we'll look after you.'

Ado goes across to the table where the clothes have been placed. 'We've found you something traditional, naturally. Light enough to move around in and providing you with space to conceal your handgun. This cloth will go round your head and cover your lower face.'

'Good, tell your man to put them in the car.'

'You're not going to change here then?'

'No, I'll have to blacken my face and hands first. I'll do everything at the barracks, out of sight.

Chapter 28

Aminah's eyelids weigh heavy. Even if they were ready to open she has no desire to re-enter the reality they will reveal. But her ears are functioning. She hears men's voices. Their words are incoherent, their tone deep and ponderous camouflaged by the sound of a car engine. She's never felt this tired and her entire body aches. The rope across her chest and arms keeps her upright. Side pressure from someone or something stops her from sliding down. Depending on the bumps and contours of the road, her head flops onto her shoulder or bounces against her chest. She can't ignore the pain they provoke and reluctantly she is dragged back to consciousness. She's in a car, going where? Think, think. It dawns — a rendezvous. They are going to free her in exchange for Abdullahi's daughter. She should be excited, rejoicing even, this is what she'd been praying for, but what freedom is she going back to? And in what state? She's been kidnapped, raped, beaten, disfigured and she's probably pregnant. Everything has changed for the worse. Her face will signal her disgrace for the rest of her life. Those who are able to look her in the eye will not see her as the person she was. As for her family, what a burden she will be to Jamilah. Her sister's had so much to deal with already, she doesn't deserve to be lumbered with a pregnant 'bitch', the former plaything of terrorists. Imagine the battles Jamilah will have to fight on her behalf. What sort of reward is that for everything her sister's done for her? She'll have to leave, try to pick up her studies, ideally get a scholarship to another country. Maybe she can be a doctor after all.

There's a bang as if the car's been struck by a missile, but it's just a bigger pothole than usual and more than enough for another surge of pain to jolt through her. Not only her it seems, for there's a howl beside her followed by angry words directed at the driver. Her eyes stay shut, she doesn't know who made the utterance and she doesn't care. But her memory is kicking in. They made her drink something. She was drugged to make her compliant. There was something else too. They were changing her clothes while she was losing consciousness or maybe they were raping her again? Wait, there was a woman helping. Maybe they were trying to improve her appearance before the exchange. The thought makes her aware of the covering across her face. These hypocrites: one minute, full of false piety, they remonstrate with you for not covering your face properly; the next, they are raping you. The banging and bumping stops. They must have slipped onto a better road and the calm helps her drift back to sleep.

She wakes up. Her head rests on her shoulder, her eyes stare into the side of the car. It's dark outside. Men's voices again; their words discernible, their voices all too recognisable. She straightens her neck. Gambo is driving, Rashidi is beside her in the back, a bloodstained bandage covers most of his face. It wouldn't take an internship at the hospital to see it's in dire need of changing. It gives her comfort to reflect that for the remainder of his miserable life, he will be subject to ridicule too, though stigma's always worse for women. She closes her eyes and feigns sleep. The rope is tight around her chest and her hand is numb, but she'll put up with discomfort to avoid communication. They wouldn't do anything to alleviate her pain anyway. There's something else she feels she should remember; something important. It seems a long time since they set out. It's bugging her. She'll keep her ears open; they might say something to jog her memory.

The car slips off the road and stops. Gambo says something on his mobile. She opens one eye a little. Rashidi leans forward on the passenger seat, trying to listen in. Someone is giving them instructions, for they don't speak and in seconds, the call is over. Rashidi leans back in his seat. Gambo turns round to speak to him and catches her eye.

'The bitch is awake.'

Rashidi turns to face her. 'That's a shame', he growls, eyes full of hate.

'Everything's in place,' says Gambo ignoring her. 'Time to get ready.'

They get out of the car. Gambo opens the door and pulls her out. The sudden movement makes her unsteady. Rashidi approaches her with a knife. She is light-headed. So this will be her fate! Slaughtered at the roadside. He spins her round and shoves her up against the car, his arm pressed against her back. The rope squeaks as the knife cuts into it, then her arms are free and blood rushes to her hands. She wants to stretch, but Gambo presses her face against the roof of the car. Rashidi pulls her arms behind her and presses his leg into her back to keep her still. He slips zip-ties around her wrists and pulls them tight. The remains of the rope drop to the ground and curl like a snake around her feet. Gambo releases his grip on her and returns to the car. She looks up at the stars and inhales. Now the rope is off, she expects to breathe more freely, but the constriction in her upper body remains. Reality bites like the crushing jaws of a hyena. It wasn't just the rope causing the tightness in her chest, it was the suicide belt they wrapped around it before they set out. The pushing and pulling had felt malevolent even as the drug took hold. When she had caught sight of the red and black wires, she had fainted.

They hadn't sought to revive her, leaving the drug to do its work instead. What are they planning? What can she do? Wrapped in a vest of death, she feels more of a captive than ever.

'Get in, bitch,' says Rashidi pushing her back into the car. 'You're only a mile from paradise!'

They laugh. Their laughter is always cruel, never joyful. She'd thought there was nothing more these people could do to her, other than kill her. She was wrong. They're going to kill her and use her to kill other people too.

Chapter 29

Abdullahi's daughter is staring out of the car window again. Farida, she's called. Who cares? If she turned round now, he's sure the same look of contempt would be glued to her face. As if she could read his mind, she turns around and he's not disappointed. He'd expected her to be nervous, frightened even, surrounded by Giwa's men all guns and boots and twice her size, but when she was brought out, she looked bold and defiant. She looks more like a teenager now — everything's unfair, her pain unique. This reminder of her youth is unwelcome. She's right to feel aggrieved. It is unfair. She didn't choose her father. She hasn't committed any crime and she should never have been held prisoner. The henna designs on her hands are symbols of life but the plastic restraints around her wrists are portents of death. Would she display the same disdain if she knew she was en route to her execution? De Witt isn't happy about it, he made that clear. But there he is, driving her to her fate and like Ado, an accomplice.

What a change in his appearance! Front and back, he looks for all the world like a Fulani with his robes and a cloth wrapped around his head and face. His hands gripping the steering wheel are black, likewise his ears, neck, and face. How would that play with his old comrades in the Veldt? The girl has paid no attention to de Witt. His voice would betray his real identity, but a driver's not expected to speak unless spoken to. As usual he's doing his job and doing it well. His presence soothes Ado's nerves. It helps that the operation is underway and he's in a proper car, dressed as himself and not having to worry about being recognised.

Progress is good. No hold-ups. Ado retains a protective hand over the holdall resting between him and the girl. Five thousand dollars, huh, a drop in the ocean compared to what they've given Abdullahi in the past, but it was still against the boss's nature to authorise its release, even though Abdullahi wouldn't be living long enough to spend it. The turning for the old mosque is coming up. He pats de Witt on the shoulder even though it's unnecessary; de Witt is already indicating, and the car decelerates and turns left. He shouldn't have touched him, a Deputy Governor doesn't touch a driver like that, he just barks instructions. So what if the girl noticed and thinks it strange? It doesn't change anything, but it's a reminder for him to relax, remember his lines and act accordingly. He peers out from side to side, relieved not to catch sight of Giwa's men. When he leans forward to look past the girl, she lurches back as if he has something infectious. The road gets bumpy and Ado shouts angrily at de Witt in Hausa, restoring appearances. Ado looks back down the road. Darkness, no sign of life. He hopes Giwa's men are as disciplined when Abdullahi's car comes into view.

They reach the mosque. All appears as it should do — still and calm. De Witt brings the car to a halt in the bottom corner of the car park, as planned. He switches off the headlights and takes out his phone, probably messaging Lieutenant Coetzee.

'What happens now?' the daughter asks. It's the first time she has spoken since they left the barracks.

'We wait for your father.'

Chapter 30

They turn right into a minor road. It's unlit, bumpy and sets Rashidi off again. Aminah too, only in a different way.

'I don't understand; why bring me all this way to kill me? Doesn't your leader want his daughter back? How can that happen if you blow me up? ... Well? ... Answer me!'

'Just shut up,' says Gambo, keeping his eyes on the road. 'Do as you're told, keep quiet and you'll be okay'.

'Are you serious? "You'll be okay?" That's what you say to someone with a suicide vest wrapped around her? I can't believe you people. Are you really that stupid?' She sobs in frustration.

'Look, bitch', says Rashidi, 'as much as we'd like to, we're not going to blow you up. You're not a suicide bomber. You're a decoy, that's all.'

'What do you need a decoy for? If they give you his daughter and you give them me, why can't both sides be happy with that?'

'Yeah, sure,' says Gambo, 'the Governor will be so happy for Abdullahi to get his daughter back and see you reunited with your family. Are *you* really that stupid? You think Yakubu can be trusted?'

'But —'

'He told you to shut up,' says Rashidi.

'Time to gag her, anyway,' says Gambo, pulling over. 'Listen,' he snarls, 'if you resist I'll be happy to drag you out of this car, stand on your throat and put the gag on you myself, right?'

Aminah says nothing and leans back in the seat, trying to process this latest twist. Rashidi gropes for something in the side panel of the door. Duct tape. He pulls her around to face him. The smell from his dressing is foul.

He pulls down her scarf to expose her mouth. His bloodshot eyes dart to the wounds on her cheeks.

'Habibi, what happened to you?' he says. 'Fallen into some bushes? You should be more careful.' He pulls back a strip of tape, bites the corner, and winces as he tears a strip away.

Gambo shakes with laughter in the front.

'Take a look in the mirror before you joke about disfigurement,' says Aminah.

Rashidi's jaw trembles with rage. He stretches the tape across her mouth, pressing it so hard that it sticks to her teeth. He tears off another strip and doubles it over the first. Her face feels as tight as her chest though her discomfort is mitigated by seeing the water in his eyes, and knowing she's won that little battle. He pulls the scarf back across her nose. Then she panics and shakes her head. She won't be able to breathe if her nose and mouth are covered. She doesn't want to die of suffocation, that would be worse than … But twitching her nose loosens the scarf, and she finds she can breathe, she just has to adjust to doing so through her nose. In a way, she's glad to focus on her breathing so she can keep her head clear and figure out what is going on. Yet when she closes her eyes, she thinks of her brother and sister. She recalls how Ahmed put his arm around her shoulder and told her not to look when their father and uncle were being slaughtered. She can feel his arm around her now. She can feel Jamilah drawing her close in a warm embrace, gently kissing her wounds and welcoming her home. These are good thoughts, good omens. Her family have come to reassure her all will be well.

'We're here', says Gambo.

Looking past his shoulder through the windscreen, she makes out the façade of an old mosque. Her sister never took her to the mosque except when it was deemed necessary. It was at school that her faith had strengthened, the same place these so-called fighters for Islam had come to undermine it. Whatever religion they believe in, it's not hers. They pull into a car park. A 4x4 is parked in the corner, a driver in the front seat and two people in the back; one must be the daughter. They draw up parallel with the other vehicle and stop, creating a gap of twenty metres between them. Gambo switches off the headlights.

Both cars sit in the darkness. The only sounds are the intermittent chirping of crickets and the far-off drone of traffic. Dark clouds are keeping the moonlight at bay, as if they're colluding in keeping this meeting covert. Unexpectedly, they pull apart and moonlight permeates the car park enough for her to see the weeds and broken stone. It illuminates the sharp metal crescent that juts upward from the top of the main minaret. She catches a movement on the roof and screws her eyes to locate its source, but the clouds regroup and it's hard to make anything out. She is sure she saw something, like when she's caught the dart of a mouse in the corner of her eye, turned to look and can't see anything but knows it was there. There are probably security forces all around. She should feel reassured but isn't. They could make an exchange safely, without fuss, if they wanted, but they're not thinking about her safety or liberation. They want more and everyone knows how trigger-happy the security forces can be. Gambo and Rashidi confirm their mistrust by carefully taking out handguns and resting them on their laps, out of sight from the people sitting in the car opposite. She suspects they were too busy eyeing each other up to take a moment to look up at the roof. Over Rashidi's shoulder, she sees a side window being wound down in the other vehicle.

'Salam Alaikum,' says a man she doesn't know. He looks important.

Gambo winds down his window. 'Walaikum Salam.'

Beside her, Rashidi winds his window down a quarter, looks out, but says nothing. The driver of the other car gets out and stands by the door of man in the back seat. The driver doesn't open the door but watches them intently. There is nothing to indicate he is armed.

'I'm Deputy Governor, Ado,' says the man.

'Do you want us to clap?' says Gambo.

'What's up with your leader,' says the Deputy Governor, directing his words towards Rashidi, 'lost his voice?'

What does he mean "leader"? thinks Aminah. He must think it's Abdullahi in the back seat with her!

'Bad tooth,' replies Gambo, 'but he doesn't want to talk to you anyway.'

'Why did he come all this way to meet me, then?'

'He's here isn't he? says Gambo, 'Let's see the money.'

'I see your leader's heart's in the right place,' says the Deputy Governor, glancing back at the girl in his car. 'What's a daughter's freedom compared to five thousand dollars, eh?'

Rashidi doesn't respond.

'Enough of this nonsense,' says the Deputy Governor. 'Toothache or not, we need to talk before you get to see any money, And I need to see Aminah.' He bends his neck as if he is trying to see past Rashidi. 'I presume that's her in the back with you?'

Aminah is excited to hear her name. She's been singled out. It must be Jamilah's doing, but Rashidi is still refusing to speak. The Deputy Governor turns his attention back to Gambo.

'Look, I'm here on behalf of His Excellency, Governor Yakubu. I agreed, in good faith, to come to this forsaken place, in the middle of the night, to talk with your leader and I've brought his daughter with me. I'm not prepared to sit here and shout through a car window.'

Gambo spits on the ground. The Deputy Governor directs his attention back to Rashidi.

'If you want the money and your daughter, we have to do an exchange. We discussed all this. Let's meet in the middle, do the transaction, then we can move on to the main business of the night.'

Gambo applauds slowly. 'Beautiful speech. Abdullahi is right,' he says, glancing back at Rashidi. 'You are full of shit. Nothing's going to happen until you bring us the money.'

'Or what,' says the Deputy Governor, addressing Rashidi, 'you'll go home without your daughter?'

He meets with no response.

'Okay,' says the Deputy Governor, 'if that's how you want to play it, I'll make the first move.' He manages to sound both confident and condescending. He taps his driver's arm. The driver opens the door, and the Deputy Governor climbs out and spreads his arms apart to show he is unarmed. Aminah is impressed by his sangfroid. His smart clothes show he's a man of standing. He leans back into the car, takes out a holdall and holds it up for them to see. He pulls the rear door open wide so they can see the girl inside. 'Money and daughter. See? Now show me

Aminah, and I will need to talk to her before you get anything.'

He sounds as if he's talking to two misbehaving schoolboys. That said, they're not helping their case by being so uncooperative.

'Look, these girls have suffered enough. Let's get this over with, then we can negotiate the next exchanges and get them home.'

Would he be so sure of himself if he knew Gambo and Rashidi had their guns trained on him? Or that Abdullahi was not the man sitting beside her in the back of the car? Then again his bravado is underpinned by the presence of security forces. Gambo and Rashidi must suspect that too which is why they're in no hurry to get out of the car or why they don't shoot an unarmed Deputy Governor when they have the chance. But what are they planning and if they know it's a trap, why did they come? Why is Rashidi pretending to be Abdullahi? Where is Abdullahi? Why have they put a belt around her? Is she really a decoy? What is their plan?

Chapter 31

Jamilah checks her phone again. Ten past ten. Surely the exchange should be sorted by now; how long do these things take? All the arrangements would have to have been agreed in advance, especially if a man like Francois de Witt is involved. She's seen the movies: two vehicles roll up, two groups get out and face each other, there's staring, some shouting, maybe some gun-pointing and always a lot of tension. Ultimately, each hostage is sent walking towards the other, they pass en route, exchange a look, reach their respective sides and usually, that's it. Well usually, but, she has to admit, sometimes it doesn't end well. There's a double-cross, a trap, a shoot-out and people get killed. She nibbles at her nail seeking reassurance from de Witt's words, "Don't worry," he said. "I'll have my guys with me. We'll get your sister back. I promise." He will. She trusts him. The movies are not the real world. They have to have drama. There's no need for drama tonight. She gets up and goes into the kitchen. She turns on the tap to watch the water gush down the sink. She has to trust him. He's done everything he said he would, and he made a promise too. But Ahmed is right; at the end of the day he works for the Governor, and everyone knows the Governor's corrupt, and she knows more than anyone how corrupt Giwa is. As for these men who have her sister, it goes without saying they're corrupt. Can any of these people be relied on to do what they say?

She returns to the sofa and picks up her puzzle mag. She can't focus and picks up her phone. She hasn't heard from Ahmed since he stormed out the previous night. She can only hope that when their sister's released, he'll be more like his old self. And not her son, but her grown-up little brother! She smiles, thinking back to their last night together when Aminah had cooked for them. Aminah's the youngest but can seem the most mature — why she's even taken to giving advice to her big sister who didn't like it at the time, but who would do anything in the world to have her back home advising her till the cows came home! If only that phone would ring, and she could hear Aminah's voice. But it's too early. Francois said he'd call later, near midnight.

When she gets her sister back, she can imagine getting her faith back too. Only Allah could have sent a man like de Witt to the clinic. Ahmed will surely change his view of Francois. She'll invite him to dinner again to celebrate Aminah's homecoming. This time, she and Aminah will cook for the four of them. It will be the best meal ever! That poor man has had such a tragic life and while it's led him into a dubious career, he has a good side to him and … well, that kiss! She's blushing again. It's the first time in her life that she's experienced … passion. He's older than Salim, the only man she ever talks to, but no man has ever aroused such feelings in her. What will happen next? She's never been in a "relationship" before. Why is she even thinking about this? She picks up her magazine and searches for another hidden word in a square full of letters. It seems to be the only form of distraction at her disposal. Her phone buzzes. She jumps. This is it! But it's not. It's a text from Ahmed:

"Sor bout last night sis, will put things right 2nite. Don't worry. A. x"

She rings his number; it goes straight to voicemail.

Chapter 32

'It's all there', says Ado with growing frustration. What's the matter with Abdullahi? Why is he being so uncooperative? Why is he letting his driver do all the talking? His driver has never said a word at their previous meetings. Can his toothache really be that bad? 'Let me show you.' He walks forward to the midway point, leaving de Witt standing by the car. He places the bag on the ground, kneels down, unzips it, and takes out a wad of notes held in place by an elastic band. He holds it up. 'One thousand dollars.' He flicks the corner of the wad with his thumb. 'Fifty twenty-dollar bills.' He holds the wad out towards them so they can make out the face and denomination, then twists it round so they can see front and back.

'Show us the rest,' says the driver.

Ado takes out four more bundles and lays them out side by side on the ground with the first one. He can't resist glancing up at the mosque. 'Satisfied?' he asks.

No reply.

'Bring out the girl and you can have it.' He puts the bundles back in the bag. 'And your daughter too.' He directs his words to Abdullahi in the back seat.

'We need to count it,' says the driver, 'Bring it over here.'

Ado glances at de Witt; he doesn't understand the language but will surely have an idea that things are not progressing as anticipated. If he's concerned, he's not showing it, remaining as impassive as a driver should.

'I want to talk to the girl first', says Ado.

'You can't. She's gagged.'

'Well, take the gag off!'

'Not until we've checked the money.'

Ado turns his back on them and addresses de Witt.

'They insist on counting the money before I can talk to Aminah,' he hisses.

Ado sees Farida glance up. Did she hear him speak English? De Witt nods as if he has received a command, walks forward, picks up the bag, and takes it over to the car where he drops it on the ground below Abdullahi's window. He steps back a few paces, looking like he's waiting for his next command. That's clever, thinks Ado, he's stolen a look inside the car and as soon as Abdullahi opens the door to pick up the money, he'll take him out.

'Tell him to back off,' says the driver.

Ado moves forward and shouts in Hausa for de Witt to step back, tugging surreptitiously at de Witt's sleeve to make the meaning clear. De Witt complies but they are still closer to the car than they were before. The driver opens his door and emerges with a gun. Ado is paralysed with fear. He's never had a gun pointed at him in his life. He doesn't want to die, here, on this night, in this miserable place. But the driver just motions for them to back off. Ado is happy to retreat back to the halfway point with de Witt and stand behind him which apart from offering greater protection, will allow him talk to de Witt without being heard. Abdullahi's driver stands between them and the holdall, blocking their view of Abdullahi and pointing his gun at them again. The rear door opens, and Abdullahi's hand reaches round to drag the bag towards him and lift it into the car.

'What do we do now?' Ado whispers in de Witt's ear. 'We're losing control.'

'We take it back,' says de Witt. 'Demand they bring Aminah out now.'

Maybe he sees the fear in Ado's eyes but before he can respond, de Witt pulls out his own handgun. He's too quick for the driver to do anything. Bracing himself for an exchange of fire, Ado leans further behind de Witt. But nobody fires. De Witt has raised his free hand. His fingers are spread out and he is making downward calming movements with his hand. Ado senses this signal is not only for the driver but everyone else with guns. De Wit is trying to keep his plan on track.

'This has gone on long enough', says Ado, surprising himself with his authoritative tone, 'you've got the money, now get the girl out here!'

The driver says nothing and stares back defiantly. There's a grunt from the back seat. Abdullahi must have satisfied himself that the money is all there. The driver walks round to the other side of the car, his gun still trained on them. The car gives him cover, he probably thinks he could shoot them both and stand a good chance of not being shot himself. He opens the rear door on the other side of Abdullahi. This could be an opportunity for de Witt! He could signal to his men to take out the driver and step forward and shoot Abdullahi. But the driver is too close to the girl, and he knows de Witt wants to get her out alive. The driver pulls her out from the back. De Witt uses the opportunity to edge closer to the car. Ado follows without thinking and is rewarded with a view through the rear window. It fills him with unease. Abdullahi has never bothered to hide his face from Ado in the past, yet now he has a bloodstained bandage around it that hardly impacts on his mouth or the tooth that is supposed to be bothering him. Abdullahi's never missed an opportunity to insult him, yet tonight he hasn't spoken a word. Ado can see the muzzle of a pistol, which doesn't surprise him, but the hand holding the bag lacks that ring he's always worn, the one with the Arabic writing. He feels clammy. He whispers in de Witt's ear. 'That's not Abdullahi.'

'How do you know,' de Witt fires back.

Ado is shocked by his lapse but recovers. 'It's a feeling. Why hasn't he spoken to us, why isn't he getting out of the car? Why isn't he showing any interest in his daughter?'

'Speak to Aminah', says de Witt, 'then you'll know if it's him or not, right?'

The driver has pulled the girl out of the car and while keeping his gun pointing at them, drags her round to face them. Her clothes are dirty and torn, her hands are bound behind her back. Her face is covered but not her eyes which express terror — hardly surprising, as the driver's gun is now pointing at her head.

'Uncover her face and take off the gag!' says Ado. 'I need to talk to her.'

'Do it yourself,' says the driver, shoving the girl towards them. She loses her balance and falls down in front of them. There's something unnatural in her movement. She squirms away from her liberators and back towards her kidnappers! He's read about people like this who develop a bond with their captors. Even when they're liberated, they're still drawn to them. He looks back at Farida sitting calmly in the back of his car. Her father hasn't said a word about her, and she hasn't called out to him. She doesn't seem in any hurry to leave her captors either. What's going on? Her door is locked, but Ado's isn't. Her hands are tied, but it would be simple enough for her to get out of the car. She's young, mobile, and nobody's pointing a gun at her head.

In contrast, Aminah looks pathetic, lying on the ground twisting like a seal to avoid the driver's hand yet pushing herself away from her liberators. Her head shifts one way, her body the other. She cries out, a mix of pain and frustration as she resists attempts to be pulled to her feet. The driver tears off the covering around her head and tries to drag her up by the hair. Despite the pain and threat of being shot, her resistance intensifies. Her face covering slips and Ado sees open wounds and scars but, more importantly, a profile that is consistent with her photo. He squeezes de Witt's shoulder. De Witt nods back. He must be as bewildered as he is at Aminah's behaviour and it's not helping Ado's nerves. They would have been better off choosing another girl for the exchange.

His reflection is interrupted by the incongruous sound of hip-hop music that appears to come from the mosque. It's a ringtone, the sound is tinny but clear. The driver stops grappling with the girl and looks to pinpoint the source, his eyes bulging. The owner's attempt to extract the phone and shut off the sound creates shape and movement. The driver sees it and doesn't hesitate to fire, igniting the kind of undisciplined response that de Witt had feared. A couple of men return fire instantly and it quickly turns into a hailstorm. De Witt ducks down and scrambles against the corner of the car. Ado hits the ground in front of him. The driver slumps down beside Aminah, bleeding from the head, chest, and mouth. Aminah tries to squeeze sideways under the car as if more afraid of his lifeless body than facing the same fate. The shooting subsides. The barrel of Abdullahi's gun pokes through the gap in the side window. De Witt is up on one knee, his left hand supports his firing arm, and he discharges his bullets into

Abdullahi's head. He slumps back in his seat and his gun drops to the ground.

De Witt signals for everyone to stop firing. A silent pause quickly gives way to an eruption of cheering and shouts of mutual congratulation. Ado shares the exhilaration. It's over, they've done it! Not the way it was planned, but then de Witt did say, "be prepared for the unexpected." Abdullahi and his henchman have been eliminated, the girl and the money are safe, and the daughter's still in custody! Alhamdulillah!

Ado gets to his feet; armed men spring up around him like mysterious night plants bursting from the earth. De Witt is back on his feet too but unmoved by the celebrations. For him, it's just another operation, but Ado's never had such a visceral experience. The taste of dirt in his mouth makes him feel more connected to life than he's ever been. There's a cut on his hand; a battle wound! He's in no hurry to wipe the blood away. Let the cameras see his badge of honour. He's a hero. He will have much to say to the media. But first, he must retrieve the money, then check on this strange girl who's just been liberated.

Chapter 33

Two Baretta M9s and a mobile phone rest on the Sheikh's bedside table. Abdullahi and Muhammed peer through a gap in a shutter, left by a missing slat. Crumbling insect remains litter the cracked wooden sill. The iron shutter handles and shafts are flaking with rust, suggesting they hadn't been used in years. Yet earlier that day, the two of them had prised the shutters open, oiled the old hinges and everything else and ensured there would be no delay, the next time they wanted to open them. They'd had to close them to maintain the Mosque's appearance, prior to their arrival. Eventually, their nostrils had adapted to the smell of the Sheikh's piss and out of respect for the old man, they deposited their own into a bottle. These are minor inconveniences set against the first-floor vantage point offered by the Sheikh's room, offering a clear view of the car park below. They watch in concentrated silence. The enemy is all around them, even on the other side of the door.

They had arrived at dawn, well ahead of Giwa and his men. They could have arrived at midday by the time that fat pig and his infidels rolled up. The Sheikh's nephew had come to get the old man up and dressed and then took him to his village. Tomorrow, after a good breakfast, the nephew will take the Sheikh to an isolated spot and the security forces will be summoned. When they arrive, the terrified nephew will tell them how Boko Haram had come to his village in the early hours and taken him to the mosque. There they had tied him and the Sheikh up and driven them to a derelict cattle shed where they had been forced to spend the rest of that day and all of the night tied to a post with two bottles of water for company. They'd been told if they tried to leave within 24 hours they would be executed.

Even in his pre-dementia days, the Sheikh would have struggled to recognize his favourite, Abdullahi, now standing in his room, dressed in his robes, and whose hair, beard and eyebrows are dyed the same grey/white colour as his own. Over time, the Sheikh had shrunk in size, but his clothes had not. They are a decent fit for Abdullahi and the sagginess, together with his adoption of a bent-over pose and frequent cough, had been enough to fool Giwa. That piece of shit had shown no concern for the old man's health, ushering them into the room and banging the door shut as if they were cattle.

Abdullahi and Muhammed may be locked in the Sheikh's room, but it's more a case of Giwa and his men being locked out. Ten minutes before Ado's arrival, Muhammed had slipped the spare key into the lock to stop a key being inserted from the outside. They had quietly manoeuvred a chest of drawers and the old man's bed in front of the door before reassembling the component parts of the Coyote that had been hidden under the bed. And there it sits on a table in front of the shutter, flanked by its ammo box, ready to sing. It's been a gruelling day couped up in the old man's room, biding time, not making a sound, apart from the occasional deliberate cough. Abdullahi is impatient for the curtain to come up and has no doubt Muhammed feels the same. They'd been surprised to see armed white men arrive with Giwa. Typical of Yakubu to send infidels to a mosque, and typical of Giwa to work alongside them.

'What do they know about our land?' he'd said to Muhammed. 'They can't speak our language; they know nothing about our religion.'

'My father told me about such men in the Biafra war', Muhammed had replied. 'Whites hired by Nigerians to kill Nigerians.'

Now it would be their turn. Alhamdulillah! His judgement on Yakubu's intentions had proved sound, and his servants will pay for his treachery.

Chapter 34

A bonding opportunity with his new comrade in arms is too good for Ado to pass up, even before going to pick up the money.

'Well done Colonel, mission accomplished!' The urge to slap de Witt on the shoulder is held in check by the grim expression on de Witt's face.

'We're lucky to be alive,' says de Witt, reloading his pistol, his hands an oily mix of dye and sweat. 'Giwa can't control his men. They can't even be trusted to turn off their phones.' He looks at Ado with piercing eyes. 'Didn't think twice about shooting off in our direction, did they?'

'It's Allah's will', says Ado. 'We achieved our goal, Alhamdulillah! You should call the Governor. He'll want to get here soonest.'

De Witt shrugs and spits to the side.

'I'll do it.' Giwa appears behind them, Coetzee a few steps further back.

''I'll check on the girl,' says de Witt walking off.

'What's the matter, Colonel? We had to speed things up.' De Witt doesn't respond. 'Your plan wasn't working. We had to create a bit of a distraction, get you out of a hole.' He grins, looking around at his men.

De Witt stops and turns round. 'I had things under control, man. Your men could've killed us.'

It's Giwa's turn to walk away, dismissing de Witt's protest with a desultory wave of the hand. It feels like he has seized the initiative and the night belongs to him. He takes out his phone, no doubt ready to regale the Governor about how he and his men saved the day. But he doesn't dial. He's looking into the darkness, past the last of his men walking in. Ado follows his gaze and catches sight of a figure running towards them. It's a young man in jeans and a tee-shirt and he's waving as if to show he's unarmed. He's shouting and more people turn to look in his direction. It's hard to make out what he's saying, though his voice seems to have registered with Aminah, who has wriggled out from under the chassis. She presses her back against the side of the car, pushes hard with her legs, and prises herself up. The high-pitched scream she emits from behind her sealed-over mouth sounds like a monkey raising the alarm. She shakes her head violently from side to side, then runs forwards and backwards in a pattern that makes no sense. Giwa's men start laughing. As the running man gets closer, his cries become more audible.

'Don't shoot. That's my sister ... Aminah, I'm here ... Why isn't anyone helping her?'

'Don't shoot!' cries de Witt fiercely.

Amidst the laughter, someone does shoot, and as before, it proves infectious. The young man is stopped in his tracks by a hail of bullets and slumps to the ground like a fallen antelope.

Giwa goes immediately on the offensive. 'We know these people,' he says to de Witt. 'They send suicide bombers against us, girls, women, men. This was part of their plan once they'd got what they came for. We've seen it before.'

'For Christ's sake man,' says de Witt, 'I gave an order not to shoot and I'm in charge here. You didn't even tell them to open fire. Can't you control them at all?' De Witt's men, now out of cover, gather round in support of their Colonel.

'They have a standing order to shoot anyone running towards them in such a situation', says Giwa. 'I don't care who that fool was, he wasn't supposed to be here, and he shouldn't have been charging towards us like that. He's only got himself to blame.'

'Didn't you hear what he was saying?' says de Witt.

'He's her brother!'

Aminah seems to have changed her mind about staying put and runs toward her brother. She is stopped by one of Giwa's men who grabs her in a bear hug and carries her back, laughing as she wriggles and kicks, as if he's playing with a dog. He drops her by the car. She slides back to the ground, crying, defeated.

'How do you know it was her brother?' asks Giwa.

'Have you ever met him? This operation's over, old man. Time for you to take off your fancy dress and clear the stage. And take that bunch of hired has-beens with you.' He glares at de Witt's men. 'I'm fed up with the lot of you, especially you,' he says looking at Coetzee. 'You're like a fucking leech, following me round all day. Who do you think you are? What have you contributed to this operation for all the money we're paying you? I should arrest you for theft and impersonating a fucking soldier.'

Giwa's men cheer him on, relishing the Afrikaners' discomfort.

'As for your little plan, Colonel? Well, you know what happens now, so fuck off!'

There's a roar from Giwa's men.

'Not before I check on the girl,' says de Witt calmly, heading towards Aminah. Ado takes his phone out to ring his media contact, then remembers he still hasn't retrieved the money from the car. He remembers too the final act of the plan, the one de Witt had declined to take on but which Giwa had had no qualms about. He looks back at his car. Fortunately it's been spared any damage in the shoot-out. Already, two of Giwa's men are getting Abdullahi's daughter out of the car. She has just seen her father shot dead and her liberty snatched away, but unlike Aminah, who's making an example of herself, Farida appears to have accepted her fate with quiet dignity. Little does the unfortunate girl know what awaits her at Giwa's hands in the next few minutes. He hopes it will be quick.

Aminah's behaviour begins to rankle. She was handpicked for liberation and people have risked their lives for her. Why is she so ungrateful? One of Giwa's men has cut her wrist ties and she is back on her feet. De Witt approaches her slowly, making the same calming gestures with his hands that he had made earlier to Abdullahi's driver. But she backs away from him, shaking her head wildly and trying to pull duct tape from her face. He walks slowly towards her, but she waves him away.

Giwa joins his men in the ensuing laughter, relishing de Witt's predicament. Giwa waves his finger from side to side, behind de Witt's back, signalling to his men not to intervene. Despite his newfound feeling of camaraderie towards de Witt, Ado cannot help but embrace the schadenfreude of de Witt's discomfort. He can empathise with the humiliation felt by Giwa and his men at having to stomach a bunch of Afrikaners superseding them in their own backyard. But the feeling doesn't last. If Giwa were in de Witt's position, he would just send a couple of men over to grab Aminah forcibly and bundle her into the back of a truck. De Witt is trying to be more humane. He stops advancing and the girl is calmer. She makes a gesture with her hands for him to wait and points to her gag. She struggles to get her fingernails between the tape and her face. She shakes her hands as if trying to get blood into them. Her face wounds open up as her nails scrape against them. De Witt makes a tentative move forward as if to help, but she unleashes a violent roar from her throat and holds out her arms making it clear she wants him to stay put. He heeds her appeal and turns to whisper something to Coetzee. It looks like he's run out of patience and is going to take a leaf out of Giwa's rulebook. Maybe she senses this, for she looks around frantically for somewhere to run. Amidst the stand-off and the laughter, Ado begins to feel uneasy about the way the girl is behaving, even accounting for the suffering she has endured. Is it hysteria or something more?

The laughter falls away unexpectedly. Giwa is shouting at the two men escorting Farida, but they are ignoring him and have reached the road. He turns to his Sergeant, saying he doesn't recognise them; the Sergeant replies that he cannot see them properly. The two escorts quicken their step and cross the road, Farida in tow. Giwa fires his pistol in the air and one of his men moves forward to challenge them, but he's immediately shot by one of the escorts and the other drops to his knee and fires at Giwa, hitting him in the chest. The Sergeant stares at his fallen boss in disbelief which gives time for the other escort to open fire on him too, and he is as accurate as his comrade. A sense of shock seems to hold back the natural response of Giwa's men as they stare at their two leaders' bodies and try to process why their comrades have killed them. Farida crouches down behind both escorts who fire at anyone close by and the three of them manage to scramble behind a pile of worn tyres on the perimeter of the tyre factory. Giwa's men spring to life firing after the escapees.

Ado dives to the ground for the second time. Ten metres away, Giwa lies motionless, a symbol of how they have been deceived. This is not some kind of mutiny by disaffected men, it's the work of Abdullahi. He has bribed these men to kill Giwa and rescue his daughter or, more likely, they are his men in disguise. Why would he do that when he had a deal to get his daughter back and get paid into the bargain? Because he didn't trust the deal and Giwa was a big prize. But Abdullahi's lying dead in the back of the car. His gun still lies on the ground where he had dropped it. Then Ado sees something else he wasn't expecting. Beyond the gun, under the gap between exhaust and tarmac, he can discern feet moving on the far side of the car. They belong to one of Giwa's men who emerges with a firm grip on the holdall. Any hope this might be a show of initiative to secure the Governor's money evaporates as the man jumps over the car park wall, and sprints away from the mosque, into the darkness. Is Ado the only one to have seen this?

Everyone else seems distracted by the shooting match that has broken out between the escorts and … Ado shuts his eyes … No wonder Farida was calm. The escorts are Abdullahi's men, likewise, the thief who has grabbed the money. Abdullahi has played them. Abdullahi … The man without a ring on his finger, who never got out of the car, whose face stayed covered and who never uttered a word. Ado had known from that single glance inside the car, that the man sitting in the back seat was not Abdullahi. When you have been up close to a man like that, you never forget the shape of his face. He wouldn't allow himself believe it until now. De Witt had eliminated one of Abdullahi's fighters, who like the driver, was expendable, whether they knew it or not. Duct tape had been put over Aminah's mouth so she couldn't give the game away. At least they've left her behind. Something can still be salvaged from this debacle — two dead terrorists and a rescued hostage. She is crouched down at the other end of the car from de Witt and has almost rid herself of the last of the duct tape. When the shooting stops she'll confirm everything; for now, his priority is to get de Witt to go after the thief. The gunfire is easing off, de Witt is ten metres away but there's no way he's going over to him. He'll stay put and phone him. Good job he hadn't rung the media or that Giwa hadn't phoned the boss. Look what they would be walking into.

Chapter 35

While her two escorts provide covering fire, Farida darts into the ruins of the old car factory. Abdullahi unclenches his fist. She's safe now. He's proud of how she has handled herself. If she were a man, she'd be his natural successor. Watching his other fighter grab the bag of money from the car was like watching a pied crow raiding a nest for chicks. All three of his fighters had merged effortlessly with Giwa's forces. In the aftermath of Gambo and Rashidi's shooting, they had broken cover from behind the outer ring of Giwa's men, and joined in the celebrations, slapping each other's backs, and smiling broadly in the same moronic fashion as their enemies. They had walked into the car park alongside them and taken up their positions without a sideways glance from anyone. The infidels had thought their work was done and they'd soon be heading back to base, a rare victory under their belts and finally, some revenge to savour. Now there's not so much to celebrate and they don't know it yet, but things are going to get a whole lot worse. They've been surrounded from the moment they arrived. Almost invisible in their black kaftans and fighting under the banner of the new Islamic State West Africa Province, Abdullahi's fighters have had to be patient too, but now they are closing in relentlessly from all sides, tightening the noose.

A cheer goes up. One the escorts is hit. He's stopped firing back. If he's not dead, there may be time to save him. He deserves to be saved, he's the man who shot Giwa. If he's dead, he died a martyr and Paradise awaits. His comrade takes his chance and makes for the tyre factory. Bullets hit the ground around him, but he makes it. He's done what he had to do and will be rewarded. As for

Giwa's headless chickens, they stop firing, stand up and look for someone to tell them what to do next. There seems to be no appetite to chase after Farida and her protector, or even go and look at the man they just shot. Their eyes are drawn to the motionless bodies of Giwa and their Sergeant, almost as if they're willing them to get up and take control. Not so the group of white mercenaries crouched around Ado's driver, as if receiving instructions. Well it's time for Abdullahi to give a few instructions of his own. He looks at Muhammed, picks up the detonating phone and dials. Aminah's belt explodes. With the noise of the blast still reverberating around the mosque, they proclaim the familiar battle cry, 'Allahu Akbar!' and Muhammed throws open the shutter door. It crashes against the external wall taking off some of the rendering. He takes the reins of the Coyote, while Abdullahi places a supportive hand on the ammo. As if incensed at being kept waiting, the Coyote howls into life, spitting out empty cartridges into the stone courtyard below. Bullets pass under his fingers directly into the body of the weapon; a second later they are lodged in the bodies of the infidels and everything around them. Mortar shells descend into the car park. It's as if the Sheikh has conjured up demons from the deep, to punish these men who invaded his mosque and disrespected him.

Ado's phone drops from his grasp. Everything happened at once, a total assault on his senses. A loud bang, a flash of light, a whoosh of air and a burning sensation along his back. They must have planted a bomb in the car. The hissing in his ears and searing pain render him breathless. The ground is being churned up and there are multiple explosions all around him, duller than the car bomb but relentless. His body is jolted by hot metal piercing his body. Something hits the back of his thigh. More pain. The car park is transformed into an inferno of noise, flame and smoke. His mouth is dry with dust; each cough is agony. The earth he had so recently become attached to, is giving way. Is he going to fall through a fissure, his torn body never to be found? Men are screaming. He covers his ears and shuts his eyes. The ground shudders and cracks. He weeps. He doesn't want to die, but he lies exposed and defenceless. His whole body is being subjected to an onslaught of bullets, bombs and shrapnel and he knows he has been hit more than once. Concrete is being blown to pieces, creating secondary missiles. Perhaps it is one such lump that crashes into the back of his head and stills his tears. There is no more pain, no more fear, no more anything.

A minute after it had begun, the firing and shelling cease. The Coyote pauses for breath. It's the signal for his fighters to move in and finish the job. Cries of "Allahu Akbar" fill the air as they set out to block the escape of survivors and cut the throats of the dying. It is fitting for men of Jihad to put the enemy to the sword, face to face but Abdullahi and Muhammed maintain their position, waiting for the smoke to clear in order to identify any pockets of resistance. Abdullahi is impatient to ensure Ado and Giwa are dead. He has decided to remove their heads. He will allow a couple of Giwa's men to survive so they can tell the world what they have witnessed: how Islamic State West Africa Province had outthought and outfought the Nigerian Security Forces and their foreign allies. How once again, the President and the Governor had been taught a lesson: they will never defeat the soldiers of Jihad because Allah is on the side of the Faithful, and they are implementing Allah's will. Alhamdulillah!

Part Three

Ten days later

Chapter 36

'Maybe you should take time off', says Dr Salim.
'So I can sit around all day going crazy?' says Jamilah.
'That's how I spend my evenings.'
'Well, maybe get away for a while, a change of scene might help.'

The day Jamilah buried her brother and sister, she'd wanted to run away, never mind get away. She doesn't mean to sound irritable but Salim's not the first person to make such a suggestion. Do people think you can travel and leave grief at home? Anyway, she's not ready to stop thinking about Aminah and Ahmed, and home is where their presence feels strongest. Why did Allah keep her alive and let her family be taken?

'I know it's hard,' continues Salim, 'but you need to look after yourself. Try to eat more. How are you sleeping?'

'Look Salim, I'd rather be working, keeping busy, seeing people, following a routine. Give myself a break from trying to comprehend the incomprehensible.'

She can see he's run out of words of comfort. Like his peers, he's better at diagnosis and treatment, though she knows more than most what a caring person he is. This is the first time they've sat down and talked since the funerals and they're finding there's not much to say other than clichés. Then out of nowhere, or maybe it's because it's him, she looks down at her hands and finds herself opening up.

'Ten years ago I buried my father and my uncle, ten days ago it was my sister and brother. You could say my mother died of natural causes; you could also say she was murdered by the neglect of badly resourced health service. As for the rest of my family? There's no grey area. They were murdered. Why? Wrong place, wrong time. Where's the wrong place? Sweating in the fields to feed your family or chatting at school with your classmates? As for Ahmed, I don't know what he was doing in that place, but he didn't deserve to die for it.'

'Neither you nor your family did anything to deserve these things … I still have the number of that Counsellor I mentioned when we talked about Ahmed.'

'I know you mean well Salim, but what experience could a Counsellor draw on to help me? What could they tell me about grieving that I don't know already? You and I see death every week; we know the pattern of grief. Death can be a blessing but never when it's premature or unnatural'.

He nods.

'I'm glad you understand; for me, it's beyond understanding! … I'm sorry Salim, I forgot about your wife.'

'It's okay.'

'How did you get over her … passing?'

Salim clears his throat. 'With all my training and experience, I still couldn't save her, or A'isha, our little girl. Her time on this earth lasted two hours and twenty-five minutes. You could hardly call it a life, but it was. She was beautiful, my own little mayfly.'

This is unlike him. He never shares such personal information. It's her turn to struggle for words but he hasn't finished, and she's content to listen.

'I interrogated myself for days. Why had my wife and daughter been snatched away from me, surely I could have done more? Why was I left to mourn them and not the other way round? I know it's a worn out cliché, Jamilah, but time does ease the pain. I determined to be the best I could at what I do, so that next time I'd be better prepared. And I am, except there's never been "a next time" and there never will be. I never re-married. I didn't want to be in a position to test myself ever again on my wife and child. What normal person would?'

Jamilah wants to put her arms around him.

'We're not unalike', he says. 'We have dealt with family tragedy in similar ways. I know my wife would never have blamed me for what happened; in the same way, I'm sure your family would never blame you. I admire you, for what you have done in the face of so much adversity and the person you've become.'

Jamilah feels a lump in her throat. He's the only person who ever praises her. And now she has a better understanding of why he's helped her so much. He couldn't help his wife and daughter, but he could help her.

'Your loss goes deeper than mine', he continues. 'The possibilities of maternal and/or child mortality are always present in pregnancy. For you … to have such trauma happen twice is as unnatural as it is incomprehensible.'

'Why do I need a Counsellor when I've got you, Salim? You're always here for me.' She sniffs and dabs her eyes. 'The Director called me in the day I returned to work. Offered his condolences, which I know is kind and respectful. Said I needed to connect with Allah, that I should talk to his Sheikh, and he would help me understand why these things happen and guide me on how to go forward.'

'Maybe it's worth a try?'

'No. Allah let these things happen. He allows these men to roam around killing in his name. He never protected me when I was a girl, and he didn't protect Aminah or any of my family. I know it's wrong to say it, but it's too late for Him to help me. Why did He let it all happen in the first place?' The tears come. 'It's wrong Salim.'

Salim gets up from his desk, hands her the tissues, grabs a chair and sits down beside her. He puts his arm around her shoulder and her head falls against it.

'Listen Jamilah. We can't blame Allah when bad things happen. When an aeroplane falls from the sky it could be because of lack of maintenance, pilot error, or the airline insisting the plane fly in bad weather. These things are caused by human beings. It wasn't Allah who killed your family, it was human beings, even though there's a strong argument for considering them as something else. Life is a continual struggle between right and wrong. It can seem perfect when good things are happening but without evil how could we know what good looks like? Without that tension, life would be bland, but it isn't, it's full of opposites.'

'So you think we should accept evil acts as part of life's struggle and move on?'

'No. We must recognise good and evil co-exist, make choices about what is right and what is wrong and lead our lives accordingly. I think it's in our nature to do the right thing but it's a struggle, and it's probably supposed to be. We are put to the test. We have the Quran and the teaching of the Prophet to guide us, the Christians have their Bible and their prophet, the Buddhists and Hindus have their equivalents too. As far as I know, there is no established religion dedicated to evil and while Satan exists he provides no equivalent to the Quran. Yet, across the world, people kill each other in the name of religion or more accurately a twisted version of it, and that's how Satan does his work. So, Jamilah we can't blame Allah for the sins of men who misinterpret his word, or for those of men like Yakubu who have been given the opportunity to do good but choose to use that power to do evil.

'But your wife and child, Salim, how can their death be justified?'

'We are human beings. Our bodies are vulnerable to disease, malfunction, inherited genes, accidents, etc. I would like everyone to live a long and healthy life but maybe such a thing can only be fully appreciated because there are many who don't.'

'You've thought it all through.'

'I've had plenty of time. What do you think I do with my evenings when I'm not here with you?'

'I don't want to go home', she sobs, 'but Ahmed's Arsenal shirt still hangs over the chair, waiting for me to sew the sleeve for him. His souvenir mug still sits by his bed; it's cracked but he wouldn't let me throw it out. Aminah's books, the doll she still keeps − kept − by her pillow. She was so bright, Salim. Far cleverer than me. Reading medical textbooks while still at school. She could have been like you. Their toothbrushes are still waiting for them in the bathroom. I've washed and ironed their clothes and put everything away like I've always done. I miss them so much. I can't speak to them, can't ring them and it's all so quiet. They've stopped teasing each other, stopped teasing me. When I hear a motorbike approaching I wait for the sound of his key in the lock but … I can't believe they're gone. They're still in the house but they're not.'

Salim holds her tighter, and she presses her forehead into his white coat. He strokes her hair. Her sobs decrease.

She feels secure with him and something else that reminds her of de Witt. What was she thinking? How could she have been so intimate with that man? She's angry she let herself trust him and angry that he lied to her. Breaking a promise is the same as lying. She had waited for his call through midnight and into the early hours, her hopes turning into dark despair. Nothing from him, nothing from Ahmed and nothing from Aminah. In the morning, when the news reports started, it was like reliving Aminah's abduction all over again, only worse. This time the police came to her. A solitary policeman presented himself at reception asking to speak with her. He told her Aminah had been blown up and Ahmed killed in the crossfire. He was young, he was nervous, he couldn't find the right words, but at least he'd come in person. Salim had gone to identify the bodies. She was used to death but couldn't bear to see the damage Abdullahi and Yakubu's men had inflicted on her siblings. There was no news from de Witt. The policeman hadn't known who she was talking about. She'd tried his phone. Nothing. After a few days, she assumed he'd been killed with the rest of them. The doorbell sounds. She lifts her head from Salim's shoulder to let him stand up.

'Thanks, Salim. Oh no, I've made a mess of your coat.' She takes a tissue and starts to dab a wet patch where her tears had collected.

'Don't worry,' he says. 'I'll grab another. You get the door.' He picks up a file and hands it to her. 'You see her first and call me when you need me.'

Jamilah knows this means the patient must have experienced some sexual trauma and it won't be a routine visit.

'That's if you feel up to it?' he says.

'It's my job.' She raises a smile for him and goes to get the door.

The visitor is alone. Young, around twenty. She seems nervous but not intimidated. Like most of Salim's clients, she's dressed in fashionable robes that don't come cheap. She's prettier than most and smells expensive too. A Big Man's girlfriend she thinks, especially as there's no mother with her. Jamilah switches on her welcome smile and ushers her patient into the consulting room.

'I'm so sorry for your loss,' says the young woman sitting down. 'I can't begin to imagine what you're feeling.'

'Thank you.' Not for the first time, Jamilah realises she's associated with a personal tragedy that the whole world seems to know about.

'It's brave of you to come back to work so soon. I could never have done that.'

Jamilah hears herself say, 'Well, life goes on,' which provides her with a stepping stone back into her professional persona. 'Can you confirm your name for me, please?'

'Iman Yakubu. Mrs.'

'Are you related to —'

'Yes. His wife.'

'His wife?'

'Number three.'

'Oh ...'

'You thought I was his daughter, or probably his —'

'Sorry.'

'No need for apologies. I look younger than I am. It's one of the things that appeals to him. Look, I can be frank with you, right? Patient confidentiality and all that?'

'Yes,' says Jamilah not sure if she's in the mood for an intimate conversation with the wife of a man who has brought her such misery. 'Oh, and sorry I didn't recognize you.'

'Why should you?' she smiles. 'He wouldn't be seen dead with me in public. That's for wife number one, who's almost as old and miserable as he is, and of course the mother of his children, well the ones he's prepared to acknowledge. As for wife number two, she's the wrong side of thirty, much too old for him. Lucky her. She's got her life back. Lives in a beautiful apartment in Abuja. No, I'm the slave who's confined to the kitchen and bedroom. There to serve up food and sex. He doesn't eat with me, sometimes he doesn't have sex with me — I'll explain that later. He never watches TV with me, and he certainly doesn't talk to me, other than to issue commands and insult me for not doing things to his liking. He's a pig.'

Jamilah takes a mental deep breath. She can't recall a patient, or anyone she's ever met, being so quick to share such details of their personal life with someone she's never met before. She's been quick to take advantage of patient confidentiality, that's for sure, and it feels that she's been waiting for such an opportunity for some time. Jamilah's intrigued but reluctant to engage in what sounds too much like gossip and less like background information relevant to her patient's condition. She returns to the script.

'Date of birth?'

'Which one?'

'You've more than one?'

'Well there's the date my mother told him and there's the actual one, I can get you a birth certificate for either. Does it matter? ... I suppose it must. Okay, you can put down that I'm twenty-two years old as of yesterday, and that's the truth.'

'Happy birthday.'

'Thanks,' she smiles, looking radiant, 'but it wasn't.'

'So, Mrs Yakubu, can you —'

'Please don't ever call me that,' she holds up her hand, 'at least not in private. Iman, please. Do you mind if I call you Jamilah?'

She has no interest in forging personal relationships with the privileged elite, but she is warming to this patient and in any case, Jamilah is her name. 'No, that's okay. So, Iman, can you tell me why you are here?'

Chapter 37

The mid-day prayer is over. The anaemic water of Lake Chad looks like it has lost heart and is ready to accept its extinction. Rebirth comes bit by bit as its surface is transformed, and drawn invisibly upwards to drift silently with the kites and wait for an obliging current to take it on its migratory journey east to Sudan, or perhaps south to Cameroon. Abdullahi makes his way to the plastic chair placed in the shade of an acacia tree. Patience is not an issue for him. A two-day-old newspaper has been left out for him, but it can wait. He sits down, rests his feet on a half-empty water container and scans the lake's shimmering horizon. A flurry of mosquitoes descends on him. Even in their agitated state they seem wary of his indifference and move on. He closes his eyes, leans back and, locking his fingers behind his head, reflects on his current situation. Like any leader worth his salt, he knows when to press an advantage and when to preserve it. His full-time fighters are back in their cells in safe camps, lying low, looked after by their wives and slaves. The hired hands have been sent back to their villages and the poorer parts of town, with instructions to hide their weapons, re-assume their mundane existence, and spend their money with discretion. The security forces chase shadows as Yakubu wrings his hands, while he and his men recharge, bide their time, and get ready to strike again.

His eyes open at the sound of splashing. One of his men has wheeled his motorbike into the water and is knocking chunks of dry mud off the tyres and frame with a well-worn brush. The rains have begun, and the bikes are more important than ever with their ability to scramble through the mud. The reeds and papyrus surrounding the camp been given a new lease of life and provide cover for the fishing boat nestling against the bank. The vessel is seventeen metres long and decked out like a traditional lake boat with reed awnings fitted across the deck to provide protection from rain, sun, and aerial surveillance. It's where Abdullahi and his men sleep and, if required, can accommodate a hundred people and a dozen motorbikes. Their current cohort requires a quarter of the space. At the water's edge, ambatch trees flaunt their yellow flowers and along with their saw-like leaves, provide added cover. An egret comes to rest on a branch near the man washing his bike, no doubt hopeful he will stir up some food from the fertile mud lying below the shallow water.

In another familiar ritual, one of the slaves appears in a green wrapper, drawn up to her knees. She tosses off her flip-flops and wades gracefully through the shallows. On her head she carries a green plastic basket filled with clothes on top of which sits a large slab of green soap. Is she making some kind of fashion statement? Does she even know she's doing it? These women ... The man washing his bike watches her work. Abdullahi knows like him, he's only interested in the obvious. They admire the outline of the girl's buttocks and the sculpted turn of her calves. Humming to herself, she pulls the basket of clothes out from the one in which it has been sitting and drops it into the water. She wedges the empty basket between the reeds, ready to receive the freshly wrung clothes, then, bending from the hip, feet apart, legs perfectly straight, she starts washing the clothes. Abdullahi isn't sure if she's singing or mumbling a prayer but wonders what she's got to be happy about.

'Hey, bitch. Shut up!'

She looks up in alarm and scrubs harder, in silence.

About a hundred meters away, a local man waters three camels. Abdullahi knows the man can see him and the camp, but that, if asked, he'll swear he's seen nobody in the vicinity. He sniffs the salty air, eases himself up and pulls the newspaper out from between his backside and the chair, ready to read the latest fairy tales.

'Huh, listen to this,' he says to the approaching Muhammed, "At a specially convened press conference this morning, His Excellency, Governor Yakubu announced that the vile murderers of Assistant Governor Ado, Commissioner for Police Giwa, and over sixty members of the security forces and innocent civilians, were hunted down, surrounded, and killed, in the early hours of this morning. A total of fifty-two terrorists perished, proving no match for the combined might and bravery of federal and state security services who received minor injuries but no fatalities."' He tosses the paper aside. 'How does it feel to be killed again, Muhammed? Tell you what, let's ask Ado how he's feeling today. Bring him out here.'

Muhammed laughs and heads off to one of the storage shelters constructed from mud and reed. He returns with a sack and turns it upside down, emptying out the heads of Ado and Giwa. Ado's bumps across the ground and comes to rest at Abdullahi's feet. Giwa's settles a little further away. Muhammed pulls up another chair and throws the sack over the seat. He lifts Ado's head and places it on top of the sack, adjusting it so it leans against the chair in an upright position.

'Sit down, Mr Deputy Governor,' says Abdullahi, 'you are welcome.'

'I think he's bitten my finger!' says Muhammed.

'Ignore him, Your Excellency,' says Abdullahi, 'make yourself comfortable.'

One side of Ado's head is covered in sand and dirt, the other shows signs of decomposition. Abdullahi picks up the newspaper and waves the flies away. 'Have you read this?' he holds the front page up to Ado's face. 'You see how your boss continues to lie to his people?'

Muhammed laughs. The man in the lake stops washing his bike and looks on intrigued. The girl turns her back on the scene and scrubs harder. Other men gather round to look.

'What's Muhammed's poor mother going to think when she reads he's been killed? What, nothing to say?' The laughter spreads. 'Well, that's a first.' He leans towards the head and sniffs. 'Humph, I remember you once said I smelt like a dead dog in the sun, well the shoe's on the other foot now!' He kicks over the chair and Ado's head falls to the ground. Abdullahi switches his attention to Giwa.

'As for you, you fat pig, you don't even have the balls to look me in the eye'. He kicks Giwa's head towards the water. More laughter. 'Enough. Pick them up and bury them in the latrine.' Muhammed throws the sack to one of the newly appointed burial party.

'You see comrades', says Abdullahi, 'this is what happens to infidels. However', he raises his finger, 'when Allah calls you, you will transcend in glory from this earth. Paradise awaits you. Alhamdulillah!' Spontaneous whooping and applause follow. 'These two thought they were powerful,' he points to the sack. 'Look where they have ended up. They thought they could defeat the servants of Allah, yet their heads are no longer with their bodies and soon, they will lie rotting in our shit. But, believe me, the Angel of Death will do a lot more to them before they are thrown into the fires of Hell. Allahu Akbar!'

Everyone joins in, fists pumping the air in their usual way.

'Okay, you two, get on with it, the rest of you, back to what you were doing.' He turns to Muhammed. 'Get the Sat phone and the small boat.'

Ten minutes later they stop at an islet formed, like so many others dotted across the Lake, from submerged fossil dunes and aquatic plants bound together by reeds and trees that have taken root. Muhammed cuts the engine and Abdullahi jumps on shore and heads straight for the shade of a solitary acacia. As Muhammed drags the boat onto the bank, Abdullahi takes the Iridium phone out of its case and dials a long number. After a couple of attempts, he hears a voice at the other end and responds with a code word in Arabic. He is told to wait. His ear presses hard against the phone. He hears voices in the background talking in Arabic and his heart races. A minute passes: it feels much longer. At last, a voice speaks to him in English. He responds with the second code word and is told to wait again. He turns to Muhammed unable to restrain his joy. 'I'm through! This is Mosul', he says pointing to the phone, 'I'm talking with the Caliphate! Alhamdulillah!'

218

Chapter 38

Jamilah watches slivers of cloud flash past the wing. When the plane plunges into a sorbet of grey cloud she continues to stare. Six weeks ago she'd never been on a plane, yet this is her third flight to Abuja and another indication as to how much her life has been transformed. She has hardly been outside her state, never mind the country and so the capital has made an impression on her. The bold architecture, huge hotels like fortresses, multi-lane highways, majestic mosques and churches competing to outdo each other in grandeur and height, and, towering above them all, the monolithic Aso Rock, heavy and dark, like a warning. Jamilah has no fear of flying. She didn't need Salim to tell her she's more likely to encounter death on the roads than in the air. While other passengers grip the armrests when turbulence hits, and the Christians cry out to their Lord Jesus for mercy, Jamilah has no fear, not even when they pass through dark clouds, and she sees the lightning forks in the distance. If the plane goes down what has she got to fear from death? No family to shed a tear for her. Who knows, she might be reunited with them in another place. Ah well, the plane's still flying and there are other things to think about. Previously she'd gone to the capital to lobby for the release of her sister and all the other girls, today, it's Iman and de Witt who occupy her thoughts.

She's never met a woman like Iman before. In some ways, she reminds her of Aminah, with her looks and self-confidence; in other ways, of herself — living a nightmare while maintaining an outward appearance of normality. Yakubu is worse than she could have ever imagined. Blessed to have this beautiful woman for a wife, he slaps her, hits her with his cane, shouts at her and, fuelled by

Viagra, makes disgusting sexual demands on her. He thinks he's entitled to do anything he wants to her because she's his wife and he supports her family — which, according to Iman, he can easily afford. As for Iman's family, they are demanding and won't forgive her if she leaves him and the well dries up. Her mother thinks it's just a question of managing him better. Easy for her to say. He watches porn every night and has acquired sex toys. Ugh. At first, Iman viewed them with relief because he enjoyed watching her use them, which meant he kept his hands on himself and away from her. But Yakubu is a man who always wants more and has to be in control. He acquired bigger toys and wanted to be the one who used them on her. He was vicious and vindictive. Disgusting. How could a man be so cruel, especially a husband to his wife? Jamilah shudders. When Iman started bleeding, he became alarmed, and not for the first time, he called Salim.

Salim is fearless. Having agreed with Jamilah's conclusion that Iman had suffered no lasting damage — but only through good fortune — Salim had phoned the Governor. She and Iman had listened in awe as he told Yakubu that the behaviour that had caused his wife's injuries must stop and she must be allowed time to recover. As a good Muslim and Governor of the State, didn't he have a responsibility to set an example? He must respect his wife and exercise self-control. In the meantime, he could be assured she would have the best of care. He would send his Assistant, a Senior Nursing Officer, to monitor Iman's progress. They waited for an outburst that would see Salim recoil from the phone, but the Governor listened, hardly spoke and like that, the call was over. Iman said it was the first time she'd ever heard anyone stand up to Yakubu. If Salim were in charge of Kano, she said, imagine how better off everyone would be. Jamilah wonders if one reason for Salim's readiness to admonish Yakubu is because, like her, he feels he has nothing to lose. Is that what losing your family does to you?

Iman had phoned her the morning after their encounter to say the Governor was following Salim's orders — that was the word she used, not advice. He'd left her alone and was watching porn on his own. He hadn't apologised but he wasn't shouting at her so much, though she didn't expect that to last long. She said she was looking forward to Jamilah's visit, and well, Jamilah feels the same. She admires Iman's spirit, particularly her ability to mock Yakubu despite the way he treats her and living with the threat of what more he might do to her. That's her way of coping; maybe Jamilah could learn from her. She'll bring the house call forward and go see Iman the following night after she finishes her hospital shift.

As for de Witt, well once again Salim proved her rock. Through his network, he tracked the Colonel down to a private hospital in Abuja, where he is registered as a businessman under an assumed name. That subterfuge could not keep the whereabouts of an expatriate with gunshot wounds and a South African accent from reaching Salim's ears. De Witt is out of intensive care and recovering. The hospital director got agreement to her visit from de Witt but cautioned that Yakubu wants de Witt out of the country as soon as possible and has the President's backing. Anything that would compromise or delay that outcome, would be more than frowned upon. Two of de Witt's men are staying by his side until he is ready to travel. They camp in his private room and restrict access to outsiders. Apparently, it almost led to a confrontation with hospital security, but it seems that the Governor is content with a stand-off, satisfied that de Witt will be out of his hair soon enough. Some federal security people hang around reception in plain clothes, making a poor job of disguising their presence. Though glad de Witt is alive, Jamilah is still angry with him. She should have listened to her brother.

Chapter 39

With no luggage, Jamilah exits the airport quickly. There is no shortage of taxis, and she picks a driver who convinces her he knows where she wants to go. The driver zigzags at speed between the lanes of the highway as if Jamilah is in need of emergency treatment. She doesn't tell him to slow down, and they reach the hospital unscathed. It's a new complex on the outskirts of Abuja connected to the highway by a dedicated slip road. Clearly, the owners have influence as well as money. Jamilah tells the driver that if he wants to wait an hour, he can have the same fare back. He agrees and gives her his card with his number.

She marvels at the facility's modernity. So much glass, such space. Once through its automatic doors, the temperature drops at least ten degrees. The gentle hum of the A/C is therapeutic. She envies the staff. How much easier it would have been to cope with the market bombing in this place. The receptionist gives her directions to de Witt's room with more charm and a wider smile than Jamilah could ever muster at Salim's clinic.

One of de Witt's men sits on a chair outside the door. He gets up just enough to turn to rap the door and turn the handle. Another man inside pulls the door open and as soon as she enters, leaves without saying a word. And there he is, propped up and waiting. She goes to his bedside. There's a drip in his arm which she checks instinctively before giving him a quick visual examination. He's pale and there are abrasions on his face, hands, and arms. He looks in discomfort but manages a half smile. She resists the temptation to look at the notes at the bottom of the bed. In contrast with the last time she saw him, in fact, with all the other times she saw him, he looks vulnerable and older. She doesn't return his smile and yet despite her anger, she bends down to kiss his forehead. Residue from their last encounter, she decides.

'So Colonel', she says looking around the room, 'I haven't heard from you in a while, how are you?'

'Alive. I'm sorry about Aminah and Ahmed.'

Jamilah sits down. 'No, they weren't so lucky. I buried them last week. I don't know what happened with Ahmed, but you didn't bring my sister back. You promised, and I believed you.' She fights back the tears.

'I know. I'm sorry. I lost good men too.'

'Good men? They get paid to kill or be killed, just like you. My sister and brother were innocents, their lives ahead of them. Why did they have to die and not you?'

'Because my plan didn't work. Look, turn the TV up a little so we can talk ... There had been a history between Yakubu, Ado and Abdullahi that I was kept unaware of. Things that completely undermined my planning.'

'Sounds like you're losing your touch. I warned you not to trust those people.'

'You did. Giwa kept saying how Boko Haram were undisciplined, poorly supplied and backward. Huh, not only did they have automatic rifles and mortars which they could deploy with accuracy, they had an advanced heavy machine gun and man, they knew how to deploy that. It was Giwa and his men who were undisciplined, while Abdullahi and his men had the strategy and the resources. The Governor demanded we kill Abdullahi —'

'You never told me that! Why couldn't you just make an exchange? Why do you people have to be plotting all the time?'

'A simple exchange was never going to happen, Jamilah. I couldn't tell you that, but I was confident we could eliminate Abdullahi *and* get Aminah out safely. In fact, killing him increased our chances of doing so. My plan was good.'

'Except it wasn't. They hadn't told you everything.'

De Witt shakes his head. 'Ado had been having secret meetings with Abdullahi way before Yakubu was Governor. They assumed Abdullahi would be comfortable with the same one-on-one meetings they'd had in the past.'

'You never mentioned this before."

'I only learnt it after the ambush. Abdullahi knew it was a set-up — another case of them underestimating him. *His* men were waiting for us, not the other way round. My men managed to shoot their way out through the smoke and confusion. Two didn't make it; I could have been the third, but my guys got me out. Ado didn't realise he signed his death warrant when he set up that meeting. He had his phone out and one of my guys was smart enough to grab it as we made our move. It was instinctive and, as it turned out, significant. While I was in here trying to stay alive, my guys got to work on the phone. They were able to identify the number Ado used to call Abdullahi and they downloaded texts and dates of calls that proved that the two of them had been in regular contact while Yakubu was running for Governor and not just by phone, but in face to face meetings. Yakubu had been funding Boko Haram to carry out atrocities that made the incumbent look weak. Ultimately they sabotaged his chances of re-election.'

'So he would have financed Aminah's kidnapping.'

'Probably.'

'That's too depressing. To think someone would be so desperate for power that they would sink that low .... Yakubu is as complicit as Abdullahi.'

'At least you have the comfort of knowing Ado and Giwa have paid the price.'

'May they rot in hell. I take some comfort, yes, but it will never compensate for the murder of my family. And Abdullahi and his men are still out there, and he and Yakubu are still getting away with murder.'

De Witt looks drained. He probably hasn't spoken so much since he was wounded but she needs more information from him. 'How did Ahmed come to be there?'

'I can't say for sure,' says de Witt. 'Like you, he knew when the exchange was due to take place, but not where. He must have gone to my hotel that morning and followed me on his bike — first to Ado's office, then to the barracks. He could have waited for us to leave and while he wouldn't have recognized me in the front seat — I was disguised as a driver — he would have recognized Ado and the car. He could have followed us down the mosque road before Giwa's men had time to shut it off, but they would have seen him. More likely he knew the road was a dead end, got off at the turn-off and continued on foot. Sorry, can you give me some water?'

Jamilah pours some water into a glass and helps him drink.

'He would have hidden somewhere to watch the exchange. He wouldn't have known there was a ring of our men already in place or that unbeknown to us, Boko Haram had us surrounded in turn. Maybe he did but was smart enough to stay hidden. It's a miracle no one noticed him. Perhaps he would have survived if they had, but there's no guarantee; no one wanted to give their positions away.'

'He would have wanted to have been there for Aminah ... feel a part of her rescue.'

'The person we'd assumed to be Abdullahi was already dead, but Giwa's men shot Ahmed as soon as he broke cover. I could see it was him. He was shouting that he was Aminah's brother and holding his hands in the air to show he was unarmed. I commanded them not to shoot but they ignored me.'

'Why?'

'Giwa said he could have been wearing a belt. It was procedure. But you could see from his body shape that he wasn't. I'm sure they knew that too, but they didn't care.'

Finally, she knows. She lowers her head, determined not to show any emotion.

'Are you going to be okay?' he asks.

'What sort of question is that?' She stands up and walks off. 'What kind of world do you people live in? This was just an unsuccessful mission for you. A setback. You'll be patched up and on your way to somewhere else soon. I have to stay here and live with all this, so no, I won't be okay. Especially while Yakubu and Abdullahi are still around. I'm sure it's only a matter of time before they come for me too.'

'I'm sorry, Jamilah.'

She breathes in. 'I hope you get better soon. I have to get back.'

'I wish … I could have done more, saved your sister … got to know you better.'

'Well, you didn't, and you won't. I can't blame you for her death, just for not keeping your promise. You were considerate towards me, and I appreciate that, but ultimately …'

'I came up short.'

'Yes.' She extends her hand. 'Goodbye, Colonel.'

'Goodbye, Jamilah.' He leans forward and with a grimace of pain covers her hand with both of his. She had forgotten how large they were. 'Be careful.'

'You, too.' She slips her hand free, turns and heads for the door.

'Wait,' he says. She stops. 'Open that second drawer.' He points to a bedside cabinet. She pauses, comes back, and does as he asks. 'It's Ado's,' he says. 'Take it. It's of no use to me now.'

'What use is it to me?'

'Ado assumed he'd still be alive today, otherwise he might have been more careful with the information he kept on it. We got what we wanted from it, but it contains other treasures Yakubu would prefer to remain buried.'

'Sounds like it could get a person killed.'

'Yes, but Yakubu won't be thinking about it. He'll assume, like Ado, it no longer exists. Only me, my men, and now you, know it exists. We'll be gone soon. Take it. Hide it. Use it or throw it away, it's up to you, but if you want to seriously damage Yakubu, this phone will provide the means. It won't do Abdullahi's credibility much good either if their collaboration ever comes to light. All that Islamic purity he professes to uphold and yet he's ready to do a deal with the devil?'

She wasn't expecting this. She's unsure how to react but slips the phone into her pocket anyway. De Witt slumps back in the bed with a look of relief on his face.

'We altered the account information and we've paid a year's contract in advance. All it needs is a recharge.'

He looks frail. She can't imagine him ever continuing his career, at least not in the field. 'Where did you get hit?'

'Shoulder, arm, thigh and calf, right hand side basically. Nasty piece of shrapnel in the chest to go with. If it wasn't for my comrades … I lost some good men, friends.'

'Don't feel too sorry for yourself, Colonel. Costs of doing business, right?'

'Ja. Take the envelope too.' He's struggling to keep his eyes open.

'What's in it?'

'A couple of phone numbers and an email address should you ever wish to contact me.'

Jamilah doesn't respond, nor does she take the envelope.

'And Ado's password — 1,2,3,4 — arrogance or naivety, take your pick, plus notes on the contacts list, messages, and texts.'

Jamilah picks up the envelope and glances inside.

'Very thorough. I really must go, and you need to sleep. Goodbye, Colonel.'

This time she does leave. He mumbled farewell barely reaches her ears.

Chapter 40

'The Caliph knows what we do!' says Abdullahi, tugging hard at his beard to keep his joy in check. 'He spoke my name, called me "Brother". Alhamdulillah!'

'Alhamdulillah!' Muhammed looks at his leader expectantly, but Abdullahi walks past him and gets into the boat where he lies back, eyes closed, allowing the sun to burn his face. His skin is more than a match for it, but he welcomes the connection; that same sun will be beating down on the battlefields of Iraq creating another bond between him and his brothers there. His fingers skim the surface of the water as re-runs the conversations with his ISIS comrades and his sense of being with them in Mosul, at one with the Caliphate. He gives silent thanks to Allah for bringing him to this pinnacle, and for all the victories and the gifts he has bestowed on him. He speaks aloud,

'"And my success is not but through Allah. Upon Him I have relied, and to Him I return. Alhamdulillah!" '

'Alhamdulillah!'

'I know our brother, Yusef looks down on us. I wish he could be here to share in our triumphs over those who slaughtered him. He taught us so much. As ignorance of the fundamentals of our faith accelerates, and the politicians allow the ways of the infidel to corrupt our youth, our so-called religious leaders do nothing. They are apostates, the servants of their political masters. Instead of railing against them, they divert their eyes.'

'They're more concerned about getting money to build luxurious mosques', says Muhammed.

'Yusuf would scorn that vanity', says Abdullahi. 'He was always humble. He preached that rebellion against the laws of Allah was producing strife, chaos, and misrule. Our only option as Believers is to wage war until Islam prevails. It's happening everywhere — Iraq, Syria, Afghanistan, Mali, Burkina, and we can strike anywhere in the west, where the infidel used to think he was safe.' He sits up as the boat rubs against the shore. 'Always remember, Islam is determination. Once we move forward we don't stop. We don't go back.'

"I will never go back', says Muhammed, securing the boat.

'Good', says Abdullahi, stepping into the shallow water, 'and should I join Yusuf before you, I expect you to continue on the path he has shown us'.

'Inch 'Allah.' Muhammed hears something. His eyes search the sky.

'A-jets!' shouts the lookout.

They dive into the reeds, as two Alpha jets scream past overhead accompanied by the whoosh of rocket fire. Abdullahi hears a thud near the islet they had just come from and sees a fountain of water project upwards. There's a direct hit on the man and his camels and a split second later his village explodes. The jets ascend sharply, veer to opposite sides and circle round to unleash their remaining rockets. They repeat the manoeuvre above the lake and return a third time to strafe the burning remains with gunfire. They are gone as suddenly as they had arrived; the village has all but gone too. Abdullahi hears a solitary scream. How could anyone have survived that? A camel bellows back from the lake, trying to stagger to its feet. It looks like one of its legs is missing. It flails for a moment, before sinking into a mix of water and blood. An unusual ripple of waves, looking as surprised as anyone, passes across Abdullahi's feet. He stands up; around him others take their cue. Smoke climbs up to the sky, the sun and a slight breeze serve to feed the flames below.

'Another pinpoint airstrike by the brave pilots of the Nigerian Air Force,' he tells them, trying to banish their fear.

'Was it the Sat phone?' whispers Muhammed.

'They were here too soon for that', says Abdullahi. He turns to his men who have started to gather round him, 'You see how Allah protects us. Someone from that village squealed but he has brought the wrath of Allah on to his own miserable people and kept us safe.'

'Alhamdulillah!' cry the men.

'Alhamdulillah! Soon, it will be our turn to strike back in vengeance. More funds are coming, more weapons. Our brothers in Mosul see how we fight, how we assassinate Deputy Governors and Commissioners of Police. They tell us to aim higher.'

'Allahu Akbar!'

As the men shout, Muhammed says to him, 'Yakubu won't be easy.

'Didn't you just see what happened?' He strides out into the open. 'It's all right they won't be coming back.' One of the slaves runs past in panic. He addresses one of the wives, 'Sister! Stop her screaming, otherwise I'll give her something to scream about!' He turns back to Muhammed, 'If it were easy, it wouldn't be worth doing. Allah will show us the way.' All his fighters have assembled now and the women look on. He stands feet apart, chest out, hands on hips. 'They won't be coming back. They can't wait to get back to base to tell everyone how they slaughtered us. They'll be wetting themselves thinking about all the backslapping and handshaking, the congratulatory phone calls from the President, the Governors, the Chief of Air

Staff, the generals — all those buffoons queuing up to tell them what big heroes they are. But my brothers, look around you. Are any of us dead? Do you see any broken bodies?'

Heads shake in unanimous agreement.

'Look over there', he points towards the village. 'Listen to those screams. They're suffering because Allah, the only true god, protects us and wreaks havoc on those you would betray us. Alhamdulillah!'

'Alhamdulillah!' they cry.

'Let this be proof to any doubters amongst you — and any stupid girls who still deny the faith, Allah spares us for a reason. The television and newspapers will be full of how the President's brave boys hunted us down and slaughtered us.' He nods his head in mock gravity. 'What are we going to do?' he holds his hands up in mock despair. 'We've been killed so many times in the past week, my back hurts from having to get up each time.'

There is laughter all around.

'How many times can a man die?' He's into his stride. He sees the sparkle in their eyes. 'But we aren't dead, are we brothers?'

Heads shake all around.

'The people of that village betrayed us. They are dead, not us.'

Affirmative grunts develop into a chorus of "Allahu Akbars". He motions with his hands, and they fall quiet.

'Today, I spoke to our brothers in Mosul. We have their respect'; he allows time for the words to sink in. 'They admire us, as we do them. We are as one. We share the same enemies, the same Jihad.'

Spontaneous applause breaks out.

'I told them how honoured we felt to be part of the true Caliphate. They said they were honoured to have our allegiance.'

The men respond with a chorus of Alhamdulillah's and clenched fists.

'We remain on this earth to carry out the sacred duty bestowed on us by Allah. Alhamdulillah!'

Cries of "Alhamdulillah!" echo across the lake.

'But brothers', he holds up his finger, 'we will bide our time a little longer. Let these infidels think we are dead. Let them drop their guard. They will look even more ridiculous when we strike again. But we must leave this place. You', he points at a fighter close by, 'go and watch the trail. They'll be coming with their cameras and sticks to pick through our bones. They might be stupid enough to try to get a truck through, I suspect they'll send a helicopter. Fa'idah, you and the rest of the women pack up and make it look like we were never here. Muhammed, take half a dozen men and go to the village. Strip the clothes of anyone who has come back, slaughter them and burn the bodies. Make it look like they were killed in the bombing. Leave one of our banners there, half burnt, some of our older weapons, and a few bikes. Make them think this village was our base and those charred bodies are ours. Locals will tell them it was a village, but the security forces will tell them to shut up. Bring back their clothes along with whatever food and fuel have survived. The rest of you load the motorbikes and weapons onto the boat, then help return the camp to its natural state. Don't forget the cement.' He walks towards them; they move aside to let him through. 'We're going to Chad. On a fishing trip. We'll lie low for a week, then resurface. We'll pay Governor Yakubu a visit — ghosts back from the grave!' He clenches his fist and raises it in the air. Again, they shout as one: 'Allahu Akbar!'

'Now, go!' he claps his hands. 'I want us underway in an hour.'

Chapter 41

In the taxi back to the airport, Jamilah wonders if she'd been too hard on de Witt. The last time she'd seen him, they had kissed in her apartment. Hard to believe then that their next encounter would be in a private ward in Abuja with him barely alive. Well the door is firmly shut on that episode. She'd been in a heightened state, desperate for someone to do something to get her sister back. She'd been grateful and vulnerable to affection. He'd been her knight in shining armour and had carried her off to a place she'd been willing to go. Now, his armour is forever tarnished. He couldn't deliver on his promise, and she can see him for what he really is — a failed mercenary — and for what he always was — a privileged child of Apartheid. Ahmed had been right. To think she'd taken sides with de Witt against her own flesh and blood.

She sees the driver glancing at her in the rear view and glares back at him. Her brother had been right about the Governor too. Not only does Yakubu maintain the conditions for terrorists to exist, he also provides them with the resources to flourish — as long as it helps him do the same! Even his response to combatting terrorism is corrupt: rapists and murderers like Giwa are put in charge; money for weapons gets diverted to him and his cronies and all the while, innocent people are slaughtered, and the people left behind have given up all hope that anyone is going to do something about it. Men under Giwa's command murdered her father and uncle; ten years later, they did the same to Ahmed. Yakubu was never interested in getting Aminah back. It was a sham exchange so he could kill off Abdullahi and protect his reputation.

But Abdullahi had known who he was dealing with. Aminah had fallen into Abdullahi's hands thanks to Yakubu's money. Now she's dead and Yakubu sits in his mansion abusing Iman, while Abdullahi remains free to carry out his next atrocity. They still have families, she has nobody. She has to stop feeling sorry for herself and do something. Her hand goes into her pocket and grasps the phone. Working hard to secure a future for her siblings was a survival strategy that worked for a while but failed in the end. She's never going to get over their murder by working hard and trying to integrate herself back into the life she had before. That life has gone. Why should she bow her head, move on, and let these people get away with it? Her family needs justice and there's only one way to achieve it. She has to kill these men herself. Yet can she, a nurse, dedicated to saving lives, really do such a thing? It's against the ethics of her profession and against the teachings of her religion. But it's even more fundamental than that. According to Salim, life is about knowing the difference between right and wrong, making your choice and acting accordingly. Is killing always wrong? Euthanasia involves killing a person to end their suffering. A rabid dog gets put down before it can maul a baby. Antibiotics kill the bacteria that is killing a patient. Yakubu and Abdullahi are like a disease. Killing them would save the lives of others and prevent a lot of suffering. She would be an antibiotic for humanity. How can that be wrong?

But she's not trained to kill. How could she get close to a powerful politician surrounded by state security or an elusive, ruthless terrorist in order to kill them? What resources does she have? Resolve, determination, nursing skills, and a phone that she doesn't know what to do with. She takes it out of her pocket. An iPhone, a newer model than her own. It needs recharging, just like her. She slips it back into her pocket. She's not going to be switched off this time. It's time to act, avenge her family, and do some good. Only then can she think about getting on with her life. She needs a plan, allies — ones she can trust — and, just for once, a dose of good fortune.

'Driver! What's the matter with you? Slow down! Why are you trying to kill me?'

Chapter 42

'You can't find the passwords?' asks Yakubu. 'They told me you were intelligent. What fucking use are you to anybody? Turn his room inside out, check his computer, get into the …'

'Hard drive?'

'Yes, the fucking hard drive, what the fuck else?'

'We need a password to access his desktop, sir.'

'So get it! Ado wasn't a fucking computer nerd, go find someone who is and put him to work. His personal laptop will be at home, go and get it. Ring his wife, talk to his secretary.'

'His wife hasn't come back from her village sir, and the secretary's still on leave.'

'Oh well, let's not inconvenience them, shall we? Let's just sit around and wait for them to come back. What the fuck's the matter with you …'

'Danjuma.'

'I know what your fucking name is. They've got phones, Danjuma, they'll have numbers, ring them, Danjuma. No, don't tell me; you've tried that already and they're not answering. Just go and find them. And don't come back here until you have, right?'

'Yes, Excellency.'

'And Danjuma …'

'Excellency…?'

'Stop telling me why you can't do things. Do what I tell you to do and don't bother me again until it's done. That's if you want to be anything more than an office boy around here. Got it?'

'Yes, Excellency.'

'Well, what are you waiting for? Fuck off!'

The Governor takes off his sunglasses, wipes the sweat from his brow and sits back with a sigh. He reaches in his drawer for his Beta-blockers, knocks a couple back and takes a deep breath. It was his first wife who had advised him to get someone younger to replace Ado, someone with fresh ideas, someone he could mould. Naturally, she had someone in mind — her cousin's son, Danjuma, just back from London with an MBA. Unlike Ado, he'd been wet behind the ears before he went off to study; now he's back he doesn't seem any the wiser. At least he was able to complete a course unlike that useless son of his, always asking for money and never earning it. Always starting things and never finishing them. His mother's son to a tee.

He never thought he'd miss Ado. That man did everything for him, didn't need to be told, knew whom to speak to, understood how to get things done and ... knew how to handle money. How he could do with Ado now. An hour earlier, his lawyer had given him the good news that the purchase of the apartment in Dubai had been agreed; the problem is he can't access the offshore account to pay the deposit. Ado dealt personally with such matters and kept him out of the spotlight. He hits his desk with his fist. Why did Ado have to go and get himself killed? How fucking irresponsible. He'd told Giwa to ensure that de Witt never made it out of that ambush alive. He hadn't expected him to survive and Ado and Giwa not to make it, and, in the name of Allah, lose their heads too. De Witt and his fucking plan! So much for professional expertise; couldn't even outwit a village bandit.

His phone rings. His secretary informs him that Mr Haruna the new CP is waiting to speak to him. He's not in the mood to see anyone but she says it's urgent, so he tells her to show him in. They exchange the usual greetings and Mr Haruna sits down.

'So, Mr Haruna, what news have you brought for me today? I only want good news, you understand, or you can fuck off, like that useless assistant of mine.'

'More than good, Excellency', the CP smiles, 'we've wiped out Abdullahi and his unit. For real, this time.'

'Alhamdulillah!' The Governor gets up from his desk. 'Come Commissioner.' He takes his arm, and with his stick points the CP towards the sofa on the other side of his office. 'I've been waiting a long time to hear those words. Sit down. Would you like something? Tea, coffee, coke, water?'

'I'm fine, thank you sir.'

'So, tell me all; spare no detail.'

'Yesterday morning intel came in about a Boko Haram unit, led by Abdullahi, having set up camp in a small village near Baga Kawa.'

'Lake Chad? So that's where the little rat was holed up.'

'Yes, sir. Two NAF Alphas were sent to deal with them under the command of Wing Commander Gana and, at 13:00 hours yesterday, they hit the camp full on. Direct strike, no survivors.'

'Alhamdulillah! This Gana deserves the highest commendation. I will personally recommend him for the Nigeria Star.'

'Well deserved, Excellency.'

'I presume, unlike the fiasco the other day, this strike has been verified?'

'Yes, Excellency. They held back informing us in order to be sure. A Puma helicopter touched down at the site while it was still daylight. They confirmed at least twenty bodies, along with the remains of assault weapons, motorbikes, and one of those white and black flags they like to wave. We've some photos.'

The CP takes out a large vanilla envelope from his briefcase and hands it to the Governor who takes off his sunglasses to examine the photos closely.

'Undoubtedly there were more fatalities', says the CP. 'Bodies at the centre of the strikes would have been totally incinerated. They were taken by surprise. No time to react. Both pilots scored multiple hits — as surgical a strike as we could have hoped for. Unfortunately, there was evidence of women and children amongst the dead. Wing Commander Gana hadn't expected that.'

'I assume he was reminded that the women they drag around with them are suicide bombers and their children the terrorists of tomorrow.'

'Of course, your Excellency.'

'In my view, such casualties are inevitable', says Yakubu, feeling statesmanlike. 'Gana shouldn't dwell on it; he has avenged your predecessor, my Deputy Governor, and hundreds of our security services and civilians.'

'And Gana's comrade too. You remember that Wing Commander they shot down a couple of years ago?'

'Yes, and who they beheaded on camera. Look, you're absolutely sure it was Abdullahi?'

'We don't have DNA, or dental records or photos, as you know, Sir, but he was well-known in the area. His wife still has family there. He was specifically identified in the local intelligence reports.'

'You must come for dinner, Mr Haruna, so we can get to know each other a little better. Bring your wife too. I'll get my secretary to fix something.'

'It would be an honour, Excellency.'

'Good, now I'm sure you have work to do.'

As soon as the door shuts, Yakubu hauls himself up from the sofa more easily than he has managed in a while. He rubs his hands together. The deaths of Ado and Abdullahi mean there is no one left alive who can testify that he had funded terrorism. That loaded gun is disarmed for good. He returns to his desk and pours over the photos again. The frustration at being unable to access his account is trivial. He will sort that out.

Chapter 43

'You're going to be fine,' says Jamilah, pulling off the disposable gloves. 'Healing up nicely. A benefit of youth, as Salim would say.'

'I'm still sore', says Iman.

'That's to be expected. Take the ibuprofen when you need it. Leave a minimum of four hours between each dose.' She walks into Iman's bathroom and drops the gloves into a waste bin. 'Keep using the gel for a couple more days', she says coming back in. 'And try not to wear any underwear. If you do, make sure it's cotton and loose-fitting.'

'Ha', says Iman, 'You think I'd keep such a garment in my wardrobe.'

Jamilah smiles but doesn't respond. 'You can bathe or shower but no more than twice a day. Make sure the vaginal area is completely dry before getting dressed and keep it dry and clean.'

'Fine by me', says Iman, 'the problem's keeping him away from it. Especially if he discovers I'm not wearing any underwear!' She gets up and reaches for her robe.

'There can't be any sex or foreplay and especially none of those … things he put inside you!'

'I'm not the one you should be talking to!' says Iman, glancing at herself in the mirror. 'For now, at least, he's following Dr Salim's instructions. That man is amazing. The way he talked to my pig of a husband.' She rolls her eyes like a teenager.

'Salim's well connected. He provides services that all those men like the Governor seem to need from time to time. He's the best and he's discrete and for these people that means he's indispensable.'

'Where His Excellency the Governor's concerned, no one is indispensable.' Iman sits down at her dressing table, 'Mind you, Salim delivered all the Governor's children. That counts for a lot, including, I understand', she whispers conspiratorially, 'some of the unofficial ones. And babies aren't the only thing he delivers.'

'Meaning?'

'He's Viagra supplier-in-chief for the pig and all his cronies.'

'He's more discrete than I thought', says Jamilah.

'No fakes or generic brands. Salim gets them the real thing, very privately. That's why the Governor keeps him sweet!' she laughs. She focuses on her reflection, moving her face from side to side. Jamilah looks on in fascination as Iman applies eyeliner that she clearly doesn't need to enhance her beauty. Given who she's married to, why would she even want to make herself look more attractive? Perhaps she does it for herself, or just to pass the time, or both.

Iman turns to face her. 'I suppose I should be grateful too.'

'Why?'

'Without the Viagra, I'd have to work even harder to get his stupid dick to respond! Don't look so shocked, Jamilah. Let's have some tea.'

'I can't, I have to be back.'

'Back where? Home? There can't be much waiting for you there. The Clinic? You're doing a house call for Salim, having tea with me is quality care, a response to your patient's needs, right? Don't you have a duty of care? Anyway, he'd hardly expect you to travel back to the clinic at this hour. What are you going to do there?'

'But your driver …'

'What about him? You don't think he enjoys getting paid for sitting around on his backside? He'll be ready to go when you're ready to go. Sit down and relax.'

She lets Iman lead her back to the bed and sit her down, marvelling at her new friend's confidence. Iman picks up the house phone and rings down to the kitchen for tea. She turns her chair to face Jamilah. 'They'll bring us cake too. Not any old cake; beautiful cream and chocolate cake, yum!' Iman scrunches her eyes. 'We ladies deserve to be pampered now and again, right?'

'And again and again!' Jamilah surprises herself by making a joke. Iman's eyes light up in recognition and they laugh together and hug. Jamilah hasn't had a friend since she left the village; she is realizing how much she has missed it.

'What, was I saying?' wonders Iman. She slides her arm around the back of the chair. When she crosses her legs, her satin robe falls gracefully to one side exposing her bare legs which are equally smooth and shiny. A flipflop dangles from her big toe. Her finger and toenails are painted blood red. It is obvious why men would find her desirable, why Yakubu would choose her amongst so many. Sitting in her clinic uniform and work shoes, Jamilah imagines how she must look through Iman's eyes. There are still bits of varnish she hasn't chipped off her fingernails, a remnant from her night with de Witt, and she would never think of painting her toenails. She presses one leg behind the other conscious of the fine black hair on her shins. Why would she want to shave her legs? Everyone knows once you start shaving your legs, you have to keep doing it. The hair grows back stronger.

'Oh yes, the pig', says Iman, recapturing her train of thought. 'Let's just call him "the pig". Does that work for you?'

Jamilah can't stifle a snigger and once out, laughter takes hold. 'Yes, that works for me,' she says as they calm down.

'Oink!' says Iman, sending them both off into another laughing fit, fuelled by more cries of 'Oink!'

There's a knock at the door. Iman gets up, composes herself and goes to let the maid in. A tray with tea and cakes is placed on a small table and as the maid departs, Iman beckons Jamilah over to join her. When Jamilah gets up, Iman tells her to kick off her shoes and loosen the buttons on her top. Jamilah obeys while Iman pours the tea.

'Help yourself to sugar and milk and eat as much cake as you like, I can order some more. You can even take some home with you', she whispers conspiratorially.

'Thanks, I'll be fine.'

'It's me who should be thanking you. You're so caring. You've come all this way to make sure I'm okay.'

'It's my job, Iman, but it's nice to see you again. I haven't laughed like that since my sister … We used to have great times together.'

Iman gives Jamilah's hand a squeeze and says, 'I know. And I'm taking it upon myself to ensure you laugh a lot more in future. So, as I was saying …' she holds her hand up as a warning, 'the pig'. A brief silence follows before Jamilah loses her composure, another "oink" follows from Iman, and they're off again.

Iman picks up the thread. 'Okay, him. At the start when the Viagra worked the way it should, he didn't need any help from me to get it up, other than be there to provide visual stimulation.. So, I was grateful for that. And I knew how to get him to come quickly — I'll spare you the details. Then it began to be a problem and he'd take an extra dose. Even I know that's not good for a man of his weight and age, especially with his high blood pressure. Sometimes it works but most times it doesn't. It doesn't help that he comes to bed bloated. He's a pig who eats like a pig.'

'Once men have erectile dysfunction, they lose confidence', says Jamilah, wearing her nurse's hat, 'and find it even harder to get an erection'.

'Exactly. For most of my marriage, Viagra was my friend. Those days are over. Now, he expects me to do what nature can't. I'm good with men but not a miracle worker. I told him he should take more exercise, eat less, and lose weight. He shouldn't expect to be humping me every night the way he did when we first met. Naturally, he blames me. At first, he used those "things" as a way to take his frustration out on me. Then, as I told you at the clinic, they became a way to punish me'. She sniffs. 'And I think that's how he gets his pleasure these days. I'm worried, Jamilah. I can fend him off for a few days, maybe longer, but he's a very cruel man. He can't perform but he still has urges. He watches porn all the time as well as those gangster movies. I think he mixes them up. He'll want me back in his room soon. He'll get frustrated again. He'll lose control and really hurt me next time. I just know it.'

It's the first time Jamilah has seen Iman cry. She leaves the bed, kneels down beside Iman and takes her hands in hers.

'It's okay, we'll find a way ...' More words of reassurance fail to arrive. She draws Iman's head onto her shoulder and hugs her.

'I told you, Jamilah, as far as he's concerned, everyone is dispensable. There's not a good future for me here. He gets what he wants and destroys anyone who gets in the way. There's no one to constrain him, especially since Ado's gone. Salim can't be here to protect me.'

'You'll have to leave him.'

'Easier said than done.' Iman grabs a tissue and blows her nose. 'I told you before. A woman like me doesn't leave a Governor. My family would hate me, and he wouldn't accept such a loss of face. He'd hunt me down ... put pressure on my family. The best I can hope for is that he gets bored with me before he kills me. Throws me out. I wish he would, even though I'd end up with nothing.'

'Why should you end up with nothing after all you've put up with? Why should you be the one who dies? Why can't he die?'

'Oh, you can't believe how much I've dreamt of that,' says Iman, sitting up. 'I know a wife shouldn't say such things about her husband, about anyone, but ... the things he's done. Not just to me ... I've heard things. He doesn't talk like normal people. He has to shout all the time, even on the phone. I could tell you things ... I'm sorry, I do wish he would die.' She starts crying again.

'Don't be sorry. I'm a nurse and I shouldn't say it either, but if ever someone deserved to die it's your husband.'

'The pig.' There is no laughter. Their eyes meet. Jamilah waits for Iman to say more but instead she breaks eye contact and turns away. Her back and shoulders expand as she takes a deep breath. When she turns round again, her face is bright, her smile is back.

'I know what we're going to do,' she says standing up. 'Give you a makeover!'

'What?'

She takes Jamilah's hand and leads her across to the dressing table. Jamilah wonders if her friend is regretting what she's just said, or maybe the words have scared her. Whatever it is, she's showing her ability to ride her emotions and act as if nothing has happened. Doubtless, a skill that serves her well in dealing with Yakubu.

'We're going to make you look even more beautiful, Senior Nursing Officer. You're always looking so serious. Like you're about to tell someone off.'

'That's because I usually am', says Jamilah.

'Ah, there it is again.'

'What?'

'That smile. When you smile, when you laugh, your face lights up and wow, the transformation!'

Jamilah finds herself blushing. 'I'm not beautiful. Aminah is, was, the beautiful one in our family. I still get acne. Can you imagine, at my age?'

'I know what I see. And you don't have acne; okay, a bit there, but only because you made me look for it. Anyway, I know a way to hide it, and get rid of it.'

'Really?'

'Trust me, but first things first.'

Iman positions Jamilah in front of the mirror. Despite her awkwardness, her reflection appears calm — probably because she's still in uniform. Or is it something to do with a feeling that something has happened between them, something that has brought them closer together. As she observes Iman selecting which beauty products to apply to her face, Jamilah has a sense that something has been set in motion. They've shared intimate thoughts; the way good friends do. Are they going to become allies too? There's a bond between them, she's sure Iman feels it too; maybe she's more aware of it than her. A pause is good. Let things sink in and see where they go next.

Chapter 44

It's five forty-five in the morning and it's been some time since Yakubu could get down on his knees and up again so easily. The soles of his feet have been reinforced over the years by a waxy wedge of cracked yellow skin that acts as a shock absorber each time his bodyweight bears down on them. His big toes are pushed inwards by fist-size bunions, the legacy of teenage years spent yomping for miles in tough, ill-fitting army boots. He's slept well; his mood is up. One hand grips the side of the wooden chair on which he usually performs the Fajr prayer; the other hand reaches for his cane. He bolsters himself with a couple of deep breaths before hauling himself up with more enthusiasm for a new day than he's had since the disaster at the old mosque. Revenge does indeed taste sweet.

He assesses himself in the mirror. His stomach thrusts out, the way his chest used to, creating a plateau on which his grandchildren could happily sit if he would ever let them near him. His man breasts droop to the side resting on the great belly which curves outwards, downwards, and finally upwards to re-join his abdomen at an indeterminate point. He puts this unflattering shape and the undeniable way it spills out over his barely visible boxer shorts down to the fact that he's sitting. If he was to stand up it wouldn't look half as bad. He never thinks of his buttocks, other than as a necessary inconvenience when he struggles in the toilet. The fact is he hasn't seen them properly in a long time and has no desire to. On the other hand, he likes to think his stout legs are like pillars carved out of the Zuma Rock. He scrapes the palm of his hand across the stubble of his large head, slips on his dark glasses and bellows for his wife, who rushes in on cue, ready to perform her first task of the day.

'Good morning, Sir. Did you sleep well?'

'No thanks to you. At least I was spared your miserable whining. I'm putting an end to that nonsense. Tonight you will be back in my bed. Try to behave like a proper wife for a change.' He snorts, pleased with himself.

She remains silent. How does she manage to look so perfect, all the time? She picks up his vest, slips her hands through the armholes and lifts it up above his head. He pushes her away roughly.

'Wait until I've put my watch on for fuck sake.' She approaches again with the vest as he clips the heavy watch around his wrist. 'Take that pathetic look off your face. What's the matter with you woman?' He swings his arm round and catches her hard on the side of the face with the back of his hand and the face of his watch. She spins away but the bed breaks her fall. 'You need a good fucking seeing to that's your problem.'

'But, Sir,' she says holding her cheek, 'you heard what the doctor said, I'm not fully healed, we have to wait.'

'I don't care what the doctor said. Fuck the doctor. You might pull the wool over his eyes, but you don't fool me. There's nothing wrong with you. You're lazy, ungrateful, you think you're some sort of madam, well I'll fucking show you. Oh, for fuck sake don't start blubbing. Get off that bed and start moving. I have a press conference to go to!'

'Yes, sir.'

'Give me the vest, I'm not a baby. Get the black babban riga out, the one with the gold lining, and the matching fula. Hurry up. And make sure to have a good breakfast ready, I'm as hungry as a lion this morning.'

'Yes, Sir.'

He watches her walk to the wardrobe and can't help admiring her elegance, her feminine shape. She opens the door and reaches up with both hands to extract the robe. His eyes are drawn to the pull of her robe against her outstretched body. He is captivated by the line of her long back, the way it dips at the waist, rises over the curve of her buttocks, and flows down over her stretching thighs. He feels something stir and it lifts his spirits even more. He's pulling out of his depression and recovering his backbone. She carries back the heavy garment by its hanger, ensuring it doesn't drag on the carpet.

'Good. Come closer and hold it up for me. Higher. Now, turn around.'

'What?'

'You heard, turn around and keep holding it up.' She does as he says. He reaches round under her arms and takes hold of her breasts in his large hands. He hears her sharp intake of breath and thrusts his groin against her buttocks. 'I feel ten years younger', he growls in her ear.

'Yes, sir. But be patient. Show me tonight. You mustn't be late for your press conference.' She breaks away and places the robe across the bed.

'How dare you disobey me!' He grabs her arm and is about to slap her again when she wriggles free.

'Please sir, I couldn't hold it up anymore, and you wouldn't want me to drop it on the floor. You are so ... virile this morning. How could I concentrate? You know how to excite me. I'll make it up to you later. I promise.' She draws his hand towards her and kisses it. She looks up at him and he feels her tongue slip into the space between his fingers.

'Humph!' He looks down at her face, unable to withdraw his hand. Her cat-like eyes look back at him, along the length of his outstretched arm.

'Wait until tonight', she purrs. 'If we wait, it will be even better. Just like old times!' She releases his hand. 'Now, it's time to get you ready so you can put these media men in their place!' She slips behind him and puts her hands on his shoulders. He remains still and allows her to ease him gently back down into his chair.

Chapter 45

The idea comes as Jamilah is at the crossroads of sleep, held back by a jumble of dreamlike thoughts, the kind that seem real at the time, but disappear once sleeps takes over. This is different. Is it Aminah and Ahmed tugging her awake to keep the idea alive? Her eyes open, her mind is clear, and she is ready to act. She throws the duvet to one side and heads to the bathroom. In the shower she rehearses what she's going to say. She dries off and slips into her dressing gown and flip-flops. She disconnects Ado's phone from the charger and sits down at the table. She re-reads de Witt's notes and makes her own. As well as Yakubu and Ado's dealings with Boko Haram, there's evidence of other questionable activities. Salim would have a better grasp, but she can't show him anything, at least not yet.

She has an hour before she must leave for work. She finds a number for Abdullahi in the Contacts List and, without hesitating, presses the automatic dial. The ringtone at the other end produces an adrenaline rush. She's about to talk to the man who killed her sister. Each unanswered ring calms her down a little more and helps her take on the focused, professional mode she adopts each time she puts on her uniform. After a dozen rings, she hangs up. That was a good thing. She was too on edge. She must regroup. She takes a deep breath and redials. No response. She gets up, walks around the room and stretches. At least she knows the phone is working, otherwise there would be no ringtone, right? Whoever has it should see Ado's name on the screen. Unless this number is for a burner phone Abdullahi used just to contact Ado, and he doesn't carry it around with him? Maybe it's just too early in the morning? But these are fundamentalists living in the bush. They'll be up before dawn, ready for morning prayer. She tries again; someone picks up but doesn't speak.

'As-salamu alaykum', says Jamilah.

She hears a man instruct someone else to put the phone on speaker.

'Hello', says Jamilah

'Who's this?' says a gruff voice.

'A relative of one of the innocent people you've murdered.'

'Madam Ado! Wa-Alaikum-Salaam. Your husband wasn't innocent, Madam. We did you a favour, he would have bored you to death.' Laughter follows.

'I'm not Madam Ado,' says Jamilah. 'And I'm glad you think murdering people is funny. Some of us who must clean up your mess don't find it funny, especially when it consists of dead children or what's left of them.'

'Haven't you noticed, bitch, we're in a war, there are always unintended casualties.'

'Is it unintended when you strap bombs on young girls and send them to the market to blow themselves up? You know full well there will be children around when they do it. You send children out to kill other children.'

'Spare me the lecture, bitch. Who are you?'

'My daughter was one of those innocent schoolgirls you strapped a bomb to and blew up.'

'Ah, yes, now that was intentional. Those schoolgirls are not innocent. They're corrupted by western education. They turn their backs on the Prophet, disrespect our traditions, think they have an equal voice, think they know better. They shouldn't be in school. Why did you send her there? It's your fault she's dead. Anyway, how did you get this number? What do you want?'

'To talk to Abdullahi.'

'Haven't you heard the news?' the man laughs, 'He was blown up yesterday by the brave boys of the Nigerian Air Force.'

Jamilah's hopes that Abdullahi had been killed have been dashed before. The media can't be relied on and something in this man's tone serves as confirmation.

'I'm talking to Abdullahi, now,' she says, surprised at her assertiveness. 'This is your number; you've already admitted it as much.'

He doesn't reply.

'Okay, let's pretend you're not him. I want to give him a message.'

'We're listening.'

Jamilah looks at her notes. 'Governor Yakubu is our common enemy. I know why he's your enemy; you don't know why he's mine, that's unimportant. I will kill him for you, and you won't have to lift a finger.'

'You have our attention.'

'In return, you will release one hundred girls you have taken captive, including the dozen you took six weeks ago during the elections.'

'Why would Abdullahi agree to that?' says a new voice.

'And why should he let you have the pleasure of killing that piece of shit?' says the man she is sure is Abdullahi.

'Because the phone on which I am talking to you, belonged to the late Deputy Governor. It is now in my possession, and I will ensure it's delivered to people in the media who, with a few pointers from me, will access all the information he didn't delete from it. Information that will greatly damage the reputation of you and your organization.'

'What are you talking about?'

'This phone contains texts and voice messages between you and Ado, going back to before Yakubu was Governor. They provide evidence that Yakubu was paying you millions of Naira to finance your activities. Whatever mealy-mouthed reasons you might put forward for taking his money, the fact is, he was paying you to help him get what *he* wanted. You were doing Yakubu's work, not Allah's. You helped the man you call an infidel to get elected Governor. Is that the purpose of Jihad?'

'That's bullshit.'

'Is it?' She doesn't need her notes anymore. She gets up and paces the room. 'You think that's how your men will see it? How the other factions of Boko Haram, would see it, the ones who would like to recruit your men? Is that how your founder, Mohammed Yusuf, murdered by the very people you have helped, would see it? The media will portray you as a bandit in the pay of a corrupt Governor, not the Jihadist you profess to be. What will your brothers in Islamic State and Al Qaeda think of your Caliphate when they learn it was funded by one of the most corrupt men in our country.'

'You don't understand a thing!' he roars. 'We have an army to sustain. We can't raise taxes or divert public finances. We have to survive to carry out Jihad. Why shouldn't we take from the rich? He was funding us to do our work, not the other way round.'

'Then you don't care if the media start publishing details of your collaboration.'

'Look bitch, I've already explained. And I can tell you if you do this, you will be joining your daughter in hell.'

'I've nothing left to lose, I'm not afraid of you.'

'Talk is cheap, especially at the end of a phone. Maybe you haven't thought about what we'll do to you before we kill you.'

Jamilah remains silent. She has continued to block out what she suspects they did to Aminah. This man is so evil, he scares her, but she will not be intimidated. Not for Aminah's sake.

'You're making this up. Why would Ado keep all that information on his phone? It would be more damaging for him and Yakubu?'

'Because he never expected to die, or that his phone would ever leave his possession. Like you and Yakubu, he was arrogant. He thought it was other people who got killed and that he would live a long and comfortable life.'

'We'll call back in ten minutes.' The line goes dead.

Jamilah slumps back in the sofa and swallows hard. Her palms are sweating, her cheek is smarting. She didn't intend to say all that but it has invigorated her and at last, she's been proactive. It's like a weight off her shoulders. She cries, not because of despair, but to ease tension. She's not done yet. She looks at the phone. What a powerful instrument it has turned out to be. For Ado, an instrument of corruption and death; for her, a means to unlock redemption.

Chapter 46

'That thing she said about cleaning up our mess', says Muhammed. 'Sounds like a doctor or a nurse.'

'Doctors don't clean up mess', says Abdullahi. 'A nurse more like, not a typical one, and not as clever as she thinks.'

They're sitting in the charred breeze block hut of a deserted village they'd overrun six months earlier. It would have belonged to the chief as the rest of the huts are made from baked mud. Breaches in the corrugated steel roof permit narrow shafts of light to pierce the room, illuminating motes of soot that still float in the air and settle unobserved on their clothes.

Abdullahi's beads shift rapidly across his fingers. 'She mentioned the girls we took before the elections. Said she's the mother of a schoolgirl we put a vest on ... She's the mother of that stuck-up bitch we blew up at the ambush.'

'Aminah?'

'Even sounds like her.'

'Do you think she really has Ado's phone?'

He slaps Muhammed on the side of the head. 'How else would his name have come up when she rang us? Why didn't you turn the thing off before you threw it in the sack?' He slaps Muhammed's head again. 'Did you think Ado might want to contact us from hell?'

'I didn't think we'd need it again.'

'For once your inability to thinks might prove useful.'

'I wonder how she got hold of it,' says Muhammed.

'Maybe she knew someone at the ambush. Maybe Ado left it in his car. One thing is for sure, she's right about him. He would think he was so damned important he didn't have to bother about deleting things. I'm not happy about that phone.' He gets to his feet. 'Our men wouldn't have a problem about me taking money from Yakubu. It bought us food, fuel and how else could we have acquired the Coyote?'

'It allowed us to do His work, not Yakubu's', says Muhammed, 'and it doesn't make any difference who the Governor is, they're as bad as each other'.

'Exactly. But I know the way these media people work; they're only looking for headlines. I want that phone.'

One of the slaves enters the hut with tea on a makeshift tray. She keeps her eyes on the ground, kneels, and sets the glasses between them. As she goes to get up, Abdullahi grips her hair. He pulls her green wrapper apart and grabs the inside of her thigh. She's about to scream but is silenced by his finger on her lips. She stays still and his hand returns to her thigh prising it away from the other. He slides his finger slowly up to the top of her thigh and stops. She tenses up, holding her breath, squeezing her eyes tight. He doesn't move; he's enjoying the fear in her face, the beads of sweat that trickle down her temple. When she exhales he shoves two fingers roughly inside her. She clenches her fists and tries to suppress a scream. The noise that escapes her throat is like the yelp of a wounded goat. He pushes her away.

'Get out! I've no time for you now.'

The girl stands up and pulls her wrapper back in place. Fresh tears run onto her crumpled lips. She wipes them away and picks up her headscarf and tray and rushes away from the laughter. He licks his fingers.

'Did you hear what she said about Yakubu?'

'No, I didn't Muhammed, I must have missed that.' He sips his tea.

'Whoever heard of a doctor or a nurse committing murder?'

'Or killing a Governor.'

'We killed her daughter,' says Muhammed, 'yet it seems she hates Yakubu more than us.'

'Who knows how a woman thinks? She can't get her daughter back, maybe getting a bunch of bitches back is the next best thing.'

'And how's she going to kill Yakubu?'

'She's all a big puzzle to you, isn't she?' says Abdullahi. 'Who knows and who cares? If she's a doctor or a nurse, maybe she has an inside track.' He shifts his beads again. 'Remember when you asked me how we'd kill Yakubu, and I told you Allah would show us the way?'

Muhammed nods.

'Well, He just has and however she plans to do it, it's Allah's will.'

'So we release the girls?'

'Yes, but she's not having a hundred and I want that phone.'

'She'll see that as her insurance.'

'You think? Well, that's not going to work. She'll be our enemy as long as she has that phone. If she hands it over, we might think differently. Call her back.'

He throws Muhammed the burner. He dials and puts the phone back on speaker.

'We're interested', he growls.

'I thought you would be', she says.

'If you kill Yakubu, you get fifty girls.'

'I want a hundred, nothing less. This is a Governor we're talking about. I'm doing your dirty work for you. It has to be worth it for the risks I'm taking. You don't have to lift a finger; I could get killed.'

'Yakubu offered me ten thousand dollars per girl.'

'Why didn't you take it? You have so many.'

'Don't believe everything the media tells you.'

'I don't, or I'd be talking to a dead man, wouldn't I?'

'That's funny.'

'Do we have a deal or not?'

'No. You can have fifty, and I want Ado's phone too.'

'Why would I agree to that?'

'If you kill Yakubu and we give you the girls, why would you need it?.'

'I've already told you. What's on the phone can damage you, otherwise you wouldn't want it. You're a murderer and the threat to expose you is my protection. If anything happens to me, someone else will ensure the phone gets to the media.'

'You think you've thought this all out but you're not thinking clearly. Keeping the phone is a reason for me to find you and kill you. I *am* a murderer and if your little plan succeeds, you'll be one too. And I will know it. I expect you're not planning a suicide mission, as you find them so distasteful.' He glances at Muhammed but there is no reaction to his joke. 'All we'd have to do is let the media know the person who sent them the phone was the Governor's assassin, a woman who lost her daughter in an ambush that went wrong. Not only will the media be all over it, but the security forces will also jump at any lead that could result in them unmasking the Governor's killer.'

There is silence at the other end. Abdullahi smiles triumphantly and this time Muhammed nods his appreciation. 'While you're thinking about that, bitch, does the name Aminah ring any bells?' They laugh.

'I'll ring you back in ten minutes', she whispers and hangs up.

Chapter 47

Jamilah slips her hand inside her dressing gown to lift the damp towelling away from her skin. After the first call, she'd held the initiative. She'd been doing well on the second one too, employing her haggling skills from the market to good effect. She'd almost forgotten she was bargaining for people's lives, then she found herself bargaining for her own. She had remembered the deal she'd struck to save her little brother's life. She's not cut out for this conniving. The situation is unreal. Two months ago she would have been getting up for work, setting the breakfast table for Ahmed, Aminah too if she'd been home. This morning she's on her own, using the phone of a dead politician to talk to her sister's killer. She can't allow herself despair, she needs to regroup and get the initiative back ... He's right, as long as she has the phone she'd be a threat to him. Why did she give him enough info to work out who she is? Because she let her emotions get the better of her, and like de Witt and the rest, she had underestimated him.

She picks up the framed family photograph. They all look so happy. She's sitting between her siblings, arms around their shoulders. Salim was the cameraman. She'd just been made SNO, and they'd gone out for a little celebration. Her fingers touch their faces and her lips offer them tender kisses. She flops back down on the sofa, grasping the photo to her chest. How dare Abdullahi kidnap Aminah and end her life so cruelly? If he hadn't taken her, Ahmed would be alive too. She squeezes the photo harder as if the spirits of her brother and sister reside within it; she wants them to pass into her. A surge of energy cascades simultaneously down her chest to her toes and up to the roof of her skull. Behind her eyelids, a band of bright yellow light spreads across her face like warm sunshine. She feels bathed in love. She picks up the phone again and redials. She speaks the moment it is picked up.

'There's other info on the phone that would be damaging to Yakubu — business deals, bank transfers and so on. Once he's dead, I can delete the references to you and keep the rest, then send the phone to the media. The Governor's reputation will be trashed and panic will spread amongst his former associates. It would reinforce what you have been saying — politicians are nothing more than corrupt infidels.'

'You're starting to grow on me, bitch.

'So you agree?' says Jamilah.

'No. Why should we trust *you*? Aren't we the ones who killed your daughter? Even if you did delete references to us, some expert would find a way to access them. I've told you already, you're not as clever as you think. We'll be satisfied hearing Yakubu's on his way to hell, we couldn't give a fuck what happens to his reputation after that. I want that phone. Either you give it to me, or we'll come and take it, and that won't end well for you.'

'If I give it to you, how do I know you won't track me down and kill me anyway.'

'Because, bitch, you'd no longer be a threat to me, and I don't like to waste my time. More importantly, I won't kill the servant of Allah if she does His will. You kill Yakubu and give me the phone, and I give you my word, under Allah, that you will not come to any harm at our hands.'

Jamilah has a sense that an oath like that is not made lightly by a religious fanatic.

'Okay, I respect your word', she says, 'but I want another fifty girls for the phone.'

He laughs. He knows he holds the initiative.

'Twenty-five', she says, instantly realizing she's lowered her bid without waiting for a counter offer.

'I'll release twenty-five when I get the phone, fifty when you kill the infidel. That's the deal. Do not try my patience any further.'

'Okay', says Jamilah, trying to disguise her relief. 'When you hear the announcement of Yakubu's death, you release fifty girls. When I give you the phone, you release the last twenty-five.'

'No. I'm not having you walking around with that phone a minute longer than you have to. You'll probably end up getting captured trying to kill Yakubu and have the thing fall into his hands. Listen carefully. You give us the phone, you get twenty-five; you kill Yakubu, you get fifty.'

'And you swear in the name of Allah to release them immediately when I do what you ask?'

'Not what I ask, what Allah has decreed. I swear in His name.'

'And you won't come looking for me afterwards?'

'I've already said so, don't you fucking listen?'

'How do I get the phone to you?'

'My daughter Farida, who, supposedly was going to be exchanged for your daughter, will call you on Ado's phone and fix a time and a place. After you give it to her, get hold of a burner and use that to communicate with us.'

'Okay,' says Jamilah.

'Alhamdulillah! We're allies now. If you need an AK47 or an RPG, let me know.' The two men laugh again. 'If this works out, we'll think about letting you join us on a permanent basis.'

'I'll wait for your daughter's call.'

'Inch 'Allah. Listen, we need a name for you. Let's keep things on a business footing. How about "Bitch?"' They laugh. 'With a capital B.'

'Call me, Aminah.' She cuts him off.

Chapter 48

Ado's phone rings as Jamilah turns the key to her locker. The screen displays an unknown number.

'As-salaam-Alaikum.'

'Wa-Alaikum-Salaam,' says a female voice.

'Hold on, I'm going outside', says Jamilah, slipping past a colleague and out into the hospital grounds. She sits on a nearby wall, checking there is nobody in earshot. 'Farida?'

'You have something for me.'

'Yes.'

'Meet me at the entrance to the old market.'

'Where your father killed all those people?'

'Five o'clock. Come alone.'

'How will I know who you are?'

The line goes dead. Jamilah takes a moment to capture Farida's name and number on both Ado's phone and her own, then heads back to the wards. Pulling open a fire door, the Ado's phone presses against her thighs, reminding her that while her own phone has little worth, Ado's is worth twenty-five lives. She mustn't lose it. If she could meet Farida now and hand it over she'd feel a lot easier. It seems strange to refer to Abdullahi as someone's father, moreover the father of a daughter who could be Aminah's age. While it makes him seem more human, Jamilah's under no illusion. How does Farida deal with having a mass murderer for a father, a man who thinks nothing of killing girls her own age? If the call is anything to go by, it doesn't seem to bother her. She's inherited his arrogance. "You've something for me", she'd said. An adolescent talking down to an adult, never mind an SNO. She'd ignored Jamilah's questions, then had the nerve to hang up on her! There was no chance to ask when her father would release the girls. She'll make sure to ask at the rendezvous before she hands over the phone and she'll make sure she gets an answer. A colleague approaches,

'Good morning, Sister.'

'Good morning, nurse,' says Jamilah without breaking her stride. The nurse falls in alongside her.

'We've a problem with a diabetic, Sis —'

'You've called Endocrinology?'

'Yes, Dr Bello said he'd be here in ten minutes. The patient is sixty-five and presents with fever and shortness of breath.'

'Heartbeat?'

'Rapid.'

Jamilah looks at her, expecting more exact information. The urgency induces a well-practiced half-run, masquerading as a fast walk.

'The patient says he's taking his insulin, but it could still be Type 1-related, couldn't it?'

'I presume we're giving him oxygen.'

'Yes, Sister.'

'Go back to your patient. His breathing will get easier. Keep him comfortable 'til Dr Bello arrives. I'll go to the insulin store just in case.' She peels away and without looking back says, 'I'll join you in a couple of minutes.'

Jamilah heads to her office. It can be considered an office, rather than a broom cupboard because it has the initials "S.N.O." embossed on the door, full stops included. She switches on the strip light, which greets her with its usual ten-second flicker. There are no windows but enough space for a small desk supporting a temperamental desktop, matching chair, and narrow bookcase, all made by the same local carpenter with a focus on functionality and value for money. De Witt's facility is a world away. A year planner, pinned on the wall above her desk, captures shifts and holidays. It renders the calendar on the opposite wall redundant, but its colour photograph of a Fulani horseman at the Durbar, his stallion rearing up on its hind legs, lifts the gloom. As she slips the key for the insulin store into her watch pocket, another thought strikes her. One that could play a primary role in her pact with the devil.

Dr Bello is a young man, tall and not much older than Jamilah. With his fine features, long lashes and creamy-brown complexion, he's handsome and knows it. The sort of junior doctor her nurses get excited about when he strides onto a ward, wearing his stethoscope like a medal and his white coat left unbuttoned, allowing his coattails to rise up and flutter like a cape. At times he seems as immature and affected as them. Still, he works hard and knows his field, and he's managed to get to the bedside five minutes earlier than estimated. The finger pressed against his lips seems to indicate that he is reaching a preliminary diagnosis. He releases it and walks to the bottom of the bed, a little too theatrical for Jamilah's liking. He swivels round to face her, his back to his patient.

'It's not an insulin issue, *per se,* Sister. As you know, diabetes predisposes to certain types of infection and, especially given this man's age, death. I believe it's pneumonia.' He talks as if he has made a medical breakthrough. 'So it's not insulin he needs, it's antibiotics, though his Type 1 will complicate things, and he'll need to be monitored.'

She's glad the insulin pens she brought from the store are still in her pocket.

'Amoxicillin', he says, 'five hundred milligrams, three times a day and we'll monitor progress. I'd find him a corner slot for the first twenty-four hours. The risk of infection is low and disappears soon after the antibiotics kick in. He'll need rest too. I'll get the TB people to pass by and take a look at him just to be on the safe side.'

'Excuse me, sister,' another nurse interrupts. 'There's a woman at reception who would like to see you.' Jamilah observes that while her colleague is delivering a message to her, she's mostly looking at Dr Bello.

'Did she have a name?'

'No, but she looked … important.'

Jamilah turns to Dr Bello, but he's looking at his admirer with what he probably thinks, is a seductive smile. She turns back to the nurse.

'Okay, thank you, nurse, but remember to ask for a name in future. You can get back to what you were doing.' The nurse nods to Jamilah and smiles at Dr Bello. Jamilah thanks him and takes her leave, certain his eyes are not following her in the way they had just followed the messenger.

As soon as Jamilah reaches reception, a woman gets up and comes toward her, holding part of her robe across her face as if she doesn't want to catch anything. Despite the attempted cover-up, Jamilah recognises Iman, by the quality of her clothes, her height and her elegance. She and understands why her colleague was impressed.

'I'm sorry to show up like this, Jamilah … without an appointment or anything.' Jamilah senses an edge in her voice. 'I had to come, you're the only one I can talk to.' There are tears in her eyes.

'It's okay. Let's go somewhere private.'

She puts her arm around Jamilah's shoulder and leads her to her office. She shows Iman the chair, offers her a box of tissues, then draws up a small stool to sit alongside her. Without saying anything, Iman shows her face. Make-up can disguise bruising, but not the swelling below her right eye.

'Yes, the pig. It didn't take him long to revert to his old ways.'

'I'm sorry, Iman', says Jamilah, taking hold of her friend's hands.

'I hate him. I'm leaving him. If I stay there he'll kill me. I know he will. He has such mood swings. This morning, I don't know, he seemed rejuvenated. I can't face him tonight. I'm not well.' She lets her tears flow.

Jamilah strokes Iman's arms, trying to think. If Iman leaves, the means to access Yakubu leaves with her. Jamilah will be unable to carry out her plan and all those girls will continue to suffer a living hell or meet the same fate as Aminah. She can't lose that access, especially when her plan is falling into place. She needs time to prepare and before she deals with Yakubu she needs to see evidence that Abdullahi will stick to his word and release the first group of girls.

'No one would blame you for leaving him, Iman, but ...'

'What?'

'You said if you left, your family would hate you, right?'

Iman nods.

'And after all the depravity you've put up with, you'd leave with nothing, right?'

'Yes.'

'That even if you left, he wouldn't accept it. He'd come after you; terrorise your family if he had to, and then he'd make you suffer even more.'

'Yes, but what can I do, I can't go back there and wait for him to attack me.'

'Well … we discussed another … alternative to your leaving, didn't we?'

'Yes, but how … how could we, the two of us …?'

Jamilah opens her door and glances outside. Satisfied, she closes it quietly and kneels in front of Iman. Taking her hands in hers, and looking her friend square in the face, she speaks with quiet determination. 'We can do it, Iman. Together, we can kill him. I have a plan, but I need another day to set it up.'

'What plan? Tell me.'

'I will, in a minute, and I think we will be able to do it and not get caught. But there's a terrible thing I have to ask you … can you be with him for one more night? Somehow try to contain him? After that, your suffering will be over for good. You'll be able to make a new start. You won't be blamed and I'm sure you'll get enough of his money to make you and your family comfortable.'

'Wow, that's a lot to take in Jamilah. We talked about it and yes, I want it but I never imagined we'd find a way to do it. But … he was different this morning. I had to promise I wouldn't disappoint him tonight or else I think he'd have raped me right there and then. He's going to expect me to do whatever he wants tonight.' She turns and looks into Jamilah's eyes. 'If I try to back out he'll say I led him on, and he'll feel justified in beating me.'

'I know. It's a terrible thing for me to ask.'

'What happens if your plan fails? Can you imagine what he would do to me, to you, to my family? I don't know what you've cooked up, but it feels like too much of a risk. Jamilah, you're a true friend. The fact you'd be willing to take such a risk for me is the kindest, bravest thing anyone has ever offered to do for me. I can't ask you to endanger your life for me.' She squeezes Jamilah's hands. 'It would be wrong, especially after all the things you've been through.'

'That's just it, Iman. It's not just for you, it's for me too. Your husband financed terrorists, the people who kidnapped and murdered my dear sister. His CP raped me ten years ago and I watched as my father and uncle were slaughtered. He could have stopped them. Your husband promoted him, his men shot my brother in cold blood, the brother I'd saved from meeting the same fate as our father. Yakubu could have got my sister back alive but was only interested in killing Abdullahi, his former partner in crime. I want your husband dead as much as you do.'

Iman sits up.

'Listen, it's not only for you and me.'

'I know, there are a lot of people who wish him dead.'

'That's not what I mean. What would you think, if I told you that by killing your husband, we could save the lives of fifty girls being held captive by Boko Haram?'

'What?'

'You heard me.'

'I don't understand.'

'I can't explain it all now, you have to trust me. But I swear, it's true.'

'I believe you. I trust you.'

'It's a terrible thing I'm asking, Iman, but if you stay with him just one more night … you said you know how to handle him, make him ejaculate quickly, whatever. If you can contain him and keep yourself alive tonight, then tomorrow evening, I'll make a house call, just like before, only this time, I'll come earlier and when I leave, he'll be dead. Nobody will blame you. You'll be in the clear.'

'You seem so sure. How are you going to manage it?'
There is a knock at the door. 'Sister, are you there?'

'Yes, I'm coming straight away. I have to go Iman. I'll explain later on the phone. Will you trust me, and do as I ask?'

'Yes. I can and I will.' They seal their alliance with an embrace.

Chapter 49

Muhammed scrolls through a list on his laptop. 'Are you sure about this?'

'Allah decreed it.' Abdullahi stands with his back to Muhammed, adjusting his robe. He glances back at him, 'You question His command?'

'No, no, of course not,' says Muhammed.

He turns back and looks down at the half-naked girl kneeling at his feet. 'Get the fuck out!' She gets up, wipes her mouth, pulls her wrapper up and tee shirt down. 'That was pathetic, you're pathetic.' She runs quickly to the broken door. 'You're not going to last long around here.' He slams the door at her departing back.

'I suppose having less of them around takes pressure off our food stocks,' says Muhammed. 'Makes it easier for us to move around as well. It's just … these girls are good for the men's morale.'

'You mean some of them sign up for the women more than Jihad.'

'Yes, judging by the questions new recruits ask me, but in general, it's good for everyone's morale. Isn't it?'

'I don't think it helped Rashidi and Gambo's morale much. In future, send the ones who ask these questions to me.'

'It's not just that, the well-educated girls, you know how the Arabs like them. They bring in good money.'

'Well-educated? Well-educated in what?'

'I mean the … the ones who speak cleverly.'

'We can't move them on at the moment though, can we? And it's time-consuming splitting them up and moving them when Yakubu's infidels and the NAF are out looking for us. Better to off-load now in exchange for the phone and Yakubu's fat ass. We can do a re-stock later.'

'But ... we're giving up so many and getting none of our people in return, you don't think people might see it as a sign of ... weakness?'

Abdullahi grabs the bigger man by the throat, 'No, I don't! And I'm getting fed up with these fucking insubordinate questions and having to fucking explain myself to you. I'm dealing with a woman who says she can kill our enemy and who doesn't have the power to release our people, have you forgotten that?' He releases his grip and pushes Muhammed away. 'Do you not remember Surah Al-Ala ayat, seven? "Accept what Allah wills. He knows what is manifest and what is hidden. And We will make thy way smooth to a state of ease." Do you understand?'

'Yes,' Muhammed nods.

'Then have faith. These girls are expendable and replaceable. On the other hand, think how we will humiliate the President, the Governor, the so-called Security Forces, all of them, when our video is broadcast tomorrow. Imagine their faces when they see me, back again from the dead. Think what that does to whatever's left of their credibility. And imagine their confusion at seeing me release those bitches. A sign of weakness? No, a sign of strength. An expression of our power because they couldn't get them back and I chose to release them.' He smiles broadly and lifts up a machete. Muhammed looks nervous but Abdullahi is playing with him. He swishes it in the air a few times.

'When that bitch, guided by the hand of Allah, sends Yakubu to hell, his associates will be glad to see the back of him, and just when they start to forget about him, we'll start drip-feeding info from Ado's phone to the media and take pleasure in destroying them.'

'Ah …'

'Alhamdulillah! You've switched on the lights again. Not weakness; strategy on our part, humiliation on theirs. And all we have to do is — ?'

'Handover some bitches.'

'And our way is smoothed to a state of ease.' He throws the machete at a vertical support at the other end of the hut. Its blade drives deep into the wood and shudders. 'Now, select the girls, set up the venue, and don't forget the camera.'

Chapter 50

Jamilah skirts between the potholes and end-of-day flotsam scattered around the empty market. A few stragglers shuffle past, carrying square nylon bags full of cut-price fruit and veg, always on offer in the final hour of trading for those prepared to hang around and haggle. She heads towards the arch that the old people of the town still refer to as the entrance. There are fewer folk around than she remembers for this time of day. People are still wary following Abdullahi's murderous assault. She's not sure where exactly the explosion took place. Market people are resilient; any space created by the bomb would have been quickly filled and evidence of blood and bone washed away. She often wonders about that poor girl they strapped a belt to. She was younger than Aminah but not by much and she had a baby and a little girl with her too. When Jamilah was preparing for casualties to arrive that day, she could never have imagined that her sister would suffer the same fate as that poor girl and at the hands of the same people. Or that weeks later, she would be following in the girl's footsteps to meet the daughter of murderer-in-chief, Abdullahi.

Some election posters have survived but the candidates' faces are mostly torn off or covered by new posters. One of Yakubu's remains intact because someone had managed to paste it up high, out of reach. It's ironic that he should be staring down on the scene of this meeting where his killer-to-be plots with the daughter of his greatest enemy. Tomorrow she will see his face for real, hopefully for the first and last time. She approaches the arch. It's five o'clock. There's no one else waiting, apart from two beggars, legs swollen with Lymphatic Filariasis, propped against a nearby wall, a towel spread in front of them on which she sees a few coins. They're trying to make eye contact with her, but she's too far away for their routine to be effective. She pretends to look for something in her bag. The voice of a young woman sounds behind her.

'As-salaam-Alaikum.'

'Wa-Alaikum-Salaam', replies Jamilah, recognising the voice and turning to face a slightly built adolescent. Given her dismissive tone on the phone, Jamilah is surprised at how young she looks.

'You were expecting someone older.'

'Yes.' Smaller too, thinks Jamilah.

'Well, you don't look old enough to be the mother of a sixteen-year-old girl.'

'I'm not. They were going to exchange you for my sister, Aminah only your father blew her up.'

'This is Jihad. Those infidels weren't going to exchange me for anyone. They planned to kill my father and I don't think for a minute they would have spared me after that.' She sounds like an exasperated teenager explaining the obvious to a dumb parent. 'They were found out and paid the price and your sister was part of it. Blame him.' She glances up at Yakubu's poster.

'But she didn't deserve —'

'Just give me the phone. I haven't time for counselling.'

'Your father deserves to die, not least for sending an adolescent girl, a child, and a baby into this market, to be blown up along with a lot of other innocent people. How can you live with that?'

'They were Allah's to give, and Allah's to receive.'

'What?'

'Look, you don't understand and, I've no time to stand here and educate you. Give me the phone if you want those girls released.'

She sounds just like her father. Her small narrow face and thin lips are almost hidden by her hijab, but she's still a girl with a pimple on the corner of her nostril to prove it, yet her piercing eyes and sharp tongue project a mature, harder edge. Jamilah takes a brown envelope from her bag and hands it over. Farida takes the phone out and switches it on.

'Password?'

'It's on the envelope.'

Farida takes one look and shakes her head. 'That figures.' She scrolls through contacts and texts for a minute, then hands Jamilah a piece of paper with a number on it.

'Ring this.'

Jamilah rings the number using her own phone. A few seconds later, Ado's phone rings in Farida's hennaed hand.

'Turn it off.'

Jamilah complies.

'Little did that smug infidel realise that night when he was sitting beside me in his fancy car with his bag of money, that within an hour he'd be dead, and two weeks later I'd be standing here with his phone in my hand. You see who's winning this war, who has right on their side?'

'No, I don't. Neither your father nor him,' she looks up at the poster, 'have right on their side. But you have the phone. When will your father release the girls?'

'He keeps his word. Rare in our country, don't you think?' She dials a number on Ado's phone. 'He's curious about you.' Before Jamilah can respond, Farida raises her hand. 'Papa, it's me. As you can see, I have it … I will. By the way, she's the sister, not the mother. And the ways she's dressed, a nurse, never a doctor.'

Jamilah pulls Farida's arm, 'Ask him about the girls.'

Farida brushes Jamilah's hand away, 'Hold on papa. She wants to know … okay.' Farida hands the phone to Jamilah. 'Ask him yourself.'

But Abdullahi doesn't give her a chance.

'Look, Bitch, I gave you my word. Watch the TV tomorrow and get yourself a burner if you want to talk to me again. Hand me back to my daughter.'

Jamilah hands back the phone. Before Farida speaks to her father she looks at Jamilah as if she thinks she's dumb.

'Why are you still here?'

Jamilah stares angrily at this strip of a girl who feels she can dismiss her like a servant. Farida returns her stare with interest.

'Go! And don't think we won't check for bugs.' She shakes the phone.

Jamilah turns and walks back the way she came. Such insolence and stupidity. As if she'd jeopardise her life and put a bug in the phone. After a few paces, she stops and looks back. Farida walks towards a man sitting on a powerful motorbike. She hadn't seen him earlier, but he probably had his eye on them all the time. Farida grabs hold of the driver's shoulder and climbs on the back of the bike; no side-saddle for her. The bike roars as if welcoming her on board. She seems like some evil princess, a part of the darkness into which she's being transported. Another bike with two men on board emerges from the shadows and follows. Such a slip of a girl but her demeanour belies her appearance. She talks like her father, has inherited his self-belief and doesn't lack courage. It's not just teenage bluster, she was being held prisoner by Giwa, and that couldn't have been easy. Farida was supposed to die that night; instead, it was Ado and Giwa. And while de Witt, professional soldier and military mastermind, lies in a hospital bed recovering from his wounds, Farida, all five feet of her, moves around the country doing her father's business. No wonder she acts as if she's bulletproof. Maybe they are winning and, if Jamilah's plan for Yakubu succeeds, the elimination of their biggest threat will only add to the argument. But that's no reason for hesitation on her part. The lives of the girls she is going to liberate are more valuable than Yakubu's. Once she ends his life, she will find a way to end Abdullahi's. Impossible? A couple of days ago she could not have envisaged communicating with him, now she's just met his daughter. Tomorrow she will come face to face with Yakubu; that's another miracle.

Chapter 51

Traffic is in full flow which at this hour means "go-slow." Jamilah feels in need of peace and quiet to collect her thoughts. She'll go straight to the clinic, pick up something to eat en route and get there before Salim. She gives the auto-rickshaw driver directions to her favourite street vendor and pulls down the side flaps of the vehicle to help keep out the fumes. When she settles back she's surprised how the cacophony of horns, grinding gears, belching exhausts, and rattling engine parts, fail to derail her thoughts. It must be the adrenaline. The stop and start of the traffic is symbolic of her day. It started early, negotiating with terrorists, then progressed to propping up the wife of a Governor so she could join her in killing her husband, after which it moved to a rendezvous with the daughter of a terrorist and the handing over of a phone belonging to an assassinated Deputy Governor. All this, while she carried on with her job as if everything was normal. So much depends on her friend, Iman staying the course for one more night. It was a terrible thing to ask of her, but if the plan works out, she'll be in a much better place. She decides to text her, gets her phone out, then calls instead.

'Hi, Jamilah.'

'Hi, how are you?'

'Hanging in there, I suppose. Hopefully, I won't be hanging from the ceiling later.'

'I was thinking about you, how brave you are.'

'I don't know about that. It's something I have to do. Do it and get through it, right?'

'Right. How's your cheek?'

'I'll live.'

'And the Pig?'

Iman laughs. 'In a meeting, probably fed up and looking forward to his two favourite pastimes — overeating and abusing his wife.'

'I've got an idea!' says Jamilah, suddenly inspired. 'You oversee his meal preparation, right?'

'Amongst a hundred other things.'

'Why not put something in his dinner tonight to make him sick? Knock him out of his stride.'

'That's a great idea! Have you anything in mind?'

'Hmm, we have emetic medicine at the hospital but with all this traffic there's no way I could fetch it and get over to you in time. Wish I'd thought of it earlier. Wait, have you any food that's gone off?'

'Yes! I took some prawns from the freezer a few days ago and put them in the fridge but they smelt off today. I threw them out, not more than an hour or so ago.'

'Can you retrieve them?'

'Probably. He can have them. I won't clean them; in fact, I'll add some nasty things to them.'

'You can't poison him; they'll know it's you!'

'No, I meant bits of dirt and stuff. I'll undercook them, add extra sauce, and slip them on the table with the rest of his food. He won't blink. They'll be gone in a second.'

'Wait, I've a better idea,' says Jamilah, matching her friend's enthusiasm. 'Mustard seeds. They'll do the trick. Back in my village, if a child consumed poisonous berries, he'd be given mustard seed dissolved in water and be sick in a few minutes. For a pig-sized stomach it'll probably take twenty. Quicker than waiting for dead prawns to digest and easier for you to administer.'

'Great! You're a genius Jamilah!'

'You can put your hands on some?'

'Of course.'

'Right, grind a couple of teaspoons of seeds and mix them with a small glass of water. Pour the mixture into a large glass of his favourite fruit juice. There'll still be a mustard taste, but by the sound of him, he'll gulp it down first before he complains.'

'He likes mustard! He likes anything! Sounds perfect. Thanks, Jamilah, you're such a great friend.'

'I should be thanking you, Iman. Look, I'd better go and leave you to find your mustard!'

'Wait Jamilah, you were going to tell me about the plan and the girls. That's what I thought you were ringing about.'

'Yes, yes, sorry. It's very noisy here, I'm sure you can hear the traffic. I'll call you back in half an hour, okay?'

Iman agrees and they disconnect. Jamilah wonders if she should speak to Salim later and suggest he call Yakubu to make sure he's heeding Salim's advice — just add some insurance. But Salim would want to know why, especially as she's already reported that Yakubu was keeping his distance and Iman was doing well. Best not arouse Salim's curiosity or draw his attention to the new bond between her and Iman. He mustn't be linked to anything they're going to do. She'll remind him she's making the house call on Iman tomorrow night and, if for some reason he wants her at the clinic, she'll invent a domestic emergency and go to see Iman anyway. She doesn't lie to Salim normally, but she will if she has to.this. The rickshaw pulls up at the roadside and she leaps out to get her street food. A tall muscular youth in a baseball hat, fashionably torn jeans and unfashionably torn Barcelona shirt, ambles over to display his range of mobile phone top-up cards and protective covers. He doesn't look like a local. She looks him in the eye and tells him she wants a cheap phone and pre-registered pay-as-you-go sim. He hesitates and gives her a once-over look.

'It's for my boyfriend,' she says, with a smile that hints her make-believe boyfriend might be married.

The boy smiles back, more excited it seems by an encounter with a loose woman than the prospect of a sale. He tells her that because she's so beautiful, he'll make her a very special price. She haggles but only a little so as to bring his tedious ogling to a swift end. Price agreed, he tells her to wait a minute and ducks around the back of the food stall.

She orders *Dambu Nama*, pays up, gets back in the rickshaw, and pulls back one of the side flaps to let the smell of her food out. Carefully lifting back the polystyrene lid, she steals a shred of hot beef drenched in spicy suya sauce and pops it in her mouth. There's no time to relish it as the youth returns and hands her a phone, a lecherous half-smile on his face. It's switched on and so, it seems, is he. He tells her the password while his eyes continue to check her out. If she didn't need his services, she would soon tell him where to get off; instead, she taps in four zeros and is rewarded with a dial tone. She glances at the driver.

'Is there something you need?' The driver turns back to face the front.

She dials her own number to capture the new one on her phone, adds two top-up cards to the bill and hands the youth the money. He smiles his stupid grin again. Can he really think she would find this alluring? She tells the driver to go. The engine gasps for air and splutters into life. She settles back in her seat, but the youth stays put and asks her name. She ignores him. The vehicle moves off, the youth breaks into a trot to keep pace, holding on to the side rail.

He tells her his name and that he's added his number to her phone.

'Call me … I love tall women, real women like you … You know men from Plateau State are the best lovers, right? What's your name?'

She continues to ignore him and soon he has to let go. He stops running and his voice fades. She glances back and he waggles his thumb and little finger by the side of his face and mouths, 'Call me!' She turns around and sets her food down on the seat. How can young men like that think such approaches work on women? Maybe it works at the level it's supposed to — young women as stupid as him. Otherwise, he'd have to change his approach in the face of repeated rejection. Huh, either that or become a rapist, or a terrorist, or both. She blocks his number and enters Abdullahi's number as the sole contact on this, her new burner phone. She sends him a text:

'My new number. Aminah.'

Chapter 52

It's 9 pm. Jamilah is already in bed. She hates being alone in a silent apartment but it's easier to endure in her bedroom, where she's always been alone. The photo she'd drawn on for strength at the start of the day, lies beside her on the bed. Tomorrow will be another big turning point in her life. The plan is clear in her mind and Iman is on board, but she continues to think of things that could go wrong and what she might do to put them right. That's what de Witt would do, though a lot of use it was to him in the end. Iman is great. She came up with embellishments to the plan that Jamilah would never have imagined. She only hopes her friend will survive Yakubu's clutches tonight. She places the photograph back on the bedside cabinet and is about to turn off the light when her phone rings. Her heart races but Iman's breezy tone allays her concerns.

'Hi sister!' she says, 'it worked! I can't wait to tell you.'

'Chapter and verse,' says Jamilah, relieved and infected with Iman's zest.

'I added extra salt to the Pig's food to make him thirsty, as well as a few extra chillies to distract his taste buds.'

'Wow. That was clever. Are you sure the chef didn't see you?'

'Chef's my friend. He knows I like to cook and he's enough on his plate getting the Pig's dinner on the table without worrying about what I'm doing on the sidelines! But, don't worry, for this task, I waited until he was particularly busy doing other things'

'And …?'

'Well, the Pig was horny as hell. Wouldn't be surprised if he'd popped some of those blue pills before he came to dinner. Kept trying to grope me every time I put a dish anywhere near him. It's like having a slobbering bear trying to grab your ass with his paw.'

'I'd dump the food all over him.'

'Ha, I expect you would! Anyway, halfway through the main course, I bring the glass with the juice and mustard seed and set it in front of him. I manage to withdraw quickly so he can't get near me and go hover outside the door, as usual, only this time I'm on more tenterhooks than I've ever been in my life! There was no immediate reaction, so I began to wonder if he'd even drunk it. Finally, I get my summons. He demanded to know who was trying to poison him. He complained about feeling nauseous and thirsty, but I fussed over him. I told him it was indigestion brought on by the spiciness of the dish and hadn't I been telling him for ages to eat more slowly?'

'Clever,' says Jamilah, closing her eyes, aware that in springing the idea on Iman she'd only thought about making him sick, not whom he'd seek to blame or what he might do about it. She has to do better.

'I'm used to him,' says Iman unphased, 'he was in real discomfort and sweating more than usual, so for once, he was in no mood to argue. It was easy to persuade him to go upstairs and rest for an hour. Especially when I whispered that I wanted my big man to be the lion he'd promised to be for me, but even a lion had to rest now and then to regain his strength.'

Jamilah marvels at her friend's resourcefulness. 'What did he say?'

'Nothing. He got up, snatched his cane out of my hand and as I tried to help him towards the staircase, he pushed me away. He grabbed the banister and, swearing under his breath, hauled himself up the staircase. He was doing better than I expected until he reached the landing and ...'

'What? Tell me!'

'He made straight for the bathroom and was so sick! I'm telling you Jamilah; it was like an avalanche!'

They both laugh.

'And you'll never guess ...' Iman pauses either to calm herself or increase the suspense.

'What? Tell me.'

'His sunglasses shot off and fell into the toilet. He stared at them for a moment then was sick all over them!'

They howl with laughter.

'Shh! He'll hear you!'

'No, he won't, he's in dreamland.'

'Are you sure?'

'I went downstairs and got two security men to come and lift him up. "He's been so busy at work", Iman puts on the helpless girly voice she spoke to the men with, "he was a little shaky on his feet earlier, but he said he was just tired". I fluttered my eyelids a few times, and told them, full of concern, good little wifey that I am, "Poor man, he just needs a good night's sleep". They took in my every word and helped me get him out of his clothes. I wiped him down and we got him into bed. He was totally spent but not in the way he thought he would be! I summoned a maid to clean up the mess. Poor thing, she was almost sick herself a few times. In no time he was snoring. I assured the guards I'd be keeping an eye on him and off they went. He's still snoring.'

'I'm so glad you're safe, Iman!'

'Alhamdulillah!'

'I'm proud of you.'

'It was your idea, Jamilah. Sleep well, tomorrow we'll take care of that pig for good.'

'Inch 'Allah.'

Chapter 53

Jamilah wakes a few minutes before the alarm. Iman had called on her to sleep well and that's exactly what she's done! Iman's confidence must be rubbing off on her. To think at first it was she who had to convince Iman about the plan. As her feet touch the rug, Jamilah picks up the photograph and stares at her siblings before kissing their image. They know what's at stake. Tonight is the first step in restoring her family's honour. She makes her way to the bathroom and sighs at the sight of her acne which has flared up again. She's tried everything, it just has a life of its own. The phone rings and she heads back to the bedroom to pick it up. Thankfully Iman's lost none of her enthusiasm and it seems Jamilah isn't the only one to have slept well. Apparently, Yakubu hadn't stirred until the call to prayer.

'I peeped in and saw the big lump shuffling towards the shower', she says. 'He was still sluggish when he came out. Hardly said a thing when I came in to help him into his clothes. Can you imagine? He's Governor of Kano State and I have to get him dressed in the mornings, like a little boy! Anyway, I told him I'd talk to the chef about the spices, but it was up to him to stop rushing his food. He made a few grunts. I said that instead of focusing on what had happened last night, he should look forward to what's in store for him tonight, especially, I said — whispering in seductively in his ear — especially, as I had arranged a very special surprise for him! One that all men want but few ever get, I told him. Ha, that got his juices flowing. Listen, I have to go Jam, just wanted to let you know everything's good at this end!'

'Thanks, Iman. You're amazing.'

'I am', she laughs. 'We both are! See you later!'

Jamilah tosses her phone on the bed. Wow, she's lucky to have Iman as her friend and ... accomplice, but she's overdue some luck. If Iman can steel herself, so can she. This is the day she becomes a killer. Yakubu and Abdullahi have forced her to shift her moral compass but given the chance to avenge her family, free seventy-five innocent girls and give Iman a better life, wouldn't it be wrong not to take it? Her mind and conscience are clear.

Chapter 54

Jamilah embraces her routine with more intensity than she would normally deploy. She has to keep active, but there is a limit to the number of times she can walk around the wards supervising staff, speaking to patients, and checking on hygiene, before she looks obsessive or in truth, more obsessive than usual. The task that she will have to perform later that evening is not the only thing preying on her mind. The news channel is left permanently on in the wards but is refusing to give her the reassurance she craves. Is Abdullahi playing her for a fool? Is she going to give up the phone and kill Yakubu without seeing a single girl freed? The TVs and their remotes rest on solid shelves screwed into the wall, protected by wraparound metal rails that are un-locked each morning.

It feels like Abdullahi has remote control over her. He's got the phone and he can decide when to release the first cohort of girls, presuming he will release them. She hasn't told him this is the night she plans to kill Yakubu, or that she can't postpone it. He agreed to release the first twenty-five immediately and he's had the phone since yesterday. Surely he knows the sooner he lets these girls go, the sooner she will move to complete part two. Maybe she should call him, find out what's happening, let him know it's tonight? No, she'll appear flustered, panicky even, and he'll be even more exasperated given the way he exploded last time she reminded him of his side of the bargain. She has to take him at his word. Of course it would have been preferable to have waited until she saw the first group released but there was Iman's welfare to consider. She will have to proceed with the plan tonight whether he releases the girls first or not. She has to accept it and stay focused, otherwise she could put the lives of Iman and herself in danger.

Following a last check for holes in the protective bed nets, it's time for her to move out of the wards entirely. She heads to reception where there's a TV to distract the visitors. A colleague stops to ask a question and finally, over her shoulder, Jamilah sees what she's been longing for. She motions to her colleague to wait and asks the receptionist to turn up the volume. She moves closer to the TV, drawn by a red ticker headline that runs across the bottom of the screen which reads: "Exclusive: Abdullahi alive. Boko Haram free 25 girls." In the foreground of the picture, the earth is parched and dusty and a Boko Haram leader stands, hands on hips, addressing the camera. Behind him are two rows of girls, sitting on the ground. It's her twenty-five! The poor things look like condemned prisoners; their plain black hijabs are like prison clothes. They stare at the ground, their expressions sullen and empty as if life has been drained out of them. They have lost their individuality. They've been transformed into a commodity, like sacks waiting to be lifted onto trucks and shipped to market. But they are free! She is exhilarated. This is an achievement, the first positive thing that has happened since Aminah was taken and it's all because Jamilah decided to act.

People in reception lean forward to see if they recognize any of the girls. Jamilah's attention has shifted elsewhere on the screen. Three fighters stand behind the girls, hands resting on sub-machine guns that are strapped diagonally across their chests, barrels pointing to the ground. They too are dressed in black, but their faces and heads are covered, leaving a horizontal space for eyes that stare back dispassionately at the camera. In the spaces between these men, attached to staves pushed into the ground are two square banners. One displays Arabic writing scrawled in white on a black background; on the other, the writing is scrawled in black within solid white circles. The TV reporter translates the writing as, "People Committed to the Prophet's Teachings for Propagation and Jihad." Three heavily armed Hilux trucks, sand-coloured and camouflaged, look down ominously on the scene, the drooping branches of a few tamarind trees are visible above their powerful guns. The reporter states that these images have become familiar to the general population, but it makes them no less distressing and only serves to increase the people's frustration at their government's inability to deal with this insurrection. Yet, he says, the story unfolding here is different. It is not Boko Haram gloating about their latest atrocity. The girls on display are being set free! To underline this, the ribbon running along the bottom of the screen has a new headline: "Following a tip-off, 25 girls picked up unharmed by security forces, at 10:30 hours this morning on the main road between Maiduguri and Baga."

Pride swells inside Jamilah, dampened by sadness that her sister could not have been one of those girls, especially when she recognises one of Aminah's classmates amongst them. Abbiah is her name. Aminah brought her home once. Still, she can breathe easier now. Abdullahi has kept his word and she can continue her plan with renewed self-belief. Without her plan, those girls and their families would still be suffering.

There is a closeup of the man in the foreground who continues to do a lot of talking and finger wagging. The reporter says the man purports to be the infamous terrorist, Abdullahi. Jamilah is transfixed by him. She recalls Lami's description of him. Unlike the other men, his face is uncovered, and he is dressed differently. He wears a camouflage jacket and trousers with three green pouches across his chest. On his feet are sand-coloured military boots while the incongruous pompom of a grey beanie bounces around his skull whenever he shakes his head or makes exaggerated gestures. The lack of face covering is significant, says the reporter, for Abdullahi has never shown his face on camera before. This could be a sign of growing confidence. Is he taunting the security forces to come and get him? In one hand he holds an open notebook on which handwriting is visible but indiscernible; in the other, a miswak, which he uses to jab at the camera to underline points of emphasis. While trying to take information from what he is saying, the channel is clearly wary of offering Abdullahi too much of a platform so mutes his pontificating especially when it sounds like it is veering into a diatribe against the elite, but they are not always quick enough and when his voice is audible, Jamilah hears snippets of Arabic, Hausa, another local language, and English. Most importantly, his voice is instantly recognisable from the phone, and he has kept his word.

Jamilah's colleague speaks in her ear. Jamilah listens but her attention remains on the screen. She catches a clip of Yakubu announcing Abdullahi's death in an air raid a few days earlier. She turns quickly to her colleague who leaves with the decision she needed. The camera pans back to Abdullahi, who is directing his words at the President. Abdullahi's voice fades out as an interpreter takes over:

'Go take a look at that village by Lake Chad. The village you said was our camp. The one you blew up, killing all those innocents.' He nods his head in exaggerated fashion. 'The one where we were supposed to have been obliterated by your air force.' He holds up the cover of a local newspaper, nodding all the while, and the camera focuses on the headline which reads: "Wiped-out!" and then on the smaller print below: "Major setback for Boko Haram. Key commander, Abdullahi and unit killed in airstrike."

'Go ask your brave pilots who gave them their directions. Those courageous men of the NAF whom you're going to give medals to for dropping bombs on innocent villagers. You cannot kill me. Only Allah decides when it is my time, and I will go willingly when he calls. Alhamdulillah!'

His speech is cut but not before he is able to describe the President and his Government as "cow worshippers." The report offers its viewers a sincere apology on behalf of the channel. Even Jamilah is surprised at how much footage is being shown, but this is a big story being broadcast by a newer, more independent channel that has received a video apparently denied to more established and less independent channels, and it seems determined to make the most of it.

Another nurse appears at Jamilah's side and hands her a patient release form to sign. 'I can't believe it', says the nurse, 'why does the Government keep feeding us misinformation? Why can't our security forces hunt these people down?'

Jamilah nods her head empathetically, and as she scans through the form wonders how it is that everything seems to work in Abdullahi's favour. She takes the pen from her colleague and signs the form. Her eyes return to the screen. Abdullahi is talking again, his voice replaced by that of the interpreter:

'... These girls should never have been in school. We have liberated them from the infidels who teach them to disrespect Allah the Merciful, and the word of the Prophet, Peace be upon him. Their heads are filled with the false teachings of the west. Western education is a deceit, an attack on our religion, promoted by corrupt politicians for their own gains and those of their friends in the West. These so-called schools should be closed down and stay closed. If you re-open them don't be surprised when we pay them a visit. We show these girls the true path. Some listen, some don't, for the Satan is deeply entrenched. We discipline them as necessary and put them back on track. Some we sell. But these,' he swings back an outstretched arm towards his captives, 'these we have cured, and we return them to their families. They have sworn never to return to school and their families will respect that.'

He juts out his chin, the corners of his mouth descend, and he nods affirmatively as if to signal he has just made a statesman-like announcement. The camera pans across the girls, who remain impassive.

'Look at their faces. They are sad. They don't want to leave us ... but they will obey. Allah, the Merciful has decided.' His head nods in confirmation, as if imparting wisdom to a rapt audience.

Around her, staff and visitors watch the screen with a mix of horror and schadenfreude. Jamilah reflects that these young women owe their freedom to her and her sister, but none of them, or their families, or all the people watching across the country, will ever know.

Chapter 55

Governor Yakubu is very much looking forward to lunch. Having spewed his dinner down the toilet the previous night, there was an empty stomach to fill at breakfast, but it had told him it was too soon for a refill. However, the morning had gone well, and his appetite is back, along with his mojo. A special surprise, she'd said. He's got a good idea what that is, but he isn't going to spoil the mystery by insisting she tells him. He's glad he put his foot down and brought her back in line. Give them an inch … He hasn't felt so buoyant in months. The offshore account has been located and the transfer made. He's the proud owner of a five-bedroom apartment overlooking Palm Jumeirah. To add the word 'luxurious' would indicate a naivety about real estate in Dubai. He will run the account down further when he signs the interior design contract. "Keep converting cash to property" was Ado's mantra and he was right. Cash on account attracts attention and if it's in your name it can only belong to you. He regrets Ado isn't around to witness this latest indicator of success in a career that has seen him transition from infantryman to decorated military commander, to respected political figure to elder statesman and successful businessman.

'A good businessman takes advantage of opportunities and protects his interests.' It's common sense, but he shares it with Danjuma anyway. The boy's still a long way off, probably thought he was being hired as some kind of political adviser — what a joke! Look at him sitting there in his thick-framed glasses. The reflection of his iPad makes his lenses look like two video screens. What advice could this boy offer a man of his experience, especially when he can't even look him in the eye? That outsize mobile is never out of his hand, probably a dick substitute. As for that hint of a moustache, why bother? Ah well, he feels generous this morning and, sitting behind his grand desk underneath the framed photograph of his old comrade the President, he feels all-powerful too. He'll persevere with the boy, for now.

'Of course, you must have an eye for an opportunity', he says to Danjuma's head, 'and transforming this tyre factory site is exactly that. Naturally, it passed my predecessor by and the people of Kano need something to replace the memory of that shameful night. We will do that for them. A new enterprise to attract investors, create jobs, build homes, and create new memories. With my contacts, particularly in construction, I can get things moving and steer the ship. I'm the perfect man to lead this project and this is a perfect opening for you, young man, to observe how real government works.'

'Yes, Sir, thank you, Sir.'

'Now that we have these terrorists on the run, it's time to move ahead on other fronts. When you create wealth you create jobs, and when you create jobs you create more wealth. And with that you create gratitude. Remember that Danjuma.'

'I will, Sir.'

'Jobs will keep those young hooligans off the streets. Stop them drifting into terrorism and banditry. We can call this project an anti-terrorist initiative. Fix a meeting tomorrow morning with the State Ministers of Commerce and Industry, Land and Physical Planning, Works and Transport, Local Government, and we'd better include Planning and Budget.'

'You sacked him, Sir.' Danjuma peeps through the gap between his glasses and eyebrows. 'Last week, Sir.'

'Clueless Motherfucker.'

Danjuma, looks up, alarmed.

'Not you!' says the Governor, 'Yesterday's man. What's his name? Doesn't matter. Prioritising audit over action, focusing on value for money, as if that's everything. Couldn't see the big picture. The kind of bureaucrat who's been holding this State back for years. We need new blood, forward thinking, fast acting, people.'

'Yes, Sir.'

'What are we doing about finding a new one?'

'Hmm, nothing at the moment, Sir. You said you would think about it.'

'That's right, but I've had a lot on my mind. Add it to this afternoon's agenda. Invite his Deputy or whoever is filling in. It'll be a chance to find out if he's any good.'

'It's a woman, Sir.'

'What? In the name of Allah, we can't have a woman in charge of planning and budget. How did that happen? Look, I need eyes and ears, I can't be everywhere. She'll propose all sorts of crap — increased spending on schools and health, getting more students into university, paying lecturers on time. Where is she going to get the money for that? Oh yes, she'll be great at spending but what we need is investment in wealth creation. Some people live in a dreamworld. We need young men out there working, not lying around on their asses, only getting up for a spot of thieving or to impregnate their stupid girlfriends. Wake up Danjuma, keep me informed!'

'I will, Sir. Shall I schedule the meeting for nine o'clock.'

'Yes. Get someone to look into grant opportunities from the World Bank, what's the name of that fund?'

'The Emerging Africa Infrastructure Fund.'

'Right', says the Governor, licking his lips, 'we'll need — '

'We need to turn the TV on, Sir.' Haruna bursts in, looking anxiously around for the remote. It's on his desk. As Haruna comes over to pick it up, the Governor grabs it and switches it on.

'Channel 105,' says Haruna. The Governor thinks Haruna needs to watch his tongue as that sounded surprisingly like the second order he's issued in the last few seconds. Such thoughts are forgotten as the Governor reads the rubric running relentlessly along the bottom of the screen. He hears a reporter say that the man calling himself Abdullahi has a special message for His Excellency, the Governor of Kano State. He sees a man waving a miswak, to emphasise insults directed at him and which the reporter says are being muted because of their obscene nature.

'Motherfucker!' says the Governor.

The man's body language becomes less animated, and the voice of an interpreter interjects: 'Yakubu, you have said many times, we who fight Jihad in Allah's name, show no mercy, but you are wrong again. The release of these girls is an act of mercy. As for you, you ...' The man's voice fades as a torrent of insults flow the Governor's way, reinforced by gesticulations and a face filled with contempt.

'Who is that piece of shit? Why are they broadcasting these lies? Someone will pay for this.'

'He claims to be Abdullahi', says Haruna, backing away from the Governor's desk, as if he wants to provide the Governor with a better sight of the screen.

'What!'

The CP shrinks back a little more. The Governor's attention is back on the screen, listening to the outpourings from the man claiming to be Abdullahi, voiced by an interpreter.

'You said you would be ready to exchange our fighters and our families for the girls we have liberated, but you are a proven hypocrite and a liar.'

The Governor pulls himself up from his seat. 'Who the hell allows these lies and insults to be broadcast.

Danjuma, get me the head of this channel immediately. I want this off the air, now!'

'Our fighters will be martyrs before surrendering to infidels,' continues the interpreter, 'the only comrades you capture are those injured or taken by chance. You torture and execute them like you did our dear leader, Sheikh Muhammed Yousuf. Your forces fill up your cells with vagabonds and strays and call them Boko Haram to make it look like they are effective. What about the wives and daughters of Jihadists whom you have kidnapped and who lie starving in your barracks and prisons? We agreed an exchange with you, you responded with treachery. So we executed your CP, and your Deputy Governor then slaughtered your security forces, including your white mercenaries. Shame on you for bringing these infidels to our land.'

The Governor glares at Haruna, his clenched fists press down hard on his desk. 'You assured me he was dead! You assured me!' He bangs the desk causing his computer monitor to jolt. Danjuma has retreated to a corner of the room and is speaking into his phone, which somehow rings while he is talking. As Haruna searches for a response, the TV comes to his rescue again, regaining the Governor's attention.

'Today, I demonstrate the mercy of Allah. This is your opportunity, infidel. We will leave these girls by the roadside for you to pick up. I choose to release them. Will you release twenty-five of our women and children? The world is watching. Allah is watching. I leave you with this message, from Sūrat Ibrāhīm, 14:42, listen well: "Never think that Allah is unaware of what the wrongdoers do. He only delays them for a Day when eyes will stare in horror." You have been warned.'

The men behind Abdullahi join their leader in chants of, 'Allahu Akbar!' and the reporter reappears on screen to say it is the end of the video and his report, but he will return on the hour with an update and, hopefully, reaction from the Government and military.

Phones ring on the Governor's desk, in his pocket and in the pockets of Danjuma and Haruna.

'Excellency, there's no proof it's him', says Haruna. 'It's just propaganda. You saw the photographs. They were wiped out.'

'Were they? Were they? Did anyone actually identify his body? Is there a photograph of a dead Abdullahi, for me to look at?'

'... No, Excellency but the Wing Commander —'

'All the Wing Commander did was off-load his fucking rockets. All he identified was explosions.' He slumps back in his seat. Each time he thinks he is rid of Abdullahi he comes back like a bad smell and this time he berates him in front of the whole nation.

'But, Excellency, it could still be —'

'Get out of my fucking sight! Get in touch with those fools who insisted they had killed this piece of shit. Put them in front of the cameras this time, not me. Then you can start writing your letter of resignation.' Haruna slinks out.

'Danjuma, get working on a Press Statement, liaise with the President's Office. For now, it's "No comment." I'm ringing His Excellency to agree on our response. I can tell you now, we won't be releasing anyone in any fucking exchange. He doesn't dictate to us. We need to lay the blame for this fiasco at the feet of the people who caused it. I can only relay information on air raids on the basis of what I'm told by the people in charge of air raids. I should be able to trust in what the NAF and our security forces tell me.

They will face the consequences, not me. Heads will roll. We have set an example here with Haruna. Make sure he includes an apology for feeding me misleading information in his resignation letter.'

Danjuma looks relieved to have a reason to get out of the room. He opens the door to find the Governor's wife waiting to come in. She gives him a beguiling smile. He looks paralysed.

'Danjuma, close your mouth and stop ogling what doesn't belong to you. She's out of your league. If you were half a man I could get upset. And I want the head of that TV channel in my office yesterday. Do you understand?'

Danjuma backs out through the door, the nodding of his head increasingly vigorous with each backward step. Before ringing the President, the Governor reaches in his drawer for his Beta-Blockers. Anger is giving way to despondency. Abdullahi has just rammed another thorn into his side. His new jewel in Dubai has lost its sparkle, even his appetite has subsided. There is a familiar rap at the door. His wife is still standing there. What the fuck does she want? Is she going to say she has a fucking headache? Is that the next fucking thing?

'Well?'

'Sir, are you ready for lunch?' she steps inside, pushing the door back with her rear.

'I'll let you know ...'

Her arm stretches above her shoulder, her long fingers clasp the edge of the door. She shoots him a seductive smile which unexpectedly disarms him. Behind his dark glasses, his eyes narrow taking in every line of her angular body. No talk of headaches, at least that's something. Is he imagining it, or is that red and purple dress tighter than usual? The shoulders are padded wide, the cloth stretches over her breasts, inwards to her waist, then out over her hips, before shooting down across her thighs to form another triangle from her knees to the floor. Unlike Danjuma, she doesn't flinch from his gaze; she accepts it full on, turning sideways to let him feast on her profile, lifting her head back, pushing out her chest and letting the dress take the strain. She's taunting him, regaining power and enjoying his paralysis. Her strong buttocks look as if they could rip the seams of the dress apart at any moment. Desire floods through him, mixing uneasily with the frustration he has just endured. She stands facing him, hands on hips. Where does she get this confidence from? For a second he imagines if he stares hard enough, the dress will burst into flames and leave her naked and unscathed.

'You like this dress, don't you, Sir?'

They both know the answer. He doesn't give a damn about the dress, only what it accentuates. He goes to speak but his throat is dry.

'I'll tell them to bring lunch.' She leaves without a backward glance or being told, knowing she's scored some kind of victory. He can't disagree but tonight he will use that body to assuage his lust and vent his frustration. She will do whatever he says, whatever it takes, and be grateful. He will show her who is really in control.

Chapter 56

Jamilah makes her way back to the wards. Listening to Aminah's plea for help that terrible night was like slipping into an angry river, one that's been dragging her downstream ever since. After listening to Abdullahi's rant, she feels she's found a log to cling to and maybe she might make it to dry land and, who knows, start to rebuild her life. She passes Salim in the corridor and gives him a warm smile. He responds with a nod, professional as always. She likes that. They are both heading to the bedside of someone who needs their expertise; what would he think if he knew to whose bedside she would be heading tonight? She feels a light tug on her arm and turns round. It's him.

'You saw the TV?'

She nods.

'I'm sorry Aminah couldn't have been one of those girls.'

'I know, but at least some families will be happy.'

'Yes.' He squeezes her arm. 'I have to go', he looks as if he might say more but he tightens his lips and is gone.

He's always rushing somewhere in the hospital. He's such a good person. It was kind of him to retrace his steps and express his concern. He's the only one who would think of doing that. She has a twinge of guilt, knowing that she is using an appointment with one of his patients for her own deadly purposes. She would love to confide in him. He, of all people, would understand her motives, but even though he's just seen the first release of girls, it wouldn't deter him from trying to stop her. He'd tell her she would be risking her life and career. He'd want to protect her. But she's already chosen her allies; confiding in Salim would make him one too, unless he reported her to the authorities, and he'd never do that. On impulse, she sends Abdullahi a text:

'U kept ur word. Listen to the news tonight and keep it again. Aminah'

She's not expecting a response; terrorists don't spend time exchanging texts like teenagers. When her phone rings five minutes later she panics. She doesn't want to speak to him, especially not here on the ward, and seeing how he looked and behaved on the video has spooked her. He's become a real person and one she's not ready to talk to yet. Why can't he just text back? But it's Witt's number on the screen! What can he want? She's already heading to her office and lets the phone go to voice mail. She lets herself in, sits with her back to the door and calls him back.

'Sorry, I was busy. How are you?'

'Better than the last time you saw me.' He sounds it. 'You can't keep an old dog down, right?'

'Or teach him new tricks.'

'I'll plead guilty to the first one.'

'All that expensive treatment must have paid off.'

'It has, I'm being discharged today.'

'Congratulations. So this is a good-bye call.'

'Not quite.'

'Meaning?'

'Unfinished business.'

'What might that be?' she asks, bemused that he still has designs on her.

'What else? … You'll have seen the TV. The return of the man they couldn't kill.'

'We all watched it. Twenty-five girls set free. As wonderful as it was unexpected.'

'There's always a reason for what he does. He hasn't turned into Abdullahi, the Merciful.'

'It sounded like he wanted to embarrass Yakubu. Whatever his motives, it's still something to celebrate. Imagine how the families are feeling. I know how I would have felt.'

'So, you've no idea why he's released these girls?' he says ignoring her barb. 'Or why now, without a guarantee of getting anything in return?'

'Apart from what I've just said, no. Why would I?'

'Because you texted him twelve minutes ago.'

'What are you talking about?' She curses at her stupidity. She forgot to use the burner phone.

'Ado's phone received a text as it was approaching Lake Chad. It came from your phone and you're at work. Somehow Ado's phone has made it to Lake Chad, and you just contacted its new owner.'

'I don't understand.' Jamilah tries to think, but her heart is sinking. She can't match the duplicity of these people. She pinches her stomach, both to punish herself and somehow prise out an explanation.

'It's simple. Not only did we renew the contract on Ado's phone, we programmed a tracking device into it. A sophisticated and well-concealed one. We can even track it when it's switched off.'

'What?'

'The stakes were high; our time here was at an end. We gambled if you took the phone, you'd be able to do more with it than we could. We're a professional organization but if there is anything we can do to avenge the death of our comrades or even just harm the perpetrators, we will do it. You exceeded our expectations.'

'But they were going to check it for bugs.'

'I'm sure they did. But these are bush boys. Did they think we were going to download some cheap app you could download off the internet for fifty rand? We've access to software they can only dream about.'

'You used me. I could have been killed.'

'That wasn't our calculation. And we were right. You're still alive and as of today, so are twenty-five girls previously held captive by Abdullahi.'

There's nothing she can say. She's out of her depth. He's another one operating her by remote control.

'The phone went back to Kano with you and stayed at your place for a couple of days. Then you took it to work with you before making a trip to the market where it was used to ring a number which we know belongs to Abdullahi. After that, it went east at high speed. This morning it travelled to the site where those girls were released. We know it's him who has it, Jamilah, or should I call you Aminah?'

'You and your little games, you're just like the rest of them.'

'Look man. We didn't keep you in the loop, I understand that, and I apologise, but don't compare me to those murderers. We're on the same side for God's sake. If I'd told you the phone had been bugged you'd have been too afraid to even consider contacting him. It was a long shot but it's paid off. This time we can take him out, and I wanted you to be aware of your role in making it happen.'

'How will you do that?'

'Yakubu cut us loose. We have a contract with the Chadian Government now. We fly to N'Djamena this evening. Chad wants Abdullahi dead as much as Nigeria, Cameroon, Niger and anyone else in the region he has been picking fights. They've sufficient air power to make a lethal strike and we'll be there to ensure that's what happens.'

'But you can't do that before ...'

'Before, what?'

'He's had a chance to spill the beans on Yakubu and his cronies. Can't you see how important that is? You told me yourself it was Yakubu's money that helped Abdullahi carry out his atrocities. There's too much blood on Yakubu's hands, you can't let him get away with it.'

'The lesser of two evils. Look, your country and mine are full of Yakubus. Abdullahi is something else, a brutal killing machine. Thanks to you, we have the chance to take him out.'

'Can't you give him a day or two to use the information? Surely you can wait forty-eight hours, after all this time.'

'We can't take the risk. He might discard the phone, lose it, damage it or the tracking might malfunction. Why are you so worried about the reputations of politicians? Everyone knows what they're like. Giwa's men killed your brother; he's dead now. Yakubu lost him and Ado. This his man killed your sister. He killed my men. He's killed hundreds of people. Do you want him to go free and carry on killing? This is your chance for revenge. I thought you'd be pleased, grateful even, to know you've played a such a part. I know if he'd tortured my sister —'

'What do you mean, "tortured"?'

'When they uncovered Aminah's face, you could see slash marks … Didn't you ID the body?'

'No, Salim did. He didn't say.'

'I'm sorry I mentioned it, but now you know the kind of man we're dealing with. Look man, I have to go. There's no reason to delay. We'll strike when we're ready. If it happens before he's spilled the beans, so be it, fate will take its course.'

She has nothing more to say to him.

'Look Jamilah, I'm sorry for misleading you but when the dust settles and Abdullahi's gone, you'll feel differently. I'll send you a text when it's done.'

She ends the call.

Chapter 57

Jamilah weeps for her sister. Along she had tried not to imagine Aminah's suffering at the hands of Abdullahi and his men. She had known from reports in the media, how they had treated other girls and that it would be unlikely they would leave her beautiful sister alone. She had pushed away these thoughts, telling herself whatever they did to Aminah, it would not be the end of the world; hadn't she herself survived Giwa's assault when she was the same age? The two of them could work through it together. But to torture her with a knife? What level of evil is that? To cut the skin of an adolescent girl with the face of an angel, that hurts so much. And she was truer to her faith than they could ever be, despite all their proclamations. If Jamilah had needed further justification to achieve her ambitions for these men, she has it now. She stops crying. It no longer feels like these men are working her by remote control but that they are all being manipulated by a higher force directing a drama in which none of them can be sure what the other will do next. She doesn't know where it comes from, but she has a sense that things are moving in her favour. Is it fate or luck or the power of good? Iman had turned up at her door, so too had de Witt, and they have provided her with opportunities for redemption. That was more than good fortune.

If she implements her plan successfully and the Chadians do the same for de Witt, he's probably right, she will be glad of his duplicity. By tomorrow she will have achieved her goals. Wait, not all her goals. She has a deal with Abdullahi to release fifty more girls. Girls who could suffer the same fate as Aminah. Should she tell de Witt the real reason for seeking a delay? She'd have to tell him about her plan for Yakubu too. That mightn't matter, he can keep those kinds of secrets, but he'd probably try to stop her, not out of loyalty to Yakubu, but because he'll say it's too dangerous, not the sort of work for a nurse — he'd say nurse, but mean woman — she'll only get herself killed. If he were to agree to a delay, he'd feel obliged to share the reason with his precious men. That would mean another half a dozen people knowing about her and Iman and she can't trust any of them. They failed to rescue Aminah and were all complicit in the deceit regarding Ado's phone. What's more, if she and Iman fail to kill Abdullahi tonight, she'd have shared their secret for nothing. Well, she's not prepared to take that risk. Besides, he won't do it. He'd have to invent a reason for the Chadians and if Abdullahi got away, de Witt and his company's reputation would be in the firing line. He can't risk another failed mission, while the Chadians won't pass up an opportunity to demonstrate how their air force is more capable than the NAF. She stares at the floor. She can't remember having to think so hard. She's probably missing something … In the perfect scenario: they kill Yakubu tonight; fifty precious girls are released tomorrow; and then, the Chadian Air Force takes out Abdullahi.

She stands up as her mind races down more negative paths. What if the strike isn't successful and Abdullahi gets away? De Witt sounds confident, but he was confident about getting Aminah back. Nigerian pilots are surely as experienced as any in Chad and yet they got it wrong. Abdullahi would wonder how they'd tracked him down. His attention would turn to the phone, and she would become his enemy. Every day she'd be living in fear; and de Witt's right, he wouldn't be Abdullahi the merciful when he found her. Her eyes catch the family photo on her desk. She's the only one left. How long before they take her too? She sits down. Maybe she must leave things to fate, as de Witt said, or to Allah's will, as Abdullahi would say. Fate hasn't been kind to her in the past. She touches the family image with the tips of her fingers. How can she abandon those girls? If she were still alive Aminah would tell her not think about doing so.

Maybe she should text Abdullahi again —with the burner this time — and tell him she plans to kill the Governor in a few hours, put him on notice to free the girls. He's probably going to need more time as there'll be twice as many this time. Then again, there's still no guarantee he would do it before the airstrike.

This is too much. She can't think of everything. Tears of frustration come, and she lets them flow, hoping, like yesterday, they'll bring relief and some clarity of thought. If only she could confide in Salim. She can't. Maybe she should pull the communication cord; tell Iman it's all off, it's too dangerous, she'll have to leave Yakubu, run off somewhere. But, if Yakubu injures Iman tonight or worse, kills her, how could Jamilah live with that? The pig would be free to carry on as before. How can she abandon Iman or those girls?

She stops crying. To save Iman and have a chance of saving the girls, she has to go through with the murder. Abdullahi is not the priority here. To ensure the girls' liberation, she has to tell Abdullahi to get rid of the phone, it's the only way, even though she'd be saving the man who tortured and murdered her sister. She'll ring Farida and tell her she's just discovered that Ado's phone is bugged. When de Witt hears of Yakubu's death, sees more girls being released and finds he no longer has tabs on Abdullahi, he'll put two and two together. She can live with his wrath. He'll be gone from Nigeria in a few hours and even if he wanted to come back, which he won't, they'd never let him in. Perhaps if he'd been upfront with her, the outcome might have been different. There's a knock at the door. She snatches a tissue to dab her cheeks and unlocks the door.

'Salim.'

'I thought you'd be here.'

'What's up?'

'You've been crying.' He steps in, closing the door behind him. She sits down, exhausted.

'When my grief gets too much, I come here to take a few minutes. Part of my survival strategy.' It's not a lie, just not the whole truth.

'I just had a call from de Witt,' he says. A heavy cloak of guilt settles across her shoulders. 'I don't have to tell you what it was about.'

She doesn't speak.

'I understand why you did what you did but you know these people. They can't be trusted. I'm angry with de Witt for making you his ally, unbeknown to yourself. Worst of all, for steering you into the path of these psychopaths. I told him so. And ...' She looks up. 'I'm surprised you didn't talk it over with me first.'

'I'm sorry. Ado's phone offered me a chance to do something. I knew if I told you, you would have tried to stop me.' His silence indicates she is right. 'And twenty-five girls would still be in captivity.'

Salim takes a breath.

'So why did de Witt call you?' she asks.

'To ask me to check you were okay and, more specifically, ask if I could keep an eye on you.'

'Why?'

'He's troubled by your lack of enthusiasm for his plan to assassinate Abdullahi. ... Is there something else I should know?' His eyes search her face.

'No, of course I want to see Abdullahi dead.' She manages not to look away. 'De Witt's just being de Witt — thinking he knows more about what you're thinking than you do.' She looks away. 'He's probably got someone keeping his eye on you now, seeing you know about his plan too.' She looks back at him, but his demeanour is unchanged.

'He can't afford another mission failure,' she says, looking away again. 'If he can link up successfully with the Chadian Air Force, his company's reputation will be restored. He's just being cautious ... Of course I want to see Abdullahi killed', she looks back at him. It's a true statement but she doesn't like keeping him in the dark. Their faces are only a foot apart. 'I do and I'm sorry he's drawn you into this. He had no right to.'

She seems to have said enough as the concern on his face falls away, but it only serves to make her more miserable given he had to find out what she'd done from de Witt, and she's holding back even more from him. It's hard to keep the truth from the only man in the world who has ever cared for her, apart from her father and brother. She waits for him to say something. What can he say? "Never mind, Jamilah, just don't do it again?" It feels like she's betrayed him. She stands up, takes his face in her hands, and kisses him full on the mouth. It feels like he is going to pull away, but she slides an arm around his back and a hand around his neck to discourage retreat. He doesn't try to. His arms go around her back, draw her close and he returns her kiss. Years of professionalism and denial finally give way to passion and an acknowledgement of love. And in this action at least, there is no deception or indecision.

Chapter 58

'Jamilah! I'm so pleased to see you.' Iman draws Jamilah into a tight hug.

'How could I miss the fashion show?' says Jamilah, as her friend ushers her into her room.

'You like it?' she lets go of Jamilah's hand and twirls.

Iman looks breath-taking. Her make-up is perfect, her complexion smooth and light. Her cheeks give out a healthy glow despite the mark left by her husband's fist. Her eyes are large and mysterious. Her lipstick has been applied with precision and reflects the sparkle of her perfect teeth. A spectacular turquoise dress reveals more than a hint of cleavage and is matched by a towering head wrap. Glimpses of bare arm show through the slits cut into the sleeves between shoulder and elbow. No further embellishment to her beauty is required; regardless, a glorious neckless comprising multiple gold chains, falls gracefully over her collarbone. A gold spider with a dull pearl at its centre rests at one side of the web, its long legs poised to detect any vibration. Yet when Jamilah looks at the matching earrings, she sees the spider is in fact a representation of the sun and its rays.

How strange, that a wife should prepare to kill her husband by making herself look as attractive as possible to him.

'You look incredible', says Jamilah.

'Dressed to kill, you mean.' She smirks.

'I can see you're not having any second thoughts', says Jamilah, setting down her bag.

'Huh, not a chance. I see it more like euthanasia. He's riddled with wickedness. Terminal. We'll be putting him out of his misery. Yes, it's involuntary but he doesn't realise how miserable he is.'

'Or how miserable he makes everyone else.'

'Oh, he knows that and doesn't care. Goes to show how sick he is. We're the agents, no angels, of euthanasia!'

'That's a good way to put it.'

'Right, now listen, I have the perfect ensemble for you! You're tall like me, it'll fit like a glove, but first, let's do a little something with your face.'

'Beauty and the beast', says Jamilah slipping off her hijab.

'Tut, tut. I won't have it. You're beautiful Jamilah. Accept it. I've seen the way that Dr Salim looks at you. Isn't that what all you nurses look for, a handsome doctor? Hey, you're blushing.'

'I'm not.' Jamilah's face is burning. 'Let's get on with this.'

Iman smiles. She takes a dress from the wardrobe and hangs it on the door. Naturally, it looks fabulous, but there's no time to admire it and Iman plonks her down at the dressing table and gets to work.

'That ointment you gave me, isn't working,' says Jamilah, embarrassed again by her skin and wanting to change the subject.

'Give it a chance, it's not a miracle cure! Anyway, you forgot to ask how your patient is; but don't worry, I'm fine, thank you, your medication is working.'

'Oh, sorry, that's terrible of me.'

'Apology accepted, I suspect you might have had one or two other things on your mind … Now, that's starting to look better … Don't talk while I do this lipstick.'

'How's your husband?'

'Shush! Foul mood as always, more so today. You saw the TV earlier? Of course you did. Those girls. Jamilah, you're a hero. No, don't talk … There, that's done, just a few seconds more … Despite what you say, I don't have to do very much at all. You look fabulous. He's going to think you're one of my airhead friends, who would have given anything to have become his third wife … and who might still be hopeful', she smiles mischievously.

'I don't know how you've put up with it', says Jamilah.

'Well, we can't all go to college and become highly trained nurses … There.' She finishes tightening the tie on Jamilah's new headdress and steps back. 'What do you think?'

Jamilah knows it's her face in the mirror but can hardly recognise herself. In five minutes she's become a different person. She doesn't know how to respond.

'Wait 'til we get the dress on.'

'Where is he?' says Jamilah slipping off her trainers.

'Eating. He'll be up soon. He was having a skype call with some people. He doesn't like it. I think he's half deaf. All this "Can you hear me?" stuff, he can't stand it.'

They hear coughing next door. 'That's him.' Iman goes across to the adjoining door, opens it softly and peeks in. She gestures to Jamilah to come over. They look in together. This is the first time Jamilah has been close to Yakubu or seen him in the flesh. He's bigger than she imagined, sports his trademark sunglasses and cane, and is wearing a plain black dressing gown and open-toed slip-ons. He looks like an old bull elephant shuffling towards a watering hole. The call of the muezzin drifts in on the breeze. Jamilah wonders if it's a call to prayer or death.

Iman shuts the door carefully. 'He'll have his shower', she whispers, 'then dry off sitting in his chair. He'll stay there for the Isha prayer. He likes his routines. Nowadays that includes taking out those "things", then lying back on the bed and hollering for his wife to come in and gratify him. Come on, let's get you dressed.'

As her friend predicted, Iman's dress fits Jamilah perfectly. It's a lush green, made of fine material in a herringbone stitch, and accentuates her body in a way she would never have imagined. She reflects on how awkward and gauche she must have looked the night de Witt came to dinner. Tonight she feels confident, powerful even. It's just what she needs.

'Who's the beautiful one now?' says Iman.

'We're like two princesses going to the President's wedding', says Jamilah, smiling.

'Two queens', says Iman and they both laugh.

'In full warpaint and battledress,' adds Jamilah.

This is unreal; they're laughing just before they carry out a murder. It must be nerves. Nerves and adrenaline. That's okay, they can draw on them both.

'Are you ready, sister?' Jamilah takes her friend's hands.

'Ready.' Iman's eyes are alive. They hug.

'We'll be fine,' says Jamilah.

'I'll make sure of it,' says Iman. She releases her embrace and has a concerned look on her face. 'I'm sorry, Jam, you know you're going to have to touch him.'

'I'm a nurse. There's not much I haven't touched. Listen Iman, I know people would say this is wrong, but my conscience is clear. Ahmed and Aminah are gone, I can't bring them back, but you and fifty young girls are still here and tonight I can make sure it stays that way.' For the second time that day, Jamilah is embraced and feels love.

Chapter 59

'You're lucky to have a daughter like that.' Muhammed talks into his laptop.

'Alhamdulillah. If she'd been born a boy, she'd be sitting with us now. Her mother's sickly, weak-willed, can't deliver me a son. Farida's strong, smart, a natural leader. Takes after her father.'

Muhammed gives a quiet nod.

'You saw how she handled herself during the ambush. I can trust her to do what I ask ... What's up with you? ... Oh for fuck's sake, you're thinking about Fatma and your daughters! How many times must we discuss this. Allah calls us, we act, we're blessed. Would you deprive those girls of Paradise? That's why you went on about not releasing those bitches, isn't it? Now that we're releasing more, it's set you off again. Take any of them, take your pick. Get married again if that's what it takes to get your head straight.'

'I have been thinking about it. I don't get the same —'

'Stop thinking, do it.'

Muhammed nods with enthusiasm. Abdullahi walks to the side of the boat shaking his head. He holds on to the metal bar supporting the overhang and looks out across the shimmering water. Around the sides of the lake, fires, candles, bulbs, and gaslights flicker from small settlements. A few fishing boats are still active though most are moored up for the night. He sniffs the warm salty air, clears his throat, and spits into the water. He turns his head as Muhammed shuts the lid of his laptop.

'So, you've got our fifty?'

Muhammed nods and stands up. 'I'm going to make a few calls and confirm with the unit commanders, but yes, and they'll be ready to move. I've a good idea where we can dispense with them. I'll set it up.'

'Good.'

'What about Ado's phone?'

'Farida keeps finding new things. It's turning into a gold mine. She's going to extract and package excerpts then release them anonymously through internet cafes and directly to the media. Yakubu (should he continue to exist) and his cronies can deny it first time round, but we'll pile on the misery, brick by brick and watch them squirm.'

Muhammed reaches for his AK47, a hint of a smile on his face.

'Have you got the ring?' asks Abdullahi. They both laugh. 'I'm going to spend some time with my daughter. Come back in an hour when you've finished with your fiancée. We'll see if there's any news from the Bitch.'

Chapter 60

Governor Yakubu lies on his bed, still drying off, still cooling down. His towelled dressing gown is untied and he makes no attempt to cover his lower body. His babban riga robe has been flung over a chair and looks impatient to be folded and put away for the night. These days it's easier to get clothes off than on, though the two items he can remove and put back with ease — his fula hat and his sunglasses — are back in place. He reflects on how well the day had started, only to turn quickly to shit. He's not going to think about it anymore and, fortunately, all the distraction he needs is waiting for him in the adjoining bedroom. She's keeping him waiting. Normally he wouldn't stand for it but he's in her domain now and waiting is only adding to the tension and building anticipation of what's to come. And here she comes. Fuck, she looks hot. Hotter than any bitch on Porn Hub. He likes to see the beautiful ones roughed up, slapped, choked. He likes to see them cry, but still ask for more. That's what floating his boat at the moment. In a month or so it could be something else. He gets bored more easily these days.

'You're wearing too much,' he says.

'Don't you like it?' She poses for him, holding her arms out wide, opening her palms and spreading her long fingers out with a flourish. He loves it. The anger of the day continues to simmer but she has ignited his lust and it is coming rapidly to the boil. She places her hand on her hips and pouts. Slowly she walks toward him. He took the Viagra before he started eating so it could get a head start and it's working. Alhamdulillah! She's beside the bed, unwrapping her headdress.

'Leave it on! The jewellery too.'

'Yes Sir.'

'Master! In this room, you call me, master. How many times must I tell you. I think you're deliberately disobeying me so that I will punish you. Aren't you?'

'Yes, Master', she pouts like a little girl. 'I think I might need some chastisement, Master.'

She reaches behind her neck and unhooks her dress. She is standing right in front of him. The dress loosens, she pulls it down and withdraws her arms from the sleeves. He never tires of those breasts. They are partially covered by a lacey bra but as good as they look now, they need to be uncovered, set free. She slips off her shoes, the dress falls silently to the floor. Her lingerie matches the colour of her headdress.

'Put your shoes back on!'

'Yes, Master.'

She regains four inches in height.

'Take that off!' he says gruffly, helping his dressing gown slide to one side to show off his erection.

'Ah,' she says, smiling, 'my lion is back.' She unhooks her bra and throws it on top of the dress.

'Never mind that, take the rest of,' he points to her panties. She knows his heart is thumping, she teases him more by turning round to show off her tight buttocks and the strip of lingerie that has disappeared between them. She's trying to prise away his control, but he's not having it. She wiggles out of the lower half of her lingerie, throws it on top of the bra, then, still with her back to him, she stretches her hands up towards the ceiling and leans to one side, displaying the full length and curvature of her body.

He gasps. What's gotten into her tonight? She's driving him crazy. A couple of nights ago she would hardly do a thing, now she's like a bitch on heat.

'Come here!'

'Yes, Master.'

She puts a knee on the bed and manoeuvres her body across him, her belly over his erection. He slaps each buttock hard.

'You like this, don't you.'

'Yes, Master.'

'Are you wet for me?'

'Of course, Master.'

'Do you want me to slap you harder?' he wheezes.

'Yes, Master.'

Her hand slips in between their bodies and she tugs his erection with a strong grip.

'Beg me,' he gasps.

'Please, Master, slap me harder.'

He spanks her as hard as he can. He wants to hurt her, but he's losing control and getting increasingly out of breath. She knows how to make him come, but it's too soon. He catches sight of the dildos on his bedside cabinet. Time to move things up a gear. He slaps as hard as he can one last time. Gratified by the flush on her buttocks, he pushes her roughly to one side so he can reach out.

'Sit up and open your legs!' He has one of the larger dildos in his hand.

She hesitates.

'Take it!' He grabs her wrist and presses it into her hand. He pulls her other hand back onto his erection, but to his frustration, it is shrinking. 'Fuck this. What's the matter with you?'

'Nothing, Master. Don't I please you?'

'Fuck this. Fuck Salim. This stuff must be fake.'

'Relax, master. I can fix this. We don't need anything from Salim. You know I have a surprise for you?'

'Hmm.'

'You are always telling me your dream is to have two beautiful women at the same time?'

'Yes.' His heart beats faster.

'Well, tonight I will make your dream come true.'

She gets off the bed, dropping the dildo on the floor. She throws off her shoes and, unwrapping her head-dress, walks confidently towards the adjoining door. He hadn't told her she could get up and leave, but thoughts of further discipline are cast aside by fevered expectation and yes, a returning erection. Alhamdulillah! His wife opens the door and comes back in, naked, apart from her jewellery, and holding the hand of another desirable young woman whom she brings to his bedside. She is fully clothed, almost a clone of his wife. Tall and well put together, she can't look him in the eye. She wouldn't be the first one to avoid his gaze, and he likes that confirmation of his power.

'Master, this is my friend Jamilah. She admires you so much. Always telling me she would do anything to meet you. Isn't she beautiful, Master?'

The woman smiles nervously and looks away. She seems much less at ease than his wife. He likes that too.

'I've told her what a lion you are.' She sits down on the bed, still holding on to her friend's hand. 'Poor thing. Jamilah lost her husband last year and has been so lonely. Haven't you Jamilah?'

'Yes.' The woman bows her head and looks down at a little handbag she grasps to her chest. She might look shy, but she's come into his room, holding the hand of his naked wife. He is really liking this a lot.

His wife lets go of her friend's hand and jumps across him to settle on his other side. She positions her leg across his and runs her hand up his thigh towards his groin.

'Hmm, something's stirring here. She pleases you doesn't she, Master?'

'Why are you standing watching us?' he croaks at the friend. 'Get out of those fucking clothes.'

'I told you he'd like you, Jamilah.' Iman turns back to him, 'And I wasn't wrong about this either, was I?' She squeezes his erection but he's losing it again. The friend's still standing there, awkward, gormless.

'Get those fucking clothes off! Are you deaf?'

The friend looks taken aback but with an encouraging nod from his wife, she starts unwrapping her headdress.

'Don't take all day about it!' Hasn't she ever undressed in front of a man before? She was married for fuck sake. Her shyness is starting to annoy him, though it still feeds his lust. She's fresh, new, another version of his wife. He can't wait to see what she looks like. Why's she fiddling with that headdress? Before he can shout again, his wife's soft palm caresses his cheek.

'Master, relax.' She draws his face towards hers, kissing him lightly. 'We'll take good care of you. I promise. Aren't I always telling you not to rush your meals? Well this is the same; relax and it will be so much better.'

Her tongue slides into his mouth. Her hand is working him, reviving his erection. She presses her body against him, and he feels her breasts against his chest. He can't remember her being so aroused. He grabs her ass and then reaches for her groin.

Chapter 61

Yuck!! Gross. Jamilah can hardly bring herself to look at him. How can Iman stand it, not just his slobbering all over her, but kissing him too! He's disgusting. There's no way he's going to touch her. Absolutely not! Why did she agree to this? Iman made it seem straightforward. And she'd said she was a nurse used to the human body in all its forms. But with patients, she's the one who does the handling — for good reasons — and not the one being handled. But she can't just walk out. She's in too far and she'll never get this chance again. The lives of young girls depend on her. She has to do what she came for, if only to stop him groping her friend and avoid him groping her. The headdress comes off; the dress swiftly follows, and she sets them carefully on top of Yakubu's robe, driven not by her compulsion for tidiness but to put off, even if it's for a few seconds, the awful moment when she must get into his bed. Her small bag lies open on the floor by the side of the bed and is soon joined by her borrowed lingerie. She can't turn fully round to face him; her hands automatically seek to keep her intimate parts private a while long. She steals a look. Iman has him under control.

There are so many similarities between him and Giwa: bulk; arrogance; and a sense of entitlement, being the most obvious. He thinks he's some kind of sultan, lying there expecting these two young women to pander to his desires. He's repulsive, but Iman, the brave girl that she is, continues to feed his delusion. It's a wonder she can find anything under the rolls of his belly fat. And look at those big drooping man-boobs ... how can Iman stomach him? As if he can read her mind, he pulls his face away from Iman to look at her, his new plaything. Why would a man want to look at another woman when he has Iman? Because men like him always want more.

'What's the matter with you, you stupid cow? Turn round. Yes, right round, and take those hands away! Let's have a good look at you. A proper look. Raise your hands above your head!'

'Isn't she beautiful, Master.'

'Yes, I suppose so.'

Iman sits up on both knees, pouting. 'Master, you're making me jealous.' Then she smiles seductively, 'Come here!' She pulls his head round, diverting his gaze back to her, then pushes her breasts into his face and he slobbers over them like the pig he is. Jamilah almost retches while Iman moans as if she's enjoying it, but her eyes dart urgently to Jamilah and open wide. She has manoeuvred him on his side, facing away from Jamilah and exposing just enough of his fat backside as she needs to see. This is their chance! It's come early, Alhamdulillah! Iman grips a roll of fat on his invisible waist, as if she's in the throes of passion. Jamilah drops to her knees, takes the insulin pen out of her bag, and pulls the top off. It's primed. Iman locks eyes with her then digs her nails into his buttock. Simultaneously, Jamilah slides the needle fully into it at the recommended 45-degree angle but doesn't allow it to stay there for the recommended six to ten seconds. She forces the plunger down without hesitation discharging the full load of insulin into him. She extracts the needle immediately and hides the pen behind her back.

'What the fuck?' The Governor forces his face over Iman's arm.

'Master, was I too rough?' Iman coos in his ear. 'I can't help it.' She rolls her eyes and digs her nails into him again, in a more playful way.

Jamilah lets the pen drop to the floor. It doesn't matter if he caught a glimpse of it, the die is cast. She climbs onto the bed beside him, forcing a smile that aims to convince him she's there by choice. He looks confused.

'Look who's here,' says Iman straddling him and glancing back at Jamilah. She leans forward and whispers in his ear, 'she's so shy, but for you, master, she'll do anything you want, she just needs to be told.'

'Stand up!' he barks.

Jamilah is glad to move back from him.

'Take those off.'

Jamilah hesitates. She's not wearing anything.

'What are you waiting for?' He turns to Iman, 'What's she ... waiting ... for?' He gulps for air, then slumps back on the bed, knocking his hat forward. 'What's she ... waiting ...?' He raises his head and squints around the room, 'What's Zainab, doing here?' he mumbles. His head falls back again, his chin flops onto his chest causing his sunglasses to slip over his nose. His eyes struggle to stay open.

'Zainab?' says Jamilah.

'Wife number two,' says Iman climbing off him.

'He's having a hypoglycaemic attack. It won't be long.'

'Alhamdulillah!' Iman stands up on the bed. 'I'm going to give him an attack of my own.' She draws her foot back and kicks him hard in the groin. 'You pig!' Her foot is covered in sweat. She drops onto her knees and slaps him hard in the face knocking his sunglasses off. 'That's for the other day!' She whacks him on the side the head, knocking off his hat. They hear the hint of a groan, but no other reaction. 'Do you want to take a shot?' says Iman, wiping her foot and hands on his dressing gown.

'No. He's fallen into a coma, and you have to stop hitting him or people will think he was beaten to death.' She smiles at her very good friend. She feels … relieved; And she has no sense of guilt. Only good can come from this act. 'We need to move. Grab all the clothes Iman and put them back in your wardrobe.'

'You think?' she smirks, jumping off the bed. She too displays no signs of remorse or guilt.

Jamilah puts the pen back in her little bag and then examines Yakubu. His breathing and pulse are weak. To anyone else, it would look like he's dozing but his body and brain are being starved of glucose, oxygen, and water. He's suffocating.

'Come here and look, Iman. You see there, where I injected him.'

'That dot?'

'Yes. Can you scratch him there with your nails, while he's still breathing?'

'I'd love nothing more.'

'You see the mark your nails made earlier when they dug in, just scrape from there, right over it … Good. You can't see the entry point now. Right, you went to bed tonight as husband and wife. You attempted sex but despite your best efforts, and a little rough sex, he was too tired. You went back to your room, he fell asleep. Which makes me think there's something else you should do.'

'What?'

Jamilah looks at the dildos. 'Sorry.'

'It's all right.' Iman takes the smallest one off the bedside table. Jamilah turns away to give Iman privacy.

'It doesn't have to go all in, just enough to leave a trace should someone examine them. And remember, if asked, say you tried to do more but had to be careful because you were still tender from when he got rough with you last time.

'I know, Jam. You can turn round.'

Good. Put it back with the others. No, on its side. Where does he keep his iPad?'

Iman opens the drawer of a bedside cabinet.

'Turn it on to a porn channel. I'm sure you know where to find them,' she smirks. 'Leave it on the bed with the tissues.' While Iman gets busy, Jamilah looks in the drawer of the other cabinet. 'Thought so.' She moves the packet of Viagra forward in the drawer to where its presence will be readily noted and leaves the drawer open. She scans the room, checking she hasn't touched anything else, apart from her victim, the clothes, the insulin pen, and the bag. 'Put his hat and glasses back on. Good. Leave the bedside light on.'

Chapter 62

Jamilah checks herself in the mirror. The make-up has been removed and she's back in her own clothes. So much for glamour. She won't miss it; the key thing is she looks exactly like she did when she arrived. As for how she feels, well that's certainly different. A sense of achievement, no regrets, more confident — there'll be time to think about that later, for now, there are still things to do before she can leave. She returns to Yakubu's room where Iman is waiting for her. This girl can't stop looking glamourous even though she's changed into her dressing gown and flip-flops. On the other hand, Yakubu's the same big lump, lying in the same place and looking well and truly dead — but she still has to check. No breathing. No pulse.

'I can confirm you're a widow', says Jamilah. 'Congratulations.'

'Thank you.'

'We'll leave his dressing gown the way it is, let them find him like that. If he's to have died from heart failure, it needs to look as if he's had some kind of struggle. Wipe the iPad screen with your sleeve, the sides too. Get rid of all your prints … Is he right or left-handed?'

Iman holds up Yakubu's limp right hand.

'Take hold of his index finger and tap it on the screen. His thumb too. That'll do. Throw it to one side, face up. Good. Okay, listen Iman, I know we've been through all this before, but we have to get it right.'

Iman nods.

'It's almost eight fifteen I signed in at seven forty, examined you, everything was fine. I told you your wound was healing up well, we chatted, I admired your dresses. We heard your husband next door. At around eight o'clock you checked on him. He was heading for the shower as part of his normal routine. Soon after he called for you and I took that as my cue to leave, right?'

'Right,' says Iman. 'We said our goodbyes, you gathered your things together and left. When I went in he'd already showered and prayed and was lying on the bed eager to spread his seed.'

'Then what?'

'He couldn't function. He was tired and depressed. He told me to use that thing, even though he knew I hadn't recovered from last time. I tried a little bit but in the end he was too tired. He couldn't get it up, became frustrated and told me to get out.'

'So, you were back in your room within fifteen minutes — by eight-thirty, right?'

'Yes,' says Iman, 'and I'll say when I looked back he looked completely drained, what with all the stress of the last few days.'

'Good. Then you felt hungry so called down for some tea and cake.'

Iman nods. Jamilah glances at her watch.

'Okay, you're supposed to be with him now, so stay here 'til eight-thirty, then go back to your room, make the call for tea and stay put until you get up tomorrow at the usual time.'

'I know, I know. When I don't hear him up for the morning prayer and he doesn't call me to help him dress, I go see what's happening. I find him on the bed. I'm shocked, I scream, I run to get security — sobbing, and gasping for breath.'

'But not overdoing it.'

'Come on,' says Iman, hands on hips. 'Didn't you see me just now? You don't think I can act?'

'I do, I do!.' Jamilah kisses her friend on the cheek and then turns to look around the room.

'Right. That's it. Stay calm, do as we said, and everything will be fine.' They hug. 'Remember don't call me. I'll text my condolences tomorrow, having heard the news, then we can talk.'

'Okay.'

Jamilah goes back to Iman's room and retrieves her medical bag. Iman blows her a kiss from the doorway. Jamilah waves, smiles and leaves.

The guards downstairs give her a passing glance and one makes a note in a log book. She steps into the warm night and walks briskly towards the gates and the next checkpoint beyond which, she makes out her driver sitting in the front seat reading a newspaper. The guard isn't interested in searching her medical back as she is leaving the premises. Even if he were interested, he wouldn't recognise the weapon that had just killed his boss. He gives her a wide smile; she smiles back politely. He nips in front of her to hold the gate open and let her pass through. She acknowledges his show of gallantry with a simple nod and no eye contact. She makes her way across the courtyard, trying not to quicken her pace. The driver hasn't seen her yet. She wishes he had the engine running and the door open ready for her but clearly, his newspaper takes priority. She glances back at the grand building searching for the window behind which a dead Governor lies on his bed, watched over by his young widow. A couple of soldiers wish her goodnight and stare the way soldiers do at a young, unaccompanied woman. All these men and their security apparatus have been unable to stop a nurse from walking in and killing the sole person they were there to protect! She walks past them with the murder weapon in her bag and all they can do is leer. They have no idea their boss is dead and, if all goes to plan, they'll remain unaware for at least another ten hours. She's beginning to see why Abdullahi is successful. Political power is like an illness; it spreads out from the core, infecting the parts that hold it in place with complacency and arrogance.

'Wait!' It's a loud voice that carries a threat.

She turns in alarm. The expression of the soldiers has changed to alertness. Something is wrong. There's a light shining on her, half blinding her. The guard is running towards her.

'Stop!' He looks angry. Her heart is thumping. What's gone wrong? There's no point in running. They would either catch her or shoot her. How did they find out? It doesn't matter. It's over.

'Pass,' says the guard coming to a halt in front of her.

'What?'

He switches his torch off. She has to blink to see him properly. He beckons with his fingers. 'Your pass. You didn't hand it back.'

She looks down at her chest. It's still pinned in the same place. It could easily have come off when she was changing in and out of her clothes. But a nurse knows how to pin.

'You never asked,' she says.

One of the soldiers laughs and she realises she has undermined this man firstly by distracting him from his duties and then making it worse with a snide remark. Why did she have to say that? What good will it do her? It's like some of Iman's spirit has rubbed off on her. She decides to let more of it rub off. She's a guest of the Governor's wife, she's here at the Governor's request and one of his drivers is waiting to take her home. She stares at the guard, the way she would if one of her team had done something foolish, then, shaking her head in disapproval, unpins the pass and holds it out to him. He snatches it from her hand, all flirting forgotten, and stomps off in a vain attempt to shake off the humiliation of having his peers witness not only his dereliction of duty but also the way a nurse stood up to him. She has no sympathy. Isn't it typical he'd blame her for his incompetence? Procedures are there for a reason, not to be cast aside when a pretty nurse appears — not that she'd consider herself pretty. The driver is seeking to compensate for his earlier lack of attentiveness and is quickly out of the car, holding the door open for her. She gets in the back seat and declines to thank him. The arrogance of power is infectious.

In no time they are pulling away from Yakubu's residence. She muses that whatever happens, it won't be his residence much longer. They pass Coronation Hall and join the roundabout. She takes out the burner and texts Farida: *"It's done, hope your father can act as quickly. Aminah."* She's more comfortable contacting the daughter than the father. Besides, who knows what other tricks de Witt has up his sleeve? Her burner dings. She's not expecting a fulsome response but Farida's curt *"Ok,"* is welcome for it means Abdullahi will soon be informed of Yakubu's demise and the handover of the remaining girls can proceed.

There's nothing left for her to do but go home, wait and trust that Iman has an uneventful night. She deletes both messages, leans back against the cushioned seat and shuts her eyes. But she's not ready to relax. Her mind runs through the events of the last hour, searching for anything she might have overlooked. Her interaction with the guard was too risky. He might have insisted she accompany him somewhere … but he didn't, and it could work to her advantage. He and others watching their exchange will remember her leaving and the fact that she didn't seem nervous or in a hurry. The real risk took place in the Governor's bedroom and well, her plan couldn't have gone any better. In and out, like the needle itself. Thanks to Iman she didn't have to touch him, and he didn't get a chance to touch her. Alhamdulillah! But was it Allah's will, good planning or simple good fortune? Whatever it was, she can't pray to Allah to protect her; she's a killer now and not about to repent.

Chapter 63

Farida finishes relaying Jamilah's text to Abdullahi and Muhammed.

'Can we believe her?' asks Muhammed.

'She's doing Allah's will and she's shown we can trust her.'

'I wish we could've done it ourselves', says Muhammed.

'Yes, but why do you think no one has managed to kill a Governor before?'

'They can't protect their people', interjects Farida, 'but they make sure they protect themselves.'

'Exactly,' says Abdullahi. 'There's always resources for that. And they never put themselves on the front line. That's why Allah found us a nurse. We killed him at a distance. Show me the message.'

Farida hands him her phone.

'Aminah.' He shakes his head. 'I kind of like this bitch.'

'I wonder how she did it?' says Muhammed.

'Well for sure it wasn't a suicide bombing', Abdullahi laughs.

'She thinks she can get away with it,' says Farida.

'Must have poisoned the bastard or something,' says Muhammed.

'Not if she wants to get away with it,' says Farida. 'Too easy to trace.'

'Let's hear what they say,' says Abdullahi, 'but who the fuck cares? If ever an infidel deserved to go to hell, it was that son of a bitch.' He tosses the phone back to his daughter. 'You realise, you've got a confession right there, don't you?' He laughs.

'It's from her burner,' says Farida.

'She's learning.'

'It's not *her* phone that interests me, papa.'

'I know. What else have you found?'

'A lot, and with some help we could find a lot more. For the moment, we have more than enough to drop in the lap of the media before all the sheep start bleating about what a great patriot Yakubus, son of Kano, the usual bullshit.'

'Good. We'll bury his reputation along with his stinking body.'

'Not just his, papa.'

'I know. Focus on Yakubu first. Let the others piss themselves; each day, we'll provide a new revelation.'

'The media will go crazy for this, Papa. We'll start a fire that will burn for weeks.'

'Months.' He smiles at Farida, fearless, clever − the son he'd always wanted. 'Talking about media', he turns to Muhammed, 'I assume everything's set for tomorrow. And I'm not talking about your wedding!'

'Yes, on both fronts', says Muhammed with a grin.

'Muhammed is taking another wife tomorrow', he tells his daughter. 'We'll have two ceremonies; two celebrations and we'll video both.'

'The media people won't know where to turn, papa. Yakubu's death, the release of fifty girls, revelations about Yakubu's past.'

'They'll be confused', says Muhammed.

'Another sign that the End of Times is upon us, Alhamdulillah!' says Abdullahi.

'Alhamdulillah!' echo Farida and Muhammed.

'Let me see Ado's phone again.' Farida passes it back to him. 'You see the power of Allah? Without getting off our backsides, we have killed the Governor of Kano State. Alhamdulillah!'

'Alhamdulillah!'

'And with this phone — and still sitting on our asses — we'll destroy his allies. The "Big Men."' He tosses the phone back to Farida. 'Glory be to Allah. Let us praise Him for the blessings he has bestowed on us.'

'Allahu Akbar!'

Chapter 64

Once home, Jamilah wastes little time in climbing into bed. Her body is ready for sleep, if only her brain felt the same way. Her thoughts have moved on from the evening's events to what will happen next, but she knows the plan and there's nothing more she can do for now. She burrows down under the duvet, embracing the darkness, and her breathing slows. Her body wins and she slides into a deep sleep.

It's not a total victory, nor is it the sleep of the innocent. She finds herself standing in the grounds of the Governor's Residence. Her face is made up but the application lacks Iman's expertise. She looks cheap, grotesque even. There's no Visitor's Pass on her chest. The guard is pushing her back towards his checkpoint. Why is he being so rough? A woman takes her behind a curtain for a body search, then rummages through her bag in silence. They come out, the woman shakes her head, and the guard takes Jamilah's arm and drags her back up to the Residence. Two security men take over and escort her to Iman's room. They knock. Iman doesn't answer. They go inside. Nobody is there so they rap tentatively on the adjoining door to the Governor's bedroom. Iman opens it. One of the men offers his apologies, first to Iman and then, over her shoulder, to the Governor, whom he sees slumped on the bed. Not getting any reaction, and concerned he hadn't been heard, the man repeats his apology. The Governor doesn't react and, suspicions aroused, the guard pushes past Iman and goes to the bed and tries to rouse his boss. He speaks to someone on a handheld radio, then rushes from the room. His colleague grabs Iman and her by the arms and drags them towards the Governor's bathroom. On the way, he accidentally kicks a Visitor's Pass, and it slides across the floor triumphantly. A radio crackles. Someone is trying to get hold of the Governor's Assistant. Iman doesn't seem bothered. When the bathroom door slams shut, she bursts out laughing. It's so loud. Jamilah wakes up.

She's too wide awake to go back to sleep now and if that's what sleep has to offer, she's not interested. She settles on resting her eyes. Hopefully it'll stop them looking too baggy when she turns up for work. She wonders if Iman is awake too. How could she possibly sleep, with her husband lying dead in the next room and she the only person in the place who is aware of it? That won't last long. Soon, she'll enter his room and share what she finds with the world. What a strange scenario, but it won't phase that girl.

She switches on her clock radio. Radio Wazobia provides a soothing voice. She doesn't want to hear any breaking news about Yakubu for at least a few more hours yet. She doesn't want her phone to ring either. If ever a night needed to be uneventful, this is it.

She didn't think about Salim earlier, in case she got distracted, now distraction is what she needs. They kissed! Wow! It felt good. Really good. What made her do that? It doesn't matter, it was … wonderful. She hugs a pillow against her chest. She loves him, not like a surrogate father, not like a mentor, but as a man. When did respect and gratitude turn to love? She can't be sure. What matters is that he loves her too, of that she's sure. He's been kind to her for so long, yet cautious too. Careful to do and say the right things. Afraid if he didn't, it would look like he was taking advantage of her vulnerability. If that's not love … She squeezes her pillow tighter and thinks of their embrace. Maybe she can pick up her life again, make a new start. But

... she's just killed the Governor of Kano State. How ironic that a few hours after their first kiss, on the day when their love finally revealed itself to them, she should become a killer. That wasn't part of her plan. When the Governor's death is announced he'll think it strange she was there that evening. When he sees the release of even more girls he'll make the connection. Even though she cannot expect him to accept what she's done, she's not going to hide keep the truth from him. She had to do it and she will live with the consequences. In the end, she had followed de Witt's advice and let fate take its course — only because she couldn't decide on an alternative. She didn't tell de Witt about the girls; she didn't warn Abdullahi about the airstrike. Fate will determine whether he lets the girls go before de Witt and his Chadian allies get the chance to strike.

Then it hits her. She sits up, fully awake. What if Abdullahi assembles the girls at his camp? He could be doing it at this very moment! Surely fifty girls wouldn't be travelling around with him, but he could bring them to his camp first. No, that wouldn't make any sense. They're probably spread around a few camps. He'd arrange for them to be taken separately to the release point, why risk them making two journeys on the road. Wouldn't he? She doesn't know! How stupid of her not to think of that simple scenario. Once again she's overlooked the obvious. The bombs will kill the girls and she'll be responsible for their deaths. She jumps out of bed. She'll have to call Abdullahi. She can't have the deaths of fifty innocent girls on her conscience. De Witt will be furious. He'll tell her she was out of her depth, and he'll be right. He'll tell her Abdullahi could slaughter fifty people in a night and go out and do it all over again the following night and he'd be right. Whatever action she takes has implications. The moment of pride she felt as the car drove away from the Governor's residence, has been dealt a reality check.

She picks up her phone. There's only one thing she can do, the same as she always does when she needs help. Yakubu is dead, Salim can't talk her out of that, but she'll tell him the truth. Whether he still wants her after that is up to him, but at this moment she needs his counsel and she'll listen to him and do whatever he says. From now on, she'll be led by Salim, not fate or Allah's will. Voicemail. She doesn't leave a message. The first call will rouse him, and he'll see who was calling. She waits a few seconds, then redials. He picks up and the whole story spills out. Its recounting brings home the scope and gravity of what she's done. She cries but apart from keeping Salim in the dark, she has no regrets. She had to act she tells him. She couldn't have her life destroyed and remain subservient again. It wasn't just about revenge but saving lives too. Can he do what he's always done — accept her for what she is? She'll understand if he can't. Regardless, she loves him, admires him and will always be grateful to him.

After a pause, he clears his throat and speaks, 'Jamilah, I'm stunned. This is a lot to process. As a medical professional, I cannot condone what you've done, but as a human being,' he sighs, 'given everything that's happened to you, I can understand it.' Another pause. 'I'm coming over.'

'Are you sure? It's half past two.'

'I'm sure. There's no traffic, I should be there in twenty minutes. The drive will give me time to think. Put some coffee on.'

She flops on the bed. He hasn't cut her loose. Their bond is holding. He's coming to be with her. She springs to her feet and heads to the shower. She must look her best for him.

Chapter 65

The sound of a car. Jamilah looks out. Salim pulls in, cuts the engine and turns off the lights. He's made good time. She undoes the locks ready for his entrance and returns to the table to pour hot water over the coffee granules. She goes back and listens behind the door, opening it at the sound of his approach.

'Hi,' she says as he steps in, not quite ready to read his face.

'Hi,' he replies.

She bolts the locks back in place. When she turns, he's standing in front of her. This time he moves first. His arms wrap round her back and draw her tightly to him. Her arms slide behind his neck. They kiss urgently, as if eager to make up for lost time. The danger that surrounds them adds to the intensity but in his arms she has an overwhelming sense of security. An emotion long forgotten. She pulls away and gently pushes him inside. They sit at the table, not yet ready to speak. Salim reaches for his cup of coffee; Jamilah reaches for his other hand, her long fingers sliding between his. He speaks first.

'If you warn Abdullahi, he'll be indebted to you and you'll have saved the lives of all those girls. But for how long? He might let them go in recognition of you keeping him alive but how can we ever know what a man like that will do? But we can be pretty sure he'll keep on killing and that each time another innocent person is slaughtered, it will haunt you. When one death becomes a hundred, you'll go crazy with remorse.'

Jamilah nods, not wanting to think about it.

'On the other hand, if you don't warn him and de Witt's strike is successful, and no girls are injured, then, setting aside Yakubu for the moment, you'll be in the clear. You'll have achieved something redemptive, whether the remaining girls are released or not.'

Jamilah nods again and squeezes his hand.

'But ... if you don't warn him, de Witt's strike fails and Abdullahi survives, he may suspect Ado's phone had something to do with it.'

'But he made me give it to him. I wanted to keep it as my insurance.'

'That would work in your favour. The only thing is ...' He takes a sip of his coffee and Jamilah covers his hand completely with hers. 'Should Abdullahi survive the strike, he'll always know you were responsible for Yakubu's death. He could seek to blackmail you to do more for him.'

'He swore in Allah's name that no harm would come to me if I did as I said. I believe him.'

'Okay, but that would change if he thought you'd set him up.'

'So what do I do?' she asks.

'We have to convince de Witt to delay.'

'He won't.'

'It's the only way to guarantee the girls come to no harm. If Abdullahi has held on to the phone this long, why would he get rid of it now, especially as it contains information with which he can damage his enemies? De Witt will still get his chance.'

'I don't think de Witt will risk a delay. And it's not just down to him to decide.'

'If the raid goes ahead and the girls are killed, when de Witt had the chance to prevent it, their death will be on his conscience, not yours, and from what you tell me about him, I think he has a conscience. He is resourceful; he can come up with a reason to satisfy the Chadians. Besides, unless he agrees to a delay, which might only be for a matter of hours, we'll tell him we will warn Abdullahi. They would lose the chance to take Abdullahi out and may never get another.'

'I knew I could depend on you, Salim.' She gets up, stands behind him and wraps her arms across his chest, showering kisses on his neck and cheeks.

'What's more', says Salim, his hand grasping her upper arm, 'killing the girls would be a disaster for his company. There's no time to lose. He needs to come up with a reason for the Chadians to delay. Ring his number then pass the phone to me. He owes you this. He should never have put you in danger.'

She dials and waits. 'Voicemail.'

'Try again.'

'Same.'

'Seems I'm the only man crazy enough to get up in the middle of the night to take your call.'

'The only one who matters.'

'Okay, leave a text for him to call you back urgently.'

Jamilah does as she's told.

'While we're waiting for the Colonel, tell me again what's supposed to happen when Iman goes into Yakubu's room.'

'Presuming no one else discovers him — unlikely, but not a disaster — she'll rush down to security and raise the alarm. They'll go to his room, find him dead, call the CP and send for Yakubu's physician.'

'Okay, I know the rest: late sixties; overweight; shuns exercise; high BP; and going through a stressful time.'

'Iman will tell the doctor about Yakubu's erectile disfunction; how he was taking too much Viagra, how it made him depressed and frustrated. The guards will verify how he had vomited the night before and passed out — she'll suggest that was stress-related too.'

'All pointing to a fatal stroke or heart attack during the night.'

'Do you think there'll be an autopsy?'

'If they were to regard his death as suspicious or unnatural, then yes, especially given his status, but that's unlikely in the circumstances. One thing they won't do is check for insulin. Determination of insulin in post-mortem specimens isn't offered routinely by forensic toxicology laboratories around the world, and certainly not in this country — but you knew that already.' She looks away, embarrassed at being exposed as the scheming assassin. 'If there's no obvious trauma or evidence of foul play which, from what you've told me there isn't, then given medical history, age, and all the things you've mentioned, I would expect them to conclude that heart failure in the middle of the night was the cause of death.'

'Natural causes.'

'Yes. And as such, I can't see the coroner being troubled. But you planned for that too.' He looks up at her again. She diverts her gaze again and feels an impulse to go sit on the sofa; instead, she stays put and runs her hands down his arms.

'Salim, I had to do something. I'm not usually so conniving. I couldn't tell you.'

'I know.' His hand reaches up and gives her arm a reassuring squeeze.

'Thanks for being here', she says, pressing her cheek into his. She hugs him and kisses his head.

'The CP will check the visitor's log. You'll get a visit. You might call it a verbal autopsy.'

'I had a reason to be there, and it wasn't my first visit.'

'I knew why you were going the first time.'

'I hated keeping you in the dark, especially as Iman was your patient. If you'd known about it, you'd have been an accomplice for not stopping me. I had to protect you.'

'I've never imagined you needing to protect me. When I think of what must have been going through your mind yesterday … It's a lot to take in but I know what a good person you are, Jamilah. We'll get through this together. But you must never keep me in the dark again.'

'I promise.' She makes him stand up and they embrace. When she'd decided to engage with Abdullahi, she'd had no one left to lose; things have changed. She has another ally, an accomplice even, and someone new to protect.

Chapter 66

The first ping of her phone feels like a nudge, the second is the jolt she needs to rouse her from her heavy sleep. They had waited in vain for de Witt to ring back. The kissing and intimate contact had intensified as they quickly found the sofa and soon after, her bed. It was Jamilah's first time; her proper first time. It was how she had hoped it would be and more. He was experienced, she wasn't. She had expected the tenderness but had never imagined the passion. Maybe the seed had been sewn with de Witt. Perhaps it was because she had been impatient. She loved Salim, she wanted him, and he had wanted her. It was swift but intense. They came together locked in the same electric charge. As they slumped back in the bed, sleep was lying in wait for them. She had wanted to ask him questions but, instead, she had rested her cheek on his chest listening as his breathing slowed to the same rhythm as her own.

She reaches for her phone. It isn't there. She spies it through the open door. She looks at the clock radio. Five past seven! She'll be late for work. She looks at Salim; he hasn't stirred. She slides out of bed leaving her dressing gown hanging on the door, at ease with her nakedness. Maybe she should listen to Iman and be proud of her looks. Who could have imagined twenty-four hours ago she'd be walking across her room like this, her clothes scattered on the floor, while Salim lay sleeping on her bed? She picks up the phone. A text from de Witt.

"It's done."

She returns to the bedroom, switches on the radio and checks the online news on her phone. Nothing on either. Salim leans on his elbow watching her, waiting for her to share. She sits down beside him.

'It was de Witt. "It's done."' She holds the phone out for him to read the message.

'Sounds definitive', says Salim.

'I need to know about the girls.' She rings de Witt's number. Voicemail. She leaves another text asking him to call back urgently.

'They must have hit Abdullahi at first light. I suspect the girls were nowhere near him.'

'Oh Salim, do you think so? Do you think they're okay?'

He nods, though not as convincingly as she'd like. She keys in the news website.

'There's nothing being reported yet about him or Yakubu. Poor Iman, all alone there. I don't regret it, Salim, whatever happens. Neither will Iman. He was a monster. He would have killed her.'

'I know. We'll just have to be patient. We'll know soon. Until then, we must carry on as if it's just another day.'

'You're right, and I'm late.' She pulls herself away.

'Don't go yet. I want to look at you.' His hand stops her embarrassed attempt at pulling the duvet up to cover herself. 'If that's okay.' She turns her head away and lets the duvet fall. He strokes her face gently and draws it back to him. 'You are so beautiful, Jamilah.' She's not sure if she should smile or cry. She kisses him and his hand caresses her breast. Another ping from her phone interrupts their intimacy.

'It's de Witt. *"Will call soon."* That's it. Nothing about the girls.'

'He doesn't know about them, remember.' He takes her in his arms and strokes her back. 'This doesn't change anything. We get on with our day and wait for news. Let me know as soon as de Witt calls.'

'I will. Come on. Time for a shower, then we go.'

Chapter 67

The cries and screams persist pulling Abdullahi back to consciousness helped by the annoying ringing in his ears. Grit crunches between his teeth. His lungs work hard to expel the smoke and dust. His throat is parched like a dried-out river bed. People are lifting him. He can't see them. He can't see anything. Someone strokes his head. That can only be his daughter, no one else would dare. Water trickles into his mouth forming a foul-tasting paste that he spits out. He can't lift his left arm but manages to push the bottle away with his right. A hand is on his forehead as if he needs calming. He remembers the explosions. He was walking back from the latrine. No time to react. He recalls the whoosh of the MIGs as they cut through the morning chill, looking as if they were flying past but instead unleashing their invisible bombs. The earth had convulsed as the soil and rock were propelled upwards before tumbling back down like a landslide. His head sinks onto his chest and he passes out.

This time it's the pain that wakes him like a kick in the head. His brain jerks into gear, his senses shift to high alert. He hadn't felt this burning on his skin before; he must have been in shock. When he shifts position it's like he's lying on chards of hot glass. He can see through one eye. Farida is beside him. He's in a speed boat bouncing over the surface of the lake, engine screaming. A blanket is tied to the boat rail and one of his fighters ensures it is pulled taut to provide shade and protection from the spray.

'How are you, papa?'

'Allah has spared me again, Alhamdulillah!'

'Yes, papa, but not your leg.' She kisses his forehead.

He raises his head back and looks down at his body. There's a tourniquet above his left knee and below that, a bandaged stump. He attempts to wiggle his toes, but they're not there. He points to the water bottle in her hand, and she holds it to his mouth. He swishes the water around his mouth and spits it out. Then he drinks.

'Why would Allah let this happen to you, Papa? You're his bravest and most dedicated warrior.'

'Don't talk like that!' he growls. 'Praise Allah. He has kept me alive for a reason. He has kept you alive too. It's not my time yet, nor yours. Direct your anger at the men who dropped the bombs and the infidels who sent them.'

'I'm sorry, papa.'

'You're bleeding.'

'It's your blood, not mine. Can you see through your left eye? It's very swollen.'

'No, but I can see with this one. I can speak, I can hear, and I can think. I am blessed. Alhamdulillah!'

'Alhamdulillah!' Farida smiles and strokes his head. He winces and she pulls her hand back. 'Sorry papa, take these.' She slides her hand under his neck and brings his head up slowly. He breathes in sharply. She wipes some dirt from his mouth and puts two tablets on his tongue and the bottle to his lips. 'These will deaden the pain, papa. You've lost a lot of blood. Not just from your leg but your arm too.' He swallows, glancing at the thick blood-stained bandage on his upper arm. At least there's no pain from that.

'When we reach the shore, a doctor will be waiting.'

'Where are we headed?'

'Baga Kawa. We're almost out of Chadian waters.'

'The NAF wouldn't try to hit us in Chad. It was the Chadians who attacked us. They'll be rushing to the scene now whatever way they can. They'll want to pick through our bones. Finish off any survivors.'

'There's nobody left, papa. Apart from the five of us.' She looks around and then stares forlornly across the Lake. Maybe one or two managed to make it onto small boats. The rest are dead or dying. It was lucky you had a Plan B.'

'Not lucky. Allah has taught me to think ahead. He sent us Ali.'

A pair of bony feet appear by his head, then drop below his eye line, replaced by a long-lined face bordered by a white beard and eyebrows. His long arms are wiry and polished bright by the sun.

'No matter how they try, they cannot kill you, Sheikh. Alhamdulillah!' Ali clasps his hands together and bows, his head wrap touches Abdullahi's face. He kisses the ring on Abdullahi's finger.

'Alhamdulillah', responds Abdullahi. 'Nothing happens unless decreed by Allah.' He turns to Farida, 'Ali always knows where to find me. He's of the Baduma tribe, "the people of the reeds." You only see Ali if he wants you to see him. His boat lies amongst the reeds, the fastest on the lake. When it breaks cover, no one can catch it. He fights with us in Chad; finds the best place for us to camp each time we come back. You see? I turn my head, and he's gone.' He lets his head fall back but instead of bringing comfort, it induces light-headedness. 'So Muhammed didn't make it?'

'No, Papa. He was caught in the middle of it all, with his fiancée.'

'On the eve of his wedding! Still, he'll be reunited with Fatma and his daughters. They'll be waiting for him in Paradise. Fatma didn't want to marry him, but he had this obsession with her. I reminded her of her duty to Allah and how it was an honour to marry a devoted Jihadist. Can you imagine, my second-in-command, a fearless fighter, yet he went weak at the knees for a thirteen-year-old village girl? She only married him to please me. She saw me as a father figure. I told her I already had a daughter.' Farida kisses his cheek. 'She got too clingy. I thought once they had a baby she'd calm down, but it made no difference. Couldn't get her out from under my feet. And I could see it was affecting Muhammed.'

'What happened to her?'

'The market bombing two months ago. That was Fatma's door to paradise.' He takes satisfaction in seeing his daughter is unmoved. 'What happened with you, back there?'

'I got lucky. I was on the long boat with these two.' She points to two fighters behind her.

'It wasn't luck', says Abdullahi, feeling more light-headed.

She squeezes his hand again. 'I know, it was Allah's will. I don't think the pilots saw the boat at first, but they didn't miss it the second time. By then we had jumped off and were running along the shore, which is where we found, Ali.'

'Alhamdulillah!'

'Papa, how did they know where to find us?'

'The way they always do. Someone blabbed.'

'But don't the people around here hate their government as much as we hate ours?'

'Yes, but they're not all like Ali. There's always someone looking to get a reward or who just wants rid of us.'

'What about Ado's phone? Isn't it odd that we only had it for forty-eight hours and they knew exactly where to find us?'

'I know you don't like the bitch, but she's not that smart. She didn't want to give it to us. Thought she could blackmail us with it. We had to threaten her to make her hand it over.'

'It's not personal, papa. Did you never wonder how a nurse could get hold of the phone of a Deputy Governor? Or that when she knew she had to give it to you, she or somebody else could've put a tracking device in it.'

'You told me you had it checked out!'

'I did, but maybe ...'

'You think she's working with the government now? They're hiring nurses to go after us? If that's the case, she's just killed her employer, so how does that work? You think Yakubu would have wanted us to have proof of his double dealings? Or maybe you think she's a secret agent of the Chadian Air Force? Look, freeing girls is her big thing. She's not going to plot to kill me on the day we're supposed to release more of them. If we'd been attacked after the release, maybe I'd consider it.'

'You're right papa, I'm sorry.'

'This isn't the first time we've been the target of air strikes. You're giving the bitch too much credit. The air forces of two countries spend all their time searching for us. And don't discount the French. Those infidels are holed up at N'Djamena Airport, fighting our brothers in the Sahel. Their drones can travel further than anyone's.'

'You're right. Relax papa. We'll be on shore soon. Are the tablets helping?'

'Maybe. Don't give me anymore until I tell you to. I need to think.'

Chapter 68

Jamilah doesn't go to Salim's office unless it's essential. She sees him most nights at the clinic and why give the gossipmongers an opening? This visit falls into the essential category, though it's not work-related. He points to the usual seat, and she sits.

'So?' he leans forward, his voice lower than normal.

'He called ten minutes ago from N'Djamena Airport,' says Jamilah, sitting upright. 'He's waiting to board a flight to Istanbul.'

'And ..'

'Mission accomplished as far as he's concerned. Direct hit. Claims they dropped more bombs than the NAF. There's no signal from Ado's phone, they're saying Abdullahi is dead too. According to the pilots, no one could have survived — which means those poor girls are dead.' Her voice wavers, but she had determined before coming that she wouldn't cry. How would that look?

'No, no. We don't know that Jamilah.' He gets up to comfort her, but she shakes her head and holds up her palm to protect them both. Her bottom lip edges up but she fights the emotion away. Too many eyes watching. She must stay professional.

Salim sits back down. 'Look, we discussed this before. He's not going to be travelling around with fifty girls in tow. They'll have groups of them in different camps or all together on a permanent site. They'll only move them when necessary and at the last minute, such as on the day of a release, and they'll want to deliver them to a place that's not far away and easy to get to. Lake Chad's too remote.'

'I hope you're right,' says Jamilah. 'Anyway, de Witt sounded pleased with himself. Repeated how sorry he was that he hadn't brought Aminah back, and hadn't been above board about Ado's phone, but at least, "together", we'd gained vengeance. One day I'd understand it had all been for the best and I should feel proud, especially for managing to free twenty-five girls.'

'Well, he's right on that point. Did he say anything about the pilots seeing a group of young women?

'No.'

'That's a good sign. I'm sure he would have mentioned it if they'd been there. Did he say when they were going to make the bombing public?'

'As soon as they're sure. They don't want to make the same mistake as the NAF.'

'Has he heard anything about Yakubu?'

'Didn't mention him either but I can't imagine him having any contacts in Kano now, apart from me, and I wasn't going to tell him anything. It's a change to be the one who knows what's going on while he's left in the dark.'

'So that was it?'

She nods, thinking it wise not to mention de Witt's suggestion she take time off and join him on a holiday in Turkey.

'I assume you haven't heard from Iman.'

'I'd have told you. I'm hoping no news is good news, but they're taking their time to announce it?'

'Formalities', Salim shrugs. 'Confirming the cause of death, more specifically that it wasn't suspicious, contacting key people first — the President, Speaker of the State Assembly, Yakubu's other wives and children. Media statements will need to be prepared and so on. They'll need to adjust the chain of command so there's no vacuum in state government. He never replaced Ado. If his death only became apparent a few hours ago, which I'm trusting we can assume, the wheels are still—'. He is interrupted by a knock on the door. Jamilah glances round. It's his secretary.

'Come in.'

'Sorry to disturb you, Doctor,' she says, not sounding particularly apologetic, 'but the Commissioner for Police is in reception and wants to speak to you.'

'I'll come and collect him myself.'

'He wants to see the SNO too.'

Jamilah is sure the Secretary is staring at her back, hungry for a reaction. Jamilah's aware of sweat on her forehead but remains still, looking at Salim.

'Fine,' says Salim standing up. 'Can you wait here Sister?'

'Of course, Doctor', says Jamilah as if nothing could be more natural. The secretary leaves, no doubt disappointed at their lack of reaction. Salim pauses on his way out.

'Okay, this is what we expected, and we know what we're going to say.' Jamilah nods. 'Breathe slowly and stay calm.' He grips the door handle, stops, and turns round, 'Don't forget, you have no idea the Governor is dead, so remember to speak of him in the present tense.'

'I will,' she smiles reassuringly, as much for herself as him.

Chapter 69

Salim shows the CP into his office. A policeman remains outside, another with stripes on his arm follows him in. Jamilah can imagine the entourage waiting outside the main entrance and the stir it will have created in reception. She stands up respectfully while Salim pulls another chair over for the CP. The other policeman declines Salim's offer to sit and stands at attention behind Jamilah and his boss. It feels like they're blocking off her escape route. The uniforms and stripes make her uncomfortable. While she is sure that what she has done is right, the presence of policemen in Salim's office reminds her that the law will view it differently.

'This is our Senior Nursing Officer, Commissioner.'

The CP nods a greeting to Jamilah. 'You got here very quickly, Sister.'

'I was here already, Sir.'

'That was fortunate. I am State Commissioner of Police, Haruni, and this is my colleague, Sergeant Adamu. Allow me to offer my condolences, Madam for the loss of your sister and brother. Very tragic.'

'Thank you, Commissioner', says Jamilah, wondering if she will always be associated in people's minds as "that woman whose family members were all murdered." At least this man's a policeman, solving murders is his business.

'Please sit down. You are busy people and I apologize for interrupting your schedule.'

'Not at all', says Salim. 'How can we help you, Commissioner?"

'By answering some simple questions.' He turns to face Jamilah. 'You went to the Governor's residence last night to see his wife. What was the purpose of your visit?'

'Perhaps, I should explain', interjects Salim. 'The SNO assists me in the private clinic I run in the evenings and His Excellency arranged for his wife to go there for a consultation about five or six days ago.'

'Thank you, Doctor. This I know. I was addressing the Senior Nursing Officer; I'd be grateful if you would allow her to respond to my question.' He turns expectantly to Jamilah.

'Is she okay?' asks Jamilah. 'I examined her last night, and she was doing well.'

'Can you just respond please, Madam.' His smile struggles to disguise his impatience.

'I'm sorry, Commissioner. She had a gynaecological issue, as you would expect. Fortunately, not as serious as it might have been. I made follow-up visits on days three and five — last night being day five. She has responded well to treatment; in fact, there's no need for us to see her again.'

The CP turns to Salim. 'So I have two questions, Doctor. One, what was the nature of her "issue" and, why did she merit a home visit, rather than going to your clinic?'

'With regard to the second question,' replies Salim. 'My clinic provides private services in the field of Obstetrics and Gynaecology for a clientele that appreciates discretion and professionalism and is prepared to pay for it. If the client is happy to pay an additional charge, we can arrange a follow-up service to the patient's home. Such was the nature of my colleague's visit.'

'And the reason for the Governor's wife coming to see you in the first place?'

'That's why I dealt with your second question first. On the grounds of patient-doctor confidentiality, I regret I cannot share this information with a third party, without my patient's permission. And I'm sure Governor Yakubu would be unhappy if I breached his wife's confidentiality.'

'I have spoken to the Governor's wife, and she has informed me why she came to see you. I am simply seeking confirmation.'

'I can provide that only with my patient's permission.'

'You will have it. I give you my word. I presume you have a report of last night's consultation?'

'I haven't written it up yet', says Jamilah. 'I was planning to do so this evening back at the clinic. It's not hospital business.'

'Okay, well tell me about your visit now, verbally.'

'I arrived around seven forty-five and stayed half an hour at most.'

'Did you need all of that time if your patient was doing so well?'

'The first time I visited her, she invited me to have tea and I accepted. I have the impression she doesn't get much of a chance to talk to women of her own age. I'm not quite her age, but not much older. I didn't stay for tea this time, just a ... chat.'

'About what?'

Jamilah glances at Salim, who speaks up. 'I'm afraid, Commissioner, we are straying into the realm of patient confidentiality again.'

'I am doing you the courtesy of calling on you at your place of work, Doctor. If you are not prepared to do me the courtesy of answering my questions, maybe it would be better if we continued this conversation at mine. State

Police Command to be exact, where we can talk at greater length, and I can ask the Governor's wife to join us.'

'We are not trying to be obstructive, Commissioner. At the same time, I do not know the purpose of your visit or if something has happened to my patient. But before we accompany you to State Police Command, you must allow me to ring His Excellency, as he entrusted his wife's treatment to me in the expectation of full discretion.'

'Put your phone down, Doctor. I am carrying out an investigation and I have not finished this interview. Do you think I don't understand confidentiality? Let me tell you, in my work I deal with levels of confidentiality of far greater importance than those governing the relationship between a doctor and his patient. You will do well to understand, that this is such an occasion. So can you tell me please, why the Governor sent his wife to see you and', he turns to look at Jamilah, 'why your colleague said that the matter was less serious than it might have been? And before you reply, I can assure you your patient is perfectly well, and I repeat, has shared with me the reason for her consultation. I trust you can accept my word on that.' His smile expresses no amusement.

'Of course, Commissioner … Perhaps, if Sergeant Adamu could leave the room, I believe it would signal respect for our patient's confidentiality and the Governor's wishes in this regard.'

The Commissioner takes a reflective breath, then turns to his colleague, 'Sergeant, step outside for a moment.' The Sergeant does as ordered, and Salim wastes no time in keeping his part of the bargain.

'The Governor lost self-control while having sexual relations with his wife. Through the aggressive use of sexual toys, which he inserted roughly inside her, he caused tearing and bleeding to her labia and vaginal wall. Post-examination and before she left the clinic, I phoned the Governor whom I have known for many years. I told him he should set a better example and desist from such practices. He expressed remorse and undertook to do so — I expect he and his wife have confirmed this to you. I advised him not to make any further physical demands on his wife until her wounds had fully healed. He assured me he would not. As the SNO pointed out, she could have suffered more serious internal injury but, fortunately, she did not. Vaginal cuts and tears, if left to heal, do so quickly in a healthy young woman. It's all a matter of keeping the wounds clean, dry and free from the kind of contact that caused the injury in the first place. Our job was to advise her how to do this and check that her wounds stayed free from infection. Hence, my colleague's home visits.'

'Thank you, Doctor.' He turns to Jamilah.

'As I said before, Commissioner', says Jamilah, trying to feed off Salim's assured response, 'she was pleased to have someone to talk to. It is my view that she needed emotional support as well as physical care, which is often the case with gynaecological patients, following a traumatic or unexpected event.'

'Such as?'

'Miscarriage, stillbirth, pregnancy, infection, sexual assault …'

'She told you she was sexually assaulted?'

'No', interjects, Salim. 'She said her husband could get over-excited, and on this occasion, went too far. He regretted his actions and had sent her to us to ensure she had the best of care.'

'So what did you talk about, Madam, in your *chat?*'

'I assured her that her wounds were healing well and there was no permanent damage. I couldn't advise her on how to handle her sexual relations with her husband as … I don't mean because I'm not married myself, it's just that it's not our role. It seemed to me she was better placed to do that herself.'

'You think so?'

'She's young but seems to have a strong resolve. I think she was glad of female company. She showed me the clothes and jewellery the Governor had bought her. I think it was her way of demonstrating that despite what His Excellency had done, there is another side to him and that he clearly appreciates her.'

'Would you say that striking your wife in the face is an appropriate way to show your appreciation?'

'With respect, Commissioner', but the CP silences Salim with a raised hand and keeps his eyes trained on her.

'No, Sir I would not. I did notice the mark on her face yesterday. She said he has a temper and was under stress. Personally, I do not see this as an excuse but as you know, our laws permit husbands to "*discipline*" their wives in this way and there's nothing we, as women, can do about it.'

'She could leave him.'

'She could, but she kept telling me how kind he is, despite what he'd done. Not just to her but to her family.'

'I get the impression that as long as her husband is lavishing gifts on her and supporting her family, she's ready to accommodate any of his perverted and immoral practices. Wouldn't you agree?' he raises his eyebrow.

'With respect, Commissioner', says Salim, 'you can't expect either the SNO or myself to have an informed view on this. We hardly know the young woman. We can treat her injuries, but we're not psychologists. Who can ever know the full nature of the relationship between a man and his wife, other than the couple themselves? If His Excellency were to ignore my advice and seriously injure my patient, I would be obliged to bring it to your attention, even if she were unwilling, or afraid to do so herself. Perhaps this is why you are here? Otherwise, I cannot imagine His Excellency appreciating the nature of such questions relating to his private life.'

'With respect, Doctor Salim, I am leading an investigation and it is not your role to question why I am here.' He turns back to Jamilah. 'Why was your visit last night shorter than the previous one?'

'Her wounds were healing well, and despite her bruise, she seemed in a more positive frame of mind. I suppose that's why she didn't feel a need to talk as much or that it was necessary to offer me tea as she'd done previously.'

'Did you see His Excellency while you were there?'

'No, Commissioner.'

'Thank you for your cooperation, Sister. I'm sure you are busy. I won't keep you from your patients any longer.'

'Thank you, Commissioner.' Jamilah heads for the door which is opened for her from outside by the Sergeant.

'Doctor, a few words in private.'

'Of course, Commissioner.'

Chapter 70

Jamilah makes her way past the enquiring looks and turning heads, trying not to rush or display emotion. Those who hadn't observed Salim escorting the CP to his office to join the waiting SNO will certainly be aware of it now. Salim's secretary and the reception staff will have made sure of that; word of mouth will have done the rest. She can imagine the malicious gossip doing the rounds: an issue of malpractice at Salim's clinic; a condition misdiagnosed; a treatment poorly administered; all with fatal consequences. Those two have had it coming. Let them talk, she has other things to think about.

The interview with the CP had been earlier and more intense than she'd expected. One thing's for sure, he would never have expressed such opinions on the Governor's behaviour if the Governor were still alive, especially to Salim, whom he knows was an associate. Salim was so assured in there, he sounded like her lawyer sometimes. It seems Iman has not put a foot wrong either. Jamilah hopes she hasn't let them down. She doesn't think she made any mistakes. They had agreed not to mention Iman coming to the hospital the day Yakubu had hit her. If it ever comes to light, Iman will say she was passing the hospital and called on Jamilah on impulse to ask about a discharge that turned out to be perfectly normal. Nothing more than a brief visit, easily overlooked.

Jamilah is impatient for the CP to leave so she can find out what he wanted to talk to Salim about in private. She'll wait for Salim to contact her and get on with the job the hospital pays her to do. Her decision is made easier when two of her colleagues approach simultaneously, seeking advice on their patients, though Jamilah suspects it might be more to do with them wanting to know what the CP's visit was all about. She doesn't give them a chance to ask.

It's two hours since the CP's visit and the hospital has settled into its daily routine. Fifteen minutes after he'd left, Jamilah had seen Salim dash off to Emergency Obstetric Care and had not caught sight of him since. To those who had enquired, she had said it was a confidential issue and the CP had instructed her not to discuss it with anyone. Her reply had clearly done the rounds as no one has mentioned the visit to her since, but she knows that if anything, speculation will have increased. As each minute of normality creaks by, she grows increasingly uneasy. Why can't they make an announcement about Yakubu? Why is it taking so long? Why doesn't Salim ring her? Why haven't the Chadians made an announcement about Abdullahi? What's happened to the girls? There's nothing on the news, nothing on her phone. She heads to her office to take lunch. As she unlocks the door her phone vibrates in her pocket. It's Iman! She quickly gets inside.

'Hi Iman, what's happening?'

'Can't talk for long, Jam. They've contacted the media. There'll be an announcement soon. They'll say that the Governor passed away during the night and while it was sudden it was not entirely unexpected as he was not in the best of health. The burial will be the day after tomorrow, to allow the dignitaries and family members to be present. I'm formally in mourning.'

Jamilah leans back against the door and takes a deep breath.

'You should be offering me your condolences,' whispers Iman, 'as you can imagine, I'm devastated.'

'Stop it.'

'No one can hear me. I'm in the bathroom, can you hear the tap running? That's what they do on TV, right? Besides, Danjuma, my late husband's Assistant, is helping me through my ordeal.' Jamilah hears a toilet flush. 'He's very taken by me, and, I have to admit ... he's quite cute in a nerdy sort of way. He's been consoling me all morning. I've told him I can manage, but he keeps coming back to ask if I'm okay and is there anything I need. I give a little sob and tell him he should get on with his work. He tells me that ensuring I'm okay is his priority! Listen, we had a quiet sit-down just now, just the two of us. It seems he knows more than anyone about where all the Governor's assets are located, *and* he knows an excellent lawyer who will ensure I won't be blindsided by my late husband's children and ex-wives. All the more amazing because he's related to Wife Number One. It turns out the old cow made Danjuma's life as much of a misery as my late husband did.'

'Be careful, Iman, it could be a trick.'

'Listen, Jam, I know how my late husband used to talk down to Danjuma. But don't worry, I'll be careful. You, too. Whatever you and Salim said to the CP it worked and, by the way, Danjuma told me my late husband demanded the CP's resignation yesterday and he assumes he had the letter with him this morning but no one to hand it over to! That's someone else who should be grateful to us. I'll call you later.'

'Only if it's safe.'

'I know.'

The line goes dead, and Jamilah looks up at the ceiling. Are they actually going to get away with this? A rap at the door makes her jump. She opens it and pulls Salim inside pushing the door closed with her foot. She holds him by his lapels and starts to kiss his neck and face. She wants to go away with him, anywhere as long as it's far and they're alone.

'Whoa, calm down', he laughs. 'Everything's good. They've just announced the Governor's passing. Natural causes, burial in two days.'

'I know, Iman just told me.'

'She's okay?'

'She's indestructible. I'm a bundle of nerves.'

'You did really well.'

'You think so? I was worried the CP thought there was something … not quite right.'

'He was trying to unnerve you; make you feel guilty. That's how they operate.' He makes her sit down while he perches on the side of her desk. 'Unlike Giwa, he's a devout man.'

'Really?'

'He was shocked by the sex toys in the Governor's bedroom and the blatant use of pornography and Viagra — and unimpressed by Iman's readiness to go along with her husband's perversions. But the main thing is, he doesn't suspect her or anyone else of murder. And despite what he might have implied, he's against husbands hitting their wives.'

'Oh. Salim. I was so worried, but you were so assured with him.'

He smiles. 'Not as believable as you.'

She knows that's untrue but it's nice of him to say it.

'He thinks Yakubu made himself look foolish taking on a new wife, younger than his daughter. And that his attempts at being thirty years younger took their toll, not helped by the stress of high office, especially his humiliation by Abdullahi in the media. Naturally, I was in no hurry to disagree.'

'Why did he confide all this in you?'

'He wanted to ask me things about Yakubu and didn't consider it appropriate to include you in the conversation. Like his use of Viagra. It's something I never mentioned to you. Yakubu's been using Viagra from back in the day when it was a novelty. He asked me to get him some and it snowballed. He would ask on behalf of his associates. Even when it became freely available, he didn't want people to know he needed it.'

'I know all about it. Iman told me.'

'You're not upset?'

'If the Governor and his friends wanted to give you money for medication to treat erectile dysfunction, why should I blame you for taking it? They'd get hold of it somehow. Part of our discrete services in sexual health, right?' She smiles, happy to show solidarity. 'I think the CP respects you for standing up to Yakubu about Iman. Something he'd have liked to have done himself but never had the nerve.'

'Maybe, but I didn't have to report to Yakubu on a daily basis. I love your smile. You're amazing.' He strokes her face.

'Think so? I expect you'll want to kiss me next.'

He lifts her up from her chair and they kiss. It's better than before now they're more aware of each other's bodies. Their embrace is intense but brief. Jamilah looks into his eyes.

'We can't behave like lovestruck teenagers! At least not in the workplace!'

He laughs, then kisses her forehead.

'You should get back,' she says releasing him, 'you'll be missed.'

'I suppose so.'

She sits down. 'I'm not surprised the CP shared his thoughts with you, I'm just a woman after all.'

Salim laughs. 'Maybe it helped for him to think that. Those others too. You've outwitted them all. Not just a pretty face!' She's blushing again. 'After he saw us, there was no point in the CP continuing to hide Yakubu's death. We'd confirmed what he'd suspected and what you'd wanted him to think. He shared with me "the sordid circumstances" around Yakubu's death and that the reaction of the elite was to bury them along with his body. There'll be no talk of an autopsy or any form of investigation that would bring Yakubu's perverted behaviour into the public domain. On top of all the other problems they're struggling with, they don't need the office of Governor being tarnished, especially in a Sharia state like ours.'

She puts her arms around him again. Apart from the remaining girls, her plan has worked but she couldn't have done it without him. He looks as if he wants to say something.

'What is it?'

He sighs. 'Did you let Yakubu touch you?'

'What?'

'When you were with him, you said you undressed, I'm sorry, it's been nagging at me. Did you let him touch you?'

Jamilah takes her arms from around his neck.

'What do you mean "let"? Do you think I was there of my own choosing? Being naked in his bedroom was the only way I could get close to him to do what I had to do.'

'I know. I'm sorry, I just …'

'I did what I did ten years ago to save my brother's life. I was ready to let Yakubu touch me if it meant I could kill him and save Iman, and the remaining girls. If that offends your sensibilities, that's too bad. It didn't seem to matter last night when you were undressing me, or this morning when you told me I was beautiful, or just now when you said it again!'

'It's not that, I just can't bear the thought of that man's hands touching you. He was like a beast and you're —'

'I'm sorry for your pain, Salim, but can you begin to think of what it was like for me to be there beside him, waiting for him to paw me?'

Salim swallows. He looks moved. 'You're right, I'm being selfish. It's just that I've cared for you for so long and … it's not jealousy, it's just knowing that man could have touched you. It upsets me. I'm concerned for you and what you had to go through.'

She's not totally convinced. 'You'll be pleased to know then that I didn't have to let him touch me. Iman did all the work. You're the only man I've ever had sex with willingly. And if you want us to do it again you'd better be careful of what you say next.'

'I'm sorry, Jamilah, really sorry. Please forgive me.' He takes her in his arms, but she doesn't react. 'I should never have brought it up. Men can be stupid, I'm no different. You're so courageous. I love you and I don't want you to be angry with me. I never want you to be with anyone else but me. I want to take care of —'

She stops him with a kiss, her arms are around his neck. She breaks off, her face rests on his chest. 'You always have taken care of me. I love you too. We'll never talk about this again.'

'Thank you.'

She looks up at him. He is smiling and she smiles back.

'Okay, you should eat your lunch!' he says. 'I'll see you tonight at the clinic, if not before.'

'Right. Maybe the Chadians will have made their announcement by then.'

'Let's hope so,' he says. 'Who could have imagined the deaths of both these men, on the same day and so unexpectedly?'

'Or that we would know about it before anyone else?'

'Or that it would never have happened without you!'

'Alhamdulillah!'

Chapter 71

The fifty-five-inch screen holds the attention of the room. Iman retains the remote. There's no way she's letting Wife-Number-One think she can walk in here and take over. The mourners fill the screen, packed loosely within the grounds of Kano's Great Mosque and resplendent in their Hausa and Fulani finery. Not for the first time the Governor is keeping everyone waiting. Yet it's safe to say, as Wife-Number-One has done more than once, that in terms of prestige, the turnout falls short of what her husband would have expected. Good. The President, whom the old bag insists on referring to as "our old friend", is absent, likewise his Vice, and so it has fallen to the newly appointed Federal Minister of Special Duties to represent him. He provides the expected air of gravitas, nodding solemnly as he shakes hands with the more prestigious attendees. He has an aura of quiet authority that Iman finds appealing. That said, his performance looks mechanical and he's not alone in that regard. There has been no heartfelt outpouring of grief for a Governor who many found a difficult man to deal with. More importantly, as Danjuma had put it, and he should know, this was a Governor, who within weeks of taking office, had failed spectacularly to deliver on his promise to bring Boko Haram to heel, not only losing his Deputy, his CP and his credibility in the process, but having to watch on TV as his nemesis freed captured girls, (something he had not managed to do himself), insulting him all the while.

It's the first time Iman has been in the same room, at the same time, with the pig's other wives and the ugly daughter. What a treat! Wife-Number-One's disdain for Iman is shared by the daughter, who, unlike her mother, never has anything to say. Like her father, if she's not eating she's scowling. She's not even pretending to show interest in the proceedings, never mind grief. Whatever's on her phone is clearly of higher priority than observing her father's funeral — probably a cartoon. The old sow's sense of superiority lies not only on her being the first wife but also the mother of his two piglets. Unfortunately for them, they inherited their father's looks and their mother's stupidity. No wonder Yakubu lost patience with them and traded her in for a younger model, packing them all off to Abuja. But she remains a wife and that keeps her vanity alive. Yakubu would wheel her out on occasions when it was advantageous for him to be seen accompanying the mother of his children. Or if he was invited to dine with someone from the past whom he regarded as important and who had known the old bag in her younger days.

Wife-Number-Two is both clever and, to be fair, attractive. She had taken herself out of the firing line, on account of having divorced her husband, for which she received a generous settlement, including an apartment in Abuja. However, Iman is sure that sense of neutrality is dissolving. The battle lines are being drawn; all three are out to maximise their share of the pig's wealth. Wife-Number-One will not be shy in promoting the claims of her son, and Sharia law places him in a commanding position. Wife-Number-Two had been a lawyer in the Senate when she met Yakubu. Drawing on her expertise, she had negotiated a pre-nuptial agreement which was activated when he'd found her boring, or more accurately, uncooperative in the bedroom. She will find it hard to improve on that agreement, but she's still a lawyer and no doubt her family and friends will be encouraging her to try, and she won't be short of colleagues to advise her.

As for Iman, Yakubu had set up a trust fund for her while she has the jewellery she cajoled him into buying for her on his trips abroad. Before his demise, she would have been happy to settle for her freedom and this modest level of financial security, particularly as in Kano, a widow of her age has more marital options than a new bride-to-be, with no expectation of having to marry a much older man. With the pig soon to be lowered into his grave, Iman is emboldened to push for more, especially as she now has the unofficial support of Danjuma, her new friend, or should she say, suitor?

Huh, just look at Number One, sitting on the sofa as if she owns it. This is the Governor's residence; this is where she, Iman, resides, not her. When the old bag married him last century he wasn't even a Senator, just a senior officer living in a military house in the grounds of some dingy compound.

'Oh, dear, you're sweating,' Iman says, managing to include mother and daughter in the same broad sweep of her hand. 'Let me turn up the AC.' Having done so, she lifts an untouched glass of water from the small table in front of the daughter and says, 'I'll get them to re-fill your glass.' She nods to the maid, hands her the glass and basks in the look of twisted outrage she has brought to the old bat's face. The piglet looks blank.

Mother and spoilt son might well represent a significant alliance, but Iman has Danjuma. She never went to university but she's not naïve. Jamilah is right; Danjuma is well-placed to play a double game, but Iman is confident in both her ability to assess a man's intentions and the strength of her sexual power. She feels equipped to assess where Danjuma's true interests lie and will not hesitate to deploy a little manipulation of her own to keep him on track. She'll be a lot more generous to Danjuma than his mother's cousin would ever be, and he knows it. And she has much more to offer him than finance. Danjuma says she was always resentful that he outshone her son academically, which let's face it, would not be hard. Iman looks for Danjuma on the screen. He's easy to pick out with his height, thick-framed glasses, and familiar hat. He doesn't seek the limelight but nevertheless, is strategically placed behind the Federal Minister, ensuring his presence is noticed. Meanwhile Yakubu junior is trying to imitate the Minister's statesman-like demeanour and all he's succeeding in doing is looking like an arrogant spoilt child, which is exactly what he is.

There's a flurry on the screen as space is cleared for an old man walking slowly with the aid of a cane and clinging to the arm of a bodyguard. As he is directed to his chair, the TV commentator identifies him as the previous Governor. While it is clear to everyone that he has come to gloat rather than mourn, the commentator limits his remarks to an observation that while having been recognised as being in poor health, the former Governor has, nevertheless, outlived his younger successor.

'Who had the stress of managing all the shortcomings of a child bride', adds Wife-Number-One to the piglet, in a loud aside. Iman takes the remote and turns up the volume.

The camera dwells on a few of the Governor's former Senate colleagues. The commentator — a local, given his accent — is more at ease identifying State Ministers and members of the State House Assembly than Federal officials. Iman notices that the son is wearing his father's sunglasses. If it's supposed to be a tribute, then like him it falls short, as only Iman, who bought them, would recognise them definitively. On the other side of the Federal

Minister stands the Speaker of the State House Assembly who, the commentator states, will act as Governor on an interim basis.

A grand hearse rolls into view. Its shiny black veneer captures the reflections of the local dignitaries, officials, and party members, as it progresses along the tree-lined road. It comes to a halt in front of the Federal Minister and the Governor's son. As the rear door lifts up and the open wooden frame supporting the Governor's remains is rolled out, there is an unseemly scramble as funeral director staff and mosque officials vie to show their usefulness. A policeman in beret and khaki moves to restore order. The helpers melt away and the Governor's remains, shrouded in white cloth, suddenly lie exposed to the sun, as if washed up on a shore. Mourners, hands clasped before them, stare down at the simple frame with its long handles projecting outwards beyond the body.

Iman thinks her husband has never looked so isolated. She almost expects him to sit up and ask the mourners what they're looking at, don't they have work to do? Instead, his large shape stays silent and inert, wrapped like a package awaiting collection; ultimately, that's what he's become.

Chapter 72

While Iman is expected to watch every second of the ceremony, Jamilah has work to do. She watches intermittently, wondering what her friend is thinking. When she sees the body laid out on the ground it elicits mixed emotions. She is sure, like her, Iman has no regrets. The world is a better place without that tyrant but it's uncomfortable watching the funeral of the man they had killed. All Jamilah wants is for the day to be over, another to begin, then another, until she reaches a point where she can finally believe that a fresh start is possible.

The announcement made late the previous day by the Government of Chad, claiming to have killed Abdullahi in a lethal airstrike, had met with so much scepticism that it unnerved her. The denial from Boko Haram follows an established pattern, but there is no shortage of Nigerian military experts available to offer their informed opinion that it would be extraordinary if the Chadian Air Force had the capacity to succeed where the NAF had failed. What is certain is that her fifty girls were not set free. There were no reports of them being killed in the raid, which is good, but who knows the truth? The Chadians would never admit to something like that. Then again, if it had happened, de Witt would have known about it and wouldn't have missed the chance to show her how well informed he is.

At least Iman can move on and make a clean break. There is nothing to hold her back. Even if Jamilah never finds complete happiness or has full peace of mind, she will do her best to ensure that Salim does. His well-being is all she is focused on now.

She walks into reception and stands near a few of the visitors waiting to be called to their appointments and whose eyes are fixed on the TV. The same screen on which she had watched Abdullahi ranting about Yakubu while standing in front of the twenty-five girls he had released that day. Now it shows an Imam being escorted forward by the funeral director, one of whose aides goes before them, gesturing to those ahead to move back a little. The Imam is dressed plainly in a beige kaftan and cap. His white beard suggests a man in his seventies, though he stands straight and tall. Like the mourners behind him, he faces Mecca. Silence descends and he begins the funeral prayer. Soon they will take Yakubu to his grave and from there she has no doubt where his final destination will be.

Chapter 73

By the time the hearse reaches the drop-off point in a leafy section of Kano's Farm Centre Cemetery, the number of mourners has increased significantly as the less affluent are able to access the more expansive grounds of the cemetery than they could the narrower, well-guarded confines of the Mosque. Meanwhile the more affluent are conspicuous by their absence. Iman is warmed by this continuing lack of respect, especially as she knows Wife-Number-One will somehow regard it as a further slight to her own standing, whatever that is. She's arrogant and stupid enough to feel personal disappointment that the Federal Minister, Senators, and others, will not be accompanying her husband to the graveside, or that Governors from neighbouring states had not bothered to show up for any part of the funeral. It's clear to Iman that, in their eyes, association with failure, as represented by her late husband, outweighs respect for convention, more so, when combined with rumours of a dissolute old man given over to perverse practices unbecoming a senior figure in high office in a Sharia state.

'How heart-breaking it must be for busy leaders like our old friend, to be unable to take time out to pay their respects to your father', says the old bat with a rueful shake of her head. 'With all the terrible security issues we are facing, you can understand their position.'

The piglet appears unmoved. Iman exchanges glances with Wife-Number-Two, who rolls her eyes.

'Look how dignified your brother looks at the head of the mourners', she continues, 'His father would have been proud of him.'

Yakubu's remains are hoisted high onto the shoulders of six muscular bearers, and the view of her son is lost as the people seem to take ownership of the ceremony. A wave of outstretched hands engulfs the bearers, as people stream alongside them. One command from the pig would have restored order, however, the son is out of his depth, drowning in a sea of strangers. Iman puts her hand to her mouth to cover her smile as it strikes her that, if the old man were watching these images, he'd want to get into the ground as quickly as possible and feel the weight of the soil descending upon him. The funeral director shouts instructions and the bearers manage to keep their burden steady. Such hysteria is not unusual at the burial of a "big man" as it brings the lazy, the undesirables and the ne're-do-wells out in force, ever hopeful of reward for a service rendered or for just being there.

Another Imam appears and calmness descends. The Governor's son and the Speaker of the State House Assembly are ushered through to the graveside. Iman's attention is drawn to the face of a young man in the corner of the screen; he stands out because he looks too young to be present at such an event, more an adolescent than a man. She wonders if he's a bastard son of the Governor, seeking to draw attention to himself or better still confront the legitimate son. The camera shows a wheelchair in front of him, in which an old man, with white hair and beard and clothed generously in white robes, is seated. Maybe a former comrade of Yakubu's who got there early to ensure he was at the graveside to say a last farewell. But he looks in distress; his head is twisting from side to side. Maybe he's been waiting too long in the sun. The young man is trying in vain to calm him. It looks to Iman like he is overwhelmed by the pressing crowd rather than being overcome with emotion at the Governor's passing. A police sergeant moves across to investigate. This seems to unsettle the young man who backs off. Now he's no longer visible on the screen and the old man is left isolated. The policeman gesticulates looking like he is demanding the youth to come back. The old man continues to look agitated and is pulling at the shirt of the Sergeant. Iman's sympathy for the youth transfers to the old man. How could the boy leave him like that in the middle of a crowd and run off. The old man must be shouting for people are turning away from the grave to look. The Governor's son shakes his head in disgust. Back in the room, his mother does likewise. Things are going from bad to worse.

'In the name of Allah', says Number One, 'how can they allow rabble like that to get so close? Isn't anyone in control?'

As if they have heard her, two policemen squeeze through the crowd to help the Sergeant deal with the situation. The sergeant puts a finger to his lips gesturing for the invalid to be quiet, one of the policemen goes behind him and gets hold of the wheelchair. The other policeman gestures for the mourners gathered round to clear a path, so they can lift him out.

'About time,' says Number One. 'I don't care if he's in a wheelchair, they should throw him in jail. It'll make him think twice about turning up at people's burials and making a nuisance of himself.'

As the policemen cart the old man off, there is a dull boom. It can be heard from within the room. The picture on the screen shakes and goes blank.

Chapter 74

Like the other people watching in reception, Jamilah is stunned. People turn to each other in bewilderment. Unlike them, Jamilah knows the truth of what has just happened for she saw the young boy too. And she knows it wasn't a boy, but Farida wearing men's clothes. She recognised the narrow face and thin lips in an instant. And the old man? She saw enough of him to know it was Abdullahi. It will not be easy to identify the remains of a suicide bomber, but he showed his face on TV when he released the girls and they can compare it to the footage at the burial. Whether they confirm the inevitable claim of responsibility that will come from Abdullahi's organization will be another thing. It will be the Chadians whose credibility is undermined this time, but State Security will be under fire yet again at their failure to protect mourners from another suicide bomber. There's no time to dwell. There will be many fatalities and many injured, probably more than when Abdullahi sent two young girls and a baby into the market. Jamilah turns and heads to the wards. She must get her team ready. They know what to expect but it won't make it any easier.

The Director is speaking to Salim in an animated fashion. He sees her and signals her to join them. Salim turns and smiles. She can't smile back; she'll confuse the Director. She's still a little confused herself but one thing is clear: while the Chadian Air Force proved more accurate than the NAF, they still couldn't kill Abdullahi. He chose his own time and place to die. She will share what she saw with Salim when they get a minute. And when they get more than a minute they can start talking about what the two of them can expect from a life together. A new start is enough for now, and she's not going to lose him. She will do everything in her power to keep him safe. It will be easier now that she knows Abdullahi is gone … and all because she fought back and avenged her family.

Chapter 75

Farida grips the man's sides as the bike powers along the highway. Normally she would hold on to the side rail but today she needs contact. Her cheek presses against the man's broad back. Rain arrives without warning; she raises her head to let the heavy drops splash into her face, mingling with her tears. She never cries but today her father martyred himself and she had helped him do it. It was her failing that brought them to that place. That phone was bugged, she is sure of it. The man in the market had assured her it wasn't. Muhammed had double-checked, but those planes came in as it was getting light. They'd hadn't been in that place long yet those planes knew exactly where to find them. They hadn't been searching, they came directly to the camp and dropped their bombs. She had led the assassins right to him. If only she'd held on to the damn thing, but there was no time, bombs were exploding, planes were circling, they had to get off the boat.

Martyrdom was his alternative to surgery. Once they'd figured out who he was, he would never have made it to the operating theatre. They would have come for him and dragged him away. His death would have been slow, painful and without anaesthetic. Her father had chosen the life of a jihadist and in choosing to die like one, he'd remained true to his ideals. He knew he could no longer fight alongside his men or be as mobile as them. He had accepted it immediately. That he was content and ready to go, brings her no comfort. He'd said she must celebrate with him. While she understands his choice and his end was surely glorious, she doesn't share his joy. Rather, she seethes at the injustice. She wants vengeance. She doesn't know how, but she will get it.

THE END